without warning

Will Napier has split his adult life between Scotland and America. He now resides in Atlantic Beach, Florida with his wife and four children. His first novel *Summer of the Cicada* was published by Jonathan Cape in 2005. He is completing a collection of short fiction and is writing his third novel.

By the Same Author

Summer of the Cicada

without warning

Will Napier

JONATHAN CAPE
LONDON

Published by Jonathan Cape

2 4 6 8 10 9 7 5 3 1

First published in Great Britain in 2010 by
Jonathan Cape
Random House, 20 Vauxhall Bridge Road,
London SW1V 2SA

www.rbooks.co.uk

Addresses for companies within The Random House Group Limited
can be found at: www.randomhouse.co.uk/offices.htm

The Random House Group Limited Reg. No. 954009

A CIP catalogue record for this book is available from the British Library

ISBN 9780224073561

The Random House Group Limited supports The Forest Stewardship Council (FSC), the
leading international forest certification organisation. All our titles that are printed on
Greenpeace approved FSC certified paper carry the FSC logo. Our paper procurement
policy can be found at www.rbooks.co.uk/environment

Set in Dante MT by Palimpsest Book Production Limited,
Grangemouth, Stirlingshire

Printed and bound in Great Britain by
CPI Mackays, Chatham, Kent ME5 8TD

In memory of Dennis Bell
My grandfather. He loved a good story.

And for Brody and Alex
My smallest muses and alternative sources of energy

Prologue

Can't remember the guy's name. The one who took me to see my mother's grave for the first time. I remember his arms were cannons. Big and black and they looked about as heavy as the trees on the hills surrounding the field of headstones. He pulled the van up the long road that ran through the middle of the cemetery. While driving, he kept checking the piece of white paper beside him. He slowed down now and again – whenever he needed to check the paper. He would lift it up to his face and make a show of it like he wanted me to notice him. I couldn't see his eyes behind the shades he was wearing. He kept moving his chin like he was angling his head to look back at me in the rear-view mirror. The expression on his face never changed.

'You alright, Joe?' he asked.

'What are you looking at up there?'

'A fax. Got it sent to the home so you'd know where to find the site. The plot, I mean.'

He raised the paper in his right hand and kept driving. I looked at it for a second, not making all that much a fuss over it. Still, I leaned forward to see what it was all about. There was a line for the highway we'd come off. Smaller waves snaked off the bold highway line. 'Cemetery' was written in an egg shape drawn off the side of the highway line. We were some-where in that egg shape. On one of the smaller waves, heading towards the centre of the egg where a black spot had been drawn.

There was an X on the side of the small wave we were driving along. The few badly drawn circles were probably meant to be trees. I looked out the window to see if I could figure out what part of the wave we were riding. Figured the X was where my mother was buried.

'You holding up okay?'

'Yeah,' I said. 'Just kind of strange is all. It's been a while.'

'Long's that?'

'Since she was taken away.' Kept my eyes off him. I stared out the window. 'Since my old man hauled her off.'

He shook his head and lowered the fax-map.

'She's been dead a while. More than a year.'

'Why'd you decide to come out now, Joe?' He angled his chin up to the mirror again. 'Why not sooner?'

I shrugged my shoulders and kept looking out the window. Watched the sky over the trees. It was blue and clear. Only clouds I could see were way off in the distance. They were shaped like knives cutting low across the sky – shaving the tops of the trees where the hills rose up. Beyond the clouds the sky was a blue. So bright it made my eyes go dry.

'I don't have anything else to do. I guess that, and they finally offered it up. Asked me if I'd like to see where she was buried.'

'Hear you,' he said.

He drove the rest of the way without saying anything else. I watched the scene go by outside my window. We were passing all the same things now. Headstones down the hill to the left and headstones up the hill to the right. We were going down and at the bottom of the hill there was a small circle of gravel to turn around on. Nothing else beyond that spot but long grass and the start of a forest. From the way he was slowing the van down, the closer we got to the bottom, I guessed we were lost. Didn't say anything 'cause it didn't feel like it mattered. He could have turned the van round and driven the three hours back to St Martin's Home for Boys and I wouldn't have cared a damn. My mother wasn't going anywhere. Kind of figured if I didn't get to see her grave right then, I'd get another six-hour round trip some other day.

'What are you smiling at?' the big guy asked.

'You got us lost, man.'

'Boy, you are wrong about that,' he said. He pulled the van round the circle and stopped it in the shade. Branches of a tree hung down and touched the windscreen. He put an arm across the bench seat and turned his head so I could see my reflection in his sunglasses and I didn't like what I saw. Some runt of a guy looking all stupid, sitting pretty on a big bench seat. A weak kid hunkered up next to the door. Looked like some lost punk.

'Your mom's grave is up the hill,' he told me. 'Should be about fifty feet up this road and then right. Walk till you pass . . .' He turned his head and was looking down at something in the front seat. He raised the fax-map. 'Pass maybe twenty plots and you should be there.'

He rolled up the sheet of paper and fed it through the cage that was separating us. I took it from him and picked up the plastic-wrapped flowers from the seat next to me.

'You want to let me out?' I asked.

'Yeah, man.' He opened his door and stood outside the van. He took a good long while stretching his back. Stayed in his pose for a few seconds. I couldn't get too annoyed 'cause he wasn't a guy to get involved with. Big as he was, I wouldn't have a chance. He came up to my door and pulled the handle and swung the door open. 'Sorry about that, Joe. Forget about the handles on these doors sometimes. I'm usually driving the other van.' He pointed at the door. 'Other van, the doors can still open from the inside.'

'You're not usually driving guys like me,' I said.

He smiled at that too. His white teeth looked wet and wide

behind his dark lips. He was nodding his head with exaggerated motion. I caught my reflection in his glasses each time his head came down. Out of reflex I put my hand to my face. Ran a finger across the scar over my left eye. Kept my fingers on it for a few seconds, like I needed to make sure it was still there. Got out of the van and felt his hand fall on my shoulder.

'I'll be watching you from here,' he said. 'You need me to drive up and get you, just raise your hand.' He waited for me to nod, then said, 'See you at the top.'

His hand left my shoulder so he could aim his thick finger up the hill. I followed where he was pointing and looked up to the top of the road we'd just come from. The same one that led back to the highway. I kept nodding my head without looking at him and tossed the bouquet of flowers from one hand to the next. Tossed it back again.

'Take your time. I'm in no rush.'

'Yeah,' I said. 'Neither am I.'

Started my walk up the hill, moving out of the shade and into the heat. The sun was coming down hard with nothing to break it up before it hit my shoulders. I kept moving, knowing it was going to be a hot day. *No shade where you're going, Joe. No big headstones to lean your back against. And just look at you in those clothes. You're going to fry, boy!* I'd dressed in a white T-shirt and khaki shorts first thing that morning. Then I'd thought about it a while. Figured I needed to suffer somehow if I was going to get the full effect. I owed that much to my mother. So, I'd gone back to my closet and changed into a black button-up shirt. Black jeans. My black military boots that were already gleaming bright. I got on all those clothes and sat on my bed for a few minutes looking out the window. Staring while I tied my boots up – watching through the bars and into the blue sky beyond.

That blue sky gave me a good feeling about getting away. I'd left my dorm room and stopped to look through the windows leading onto St Martin's back green. Saw a pair of red flags sticking up out of the ground. Markers for the beginning of the forest part of the cross-country run. It was the start of two miles of uneven trails. It was a good run, but that day I wasn't interested. Just didn't have the energy for it. Checked myself one last time and walked down the hall and into the reception foyer. Moved up to the front door and touched the buzzer. Waited.

I listened for the sound to come from down the hall. Heard the faint electric hum of the speaker in the wall. The speaker crackled, then a voice said: 'Stand to the left.' I sidestepped and looked down the corridor and caught sight of the guard with the phone to his ear. He was looking at me. 'What's the name?'

'Joseph Pullman.'

'Wait.'

He disappeared from sight. They always did that when they flipped through their clipboards full of names. Lists of day-trippers and residents expecting visitors. There was another list for the work-release crew who were chalking up hours of community service. The guard took so long I figured he was checking that list for my name. With my reputation, it was an easy mistake to make. The guard finally came back into view. He was nodding his head while he spoke into the microphone on his desk.

'Transport number fourteen,' he said.

The buzzer sounded and I pushed through the front door. I walked out to the front step. The sun came down on me and it took a few minutes to blink the glare out of my eyes. Kept blinking and headed up the path to the blue van with the black number fourteen stuck to the rear fender. The cannon-armed driver was leaning up against the door talking to one of the house guards. Guard looked at me for a second. He shaded his eyes with one hand and looked up at the sky.

'Boy,' he said. 'You are going to burn down to nothing.' He looked at me again and shook his head. 'Can't you feel the heat?'

'Sure I feel it.' I looked down at my shirt. Swiped a hand across my chest like I had something to clean away. 'This is out of respect for my mother.'

But I wasn't feeling the same conviction at the cemetery. Walking up the path I wished I'd stuck with the khaki shorts and white T-shirt. I wished I'd let the driver and his guard buddy-talk about Cal Ripken and Eddie Murray and the rest of the Oriole infield while I went back to my room to change.

She's dead and gone, Joe. Who the hell you trying to impress coming out here looking like Johnny Fuckin' Cash?

Farther I got from the air-conditioned van, the more my shoulders got the itch from the heat. Sun traced me like a hunter's scope on a fourteen-point buck. Had me in the sights and I wasn't all too comfortable about it. Turned for a second and walked backwards – gravel grinding under dragging heels. Checked on the driver, looking back to see if he was talking on his oversized car phone. Calling back to the house so he could let that guard friend of his know how bad I had it. How much I was feeling it. *He's walking in the sun dressed like a priest, man. You should see this sorry sonofa . . .* But he wasn't on the phone. He'd got back in the van and was already sitting in the driver's seat with the chair slanted back. Hands behind his head. He brought a hand round to give me a wave, like I should keep going. Like he was a back-yard quarterback telling me he was planning to throw the longest pass of his life – and he was expecting me to catch it.

Remember, kid, go fifty feet and turn right. Then pass maybe twenty graves. That's where you're going to find your momma.

'I'll find her alright,' I said.

Twisted on my heels and started walking faster. Feeling good for getting away from the van. Having a sense of release for escaping all the institution routine. It wasn't all that bad. Too much shit had fallen for the house to be clean, but it could've been worse. I'd done the foster-family thing and it seemed like everybody knew that didn't work out all too well.

Court hearings and dodging therapy sessions with Collins had been getting to me. I was tired of telling them the same thing every time I was asked—

So, what happened?

Charles Vincent McLean got too personal.

And what did you do to him, Joe?

You know the answer to that one.

Every damned time. It was always followed by that long silence. I'd use those silences to think about better times than these. Collins used the silence to figure out what he was going to ask next. Wondering what he had to ask to open Joe Pullman to his core. While he thought he'd chew his pen and look at his clipboard. He'd go on reading the words he'd written like they were instructions on a better way to deal with St Martin's resident 45230. But Collins never used the silence well 'cause he was always asking me the same thing.

And what happened then?

Everyone knows the answer to that.

This is meant to help you, Joe.

I don't feel the benefit, Mister Collins. I never have.

They all wanted to know about Charles Vincent. He was a hot topic because that episode between me and him had made the papers. He was the reason they couldn't get me 'homed'. That's what they were calling it. Collins and all the other administrative people at St Martin's, and all the other professionals and shrinks I came across who were employed by the state. They all wanted me to be homed. Thing is, it's hard to home a boy like me. The boy I was back then. All the trouble had to do with Charles Vincent – my first foster brother. He belonged to the man and woman the state had assigned to look after me when someone found my mother hanging from a tree in Virginia. After my old man got arrested for killing some kid named Dean Gillespie. Charles and his brother were real interested in my old man. Thought maybe me and my old man were alike, and they pressed on me hard until I told them enough to fill that curiosity.

Are you like your father, Joseph? Charles had asked me. *You a kid-killer?* He'd sat me down in a chair, him and his brother hovering over. They kept at it. Whenever it was just us, they tried their luck.

I don't know, I'd told them. But it wasn't enough.

Come on, Charles said. He'd move his face up close to mine. *Do you have it in you? Is it in there, Joseph?*

It was all too much. Not just little Charles Vincent and his shadow of a brother. Not just the musty stink of their basement. Not the way their parents had clipped the articles about my father from the newspaper and left them on the kitchen counter for me to find. I couldn't catch a break anywhere in that house. Round that time I was never alone. I'd go outside the McLean house and the neighbours would shake their heads and look real sad at me. Some of them would try to talk to me. Thing is, I'd been told not to speak with anybody. But it didn't stop the questions from coming. I'd go back in the house and there would be new clippings on the counter top. There wasn't any space. No peace. Worst of all, there was Charles Vincent.

Come on, Joseph. I'm waiting!

So I decided to give him what he wanted. One evening, while his parents were out at the neighbour's house for cocktails, I answered Charles Vincent's question with everything I had. Then I gave him some more. Lucky for me, the judge put my reaction down to hardship. Down to the lifetime of abuse at the hands of my old man. What I did to him didn't make it into the papers. Not all the details. His broken nose went to print and so did his arm. Not how I'd pulled it back and used my knee for leverage. They left that out, but wrote about how he had suffered a 'significant break'. Papers printed stuff about how Charles Vincent needed surgery to piece the elbow back together. The work that doctors had to do to fix his eye didn't hit print, and neither did the part about his teeth.

How he didn't have any left up front. What I did to Charles Vincent was enough to land me in a courtroom of my own. I found myself in an orange jumpsuit with hands clasped over my crotch. There was a judge looking down at me from his high chair. His voice roaring words equally loud and damning as those of the judge who had roared at my father.

You've been found guilty of serious assault, Mister Pullman.

'Damned straight,' I said. Called out to the hot blue cemetery sky same as I'd wanted to call up to the judge. Instead, I'd stood looking up at him with my mouth shut and my hands stuck together. Feeling all the hate and anger swelling up inside me, I'd chewed at the inside of my cheek. Chewed it so hard the skin came off between my teeth. Sucked at the blood that was leaking out. It kept coming and I kept chewing. The judge kept roaring and the blood flowed faster and fell back towards my throat. I'd kept quiet and swallowed it down. Blood and pride together.

Walked up the hill. Counting off the feet as I went.

Thirty.

Forty.

Taking into consideration the life you have lived, Joseph, I feel it is not in your best interests to impose time at a correctional facility. However, I do feel you require supervision and guidance.

'Well, I'm getting that now,' I sang. 'I'm getting more guidance than I can handle, your honour.'

Fifty.

Turned right and started past the first grave. Looked back at the van. Couldn't see past the glowing yellow of the sun on the windscreen. Turned my head forward and kept walking. Felt like I was cooking inside my shirt and wondered how long it would be before I passed out. How long I'd have to be unconscious before the big counsellor wouldn't be able to bring me back. Till I was so far gone they'd just dig up my mother's grave and chuck me down there beside her.

After the fifth headstone I started reading the names.

Looking at the dates and making fast calculations of how old the people were when they'd died. Fifties and sixties. Mothers. Fathers. Grandfathers. There was a baby too. Born and died on the same day. Thought it was weird that it didn't have the same name as the people round it. There weren't any empty plots, either. No space for when her parents died, if they hadn't died already. No space to be added into the ground next to that baby. That got to me. At the time I figured it was because of the heat. Later I decided it was because I'd be in the same place one day. I was sure that eventually I'd be stuck between strangers. Trouble was, people wouldn't even pass my name and think it was strange. I wasn't young enough for it to cross their mind. I was my own person now. Almost a man. Maybe already a man.

I was dragging my boots through the dried blades of grass. Finally came to the grave. I looked down at the small black square with my mother's name dug into it. *Clarisse Pullman.* Seeing her name like that surprised me. I didn't think she'd have my father's name any more. Figured she'd have gone back to her old family name. Maybe she didn't have a choice. *Can't change to birth names in cases of suicide. It's just not Christian.*

The plaque was simple and shining black. Her name etched and showing the white of the stone under the surface:

Clarisse Pullman
Born May 3, 1948
Died April 16, 1987

Nothing about a loving mother. Devoted wife. Screaming victim. Just Clarisse Pullman and when she came and when she went. I dropped the flowers on the headstone and looked back at the van and watched it for a while – wondering if I was being monitored or if the big guy had fallen asleep behind the wheel. Part of me was yelling out to chance it. Cut off for the woods and see how far I could get before someone tracked me down. Then again, I didn't think there was much of a chance that I could get far enough to make a go of it. Eventually they would get me. Chances were good that they would get me before the day was finished.

He's got scars all over him. Look for the wishbone thing that cuts up over his left eye. You see that and you know we got our man.

With that I sat on the grass in front of my mother's grave. Crossed my legs like an Indian and felt the sun burning against my back. Skin on my neck was turning hot. It was a good feeling. Better than feeling the heat through my shirt. That heat straight on my neck was a different kind of burn. It hurt, but not in a bad way.

Took my shirt off and sat there looking at the headstone. Remembered my mother the way she was towards the end. Kneeling in the kitchen of our house on Westchester Drive. Kneeling like she was praying for something – screaming up at the kitchen ceiling. Screaming until the veins in her neck swelled up thick as snakes. Then there was the way she looked at me. Stared at me with her red eyes looking desperate – me watching her through the sliding glass door.

'What a mess,' I said. Reached out and touched the headstone. It was marked same as the glasses get marked when you wash them in hard water. A thin white dust coating that's left when the water dries. Ran my fingers over the headstone and left lines where I touched it. Looked at my fingers and felt the grit. Used my thumb to rub the ghost-white dust into my fingertips. 'You weren't even there.'

It felt good to hear my voice and be alone again. There was distance from everything. From St Martin's and from the trouble waiting there. It felt good because I hadn't closed the book on everything. It's not that I wanted my mother to know I was angry that she had left me. Angry that she wasn't able to take care of things like she was supposed to. She had failed me. She let it all blow apart in the end, but I didn't hold it against her that my father beat the shit out of me. Knocked me round like church bells at lunchtime.

'You didn't have half the strength I have,' I said. Looked down at the grave and figured it was probably because of her that I was able to get through it all. 'Cause of her I didn't let my old man break me. But I wasn't visiting her grave to tell her that.

I dropped down to her headstone and tried to judge where she was down there in the ground. Where her face would be, her ear. Put my face to the grass. Took a deep breath and smelled the dry earth, catching a strong smell of wild onions. Sucked it all up in my nose and, when I was full, I shouted until my lungs went empty.

'He's gone! He's gone! All that time laying his hands on me. Who's the tough one now, Ma? Me! That's who. Me.'

Then I laughed. Laughed until my stomach ached. Until my throat felt raw. Until I couldn't see from the tears swimming in my eyes. Rolled over and felt the grass against my back and the sun finding new pale skin. Blinked until my eyes were clear again. Until I could see the sky over me. Felt the dried blades of grass pressing into my back. The last of the laugh shook away from my shoulders and I put my hands behind my head and stretched my body out and took the heat that was burning against my skin.

'Goddamn, that was a crazy summer,' I said. 'You remember just how crazy, Ma. You were part of that.' Looked at her grave like she would be there. Like she'd be laing on her side. Maybe with her hands crossed over her chest. Legs crossed at the ankles. Fresh as the good days she used to have. Days when she looked like things could be different. When she was close to becoming real again.

'You want to know what happened?'

I had to stop laughing again before I told her the story. From beginning to end. Started talking and didn't look anywhere but the blue sky over me. Crossed my hands over my chest and my legs at my ankles and started talking. It took me a couple of hours 'cause I didn't leave anything out. Never stopped to look and see if there was anyone close by. Someone walking up through the paths in the woods to lay flowers on a grave. Someone getting close without knowing I was even there. Without me knowing they were there. I just kept talking. Telling the story like it needed to be told. And when I was finished I felt drained.

Felt sick in my guts.

'That's it,' I said. 'Now that sonofabitch is rotting. He's locked up and rotting away.'

Horn on the van stopped me from saying anything else. I looked up and saw the van pulling up the hill. Turning onto the waving line that reached out to the highway. Stood up and found my skin had gone tight in my shoulders. Pushed a finger against my chest. Pulled it away and saw a white impression where it had been. It filled in with red, the same as the rest.

'Look at that,' I said. 'Haven't been burned that bad before. Think I'll suffer for this one?'

Looking at the grave, I had a sense that I'd see it again. Didn't know it was going to be almost twenty years before I made it back. It would still look the same when the day came. When I would be standing over it with my son at my side. Trying to explain to him that my mother was different from real mothers. That she had problems and she'd decided to end her problems with a rope and a good sturdy tree.

Another blast of the horn and I stood up. Waved at the driver and started walking away. Looked down at the grave one last time.

'They're gone,' I told her. 'For good.'

Got back in the van without saying anything. Lay down across the seat and closed my eyes. My skin was on fire with a deep sort of itching already surfacing, but not enough to keep me from sleeping. The van rocked along the road, taking all of the bumps with force. I came in and out of dreams when the van made a turn. Each dream connected me with my mother. I couldn't see her face any more. Each time it seemed her face would be revealed, the van would move and I would wake.

I stayed awake for the last twenty minutes of the ride. My driver swung the door of the van open. I slid off the seat and looked at the entrance of St Martin's and at the gravel path leading from the van to the main door. Hopped out of the van and tried to stretch my shoulders. Thousand pins went in deep, so I let my arms down again and started up the gravel path. I felt unbalanced, so I focused on the front door and kept moving for it.

'You alright after today?' the driver asked.

'Sure. It's all good.'

He walked beside me all the way. It was already evening and the sun was low in the sky. My skin was tight and my guts were empty. Walked faster along the path and the driver kept up with me. We stopped at the door and he punched a button next to the metal speaker. A voice called back.

'Escorting Joseph Pullman into the building,' the driver said.

The electronic voice crackled something else. The driver looked down at me and shook his head. Figured it was 'cause of the state I was in – swaying and looking red raw with sunburn. Maybe it was 'cause I'd just visited my mother's grave. He was feeling sorry for me 'cause I was as alone as that dead baby in the graveyard. Before the guard buzzed us through, Cannon-Arms aimed a finger at me. Reached it out like he was going to touch it to my chest. Stopped before we connected.

'You hang in there, Pullman. There's a chance for you.'

He nodded his head and smiled so big I got a look at all his teeth. There were a lot of them and they gleamed white. He opened up his hand and left it out there in front of me. I reached up and shook it. When the door buzzed I walked through and left my driver behind. Took a left down the hall and signed in at the reception desk. The guard was watching a ball game on a small black-and-white screen. He didn't look up at me.

Two days of pain followed.

Then there was peeling.

This is your suffering, Joe. You can't have something you want without paying for it, can you? No, not you, Joe-Joe.

On the fifth day there was a knock on my door. I answered it and looked at the guy for a while without talking. Tried real hard not to smile too much and give away what I was thinking. He was the new head boy. Since Stokes got sick – since he was taken to the medical ward coughing up blood – this was the new assignment. He was just as big as Stokes, but not half as hard. Could tell that much from his smooth face and soft eyes.

'Pullman,' he said. 'Get dressed and report to Meeting Room Four.'

He walked away.

Short as he was with me, I figured it was official. Started to worry that they had connected me with Stokes' bad weed. Got dressed in my best digs and tried to decide if Oberman had the balls to finger me if they'd got to him. With all his stash, he'd be needing to make a deal just so he wouldn't go up state as an adult. So I was sweating it. Was still thinking about it when I checked myself in the mirror. White button-up with blue tie. Blue slacks and black socks. Slip-on shoes they give you for formal meetings when you're in D Class. Figured it was important to look good with the way the head boy was so tight with the facts. No smile or sneer or anything. All bottled up.

Maybe they've got something to tell you about your old man. Want to know how you're holding up after the graveyard visit. Maybe just some kind of meeting that Dean Littlejohn will put in your file to let everyone who gives a shit know what you've been doing with taxpayers' money.

Went down the hall. Nobody was out, so I couldn't stop anyone and ask if they knew what was happening. All the way to Meeting Room Four the place was dead. Like it had shut down and no one had told me before they left. D Class head boy was still around – sitting on a chair at the end of the hall reading a copy of *Franny and Zooey*. Passed him by without making like it was a big deal. Waited outside the meeting-room door and listened for voices. Wondering if maybe it was a bunch of Stokes' friends wanting to speak with me about the bad joint he'd smoked. Wanting to know how his stash got fixed with poison from the groundskeeper's shed. Wasn't likely, but it was still a possibility. The chance that I was in for a real ass-kicking.

Knocked on the door and opened it before anyone on the other side had a chance to respond.

'Joe,' Counsellor Jason Clements said. He stood from his chair and turned to me. 'Thanks for coming down.'

Clements had shaved his beard off and looked ten years younger. Almost as young as me and the other flunkies at St Martin's, only he was wearing a better set of clothes. His cost more than a couple of bucks and were made of materials that moved when he bent. Clements put out his hand. It wasn't usual for him to do that. He liked distance and was always jumpy when we were together. Still, I played along and took his hand in mine. Shook his soft palm for longer than either of us liked. We stopped shaking, and I looked at the man and woman sitting on the other side of the table. They looked weary and I couldn't decide if that look was for me or about me. Nodded my head at the man and he stood up. The woman stayed in her chair and took a better grip on her handbag.

'Joe,' Mister Clements said, 'I'd like you to meet Edgerton Meaks and his wife Mona. They are very interested in speaking with you.'

Stepped closer to the table when Edgerton Meaks reached a hand towards me. He leaned so his left hand was on the table, holding him up. We shook hands and I watched his face real close. Tried to place him. Maybe see if I remembered another Meaks. I checked his face to see if he had the same features as someone I'd run into along the way. Someone I'd had some kind of problem with.

'Pleased to meet you, sir.' He had a tight grip on me. With his hand still in mine, I said: 'Can I ask why you want to see me?'

'Well, we're . . .' Edgerton looked at Clements and seemed lost for a few seconds.

'Mister and Missus Meaks, Joe, are interested in fostering you.' He paused for a moment and made a weird kind of sound in his throat. He tilted his head like he was going to look at the visitors, but never put his eyes on them. Kind of like me when I was around a real attractive girl. I'd want to look, but there was just something that kept me from taking the chance. Made me come across as being real awkward. Clements was no better.

'Well, the possibility of it anyway.' He didn't have any trouble putting his eyes on me. Even tried for a smile.

I kept shaking Edgerton's hand. Turned so I could look at his eyes and wondered when the catch was going to come snapping into place. Tried to figure out what was going to go wrong before the whole thing even started. The woman next to Meaks was looking at me. She had a hand up to her chin. Fingers touching her white skin like her face was made from porcelain. Seemed she was afraid she'd break if she touched it too hard. While I shook the man's hand I smiled at his wife. She didn't know what to do. Her hand kept moving round her chin. Touched it all over like she thought it was going to disappear. Felt almost sorry for her. Not for the last time, either. It was almost a year later that I'd be in their house in a place called Henderson. A town that looked like it got built as a prop for an early edition of a *National Geographic* magazine. Picture heading: American Small Town Lives On.

Before we got to that stage I still needed to get them convinced that I was worth the risk they were thinking about taking. They both looked like they were slow-moving and simple people. They both wore church clothes. That concern they came in with never went away during the first meeting. It was there throughout all the meetings we had during the first few months. But they kept coming back to see me and I kept getting dressed in my best clothes and kept showing my kindest face. I saw a real chance of getting away from St Martin's if I played my cards right with Meaks and his wife.

'My name's Joe, ma'am,' I told the woman that first time. She moved her hand up to her mouth. 'Joseph Reginald Pullman. It's a real pleasure to meet you. Both of you.'

'Well, Joe,' the woman said, 'it's very nice to meet you.'

I'd stopped shaking Edgerton's hand and offered mine to his wife. She looked at it for a moment. Wasn't until she looked up and caught my smile that she set her hand in mine. I held it real gentle, like I was planning to lift her off the chair for a slow dance. After a soft shake I let it go. Was almost embarrassed at how relieved she looked when her hand fell away from mine. How she took hold of it with her other hand and set it in her lap.

'How was it you decided on me?' I asked.

'I'm sorry?' Edgerton said. He had started to sit down, but stopped. Made his back straight again. Then he pushed his hands into his pockets. Seemed to be content to stand that way for a while.

'Of all the people to foster. All the kids in all the state, I mean. Why'd you choose me?'

'Well, we heard your story. Then we read about you in the papers. Saw about your . . .' He looked at Clements for support, but kept talking. 'Read about your father and his case. When he was convicted . . . sentenced, we felt it was a shame for you to have no one left. So we made some calls and we met with some people and filled out a lot of paperwork.'

He let out a laugh that I came to trust over the years. It gave me confidence in him then, during that first meeting. 'We signed papers of all kinds. And then we finally made it here to meet you.'

'Well,' I said, 'that's real kind of you to persevere. Sure is a real kind thing to do.'

We talked for a while after that. Mainly small talk to pass the time. I took questions from Edgerton Meaks mainly, answering in a kind of unsure way. Mister Clements kept out of it and that was alright by me. I found out from the few questions I asked that Edgerton was called Pop by folks in his town. He and his wife ran a funeral home and, when he first mentioned the business he was in, he went quiet.

'It's a job that'll always be in demand,' I said.

He nodded his head and went back to asking the questions. After every one I'd take a deep breath and nod my head like I was considering the response carefully. Thing is, I didn't need the time. I was just putting on a show. They weren't the first people to come out and meet me, but Edgerton and his wife seemed genuine. They didn't seem to want to gain anything from being connected to me.

During a long silence I decided to throw them a bone.

'I went to see my mother's grave the other day,' I said. Edgerton looked at me and his right eyebrow raised up in a cartoon arch. His last question had been something concerning history. We'd talked a lot about history to that point. It was an interest of mine and we'd found it a common ground. An easy place to go to keep the awkward silences from moving into the room.

'How do you feel after seeing her grave, Joe?' Mona Meaks asked me.

She was looking at me with something different in her eyes. She was interested in hearing what I was about to say. There was something else there too. She was apprehensive. That much I could tell from the way she was holding her hands together just above the table. Holding them there like she was wanting me to see how white her knuckles had turned – how hard she was squeezing her hands together.

'Well, ma'am,' I said. 'I feel better for taking the time to speak with her. To share my thoughts. It's been a long time since it was just me and my mother. You'll know from the papers all about my father.' I looked over at Jason Clements to see how he was going to gauge my comments. He sat forward and nodded his head too fast for it to be anything less than confusion. He just didn't know how to take me and all my past baggage. 'Well, then you'll know we didn't have a very good relationship. After my mother was taken away, he sort of went away too . . . Made the house a real uncomfortable place to live in.'

Ran my fingers over the scars on the side of my head. Kept doing it for a few seconds. Usually it was out of habit. Running my fingers across them to feel how deep they were. How much the past was still a part of me. With Edgerton and Mona Meaks looking at me, I did it for show. So I wouldn't have to talk about the beatings my father dealt out. Rubbing the wounds acknowledged that I was damaged goods. Enough said.

'That's just horrible,' Edgerton said. 'And you never got out to see her?'

'No, sir. Not before now.' Looked over at Mona even when I was talking to her husband. She seemed to need more of my attention. Seemed to have a need to hear me speak about my mother. Somehow it wasn't a hard thing to do, telling Mona about the experience. 'To answer your question more thoroughly, ma'am, I feel like a burden has been taken from me. I've been able to talk about things that have been stuck in my throat up to now. Wasn't comfortable to let some of the things out. At my mother's grave it came out. All of it. And then some.'

I smiled at her. She smiled back.

'Felt good too. You understand what I'm saying?'

'Yes, Joe. I understand you.' She touched her chin again. Then she dropped her hands to her lap. Her shoulders bounced and she said: 'I understand you entirely, Joe.'

With that I sat back and let the room go quiet for a while. In that silence I decided that I would do whatever I needed to do to keep Edgerton and Mona Meaks coming back to St Martin's. I'd play the good kid and see how far the ride was going to take me. If things worked out, I'd make damned sure I kept to the same straight and narrow path that good folks walked.

That's just what I did. Kept at it for a long while too.

Chapter One

Pop was standing in front of me. He was at the other side of the table with his head shaking one second, then still as a rock the next. He'd be like that for a few seconds, standing there with his head steady. His face showing no emotion. Then it'd start shaking again and he'd look all angry and red. Veins swelling up like something was burrowing up under his skin. He raised his hand. Index finger stuck up in the air like he wanted me to look at the ceiling. Only it wasn't the ceiling he wanted me to look at. He wanted me to look at the red tip of his finger. Same one he'd just wiped along the surface of the table I was sitting at. The stripe his finger made through the middle of the table was slow to fill back in. I watched him until he'd gone back to shaking his head. Then I went back to watching his finger that he'd stuck up there between us. The red was making a slow crawl down towards his pale wrist.

I looked away 'cause I couldn't take the sight of him any more. He was old and tired and confused. He was a different man to the one I'd met as a boy. Made me think of all the time I'd known him and how much I owed him for all that time. Couldn't watch his face with those kinds of thoughts going through my head. After I looked away he started talking.

'What's wrong with you, Joe? What's happening?'

I shook my head at him and hoped he'd clear out like everyone else.

The lounge bar had been full when Edge stopped by to see me. Folks came to the Trapper's Paradise for the cheap beer and out-of-the-way secrecy. It's the two things the boarding house provides – that and three small guest rooms upstairs. Me and some alcoholic the locals called Chip were using two of the rooms. The other had a steady run of tenants, but it was never occupied for more than a few hours at a time. I'd gone down to the bar that night because the latest tenants were extra-loud. Made me feel lonely and useless for not finding the balls to speak with Carole. Tell her what she wanted to know and get back in the house.

I'd found a spare seat in the lounge. There was a time when I had better things to do than drink alone in a room filled with people. Those times kind of lost me. Or I lost them. Either way, that night I was in the bar with a purpose. I'd taken a chair and looked round at the familiar faces. Faces that sank down into the shadows when I'd looked at them. The place was full, but there was no one to talk to and that suited me fine.

After a few minutes of waiting Lenny came by my table. He's a hunched-shoulder kind of guy. There's nothing wrong with him. His spine's not bent and he's not long-time sick. He's just got lazy shoulders that make him look weak. That and he's got a quiet voice, and a mouth that moves too much for his words don't help his cause, either. He's awkward to look at and speak to, so folks don't often try. He can't look at you for more than a few seconds during a conversation – even when you're answering his questions.

He'd stopped by the table and asked what I was after. I ordered a couple of beers and a bowl of the stew he had written up on the Specials board. I pointed his attention to the chalkboard where he'd drawn a circle with shaky lines coming out of it. *Fresh stew! Get it while it's hot!* He went away with my order and I was still looking at the sign when he came back. He set the beers down on the table and told me the stew was off.

'Smells too bad to chance it, Joe. I don't really want to heat it up.'

'I'll settle for these,' I told him. Used one of my beer bottles to touch the neck of the other. It made a small clinking sound that got Lenny looking at it. He looked hypnotised for a couple of seconds, then he kind of faded off like he usually does. Not much of a talker. Even less of a cook.

About the time I got through with my first beer, Pop came strolling in. Had his hands down deep in the pockets of his coat and a white dusting of snow on his shoulders. Told me he was after some company. The way his words sounded, I knew he was there to see me about something important. More important than knocking back a few beers to pass the hours. He didn't say much to start things off, but managed to double the count of beer bottles collecting at the centre of my table.

'You doing alright?'

'Yeah.'

'Spoke with Carole yet?'

'Nope.'

'Maybe you should try . . .'

It wasn't much of a conversation, but it was enough to last us. We measured time in beer bottles, and after four each the conversation was even less important than when it started out. A dozen bottles in and the smell of bad stew was filling the room. Steaming bowls were coming through the doors leading from the kitchen. Lenny passed by on the second round and leaned in close to my head. He lifted a bowl so I could get a look in. Liquid was thick and dark and blood-coloured with a silver slick cutting a shape through it. Grey stones of meat poked up through the surface.

'You wanting to take a chance on it?' he asked.

I shook my head and he faded away again.

'You've got a duty, Joe. If not to yourself, then to Marty.'

Pop made like he was going to stand. He took in a deep breath and puffed out his chest. He stayed like that and looked at me for a while before he said: 'Don't forget about him. He's a good kid and he needs you.'

'Don't put it on me, Pop.'

'Alright,' he said. 'But you better remember he's got expectations.'

'It's shit for everybody.' Raised my bottle and tilted it at him. It was the best I could manage to emphasise the point. My energy was low, but it was something to let him know I took his meaning. 'This whole thing is real shit.'

'Well, then you go back home and straighten it out.'

I drank my beer bottle dry and looked across the table at Pop. Gave real thought to what it was I should be telling him. Tried to figure out from looking at his face how much he deserved to know. How much I owed him.

'What's going on in your head, son?'

'Nothing, Pop. Just thinking how it's all gone wrong again.'

Pop started jabbering on about something. Chances this and opportunities that. Thing is, I didn't get all of what he was saying. Over his shoulder I'd caught a shape in the doorway. Watched the shape until it moved into enough light so I could make out who was inside the shadow. It was Colin Lowell. He walked farther into the lounge and stood under the dim red light. His eyes were all screwed up and I took some comfort from the fact that I could see him before he could see me. He kept his hands in the pockets of his jacket while he looked round the place. Stopped when his chin was pointed in the direction of our table. His hands came out of his jacket pockets. My reaction was to stand and leave. Give myself a chance of avoiding him, or at least be ready to react when he was up close. He still needed to wade through a few tables to get to mine. Would need to get past Pop and I figured that wasn't going to happen. Pop didn't want the trouble between me and Colin to kick off all over again.

'Joe,' he called out. 'Wait there, Joe. I need to speak with you.'

That's the first indication I had that my body was reacting faster than my head. I'd stood up already and shoved my chair back in the same motion. Looked down and had a couple of seconds where everything felt strange. Swayed in place and felt like I'd lost something. I just stood that way, swaying from side to side, wishing I'd ditched before Colin had made it up so close.

He was at the table by then. Hands up, like he was already trying to call me down. Like he was expecting me to go back to old tricks. Show him how upset I was with the hard side of my hands. Pop stood up fast from his chair like he was thinking the same thing. He leaned towards me and put his arm out. Reached over and touched a hand to my shirt. He used his other hand to paw at Colin. Doing his best to get him moving back. Putting some kind of distance between me and him.

'It was a bad idea coming here, Colin.'

I looked round and saw the familiar faces were peeling out of the shadows. Expressions were already changing. Mouths were making new kinds of shapes. I turned my attention to Colin. He looked calm and that set something off inside of me.

'I've been here for a few weeks now, Colin,' I said. 'So we can all figure this wasn't some kind of an accident. Another of your chance encounters.'

'No, it's nothing like that,' Colin said. 'I'm here 'cause I need to talk to you.'

I stood for a while shaking my head. Listening to the sound of spoons clinking against the inside of empty bowls. Throats getting cleared. Voices talking and getting hushed down at the same time.

'We've done all our talking.'

'It's about Carole.'

'Now, you can stop right there,' Pop told him. He'd made his back straight again. Kept his hand on Colin and tried to push him away. Colin moved, but not by far. He stepped round Pop and came to the table. Pop pushed on him and sent Colin to the side. 'Listen here. Joe's got enough to think about right now. There's no need for any more trouble from the likes of you.'

'I'm not bringing trouble, Mister Meaks.' Colin looked at him, all loaded up with sincerity. Looked like he was hurt that Pop had made out like he was trying to cause more trouble. 'This isn't about anything but what's going on now. It's about Carole. Everything else is finished. That's all way in the past.'

'What do you need to tell me about my wife?' I said.

Pop stopped pressing at Colin's shirt. I don't know how many people were still round, but for some reason it seemed important. The tables were empty to my left. Over on the right too. The last of the folks were bent down and moving through the entrance door. Same way you see people move on the news when a bomb's gone off and everybody's clearing out. Smoke rising up round them.

'What's this about my wife?'

'She's been out, Joe. All over the place. Since you've been here it's been happening even more.'

'So you're following *her* now,' I said. 'Wasn't enough with me. Now you're getting a liking for Carole.'

'No. Oh, hell, Joe. Listen to me. It's nothing like that. But I've seen her round. Sure, this has got to sound real weird, but I've seen her. You need to know about it.'

'Get the hell out of here, Colin.'

'Mister Meaks, he's got a right to know. As a man he has the right.'

As a man you have the right, Joe. As a man . . .

Colin moved towards me and after that it all goes kind of hazy. He had his hand up. It came out towards me and he was wide-eyed. His mouth was moving and all that was coming from it was a long moan. A dull and quiet calling. I'd moved, but it wasn't until after everything went messy that I knew I'd moved. I was aware of my muscles burning hot. There was Colin's face one second. Then it was gone. Then it was back again. Gone. Back again. Each time he flashed up in front of me his face looked different. Worse than before. Red all over the place. His nose getting wider. Fatter. Mouth worked up in a wild shape that was shaking. Shaking like a rubber band flying through the air.

Gone. Back again.

That's when Pop's face started shaking. Then it froze. My chest was pounding. A heavy pulse took up a place deep inside my head. Thundering away. Colin's face wasn't showing any more. He was finished moving up and down. I fell back to my seat. Pushed hard against the backrest and kind of settled heavy into it. Looked up at Pop. He was standing in front of me with that confused look on his face. Head steady as a rock. Then it'd start to shake. So I watched him and concentrated on my lungs. Filling and emptying. Pop's head in front of me. Shake. Stop. Shake. His cracked lips making shapes at me, but the pulsing in my head was too loud and the shapes didn't make any sounds.

What's happening to you?

It was to be expected with all the commotion that was going on. A lot of noise. My hands were aching. Arms wet. Head felt like I was all filled up with blue electric. Charged with something wild. Through the pulse in my head came a quiet humming sound deep in there. No way to ignore it. I'd have given it more attention, but there was Pop hanging over me. *Shake. Stop. Shake.* Colin was gone, but his voice was still coming through the humming. Making its way through all the noise.

'What's happened to you?' Pop said.

I was slumped back in the chair. One of the twelve bottles of beer smashed and scattered on the table in front of me.

Looked round and saw Colin Lowell was off in the corner of the bar. Hiding somewhere back behind a fallen table. Laid out on his side with his legs moving, trying to move him back even farther. His shoes making scraping sounds against the wood floor. Kicking up the peanut shells someone had scattered during the hasty exit. His hands were up at his face. I couldn't see just how bad the cut was and how bad the bleeding was going to get. He had a slick of it on his shirt. A good load of it running through his fingers.

'Jesus Christ, Joe,' Pop was saying. 'Goddamn it, son!'

Pop looked over at Colin and I followed his lead. There wasn't much changing. He still had the red making a slow stream through the fingers covering his face. I watched him and stopped counting time in beer bottles that had only just cluttered our table. I started counting the time in Colin's strides against the floor. Feet moving over the wood. Hard soles scratching against a hard surface. Without that sound it was just Colin Lowell blubbering in the corner. I got so drawn into Colin flapping round the floor that I didn't notice Officer Jody Verring standing next to me. Didn't even see him make it through the entrance hall. Wasn't long before another officer came into the room. He went over and kneeled down near Colin. The cop tried a few times to get those red hands away from Colin's face. Each time he went for them, Colin would kick out with his legs. Shift like a fish on a hot bank of sand. Turning himself round so the cop just couldn't get a look-in.

'The hell happened here?' Jody Verring asked me.

'He fell,' I said.

'Why's there so much busted glass, Pullman?'

'He fell on my bottles.'

Verring's hand dropped on my shoulder. My muscles jumped and Verring went with them. His hand pulled away and when it fell on me again he had a tighter grip. This time he tried to turn me. I wouldn't go, so he pushed hard.

My chest connected with the table. Chin fell down and found a piece of glass. Felt the skin break and the glass go in easy, but there was nothing after that. No pain. I was numb.

'Hold it there, Pullman.'

'Sure thing, bud.'

Pop moved forward. With my head on the table, I caught sight of his belt buckle edging closer to me.

'Now you leave him be, Jody!' Pop yelled.

'It's alright, Pop,' I called out. My lips moving in the fluid covering the table. 'Just let him do his thing.'

'Joe's just been defending himself,' Pop said. 'Get your hands off.'

'Pop,' I said. 'Just leave it.'

'Mister Meaks, I'll have to ask you to keep your distance.'

Verring lifted me off the table and slammed me down on it again. I let go of a sound from deep down in my gut and it got Pop stirring.

'He's alright,' the other cop called out. I pulled up and got my chin off the table so I could see him for myself. The cop was a young guy with a long, thin nose and the sharpest widow's peak I'd ever seen. 'He's not cut. Can't see a scratch on him even.' He looked back at Colin who was twisting fish-style away from him. 'Just hold on there, sir. I'm needing to have a look at you.'

Colin was saying something. Muffled it into his hands and all I heard was this wet kind of sound. Red bubbles moved up between his fingers.

'He came in here and started throwing round accusations. Telling Joe that Carole's been—'

'Pop,' I said. 'Just leave it alone. For *Christ's sake* I don't want—'

'Shut it, Pullman.' Verring shoved his hand down hard on my back. My head went down on the table again. I'd lain steady for a while, figuring Colin was in a real bad way. All busted up from the knocking his face took against the table.

He'd had a half-dozen good bounces on it, so there was some relief that he wasn't too bad off. Thing is, if he wasn't all that bad, I didn't see why I should be bent over the table with Colin's blood soaking into my clothes. Least not with one of Jody Verring's thighs pressing up between my ass-cheeks and his hand pushing down between my shoulder blades.

'Let me up, Verring,' I said. 'You heard your man. He's not even all that hurt.'

'You can't go smacking somebody around like that and expect to get away with it. That's assault, Pullman.'

'Goddamn it,' I said. Made like I was going to stand up, and Verring pushed down hard again. Used his weight to push firm between my shoulders. This time I kept moving on him – standing up while he was trying to shove me down. He couldn't keep me there with just one hand, so he put the other one on me. Felt his baton digging into my right shoulder and I wondered how long it was going to be before Verring decided shoving wasn't enough.

'Leave him,' Pop said. 'Don't even think about it.'

I didn't know who Pop was talking to – Verring or me. Couldn't look up to see with Verring pushing so hard on me. Kept moving and felt like I was almost free from him. Then Verring slipped his arm round the front and pulled the bend of his elbow in tight under my chin. He grabbed hold round the back and started a tight choke. I leaned back into him so I wouldn't go out. Took a good hold on his arm and tried to pull it loose. Turned my head so he wouldn't crush my windpipe shut. Worked on getting enough space there so I could catch a breath. Pop was coming round the table. Moving between the scattered chairs. He kicked over the tall pot Lenny uses to store umbrellas for his guests.

'Let go of him, Jody,' Pop said. Still moving on us. 'He's going blue, damn it!'

'Verring!' The voice came out of the air, through the haze of smoke clouding up high against the ceiling. It was crawling in a dream-like way, making it hard for me to keep from going out in Verring's choke. The big arm round my neck loosed up. I took a breath and my head went light. Drained empty. Legs were somewhere down below me. Damned if I couldn't find them. They weren't connected to me any more. Not enough to hold me upright.

'Set him down in the chair and back off.'

'Sheriff, he was resisting.'

'I don't give a good dadgum what he was doing. You put him down on the chair and back off like I told you.'

With that I was getting moved to the right. Felt a heavy pressure under my arms and the earth rolled out. Then I was sinking down until a chair formed under me. My head was moving back, weighed down with cement, and then I felt a hand round my neck. The hand started rubbing. I took a few deep breaths. The hand kept rubbing until I found out the hand belonged to me. I stopped rubbing and swayed for a few seconds and finally put my hands on the table to help find the balance again. Knocked away a few shards of broken glass, so I wouldn't have them in front of me. Clearing a place to set my head down. Creating a landing point if my head filled with cement again and became too heavy to hold up.

'What in the hell happened here?' Nat Upshaw was asking me.

Cleared my throat and tested my voice. It sounded low but steady. Nat Upshaw put his face down close to mine.

'I didn't catch a word of that, Joe. Now take a breath and try again.'

'I'd rather not talk about it, Sheriff.'

He moved away to the other side of the table. He looked down at it and sucked at his lip while nodding his head. His big white cowboy hat dipping each time his head came forward. Rose every time his head went back. A ship on a slow sea. He reached up and took the hat off. Studied it for a few seconds and looked at me again. Long enough to shake his head and make me feel like a kid with a pocket full of candy and no way to pay for it. He turned his attention to the corner of the bar – to Colin Lowell and the deputy kneeling beside him.

'How's he holding up?' Nat asked.

'He's not taking his hands away, so I can't tell for sure.' The kid-cop was stooped down on his haunches. He twisted on the balls of his feet and tried for a better look. He shook his head. 'Most I can see, he's not all that bad, Sheriff.'

'Colin, quit dicking around,' Nat called out. 'Take your hands away so Jack can see your face.'

Colin dropped his hands. Real dark-looking stuff came running down from his nose and moved towards his mouth. Looked like there was a big cut at first – maybe a fat one at that. Then he went to speak and the dark mess moved with his words. Couldn't understand what he was saying. His words came out of his throat all bubbling and wet. He wiped a hand across his mouth and took a few seconds looking at his knuckles. The dark mess had moved to the other side of his face. He opened his mouth again and showed his teeth. They were all accounted for, from where I was sitting. Still, it didn't bring me the sense of relief.

The room was quiet while we all stayed dumb and watched as Colin checked himself out. He pushed his fingers into his mouth and went round touching each one of his teeth, and damned if we didn't all wait stupid-like while he did it. Then he took his nose between thumb and bloodied fingers. He yelped and looked embarrassed after that. His eyes well up and the overflow making lines down his face.

'I'm alright,' he finally said. His words muffled and rubbery. He studied the blood on his hands and spat something on the floor between him and the deputy. He ran his hands over his face again, taking inventory and making sure it was all in the place he thought it should be. 'Yeah, I think I'm alright.'

'The hell you down there hollering like that for?'

'Joe.' Nat had his hand out to keep me from going down a path that had a hard way back. 'Enough from you. Colin, all that from your nose?'

'Yessir,' Colin said. 'I think that's where it's coming from.'

'Jody, go back there and find Lenny. Tell him we're needing a towel or something. Tell him to make it damp.' Nat turned his head like he was going to speak to me. 'And, Jody, make sure you thank him for the call. This could have got worse, I'm sure.' Nat raised an eyebrow at me. Took it like he was questioning me, only I didn't know how I was supposed to answer.

'It wasn't going to get any worse than that,' I said and pointed to Colin, who was struggling to get to his feet. 'All the stuff beforehand was just words. They were getting loud. We disturbed the folks who were here and I apologise for that. Thing is . . .'

'Better be good.'

I leaned towards Nat, stuck my face over the table to get closer to him: 'He came by to tell me some things about Carole I wasn't interested in hearing.'

'Well,' Nat said with his forehead all wrinkled by his thoughts. 'Now I can see how that could make a man react. Specially one in your situation.'

'It's just the . . . I guess the moment was wrong. People were around. I felt like I had to stop him. I couldn't let him get too far into his accusations with other people listening in.'

'This all hitting the mark, Colin?'

'I didn't mean to cause any trouble, Sheriff.' His eyes flashed at me for a second, then they were away, scanning for something in the pattern on the carpet. 'Joe, I'm just trying to save you some hassle later on.'

Verring came back with the towel. Handed it to Nat, but Pop took hold of it and walked it across the room. He stuck the towel under Colin's nose and pushed until Colin's head went back.

'Van's outside,' Pop said. 'I can take him over to the medical centre. He may be better off lying down.'

'Yeah, Edge,' Nat said. He looked down at the table. Twisted his head to look under it. 'You been drinking these?'

Pop looked at Nat and then down at the four beer bottles still on the table. Nat had his boot on one of the bottles that had hit the floor. He rolled it under the sole of his boot.

'Had a few,' Pop said.

Nat nodded.

'You go on ahead. Jody, you follow and make sure they make it down there safe.'

Verring wasn't too pleased. His eyes were filled with contempt. Swimming in it. It must have been eating holes in that poor bastard's pride. Angry that he'd been so close to choking me out. Close as hell, but just not able to finish it off.

The kid-cop with the widow's peak got Colin standing and ushered him out the door. Pop followed close by, with Verring slowing when he got next to Nat. He said something, but it was too low for me to catch. The sheriff nodded his head and slapped a hand down on Verring's shoulder. He waited for the room to clear and then moved round the other side of the table from me. Looked at the surface for a few seconds and then pulled up a chair that had been knocked to the side when Colin tumbled back. He sat down. Took his time getting comfortable. Held his hat like he didn't know what to do with it. Then he looked at me. Nat Upshaw was the calm man I'd met when I first arrived in Henderson. Even-tempered and deliberate. Still, I got a sense there was something more to him. Depths that would take some hard digging to reach.

'I want you to tell me a story,' he said.

Oh, we've heard this one, Joe.

'Kind of a story are you wanting?'

'Well, we can start with what's been keeping you here.' His hands reached out to the sides. Simple gesture, but it was effective too. Made me look round and evaluate the surroundings. The dark wood panelling on the walls. Mouldering deer head over the unlit fireplace. It was a small room that felt smaller because of the dim lighting. Felt small 'cause Nat Upshaw had directed me to look at it. Made me consider where I was in life.

'Me and Carole are having some problems.'

'Most of us got that much a few weeks back when you took a room upstairs. Words are fast as the wind, Joe. News got back to me before your bag was unpacked. Probably before you even had the key in your door for the first time. Could have been more discreet about it. Bunked in with your pop for a few weeks. Put a cot in the office down at the funeral home. It's not ideal, but folks wouldn't be any the wiser. What people don't know in this town is what keeps life normal. Soon as a sniff of scandal hits the gossips, it's a dadgum frenzy.'

He stopped looking at me. Paid too much attention to the fist he'd just balled up between us. One he was holding above the table.

'Should have let it blow over and got back to things. That's what you need to do.'

I nodded my head and said: 'This isn't going to blow over.'

Nat wasn't comfortable with that. His shoulders moved and he shifted forward in his chair. His fist opened up and he spent too much time looking at his fingers. Checking his nails for something.

'Got a reason why not?'

'It's not a reason,' I said. 'More a feeling. It's not a real good feeling, either.'

'Taking it out on other folks isn't going to win you any friends, Joe. You need to get your head on straight or support is going to wear thin. Henderson's a heavy place to live without the support.'

'I'm sure it is.'

Nat nodded his head and kept his hands where I could see

them. Rubbed them together like a man out in the cold. A man remembering when times were different. A man seeing more than what was in front of him.

'You don't need that kind of trouble again.'

'I can agree with you there,' I said.

'You should go home. Get back and talk to Carole. These things can get out of hand. You can make them right or you can watch them go wrong.'

'Yeah,' I told him.

'Get your things,' he said. 'I'll give you a ride.'

Chapter Two

We didn't talk much during the drive. Nat's Bronco was skidding in the snow. More snow was falling and Nat was doing all he could to keep us on the road. I kept my eyes forward and felt a sort of calm coming over me. White flakes falling around us like ash from a fire. Watched as they gathered and danced past the headlights. The snow on the ground had a blue tint from the moonlight. The moon looked too close to be real. Close enough to reach out and shove it back up into the night sky. Shove it hard until there was nothing left but a small white spec in all that darkness.

'Those boys will be glad you're home,' Nat said.

'They're with Carole's folks.'

The shapes of ghosts formed and moved in swirls by my window. I didn't want to talk any more. I just wanted to get back to the house to lather some unguent into the cut on my chin. I put a hand to my face and felt the slick plastic of the butterfly bandages Nat had given me. A wrinkled strip from the first-aid kit he kept in his glove box. He'd watched while I fingered out a piece of glass, he'd waited until I'd taped the wound shut before driving away from the Trapper's Paradise.

'Should get that checked out.'

I nodded my head.

'What are the boys doing up in Fairfax?'

'Carole wanted to talk. Sent them away so we could do it without interruptions.'

'So why aren't you at home?'

I didn't like the way Nat was looking at me. The way he slowed the truck down so much he didn't have to concentrate on the road ahead. Just kept his hand on the wheel and his chin pointed at the side of my head.

'We don't have much to talk about.'

'Things can't be so bad.'

'Sure they can, Nat.' I looked at him and this time he looked away from me. The smile had melted off his grey face. He must have seen something in my eyes that he didn't like. 'Things can be just that bad.'

He squeezed the wheel. Knuckles white and tendons rippled up to the surface of his skin. We went back to being quiet again – stayed that way until we got back to the house. He pulled the Bronco into the driveway. He cut off the engine and killed the headlights. The house looked big and dark. I watched for movement. Something to tell me Carole was inside. The only light was coming through the family-room curtains, from the lamp on the living-room table. Carole always left it on for me in case I needed to come back for a change of clothes. Maybe show my face for a family dinner. Spend time in the place, so Marty would remember he had a father. Donald too, if he needed one.

'Go on in, Joe,' Nat said. He was watching me again. This time he had his regular face on. One that was easy to look at and hard not to like. 'Take your time speaking with her.'

'I'll do that, Sheriff.'

He put his hand out and I grabbed hold of it and gave it a tight squeeze. Nat made like he was going to say something else. Shook the thought from his head while he returned the hold on my hand. I pulled away and got out of the truck, staggering through a frozen crust of snow, moving towards my front door. Wanted to get inside so I wouldn't have to feel

Nat Upshaw's eyes on me. Got to the porch and tossed a hand in the air to wave Nat along. Used the other hand to fish the keys out of my pocket. Shook the right key loose and moved for the front door. The key didn't fit the lock. Looked to the side and spotted Edith Krantz, the old bitch of a neighbour. She had her curtains pulled wide, giving herself space to try and work out what was going on. *Sheriff pulls up and drops off the town undertaker. By gosh, it's a story that needs telling!* It's a recipe for gossip, and Chef Krantz is the biggest shit-stirrer of them all. All that crazy juice she had swilling round in her head was already boiling. Churning something up that was good and tasty. Mustering up the why to the what to the how. Last thing I wanted to do was feed her appetite. I tried not to look too loose on my feet, but it wasn't easy to keep steady.

Slid in another key and turned the lock. The door went in and I went in with it. Shut the door behind me without motioning to Nat again. I had a hot feeling burning inside my gut. For a while I stood with my back pressed hard against the door, breathing deep. Doing all I could not to lose my head. In through the nose, out through the mouth. Got a rhythm going and after a while felt like I could hold my own.

'You home?' I called out. With my words in the air I felt a pang of freedom. I'd got used to being in a room at the boarding house. I'd decided that the routine of the Trapper's Paradise was all I was ever going to have. Room to lounge bar. Back to room. Out of the funeral home. Off for a pickup. Back to the funeral home. Then off to the Trapper's, where I would lie in my room listening to the temporary tenants next door. Shower and food somewhere in all the mess, and occasionally turning up to take Marty someplace. It felt good that the routine was broken. I almost looked forward to whatever was about to come my way.

Turned and looked at the living room. The sofa and the chairs – a lot of places to settle in. Dropped my bag on the tiles in the foyer and headed to the kitchen. I had the foul taste of old beer on a dry tongue. I needed a cold one. A refresher. A nerve-killer.

The house was quiet, but that wasn't a big deal. Quiet was good. Carole didn't like music all that much any more. She'd been a dancer when we met. Nothing with poles and stages and tight silver bikinis – but she liked to move. Turn the music on and she'd get around the place. There was this crazy kind of walk she did. Moved her arms like she was in water and she'd sway her hips. Stepping slow the whole while, keeping time with the music. I'd get up close to her. Right up behind her and she'd keep going with her eyes closed like I wasn't even there.

The hell was it you called her, Joe? That name you gave her . . .

There had been a name once and I'd used it when I came up behind her. Put my hands on her and felt her push back on me. I had a name for her and I'd use it all the time. She'd push into me and she'd laugh. *Goddamn, that was a laugh.* If there was music on, she sure as hell would dance. And the louder the music got, the more she would move. *Once upon a time there was a better world than this.* She didn't play music any more. She didn't move like she used to.

I pulled the fridge door open and looked inside. A line of beer bottles standing to attention. No matter how long I was away, Carole always had something waiting for me. I reached in and took a bottle from the top shelf. It almost felt like stealing. Like I was taking from a place where I didn't belong. I waited with my hand hovering in front of the shelf, then I took another one before closing the door.

'You've been a lazy man, Joe,' I told myself. 'A bad and lazy man.'

Said it out loud almost like I was talking to someone else. I suppose I was trying to anyway. Somehow hoping Carole could hear my words. Hoping they would go some way to making some kind of amends for what had been going on between us. For all the time I'd spent away from her. The sound of my voice in the empty house brought back the sour feeling in my gut. I set the bottles on the counter and waited. Listened. Silence was all I had, so I made some noise. Fumbled round in the drawers – knocking round the knives and spoons until I found the bottle opener. Topped the bottles and let the caps rattle round like coins on the counter top. I watched until they came to a stop. One lying next to the other.

My tendency has always been to watch things fade – to take solace in being able to survive. The same way I watched Pop fade after Mona passed. Watched him go to pieces during her sickness. It took her slow, but it took him fast. The second Doc Maitland told her she was dying, Pop started to fade. Met him when he was already an old man and I took a kind of peace from the way time was removing colour from his skin. Stripping his hair to strands of ragged white cotton.

I took that same easy view with my marriage. Saw it going. Drifting. Witnessed it unravelling, and while Carole was making plans – looking for solutions – I sat and waited and played witness. I even left towards the end because it was easier than watching it up close. At first Carole had chased me. Followed me to the boarding house and brought food to my room, and she had sat with me while I picked at those meals. She would speak softly and let me have the distance she knew that I needed. Then she would leave. At first, moving close to me and holding my head to her chest. Telling me she wouldn't ask any more questions. Telling me she had only wanted to know more so that she could help me get away from my past.

Every day Carole would take a few steps back and gain more distance and I would feel more comfort. She created more quiet and I brought no noise. I watched her fade and I kept telling myself it was going to get better. It'll have to get better. I did nothing to keep her. Did nothing to close the gap. *It's just got to get better*, I'd say to myself.

It's better this way, Joe. She's taken it with her. It's all gone again.
But, that was the problem.

The first beer went down with the ease and speed of water. I set the bottle on the counter and looked at the other. Beads of condensation collecting and falling from the side. Leaned in close and waited while drops collected with other drops. Watched and listened. It was all dead. House. Sound. *Marriage.*

I pulled out the change from my pocket and tossed it on the counter. Silver spilled out. Remnants of paper money I'd spent on coffee. Change from Darnell's that still had a slick coating of bacon grease. An orange crisp of special sauce caught in the grooves. Smell of charred lard and decaying mayonnaise stronger than the copper of the pennies. The change rattled to a stop on the glass cutting board and I waited for the sound to die out before I stopped looking. Halfway to getting the bottle to my mouth I spotted the note. It was pegged to the fridge door with a magnet shaped like a tin of baked beans. Centred on the note and set just under the Hotpoint label. My name written across the damned thing:

Joe

I drank from the bottle and swallowed hard. Kept moving my eyes over the shape of my name. Knowing Carole's hand had written it. Wondering what else she had written before pegging it up on the fridge door. With the bottle tipped back, I turned my head. Still kept an eye on it. *Joe.* It was an awkward way to read a note – with my head back. But it got my mind working. Thoughts rattling away in my head – loud as greasy coins on a glass cutting board.

The hell's Carole up to?

Nothing wrong at all, man. Usually just J. J – gone out. See you later. J – will call. J – dinner's in the freezer.

This was different. All those evening classes in arts and crafts had done her proud. Sitting all night with Nancy Lowell in some classroom at the local high school. Just to get away from home. Needing to get away from the absent husband. I never complained, but I never saw anything she produced in those night-classes.

'What is it you're doing now?' I'd asked. One of the few times I'd tried to break down the thing we were putting up between us. I'd come back to the house to get a fresh suit. Me and Ted had a call for a pickup and I was looking lame and smelling stale from the mattress I'd been sleeping on at the Trapper's Paradise. I'd gone into the study to grab a file of invoices I'd left in the cabinet, and walked in on Carole. She'd been in there doing something at my desk. Didn't think anything of it at the time, but she looked scared sitting back there. Her hair looked greasy and thin. It wasn't like Carole to be unkempt. Her hands had been going through the files in my drawer, and her eyes came up and met me coming through the doorway.

'Hey,' I said. Her head snapped up. Hair stuck to her red face. She tried a smile, but it wasn't fooling either of us. She pulled her hair back and shook her head in slow motion. Blew a breath through her lips and put her hands up. She went to chewing her lip and dropped her hands.

I moved into the room and adjusted my tie. Knocked the lint off the sleeves of my suit. Kept my eyes on her the whole while. Finished with the sleeves of my suit. Carole must have taken that for a sign that she needed to speak. She covered her eyes with her hand and shook her head. Kept moving it slow.

'What is it you're doing now?' I asked her. My voice calm and paced.

'What do you mean?' she said. Her hand lowered.

'In your class.' She looked confused. 'Your evening class with Nancy. Last quarter it was macramé. Calligraphy before

44

that. See, I remember these things.' Tried to make a joke out of it. But she wasn't laughing and I didn't have the energy to raise the smile. 'What're you doing now?'

'Pottery,' she said and pulled her hair behind her left ear. Her smile was strained. The corners of her mouth quivering under the weight. She was straining, but she kept trying to put that smile on.

'When are you going to bring some of it home?'

'I don't know,' she said. 'Soon.'

'What about the macramé? You have any of that?'

'I wasn't very good,' she said. 'I left it at the class. Didn't really think it was anything we could use.'

'You need help finding something in my desk?'

'No,' she said and made a sort of laugh that neither of us was comfortable with. 'I just thought you'd have an envelope. I'm going to send Lynda a cheque. She's short this month. So I told her I'd send her something to tide her over.'

'Top left,' I said. 'Should be a couple in there. Stamps too.'

She nodded her head, but didn't go for the drawer.

'How's that sister of yours anyway?'

'Okay, I guess. Just on hard times.'

'Aren't we all?'

She didn't say anything, but she finally went for the drawer. With the envelopes in hand she got out of my chair and left the study. I took my files and left the house. We didn't speak much after that. Carole never did bring home any pottery. Two weeks later I was standing with a beer in my hand looking at a note she'd left me. Staring at the damned thing – wondering when she'd written it. Wondering what expression she had on her face when she stuck it up with the magnet. Scared as hell about what I was going to read when I finally opened it:

Joe

Now it would've been bad news if she'd used your full name, Joe. Women always use the full name when shit's in flight.

Turn the note over. Carole's gone to see her mother. She's decided she doesn't want the boys to go to her parents on their own after all. All that talk about spending time talking things through – just us, without distractions.

Have some wine.

Get some food in.

All just a king-sized load of bullshit, Joe. She must have passed you coming back down the highway.

Figured maybe she'd gone off to see Lynda. She was probably out there delivering another one of your cheques to that useless bitch of a sister. Always puffing on about welfare 'cause you just can't get enough. According to Lynda, there's never more than bare necessities. *Fat, lazy bitch knows all the trailer-trash talk-show guests on personal terms, Joe. She has all the time in the world to catch all that daytime television has to offer, but she can't find a job. She's got time to write letters to her boyfriend in prison.*

Who the fuck meets a crook over the Internet? How's that for poor? Welfare living with Internet access and low-rent mobile-trailer accommodation, all courtesy of Joe Pullman and wife.

Pushed a finger under the lip of the note. Opened it up and, before reading it, I lifted the bottle. Took a couple of heavy pulls. Kept a mouthful of beer until it went warm over my tongue. Let the bubbles fizz out and swallowed hard. Set the bottle down and took the note in two hands. Peeled back the flap and turned it over and looked at the other side. Nothing there. Just my name. Still I looked at the crease she'd made when bending it in half. Looked at it like I needed to figure out how it was all put together in case I needed to get it back in shape. So I could slip it back under the magnet and make it look like I'd never touched it. Make-believe I hadn't read it:

Joe

You can't give me the answers I need, but that can't stop me from asking the questions. I don't know when you will get this message, but I won't be here. I need time. That's your line, but I'm using it now.

I hope I find nothing, Joe. I can't stop myself from looking.

You will need to get the boys. If you can't make it, call Pop and see if he can help. That's Monday. Write it down. Don't forget again.

I'm sorry.

Carole

Lifted the bottle and filled my mouth. Set the note on the counter and kept looking at it. Opened the fridge and pulled another bottle from the top shelf. No guilty feeling. Topped the third bottle and let the cap spin and rattle. Grabbed the phone off the wall. Used my thumb to mash the buttons. A phone number I dialled only when Carole wasn't around. Dialled it all the other times we'd had problems. All the times she'd decided she needed to get away. It was without thought that I dialled Carole's parents. A reaction because it had happened before – without the note, but with Carole's sudden disappearing trick.

Thank you and good night!

'Come on, Fran,' I said. 'Pick up the phone.'

'Hello?'

'Frances.' I took a breath. Moved the beer bottle away from my mouth. 'Carole there with you?'

'Joe?'

'Listen, Frances. I need to speak with Carole for a minute. I'm beat. Had a real tough day.'

'Carole's not here,' she said. 'Why on earth would Carole be here?'

'Right. Okay.' I took a drink.

'Is something wrong?' Her voice dulled for a second. She was talking, but I couldn't make out what she was saying. I stopped drinking and tried to listen. Moved the bottle away like it was going to make some kind of difference. Her voice came back again. 'Wasn't she supposed to be home? Weren't you two supposed to talk?'

Jesus Christ, Carole.

'She's supposed to be home every day, Fran.'

'It's not like her to just leave,' she said. 'What have you done now?'

'I'm not following you.' Finished the beer while I listened to her make the dull sounds on the other end of the phone. Squeezed the bottle in my hand, trying to reshape the glass. Kept at it while walking through to the kitchen. I dumped the bottle into the trash bin.

'I'm here, Frances, and I'm waiting for Carole. We've got plans,' I said. 'I'm cooking, see. It's my turn to cook tonight.'

'But you're tired. You told me so.'

'That's beside the point.' Gritted my teeth – the only way to get through a conversation with Frances Quincy. Gnashing my teeth together until the pain was bright and large inside my head. 'She's supposed to be here. That's all. I figured maybe she drove out to your place.'

'Why would she do that? It's a long drive, Joe.'

Joe Pullman.

'Yeah,' I said. 'I'm aware of that. That's what I'm figuring now, Fran. Too long a drive for Carole to make.'

'Did you do something?' She was using her suspicious voice again.

'What's that supposed to mean?'

'Sometimes she needs to get away.' Her voice went soft again. She was talking into the back of her hand. Her wrinkled soft palm covering the receiver. Rambling her quick-fire words at someone. I felt tired and irritated, and speaking with Frances wasn't making it any easier. Part of me wished it was my hand that was over her mouth muffling her words. Part of me wished I could make out what the hell she was saying or who the hell she was talking to.

'Fran.' She kept talking. Sounding distant. 'Frances. Listen to me.' She was still covering that handset. Still talking to someone else. 'Damn it, Fran! She's not here. I didn't do anything. I just came back to fix dinner.'

Listened to her breathing. Listened to the small gulping sound she was making.

'I can have Paul call you when he gets in with the boys,' she said. 'I'll do that much.' She put the phone down. I followed suit before the sound of the dead line came pulsing out of the handset.

Went through and sat down on the sofa. Turned on the television and switched channels until I found the news. There was something happening in the Middle East. Dust and sand and smoke. A white reporter in a flak jacket was talking into a microphone. The mic was covered in grey fur. Looked like the guy was talking into an animal. My head felt empty and my thoughts were loose. Somehow I wanted to laugh, but it didn't feel like it was a good idea. Felt like I was still on the phone with Frances Quincy. Like she was still on the other end waiting for me to show some kind of guilt. I focused on the television and on the reporter, who was standing on top of a tan-coloured building. He was surrounded by a hundred other tan-coloured buildings.

I watched the news all the way through and had turned over to watch sport when the phone rang. I'd found my nerve again after the conversation with Frances. Didn't want to get into it again, so I hesitated picking up the receiver. Took my time lifting it to my ear.

'Joe, it's Frances. Paul's just back with the boys. I'll pass the phone across.'

'Thank you,' I said. Impressed that I was able to keep my voice so steady.

'Joe,' a man grumbled. 'It's Paul.'

'How's the back?' Tried to sound interested. It didn't work.

'Still there.' He coughed. 'After sixteen frames at the bowling alley I had to cry uncle. I'm expecting hell tomorrow. Think I may have to cry off early tonight. Take my pills and hit the sack.'

'Sixteen's better than usual.'

'At least I'm not laid out like one of your stiffs,' he said. There was a silence. It gave me time to get through to the kitchen and stand under the lights. Don't know why I went to the kitchen. Maybe for the beer. Maybe it's 'cause Carole was always going in there when her parents called. She'd pull out a chair and sit at the table and rearrange the fruit in the bowl while they talked. I fell onto a chair at the table. Slid the fruit bowl so it was in front of me. Looked at the bowl for a while and tried to decide if I should move the fruit around.

'So you and the boys doing okay?'

'Sure,' he said. 'Hold on, and you can ask Marty all about it while I use the head.'

There was a pause. Small commotion while Paul corralled Marty and handed over the phone.

'Hey, Dad,' he said. 'You at home?'

'Yeah, just sitting here waiting on your mom.'

'Cool,' he said. 'We went bowling in town, and coming back we passed this accident. You should have seen it. Some car spun out and went right under a truck. Didn't get to see it happen, but it must've just gone under. The cops weren't even there yet. Smoke was all over the place.'

'That's terrible.'

'Yeah,' he said, sounding less enthusiastic. 'But you would've looked too.'

Could see him standing next to the side table in Paul's foyer.

Phone, lamp and ornaments all in perfect order on the dark oak surface. Everything shining like a sailor's shoes. Like Paul's shoes when he was still on board the USS-whatever. Paul Quincy prancing round the hull of the ship telling everyone he had to use the head. Being stern and stoic because that's all he knew.

'Marty,' I said. 'You have a good long weekend. Don't give Fran and Paul any trouble.'

'Sure,' he said. 'See you next week, alright?'

'Yeah, bud.'

Another small commotion and Paul was back on the line.

'Fran tells me you're looking for Carole.'

'Yeah. She's not here. It's no big deal, Paul. Really.'

'Two of you having . . . I mean . . . She been down or anything?'

'No more than usual.'

'Huh,' the old man grunted.

Hated that. The old man's 'huh'. There's nothing Carole's parents did that got under my skin more. Not even the questions they always ask. *You two got enough money? Donald needing anything?* Even the way Frances would reminisce to Carole about old times. *Remember when you and Kevin took Donald for that vacation in Canada? Now that was a real family trip. The three of you. That was your sixth anniversary, wasn't it? And Donald loved his daddy. He's looking more like Kevin every day.* That didn't get me as deep as Paul's 'huh'. That uninterested way he marked parts of the conversation. It'd be easier if the old man would just come out and tell me what's on his mind.

Joe, you're a real pain in this family's ass. I'm bored of this conversation. I'm changing the subject in the hope you'll tell me what's going on with my daughter. Better yet, I hope you'll crawl off somewhere remote and die.

'Carole's always—'

The doorbell rang. Heavy dinging of Big Ben's chimes echoing in the foyer. Paul must have heard it in the background 'cause he stopped talking. He waited. I waited. Listened for something to happen from his end. Paul's heavy breathing filling my ear enough to make me move the phone away. Kept the phone down at my side and went to the front door. Went for the handle the same time as knuckles rapped against the other side. Turned the knob and pulled it open.

'PlumbJet,' the man said. He was tall with thin arms. A ball of beer gut was the only shape filling his blue coveralls. They were well worn and padded at the knees. He wore a baseball cap turned backwards. A thick sprout of steel-grey hair puffed from the opening in the cap. A streak of something marked his stubbled cheek. I hoped it wasn't shit.

'Yeah?'

'PlumbJet,' the man said again. I watched the guy's Adam's apple move when he spoke. Up and down with each word. That guy had a golf ball stuck in his neck. 'I got a work order for this address.' He handed over a slip of yellow paper.

I took the note and read it aloud: 'Something stinking in kitchen.'

'Yeah,' the man said. 'Don't get offended. I don't make these up. I write down only what I'm told. That's what Dispatch said was the problem.'

'Sure,' I said. Found myself nodding and didn't know why. 'You know who called it in?' The guy reached his hand and pointed at the bottom of the yellow page where he'd written 'Mrs Pullman'. I nodded my head.

'When was this called in?' I asked. The guy was looking at my hand and the phone I was holding. Paul's voice was coming through the speaker loud and clear. Put the phone up to my mouth. 'Hold on, Paul,' I said. Looked at the plumber again. 'When was this called in?'

He shrugged.

'I came by earlier and no one answered the door. So I went

to a call in Meridian. Did another job and called in to Dispatch. They told me to head back here before I finished my shift.'

'How long were you in Meridian?'

'I don't know.' He looked at me like he was getting real uncomfortable with all the questions. 'Took maybe forty minutes to drive there. Maybe the same to come back. Job was—'

'Doesn't matter,' I said.

'Well, if you're wanting . . .'

I stepped aside to let the guy past. He bent down and lifted a metal toolbox from the porch. On the side of the box was a Cincinnati Reds sticker. The box was streaked with something too.

'. . . you there? Joe?'

The plumber stopped halfway to the kitchen and looked down at the phone in my hand. He frowned for a second and then looked at me. He went into the kitchen and started whistling and I listened to him. Then looked down at the phone. Thought about pushing the red button again, cutting Paul Quincy short. Paul with his stiff back and annoying 'huh' habit. Hovered a finger for a second before lifting the phone to my ear.

'Here, Paul.' I cleared my throat louder than I needed to. 'That's the plumber arrived.'

'You got a leak?' he asked.

'Stink. Something in the kitchen.'

'That'll cost a bomb,' Paul said. He made a clicking sound with his mouth just to dig the pain in a little deeper. 'Out-of-hours service.'

'Yeah.' Felt my head easing up. 'Look. Doesn't matter anyway.'

'Just smelled it today?'

'What?'

'That smell,' he said. 'The stink in the kitchen. Just found it today?'

'No,' I said. 'Carole must have found it. I didn't notice anything. She must have called the plumber earlier.'

'So you've spoken with her today?'

Shook my head while rubbing a hand across my mouth. Realised he couldn't see me and took my hand away. Said: 'No, but I got her note.' The phone was dead silent for a second. I heard Paul breathe, otherwise I might have hung up.

'What note's that, Joe?' Paul had a voice that didn't have much expression. Rubbery and deep and always the same level and tone. This was different. This was probing in a way Paul hadn't been probing for a long time. Not to me. Sounded like a detective in one of those old black-and-white movies. Some Sam Spade flick towards the end when the crook's about to crumble.

'Not really a note. Not a letter anyway. A message. One of those slips from a sticky pad. Said she was stepping out for a while.' I cleared my throat. Started to wish I hadn't been drinking. Wished I'd stopped when I was ahead. *Plumber's here, Paul. Got to go. Better get your stiff back off to bed. Take an extra tablet for me, fella.* 'Said to expect her back.'

'Huh.' *Fucking bastard!* 'She say anything else in that note, Joe? That message she left you?'

'Not a thing. Look, Paul. I've got to go. Plumber's got a few questions for me.'

Walked to the archway leading to the kitchen. Mister PlumbJet was in the kitchen hovering at the sink. He had his nose in the air. His nostrils flaring. Then he'd turn his head, and his nostrils would puff out again. His head was turned to the sink when he stopped and looked at me. He frowned and started to flare his nose again.

'You hear from Carole, let her know to call home.'

'Paul,' I said. 'If I hear from Carole she will be home.'

'Just have her give us a call.'

'Sure.'

I hit the red button – dropped my head and took a few deep breaths. The plumber was using a flashlight to get a look down into the garbage disposal. Watched him for a second. Turned when he leaned his head to the side and lowered it into the sink and made a heavy sniffing noise. I went to the sofa and put the phone back on the charger. The plumber was making a racket in the kitchen. Let him do his thing a while. When I finally got up and turned my head round the corner, saw the guy had the cabinets open. He was leaning over the counter holding a flashlight and craning his long neck.

'Tell you the truth, bud. I don't smell a thing,' I said. 'My wife's the one that called you guys.'

He nodded his head and kept looking down into the sink.

'I smell it.' He nodded his head. 'There's something gone ripe.'

'Sure.' I walked into the kitchen. Took another bottle from the top shelf of the fridge. 'You needing a drink?'

'I'm working now. Had to sign a waiver saying that I wouldn't take a drink of anything offered from clients unless it comes from a sealed container.' The plumber turned his head and stared down his long face at me. 'Can't be alcoholic, though. Sodas are okay. But I'm not needing anything now. But those are the rules.'

'Alright, I'll be through there.' Tossed a thumb to indicate the next room. 'If you're needing anything, just holler.'

'I'll let you know when I've located the source.'

'Any idea how much this is going to cost?'

The guy shook his head.

'Not till I find the source.'

'Figured that.'

I left the room.

Hour later I was passed out. Sometime after that Mister PlumbJet was shaking my shoulder. He looked annoyed and embarrassed. His long fingers were holding onto a clipboard that he was reaching out to me. He stood over me while I looked at the clipboard. I yawned and he kept wringing his shit-covered hand. He looked at the sofas like he wanted to sit down. I got up and wrote out a cheque and clicked it onto the board for him. He nodded his head and said something I didn't catch. I was standing against the archway leading to the kitchen. When it was all squared away he saw himself out. After that I got myself up to the bedroom. Only thing I remember was a half-hope that Carole was going to be there waiting for me. I didn't put the lights on and when I got to the bed I fell down hard on her side. Hit the mattress and stayed flat out for a while. Lying in the dark, listening to the house. Searching through the silence for a sound that might have been someone moving. After a long while I gave up.

If I dreamed I can't remember.

Chapter Three

The doorbell rang four times. I lay there on the bed listening to the sound of the chime. Watched the way the morning sun burned bright through the slats of the venetian blind. The light picked out the flecks of dust floating in the air and ignited each of them. After a while I got up and went to see who was at the front door. Kept my distance from the window. Tried to keep out of sight in case I decided the visit wasn't worth my time. I was glad I'd played it safe when I saw Nancy Lowell moving away from the porch.

Stood there and watched her pacing out in front of the house. First time she'd walked to the door she'd left deep footprints in the snow. Watched while she took her time going back to her car. Stepping down in the holes she'd already made. Tossed her bag into the car and seemed to settle herself in. Looked like she was about to start it up and drive off. No big deal. No trouble at all. That would have suited me fine. Screwed up my eyes and hoped the hangover wasn't going to last too long. Hoped the sun would slide behind the clouds. Sparkles it made on the surface of the snow pushed the pain back deep into the middle of my head.

The phone started ringing. I looked at it sitting on the table next to Carole's side of the bed. That's as much interest as I gave it. Turned my attention back to Nancy, watching as she lifted her mobile phone from her lap to her ear. Watched her and tried reading her lips through the slats of the venetian blinds.

Pick up. Pick up. Pick up.

'Go away, Nancy,' I said. 'Just drive away.'

She hung up and the ringing died out behind me. I watched her dial again. The phone behind me came back to life. Waited until it died off. She tried a couple more times before her car door opened. She came back and it was almost enough to break me. Almost enough for me to take pity and go downstairs to open the door for her. Thing is, I wasn't feeling like entertaining a visitor. Especially not someone who was friends with my wife. I just wasn't up for it. All the same, watching her pushing her feet back in the shoe-shaped holes in the snow made me think she needed something. Deserved something maybe. She looked jumpy. Hands moving too fast and doing nothing.

She came back for more and I lost her when she stepped onto the porch. Still, I kept an eye on the shingles of the porch roof. She was standing down there, pumping her finger against the door chime. Sound of it was driving me nuts. I looked at the glowing snow – anticipating the long figure of Nancy Lowell in her woollen trench coat. After a while she came back into view. Still careful to put shoe into print. She turned round and looked up at the house. Looked up at my bedroom window. I was sure that I was out of sight. Far enough in the room to stay hidden. She stood with her face aimed up at the window. Whatever was on her mind was too important to take away.

She disappeared under the patio roof again and I went away from the window. Went out of the bedroom and headed through the hall and down the stairs. Was almost holding the brass handle of the front door when she knocked on the other side with her small fist. Let her have a crack at it while I got myself ready to face her.

Pulled it open.

'Sorry, Nancy,' I said. 'Kind of fell asleep.'

'You look terrible, Joe.'

'Well, that's probably about the same as I'm feeling.' Cleared my throat out of habit more than need. 'Carole's not here.'

'I'm not here to see Carole.' She turned and checked the street. Looked up and down the line of neighbours' houses like she was expecting someone was following her. Watching her. Took most time with Edith Krantz's front windows. Must have known from her times visiting Carole that the place had the most active curtains for prying and spying of any house on the block. She brought her head back round. Looked at my face and focused her eyes on something behind me. Something in the house. 'I came to see you, Joe.'

'That's odd.'

'Yes, well, what I need to speak with you about is . . .'

Got tired of waiting for her to finish the thought and asked: 'You need to come inside?'

'It is cold out here.'

Against my better judgement, I let her in. The neighbours would be watching and, no matter how hideous the prospect was, the telephones would already be in hand. Numbers being dialled. Chins moving while tongues spilled out the stories of what was happening behind closed doors. Right now I was having an affair with Nancy Lowell. A woman I disliked. A person I didn't trust – and so what was happening in other homes worried me.

Some of them will put this together later, Joe. A missing wife that you can't explain away. Oh, yes, the note. Well, anyone could write a few words down. That's no alibi. They aren't sharing that idea yet, but some of them must be getting awful curious. The Trapper's Paradise did you no favours, Joe. Neither did Colin's flat face, and now the visit from his old lady . . .

'What's on your mind, Nancy?' I asked.

'Would you be good enough to make me a cup of coffee, Joe? Tea, if it's easier for you,' she said. She was already taking her gloves off. Going for the top button of her coat. She was planning to be round for a while. 'I've been sitting in my car. Even with the heater on, I'm frozen stiff.'

'I'll brew some if you need.'

'Don't go to any trouble.' She placed her gloves in her handbag. Her attention was on something else. Since she wasn't looking at anything in particular – just the overturned magazine on my coffee table – I kind of figured there was something real important on her mind.

'No trouble, Nancy.'

'That's fine then. Coffee would be fine.'

Went into the kitchen and filled the coffee pot with water. Measured out the beans and dumped them into the grinder. Flicked the switch. The jolt and sound of the grinder sent a shock through my system. Starting with my hand and digging deep inside. Ran up to my head. Pulsing hard and making the pain more intense. The beans finished cutting and I loaded the filter. All the while I listened to the silence in the other room. Worried that I'd go back in there to find the neighbours weren't all that far off-base. Maybe they had it right on the mark.

Get ready, Joe. You're in for it now. You know her kind. Saying nothing and asking for attention. Get ready, buddy boy.

'Nancy,' I called out. 'You alright in there?'

'Fine, Joe.'

'So what is it you need to see me about?'

She shifted on the sofa. Sound of her moving towards the kitchen brought me back to reality. There was a clicking noise. She was wearing shoes, but then they always wore shoes during affairs. They do in movies and on TV anyway. Even when they were wearing nothing but a smile, they had their goddamned heels on. So the feeling was back in my stomach for a second or two. Didn't want this to be happening in my house.

'It's difficult to start, Joe.'

She was in the archway. Turned my head, eyes wide and all shocked. Let go of all the air I'd been holding.

'What's wrong?' she asked.

'Nothing,' I said and started a laugh. Just had enough air left to get one going. Not a big laugh, but it didn't need to be. Nancy was standing in the archway in her woollen trench coat. It was still buttoned to the neck, with her brown dress dangling underneath. Black tights and blue lace-up shoes finished her off. This wasn't a trip to seduce. If it was she'd lost her touch along the way. Over the years she'd been pulling in men like a fox taking rabbits from a hutch. Real easy. Somehow I don't think it's a skill that ever entirely goes away. So I laughed some more and started to feel good about things. Good as I could feel with all the mess I was in.

Nancy frowned. She looked like she was about to speak.

'Sorry,' I said. Put a hand in the air to make out like I was being sincere. 'You ever have a moment when something goes through your head that shouldn't have been there? You know, like a thought that's not placed right. Some weird idea, like it's come out of someone else's head, found a way straight into mine.'

She wasn't laughing. Way she was holding her hands in front of her made me think of widows at a wake. I choked down the rest of my laugh. It went with all of my relief. Wiped the back of my hand over my eyes and tried to make a face that apologised.

'You know what I'm talking about,' I said.

'Yes, Joe. That's why I'm here. It's why we need to talk.'

Swallowed hard.

'Sometimes I have that same thing happen to me. More than occasionally.'

Looked down at her hands because her face was too blank to read. Knuckles on her hands were turning white. Fingers had turned red from the way she was squeezing. I gave her face one last chance. She didn't look any better. Didn't have any expression that told me what was going on in her head.

'Sit down for a bit,' I said. 'I'll bring the coffee when it's ready.'

She went through and I waited for the pot to finish brewing. Wished it would take so long she'd change her mind about seeing me. Wished like hell she'd decide it was a bad idea to sit with Joe Pullman and discuss her thoughts. Seemed kind of dangerous with all the stuff that was going on in my life.

Carole, what the hell have you done?

Coffee finished brewing. I poured it in two mugs and took it back through to the family room. Set one mug on the table in front of Nancy. Kept hold of the other and took a seat on my recliner. Safest place when you're not wanting company. Same way Pop got rid of the salesmen Mona used to let in the house. He'd take his place on the blue recliner and open up a copy of the paper.

Personal space, Joe. Reflects disinterest.

Nancy didn't get the hint. She was like those salesmen with their dinnerware and vacuum cleaners. She pulled off her trench coat and folded it across her lap. What was underneath transformed her into an Amish farm-wife. Real traditional.

'How much do you know about me, Joe?'

'Not much,' I said. *You've got too much time on your hands. You prefer evening classes to bars, and you stick your nose in other people's business more than a mutt sticks his nose in a stranger's crotch. Oh, yeah, and you were a whore once . . . Transferred to a prude now, it seems.* 'Carole's good at keeping her friends to herself.'

'So you don't know about my—'

After giving me that much she cut off. Went dead quiet, but kept looking at me like she was still talking. Like I should be taking it all in. Waited for her to finish, but it didn't look likely to happen. Couldn't handle the silence, not while I was having to look at her eyes anyway. They weren't blinking.

She seemed kind of lost. It's like she was trying to get me worked up. Get me to respond.

'I know you're into night-classes,' I said. It came out fast like I'd said it just to get her to blink. Smiled at her and raised the mug to my mouth. Drank and used the motion to break the connection between our eyes.

She started to shake her head, but stopped. Gave me a shy kind of look and cleared her throat. Stared down at the coffee she'd wanted so badly. The mug was still full. Her brown lipstick not given the chance to mark the sides. She frowned and took a breath. Tight collar of her blouse looked like it was going to burst round her expanding neck. With the deep breath out she appeared less intense.

'I have an ability, Joe.' She kept her eyes on the coffee mug. 'I can see things that no one else can see.'

'Such as . . .'

'Has Carole mentioned the Spiritualist Church?'

'Nope,' I said and drank again. Watched Nancy while she stared into the steam coming off her coffee. 'But I know about it. Take it that's the one off Linston? Behind the Farmers' Market?'

'That's the premises, yes.' She nodded her head and reached for the mug on the table. Looked at it for a few seconds. Thinking about lifting it maybe. Saw something, with her crazy ability, dancing up out of the steam maybe. She finally sat back and looked at me and then at her hands. She was wringing them and rolling them in a ball. Worked at it with a real intense quality. Like she was made of clay and was smoothing rough edges on her fingers. 'I'm a member.'

'So is that what you needed to tell me? Well,' I said, 'I'm fine with that. Just don't try to convert me.' I stood and started knocking at the wrinkles in my jeans. Slapping at my thighs. Feeling a strange sort of panic. I kept slapping and hoped she would follow my lead. Stand up and get her coat. Get the hell out of my house. 'I really need to get going.'

'No, that's not what I need to tell you,' she said. 'I'm getting to that. This isn't easy, so I'll have to take my time.'

'I've got some things I need to do.'

'I'm certain you do.'

She went quiet again. My time didn't matter any more. We had all the time in the world, according to Nancy Lowell. Trouble was she was almost right about that. It just didn't sit well with me. While Nancy sat in silence I started wondering about Carole. Wondering where the hell she was at that very moment. In some hotel maybe, lying back with a cheap television on. Foil wrapped round the antenna to take away some of the salt-and-pepper haze clouding the picture. Haze of electric snow that made the people in the picture less visible. Made it harder for her to see.

Nancy was rolling her hands again. One over the other. I watched her with a real hope that Carole was going to come through the door. Drop her purse and tell me she'd done all she needed to do. No questions asked. She could take my place and listen to Nancy's confession about her Spiritualist connections. I'd take her coat and settle her in. Then I'd be off. Out the door and heading down to the parlour with a smile on my face. Not a worry in the world.

'Why are you looking at the door?' Nancy asked.

'Thought I heard something.'

She cleared her throat. Then she started to tell me just what was on her mind. I didn't interrupt or try to stop her. Drank my coffee and when it was finished I set the mug on the table. Then I leaned forward and listened some more. Still waiting for Carole to come through the door. Maybe Donald and Marty had decided to cut their visit short. They always got tired of Paul and Frances after a few days. Almost hoped Paul would show with the boys. I'd even take Paul Quincy over Nancy Lowell and her quack faith-talk.

Nancy kept talking. Words flying over words and at first it didn't make sense. I didn't need to hear about her religious side. Being as distant from religion as I am, there wasn't a reason for Nancy to bring it to me. I put people in the ground from all denominations. Catholics. Jews. Protestants. Lutherans. Henderson's even had a few Muslims over the years. Researched burial rights and traditions and conducted ceremonies for them all. Never had a complaint. Not for the service and not 'cause I'm an agnostic. A pessimistic agnostic at that. My toes were hanging over the edge to atheism, but I guess hope was holding me back. Keeping me from falling all the way in.

Checked my watch and shook my head. I was tired of playing the good guy. Nancy must have sensed her time was running out 'cause she stopped her talk about ghosts and spirits and all her other mumbo-jumbo.

'You shouldn't be such a cynic, Joe.'

'I was born this way,' I told her. 'And what I wasn't when I was born, my father put in place.'

'Pop?' she asked.

Shook my head. She swallowed and brushed at the fabric of her coat. Still using it to cover her knees.

'You don't like being around water,' she said. 'Not on boats anyway. You don't walk over piles of leaves, either. You have to check that there is ground underneath. You worry about the ground opening up.' She had her eyes closed, thinking real hard about something. Her face softened up, but she kept her eyes closed. 'There is a boy and you think about him. You visit him as much as he visits you.'

I didn't like where it was going. So I tried to cut it short.

'Didn't know you were into the local folklore.'

'The boy is near ground that always moves,' she said. 'He comes to you in dreams.' She opened her eyes and looked at me. She wasn't worried any more. There wasn't the slightest hint of concern in her eyes. 'He's always around you.'

'Okay.' That's all I could manage. I didn't say any more 'cause there was nothing that seemed right to say. My mind was wandering, but not to cheap hotels with busted television sets. Not to my wife. I was hoping more than ever for the front door to open. That silent, dead feeling was back. It was a heavy world again. Only I wasn't surrounded by police deputies. I wasn't the kid they spoke about on the television and the radio. There wasn't an officer smiling sympathetically at me, trying to make friendly while telling me about foster families. While they gave me a kid-easy definition of 'ward of the state'. It was just me and Nancy Lowell in my living room, but the world was closing in just as fast as it did when I'd lost my last family.

'That's just so you understand what I'm talking about, Joe. So you understand this isn't some fantasy. So you can spare me a bit of time.' She leaned towards me. Still keeping her distance, but inches closer, forcing me to look her way. 'Just hear me out.'

My head was nodding. I could feel my head moving back and forward. A broken scarecrow in a soft breeze.

'You'll have to hear all of what I'm about to say before you interrupt. I'm not sure I can keep going if you stop me,' she said. 'It's a tough thing to hear, and I can assure you it's a tough thing to talk about. But you're in trouble, Joe. So, listen to me and don't interrupt. Someone is dead because of you . . .'

She played with her coat. She had draped it like a skin over her legs. She kept rubbing her hands over it, tightening it into shape. She folded in all the pieces that were sticking out. Finally she lifted it and set it on the cushion next to her. She started up again like she'd never even taken a breath.

'That boy has come to visit me. He keeps coming back. So I went to the church and tried to get help. Herman Dorlund is a friend of mine. He has the gift too. So I went to sit with him and we tried together. Tried to see what was happening. To see if we could help this boy. His spirit,' she said. She waved her hand in the air. She watched it move like she could see stars trailing behind it. 'But Herman couldn't get contact. That didn't help me much at all, but Herman wasn't surprised. He told me it was because I was losing the gift. That's the trouble, Joe. Only a few of us have the ability to make contact. To see these things when we are asked to see them. It takes away the attention that some people need. Some people grow to expect that attention. Herman was hoping it was a sign that I was going empty. He's been concerned by the attention I receive, Joe. So he was upset when I was getting such clear contact. Then there was nothing.'

'Who asked you to see?'

'What?' she said. 'What do you mean?'

'When you are asked to see. That's what you said. Now, I am asking you who asked you to see?'

'Well, Carole asked me,' she said.

Nancy went silent. She stayed silent for a long while.

'So Carole is asking you about boys?' I asked. She nodded. 'Seems odd. I'll give you that one.'

'I've seen him again.' She jumped on that one. Way you jump on a new topic to get away from the ongoing conversation.

'And what does this boy have to do with me?'

'He asks for you,' she said. Her head nodding. Moving slow backwards and then forward again. Becoming a mirror of my scarecrow.

'What's his name?' I asked. 'This boy.'

'I don't know.'

We went silent again.

'I don't have time for this. I need to be someplace.'

'I've got a bad feeling, Joe.'

'So do I, Nancy,' I said, lifting my empty coffee mug from the table. My hands had stopped shaking. I didn't feel I'd shown too much of my fear while listening to her. I needed to have something in my hands. Just holding something was better than thinking about them and what they were giving up about me. 'I've got a bad feeling that I'm going to be late. I've got a bad feeling that you're spreading stories about me round town. Bad feelings are becoming a big part of my life.'

'Joe, I'm not spreading stories,' she said.

'Don't you think enough people are still suspicious, Nancy? All the fucking stories already flying around about me. No thanks to your husband. You think making up a few more stories about mean old Joe Pullman's going to make a difference?'

'I'm not doing this to hurt you,' she said.

I turned away from her, squeezing at the mug. Gripped on to it until I thought it would shatter in my hands.

'That's a fascinating story,' I said. 'Visited by the spirit of a boy.' I laughed loud enough to make her shift on the sofa. She almost stood up when I turned on her. 'I didn't know you had it in you. I can't see the relationship between me and this kid. Can you use your *gift* to tell me more?'

'No,' she said. 'No, I can't tell you any more. But I've got a feeling. So I wanted to stop by and tell you about it. I think it's because of what you . . .'

'What's that, Nancy?' Watched her for a second, then stepped forward. She didn't like me getting closer to her. Even with the coffee table between us she didn't feel safe. She moved farther back on the sofa. 'What was it that I did?'

'When you were young,' she said. 'In Maritime.'

'Maritime?' I asked and tried to smile. Tried to compose myself 'cause inside I was feeling a tension move across my chest, pulling hard. Tried to keep the mug from slipping out of my sweat-slick palm and falling to the floor. 'What's this have to do with . . .' I started and couldn't bring myself to finish.

'It's that history,' Nancy said. 'Where you come from and what happened to you.'

'And what is it you think happened to me?'

'You were involved . . .' she started.

I didn't make out like it meant anything to me. Just watched her until she couldn't look at me any more. Until it seemed like she was as spent of energy as me.

'Well, I wasn't involved.'

That's not going to convince anyone, Joe. That's a pussy voice you're using.

'You could be, Joe.' She leaned forward this time. Her hands dangling over the mug of coffee she'd never even touched. 'You could be involved in this . . .'

'Just what are you accusing me of?'

'I'm not accusing you,' she said. 'Oh, God, no. Heavens . . .'

'Then we can agree this is a waste of time. You don't need to be here.'

'He was scared,' she said. 'He told me how scared.'

That kind of did it for me. All of a sudden I felt like I'd been going along with a joke that didn't have a punch-line. Nancy was sitting in my house looking for that punch-line. Expecting me to finish off this epic tale with some serious closure. Nancy was telling me I'd been involved in something. That scared the shit out of me. I went right back to the night I picked Rachel Evers up from the mini-mart and dropped her off at the bus stop on State Road Eleven. The night I came home to Carole asking me all the questions about what happened in Maritime.

You know you talk in your sleep?

She was drunk. I was drunk and I wished like hell I hadn't let Rachel Evers talk me into driving her out to the Meridian bus station. Let her keep pushing the bottle on me when I sat with her in the van waiting for her bus to arrive. The bottle kept coming and I wasn't able to refuse it any longer. I drank and I listened while she told me about the man she was going to see. About how she was pleased as hell to be getting away from her old man. And I listened and loaded up on all the goings-on of the Evers house and I kept the bottle tipping. Her bus arrived and she leaned over to kiss me and I moved away. It wasn't anything more than a friendly thing. Rachel wasn't that kind of girl, no matter what her daddy had made her do. I'd moved away 'cause I didn't want the smell of her perfume on my clothes. Didn't want her lipstick marking up my skin. I was glad I'd made that move away from her 'cause Carole had met me at the door.

She'd moved on me fast and took a strong hold on my shoulders and shook me and told me we couldn't go any farther the way we were heading. She told me there was too much distance. Too many secrets.

What do you want to do about it?

I need you to tell me everything. No more hiding.

I'm not hiding, Carole. I'm right here.

Tell me what happened to you. Tell me why you are so – she'd stood there shaking her head and searched for a word. *Broken. Why can't you even speak about your past.*

I don't need to . . .

Marty asks you all the time, Joe. I hear him ask you what it was like when you were a boy. He's trying to connect with you.

We are connected just fine, Carole. Look, some things are better left alone.

She was talking and I kept listening and it didn't make sense to me. Why the past was so important and why it had become so important so fast. A past she knew nothing about and had been content not to go searching for.

I'd shushed her. Put a hand over her mouth and told her she needed to calm down. Told her she was going to wake the boys, but she kept shaking her head. Kept telling me she'd taken them over to Pop's house. I went to the kitchen for more beer. Needed something to take me away from her face. The look of her eyes and the redness in her cheeks. I couldn't leave the house 'cause that would admit to her that something was wrong. That I was hiding something. But she already knew that much.

What did you do, Joe?

Nothing. What are you talking about?

That boy. What did you do to him?

What boy?

Dean Gillespie.

I didn't do anything to him.

Then why do you dream about him, Joe? Why are you talking about him?

I don't. Not any more.

You talk. You talk when you dream and I listen to you.

I don't . . .

What did you do, Joe?

'I suppose that's normal for little spirit boys,' I said. 'When he comes back, tell him Joe Pullman says howdy.' I'd convinced myself it was just a hoax. Didn't know how much Nancy picked up from Carole jabbering while they drove to the high school for basket-weaving lessons. I'd been scared up until Nancy mentioned the future thing. That psychic mumbo-jumbo's a crock. Predictions and precognitions don't ring a true tune with me. Nancy had lifted the lid off the jar and let me out right then. I'd been freed. Fear left off in a fast blitz and I was left standing there pissed off and running late.

'Did Carole put you up to this?' I asked.

'God, no. Joe, this is something I'm doing for you. This is so you don't go and do something you will regret.'

'Yeah,' I said, nodding my head. Relived the impact one more time – a heavy thump that travelled through my hands and through my bones. Tried to take it all in and make good out of everything. Nancy told a hell of a story, but it wasn't the whole story. The true story.

I mulled over Nancy's words. Took her version and mine and put them together in a carbon-copy kind of way. Laid one over the other and looked for differences. Trouble was she had it pretty close, and that was a bad thing. The more I thought about it, the less I liked the idea of Nancy Lowell sitting on my sofa. I couldn't wait for her to make a decision to leave, so I decided to make it for her.

'I've got things to do.'

'Yes, Joe.'

'One thing,' I said. She looked at me with thoughtful eyes. Eyes waiting for me to ask her for help. Eyes that told me she was willing to give me just the help I was after, whatever it might be. 'Who else is in on this with you?'

'No one, Joe. It's just me.'

'And Herman?' I asked.

She looked shy for a second. Just long enough for me to get anxious. She spotted it straight off and went to make some kind of amends.

'Now, Joe. You just hold it right there. Herman's a good man. He's not going to go making trouble. When I'm having a vision I get into a state. I start rambling and I can't control it.'

'So you're in a state now?' I asked. ''Cause it sure sounds like you're rambling a load to me.'

'Herman would never do anything to jeopardise my trust.'

'It's not your trust I'm worried about, Nancy. You better head off.'

She stood up and I showed her to the door.

'Thanks for stopping by,' I said.

'Be careful, Joe.'

'I'll do that,' I said. 'Do me a favour and keep my name out of your seances until I'm dead.'

'Oh, Joe.'

'Oh, yeah,' I said. 'One more thing. Next time you see my invisible wife, tell her I'm thinking about her. Tell her that her sons are both thinking about her too. Let her know she's really shaken us all up. Let her know just how much this new adventure of hers has kicked me where it hurts. Make a big deal out of that one for me. That should put a smile on her face. Tell her that for me will you, Nancy?'

She looked at my smile. She looked uneasy.

'Is she gone, Joe?'

'Don't act like it's news to you,' I said. 'Goddamned Madam Ruby doesn't even know her best friend has gone off to pastures new?'

'I haven't seen Carole for days, Joe. I can swear to you.'

'That's amazing. So who else is putting you up to this?'

She turned and went through the door. While she walked to her car I watched the windows of my neighbours' houses. Bright winter sunshine was reflecting back at me. Couldn't make out who was standing behind the glass watching me. There were people watching, I'm sure, calculating times and making notes. Working out what I'd just done with my wife's friend. Suburban equations running through the arithmetic of adultery:

> One man minus wife. Add in midday meeting with wife's best friend. Subtract sons on a weekend trip. Add time of entry (through the front door) and exit. Equals: SOME-THING DIRTY.

I could imagine them sniggering to themselves. All my church-going neighbours sorting out creative ways of leading me into their conversations with fellow members of the Neighbourhood Watch. All of them getting quietly excited at the prospect of something having just happened behind the safety and security of a deadbolted door. Only I didn't give them much time. Nancy was in and out in less than twenty minutes. So if it was a fling, it was hardly worthwhile. But they would all have theories. Some of those bastards would be making phone calls and starting rumours. Phone lines in Henderson were buzzing with news of my bare-assed infidelity.

The truth of the situation was much worse. In the small town of Henderson there lives a self-proclaimed psychic who claims to have seen something happen. Suddenly I was involved. She'd been speaking to people and that's never a good thing. Not when I've been dropped in the deep end with an absent spouse. Women in Henderson don't leave their husbands. They spend the days complaining to friends. They spend evenings at bridge clubs. Men go to the bowling alley or to Thompson's and drink away the arguments. But you always come back. If you don't, people talk.

The curtain twitched in Gladys Munro's window across the street.

She may have worked out another story about what just took place in my home. Story she'd be itching to share, like the rest of those curtain-twitchers. Dishing it out to family while serving up dinners cooked in the microwave. Spilling the details over drinks from bottles of spirits they kept hidden away in dark cupboards. Stories the audience would act excited to hear. Stories that became vivid and real in their own little minds. As this happened in different homes – in different forms with different scenarios – the reality lay within the minds of two people; three counting Herman Dorlund.

There may just be a victim out there, Joe. And if that's not a thought that gets you shivering, you're a harder man than any of those idiots out there believe you to be.

It didn't even register to me that a phone was ringing. Sounded way off. Guess I was way off somewhere for a while. Even when I came round enough to figure out the ringing phone was real – that it wasn't more than a couple of feet from my hand – it took me a while to pick it up. Even longer to answer it.

'Yeah, hello,' I said. I listened to the quiet on the other end. Not entirely silence. Just quiet. 'Who's on the line?' I asked.

Someone laughed on the other end of the line.

Chapter Four

Sometimes in a fight you can't wait for the guy who's staring you down to throw the first punch. You take the early opportunity to shoot one on him. Fire the big punch while he's bowing up and hope like hell it takes him by surprise. Trouble is, that kind of thing only works half the time. You either miss and look like a dick or you connect and, if luck goes your way, it's enough to put him out – at least for a few seconds while you get a head start.

I drove round Henderson for a while and tried to figure out my next move. Went up to the north side of Apple Mount and parked the van in a place on the side of the road. Shut the engine off and looked across the valley at the sawmill. Watched all the smoke lifting up out of the metal roof. I rolled down the window and listened to the screaming tools echoing from inside the mill's metal sheds. Sat there long enough to get my mind back to normal – to take the edge off my nerves and remind me of times worse than these. Times when my old man's tools would fire up in the basement. Times when I wondered what he was making, and how long it was going to be before he brought those tools up the stairs and used them on me.

The headlights of another car made a sweep ahead of me as it came round the side of Apple Mount. It was moving towards the mill and I felt the need to get away before it got too close. I drove down the hill. Took the road straight back into town, where I stopped by the market and picked up a couple of packs of beef jerky from Jimmy Neilson.

Jimmy was in the mood for talking, but I only humoured him long enough for another customer to come along. Felt like it was best that people in town took me as being the everyday Joe. Figured that way they wouldn't throw fingers my way if they found out Carole was missing. Jimmy started chewing the new customer's ear and I left. Raised a hand on my way out and Jimmy did the same back. From the market I drove the van back to the house. Before I pulled up into the drive I had it figured out. Instead of waiting for something to happen that was going to knock my ass to the ground, I was going to take my swing. I'm still undecided if that swing landed hard and heavy or if it hit nothing but cold air. Things kind of went nuts round about then.

I went inside and put the van keys on the side table near the front door. Kept my jacket on and walked across the room with snow layered up on my boots. There just wasn't time to get things ready. Didn't feel the need to prepare. I went into the room and lifted the phone and dialled.

'Henderson Police and Rescue, what's your emergency?'

'Anne,' I said. My voice sounded kind of weak, so I cleared my throat and tried again. 'Hey, Anne, it's Joe Pullman.'

'Well, hello there, Joe. You needing to speak with Nat?'

'That would be fine,' I said.

'He's not here right now, but I can get a message out to him.'

'Tell him I need to see him,' I said. 'Let him know I'll be at the house for a while. He can stop by or give me a buzz. Let him know it's kind of urgent I speak with him.'

'Alright then.'

I was still holding the phone when it went dead. An electric hum sank into my ear so fast it felt like the inside of my head was filled with ants. Hung up the phone and went to

sit down at the kitchen table. I didn't make coffee and I didn't
get a beer from the fridge. I just sat there and waited. Half
an hour later the doorbell went. Got up and took a deep
breath. Thought I had it all figured out up to that point. Had
almost felt relaxed. Then I opened the door. The young cop
standing in front of me used the gloves he was holding to
slap his open palm. They made a loud cracking sound, and
all that confidence and certainty left me.

'I take it you didn't get that mat here in Henderson,' he
said. He pointed at his feet. I looked down and read the
message etched across the welcome mat on my front porch.
Another of Carole's touches that was meant to make people
feel they had found some inviting place. 'My wife would like
to have one of those.'

'Where's Nat?' I asked him.

The kid looked at me with his smile melting off one side
of his face.

'Sheriff Upshaw's out on a call . . .' He pointed to the mat
again and said: 'Mind if I come in?' I stepped to the side and
let him pass. I recognised him from the few times he'd accom-
panied me on removals. I couldn't remember his name. Would
have felt easier with Nat in the room. With this kid I wasn't
sure just how much I wanted to go into details. Just how much
background I was going to be able to give him. Nat knew me
and knew some of my past. That sort of history was important for what I was trying to do. With the young cop in the
room, it seemed that my first punch was going to miss the
mark by a goddamned mile.

'You having a good afternoon, Mister Pullman?' he said.
He was standing in front of my sofa, looking round the room
like a kid in a museum. He sat on the sofa and stopped scoping
the place out when he caught sight of the painting over the
mantel. He screwed his eyes up while he looked at it. Then
he took a notepad from his breast pocket and flipped it open.
I had a look at it while passing by him, moving to my chair,

where I hoped I would feel more comfortable. More at home. His pad was the blue-lined spiral-bound kind. Simple convenience-store notepad set inside a fancy black leather folder. He used his thumb to click the button on the end of his pen. It made a small nib poke out. Then he clicked it again and the nib disappeared.

'You need a coffee?'

'No, sir,' he said. He looked up from the notepad and frowned. 'I'm here to see if I can help out in the sheriff's absence. I understand you called up for him.'

'Yeah, I called when I got back from the market.'

'When was that?' he asked.

'Maybe half-hour ago.'

He looked at his notepad. Then he looked at me, at my boots and the legs of my jeans.

'You going out somewhere?' he asked.

'No. I just haven't changed out of the stuff I was wearing.' I'd started to sweat while sitting at the table, so I'd opened up my coat. The snow had melted from my boots and made puddles on the linoleum floor under the table. But I didn't take them off. I just leaned over and pulled a towel from the counter top. Tossed it under the table and watched it turn dark as it soaked up the wet.

'Well, like I said, I'm here on request of the sheriff. He passed the message on to me that you called. I'll do my best to be of assistance. Sheriff told me to take notes. He's asked me to make it real clear to you that he would be here if circumstances weren't what they were. Or are.' He frowned and clicked his pen.

'I'm needing to report a missing person.'

The kid-cop looked at me, then at his pad. He seemed to be reading something written in another language. I watched his eyes work from side to side just like he was reading the newspaper. His eyebrows were big brown furry caterpillars and they were lively. Both of them. They fell down and lifted back up while I was watching him. He looked up at me and the caterpillars climbed high on his brow.

'It's not one of the dead people, is it?' he asked.

'No,' I said.

'From your funeral home, I mean.' He moved himself forward on the sofa. Reached the pad out towards me and brought it back to his chest. 'A client of yours. Family member of your client, I guess it would be.'

'I was hoping that's what you meant,' I said. 'But no. It's not one of the dead people, or my clients. I'm fortunate that all of my dead clients choose not to break contract by leaving the funeral home.'

He nodded his head. I wanted to reach across and shake him back to reality. I felt like I was up against a final buzzer that was going to go off at any time and put an end to my game. While he was dicking around I had a feeling that psychic idiot Herman Dorlund was spreading word round town about the visits Nancy had with some dead kid from Maritime. The thought made my guts burn.

'Well,' he said. 'Who is it that's missing, Mister Pullman?'

'My wife.'

He nodded his head and looked at the blank sheet in front of him. While I moved on my chair he kept nodding his head. The nodding slowed until he was just looking at the pad of paper. The two furry worms over his eyes were falling asleep, slouching down and making his eyes look small.

'You can write that down if you want,' I told him. 'May come in handy later on.'

He started nodding his head again, but stopped when he lowered it to write on his notepad. He finished writing and leaned back and looked at me. We sat there looking at one another for a moment. I didn't like sitting in a quiet room with the young cop. He must have sensed my aggravation 'cause he clicked his pen again and sat forward on the sofa. Looked like he was ready to start something.

'Can you tell me what happened?' he said.

'Well, I can tell you she's not here. I can tell you I wasn't around, and when I came back she was gone. Is that enough for you?'

'Well, I could use all the details you are able to give me, Mister Pullman. You talk and I'll write.'

Spent a long while going through the motions. I told him about my morning – leaving out the visit from Nancy Lowell. I even went back and told him about what had happened the night before, starting from when Nat Upshaw drove me back from the Trapper's Paradise. Gave him times of when the plumber arrived and of the phone call I'd made to Paul and Frances. Told him what time the plumber had left. After that I went back to the last time I'd seen Carole.

'That was Friday,' I told him. 'I'd stopped by the house to pick up the boys. Carole had asked me to drive them up to meet her father at the McDonald's in Columbia. After I dropped them off I came back into Henderson by Route 43. I wanted to stop for something to eat. Passed by Darnell's and saw all the trucks and rigs and stationwagons out front and gave it a miss.'

I gave him all the details except for going by the funeral parlour. Gave him details of how I'd gone back and found my house empty, and how I'd gone back to the guest house and drank until Lenny closed the bar.

I finished the story and waited for the next question – something that would get me thinking. Anything at all would be better than the quiet. I watched the cop and sat forward. I leaned my elbows into my knees. Waited there until my knees hurt from the bones pressing in. The kid-cop looked at the notepad and I could see the page was still half-empty. He hadn't started writing again during the silence. He just read his few words over and over again.

'So, you come home and find a note.'

'That's right,' I said. 'The same note I told you about. Couple of times over.'

'Sure you do,' he said and moved his hand over his close-cropped hair. Rubbing it like he was taking some kind of ease from the action. I was annoyed that things were moving so slow. He was still in my house and there was nothing happening.

'This is not what I need right now,' I said.

'What's that, Mister Pullman?'

'Can we just get on with this?'

He nodded his head. 'I mean, I know that's what you said.' He looked up from the pad.

'Sure you do,' I replied. 'You can write it down if you want. There's nothing wrong with touching your pen to that paper. If it helps you to remember, go ahead and scribble, bud.'

He nodded again. 'This is the first missing person I've had to deal with, Mister Pullman. And I'm kind of nervous 'cause I know you're an important man in town. So this is a high-profile case.'

'Look, bud. I appreciate you're nervous. But I'm not important and this isn't high-profile. So I need you to write some notes. Once you have the whole story, I need you to take them back to the courthouse and make some calls. Put my wife's face on fliers or in a computer system, or whatever it is that you do. Then you can put the pictures in police cruisers. Then you and all your other cop friends can start looking for her.'

He sat back and let out a breath. He scratched his head and made it clear that he didn't have a clue what to do next.

'You may even find her if you leave my living room.'

'It's just. Well, Mister Pullman. If your wife left a note, I can't list her as a missing person.'

Jesus Christ!

'The note,' I repeated. 'Let's forget about the note. How about that. Just take it that my wife is gone. Not here. Missing.

Out of sight. Whatever you guys call it nowadays. Then you can have a look for her. Am I right in saying that?'

'I can't forget about the note, Mister Pullman.' He tapped that fucking pen of his against the pad of paper. 'It's right here that you told me about the note. So . . .'

'Huh? What is it?' I asked. 'What's the major problem you are having with this?'

'Well, it's a technicality, sir. But that's the criteria we have to work by.'

I shook my head and told him: 'But she's not here.'

'Yeah,' said the cop. *Officer Leonard.* I finally caught sight of his brass nameplate. Young and clean-cut. Vulnerable and a real achiever. His badge and shoes must have been polished to the last layer of metal and leather.

'Well?' I asked.

'Yeah,' he said. He made a pause that I thought was more for effect than contemplation. 'Well, she's not missing if you know she's gone.'

'I don't follow you.'

'What I mean is, she's told you she's going. That tells me that it was her intention to go through the door and not come back. When a person does that of their own free will it's not a crime. I can't put in for a missing-person report if there's not been a crime, Mister Pullman.'

I could see I wasn't going to get very far. So I went for another angle. Something that I hoped would spark some kind of interest. Some kind of *technicality* that Officer Leonard would write down. Maybe even act on.

'Her son's still here.' I sat forward again. Leaned an elbow into a knee and used my free hand to wipe at my mouth. 'Her son Donald's still living here and she's gone away. We've got a kid together, but Donald's not mine. Isn't that kind of weird? Isn't there some kind of law against that?'

'He's your stepson,' Officer Leonard said. Nodding his head with eyes wide open, making him appear to have understood what I was saying. With great interest he was following every word. 'Donald's a good wrestler too. From what I hear, I mean.'

'What? Come on now . . . Yeah, he's my stepson and he's still here, and I'm taking care of him and she's gone. Nowhere in sight. From the note she left behind she's got no intention of coming back.'

'Can I see it?'

I considered the note Carole had written. Thought about her words and how they didn't match up with what I had told the cop. Showing the note would put a mark against me, brand me a liar.

So, your wife isn't missing. Seems she's away doing something important, Mister Pullman. Nothing to worry about.

Maybe that would ring true if you didn't know my wife.

'I burned it.'

He put his pen to the paper and wrote a few words. Watching made me feel sick in my guts.

'So I've got her son to raise until he decides to leave.' I put my hands out to my sides. 'I'm raising her kid from here on out.'

'It seems that way. Yes, sir. Sure it does.'

'And that's not a crime for her to do that? Dumping responsibility? Abandoning her children?'

'Mister Pullman,' Leonard said. He closed his notebook while sucking in his lower lip. 'I think you've lost me along the way.'

'And we were doing so well,' I said falling back into the sofa.

Leonard let out a laugh. He adjusted his holster before shifting himself closer to the edge of the sofa.

'Donald . . . your stepson. He's been your responsibility since you married Carole.' He looked away. Checked the door like he was calculating the distance. Making sure it hadn't moved since he'd walked through it. 'I'm not going to outstep my boundaries, Mister Pullman. I'm not part of social services, but I'd say you've been responsible for the boy since you and his mother got together. A package deal,' Officer Leonard said. It wasn't any easier for me to hear the second time round.

'When a package is late, Officer,' I said, 'it can arrive stale. That's kind of what happened. Donald's been with us a few years. I like the kid. Care for him. But I kind of liked the package deal when it was all together. It's not a package any longer. See what I'm getting at?'

'If you're not willing to care for him . . .' Officer Leonard paused. He looked back at me and rubbed a finger over his brow. 'I could contact services in the city and have the boy placed in foster care.'

'No,' I said. 'I'm not saying I don't want him around. Christ, this is so messed up.'

'Maybe I could have Doc Maitland set up counselling, Mister Pullman.'

'Shit! He'll be fine. We all will. My son included. Screwed up, yeah. Like any kid would be, if his mother ran out on him.'

'I was meaning for you, sir.'

I sat straight, lifting a coaster from the coffee table. Looked at it and wondered how far I could throw the thing. Looked down and saw the three bottle tops from the beers I'd downed the other night. Sitting through the small hours and drinking while reading the note over and over again. Pacing and reading. Sitting and reading. Standing and reading. I watched the cop's shoes. They were gleaming on my oriental rug.

'Anything in the world more important than having mirror-black shoes?' I asked.

'Sir?'

I shook my head. Already knowing the answer. Not to Officer Leonard of Henderson Township Police Department, there wasn't. I lifted the bottle tops from the table and squeezed them in my hand until the sharp teeth cut into my skin.

'I don't need help,' I said. 'Never been that kind of guy.'

'What kind of guy would that be, Mister Pullman?'

'A kind that's not like me.'

'Do you drink often?'

'I drink.'

'Is this possibly why your wife left?'

'Look,' I said, pointing a finger at the kid-cop's face – squared it up on his straight nose. 'Don't come into my house and suggest I'm a cause.'

'Let's calm down.'

'She left everything behind. Everything. And I'm sitting here talking to you about it. And still you're asking me if I drink. Yes. That's your answer, if you still need one.'

I shook the bottle tops in my hand. Shook them at the cop and dropped them on to the coffee table. They danced round like dice. We both watched as they fell. Looked at them like a couple of gamblers betting on sevens.

'Yeah. I drink. And if you started having trouble with your wife – everything is fine, then the shit falls out the bottom of things – you'd drink too. I guarantee you'd fucking drink.'

'Okay, Mister Pullman. I'm not belittling your loss.'

'Loss?' I yelled. 'No, Officer Leonard, loss would suggest something's missing. There's nothing missing! We *know* she's fucking gone!'

'I'll have to ask you to calm down.'

'Just get out.' I stood up and moved a few steps towards the door by the time he got up from the sofa. 'I'll even open the door for you.'

'You have to understand that your wife doesn't fall within the missing person's remit. I'm really sorry for your upset, Mister Pullman. But there's nothing we can do for you.'

'I'll find her.'

'That doesn't sound like the kind of thing I want to hear.'

'What do you suggest I say?'

The cop met me eye to eye. He adjusted his belt and kept

his thumbs perched near the buckle. Rolled his shoulders and pursed his lips. It was another look for show. I wondered how much of this shit they were teaching at some backwoods Maryland Police Academy. Target practice in the morning. Hand-to-hand combat in the afternoon. Dinner and fake-gestures seminar followed by refreshments.

'I'd like to hear that you're going to get on with things.'

'Look, bud. You got mixed up in this 'cause Nat's not available. I called through to the station because my wife's gone. I thought maybe someone could do something. Offer a bit of help even. Bad mistake. If I hadn't told you about the note, you'd have put her on the books, right?'

Officer Leonard nodded his manicured head.

'Hell, man. I bet she'd be on the side of a milk carton by the end of the goddamned week. But since she decided to leave a note on the fridge door, all's not lost. She just got tired of life in the suburbs, so she's off. Leaving her sons behind. Shrugging responsibility. Hitting the road.'

'That the problem you're having with this, sir?'

I looked at the cop. Felt awkward for the first time.

'She beat you to the punch,' Officer Leonard said.

'Thanks for your help.'

'I'll make some enquiries, Mister Pullman.'

I shook my head and told him: 'Forget about it. I'll get over it.'

'Mister Pullman,' he said. 'You have to understand . . .'

'My phone's ringing, Officer. Thanks so much for your support. I better get that, in case it's my wife. I'll let her know she did the right thing by leaving a note. Such an easy way to stay invisible.'

I shut the door and caught the phone on the third ring. The line went dead. I walked back to the study and sat behind my desk. Opened the drawers and looked through the files I kept there, wondering what Carole had found. I searched with a painful thought lodged in my head: that I wouldn't know if Carole had found something. It would be gone with her, and I might never know what it was that she had found. Still, I searched and when the phone started ringing again I was out of breath. I looked at it for a few seconds. Wondering if it was worth my energy to answer it.

Chapter Five

Picked up the phone and gave a quick hello. There was a pause on the other end of the line and the sound of computer keys clicking. Papers getting moved round. Voices speaking in the background. So many noises I couldn't bring myself to make any of my own. Worried if I made any noise at all that I would miss something. Maybe something that would tell me who it was breathing down my goddamned phone.

'Hello,' I said. Listened to the clicking sound. Got impatient and was close to putting the receiver down. Finally said: 'You going to speak?'

'Is that Joseph Reginald Pullman?' the voice asked. It was a man. Heavy voice. Confidence in the words. Sounded like he was in a fair mood and that was enough to set me on edge.

'I'm really not interested in buying anything.'

'Well, that's a good thing to know. While I am not selling anything, I am simply looking to speak with a Mister Joseph Reginald Pullman. Have I found him?'

'Yeah.'

'Son of Richard Pullman, formerly of 2356 Westchester Drive, Maritime, Maryland?'

'Who is this?' I asked. The air already starting to feel thin. Lungs closing in so tight I couldn't take any more in. 'The hell—'

'No need to be irate, Mister Pullman. My name is Carlos

Muniz.' There was a clicking sound after he finished. Something hard scraped his phone. Then there was a crackling sound in my receiver. 'I am the acting representative for Mister Richard Pullman. Can you please confirm if you are—'

'Yeah,' I said. Took a breath and didn't feel any better about what I was going to hear from the guy next. Waited for the clicking sound on his end. Nothing happened. Figured the guy was recording the conversation. 'What's going on?'

'I am calling regarding the upcoming parole hearing for Mister Pullman. This is an informal phone call. You are not obligated to take part in this conversation. However, you are free to ask any questions you wish. I do have to inform you that my client has asked me to withhold certain information at this time.'

'Did he ask you to phone me?'

'He has provided me with a list of individuals who may have reason to oppose his release. Your name was on the list. Quite high on the list.'

'Maureen Gillespie?'

'No,' he said. Response coming too fast for his eyes to be searching a list. 'There are few other names beside yours.'

'It was my understanding that my father wasn't supposed to have contact with his victims,' I said. 'I'm sure you're in some kind of breach.'

'Possibly true,' he said. 'It may well have been the case if your wife had not made the initial contact. Her visit, I believe, has opened the lines of communication. It allows your father to—'

'My wife what?' I lost the air in my lungs. 'When was this?'

'I am not at liberty to divulge details of these visitations. However, I can tell you that they were recent. Your father enjoyed her company very much. He rarely has visitors. Never family.'

I sat back in the chair, looking across the desk at the door.

Had a new kind of feeling, a child-like fear of what was out in the hallway. That the door to the study was going to open and some horrible thing would come tumbling in. I needed the door to be shut. That's all that I was certain about, sitting there with the phone to my ear. There wasn't anyone else in the house. But I had that weird feeling. The feeling I get when I'm in the shower in an empty house. Still shut the door. Lock it even. *Can't blame Hitchcock for that one.* It's a self-preservation thing.

'Can you excuse me for a minute?' I asked.

'This won't take long, Mister Pullman,' he said. There was a soft click. A kind of snap that sounded when his voice paused. Could have been the nib on a pen. Maybe that Muniz sonofabitch was just clicking a pen like the kid-cop. A real annoying habit. I had a feeling Muniz was getting full use of his Dictaphone. Taking in the whole conversation so he could play it back to my old man. Sit with him in some holding facility in the state penitentiary. Both of them looking down at it while they listened to me. Smiling as they considered the tone of my voice and the words it spoke.

'Will you be present at the hearing?' he asked.

Are you like your father, Joseph?

It was like listening to the voice of Charles Vincent McLean again, and he was asking me the same question he'd asked in the basement of his father's house. I'd recorded Charles' voice in my head and now it was playing back. For a long time it had been lost. Up to that moment when the phone rang and I lifted the handset to my ear. Up to that moment it had been buried with all the other mess of my past. Buried deep enough so I wouldn't have to experience it all again. Deep down, so no one could bring it to the surface. So no one would raise that question again.

Are you like your father, Joseph?

Shook my head while I watched the door. Open, but only halfway. Wide enough so someone could walk in. Squeeze through sideways if they wanted. Could see into the clear and empty hallway, but that didn't mean it would last for ever. Didn't mean it was going to stay empty.

'Do you have an answer for me, Mister Pullman?' Muniz asked. Some sonofabitch with a Latin-twist to his northern accent. 'Will you be present at the hearing?'

'No,' I said.

'Do you plan to send a formal recommendation opposing your father's release?'

'Not sure I should answer these questions,' I said.

Another small click from the other end of the line. Muniz made a sucking sound. Blew out in a heavy sort of way. Figured he was smoking a cigarette and trying to collect his thoughts. Probably trying to pull his nerves together so he could come at me again. Get at me with some kind of intimidation.

'Your father has not declared his innocence for the past twenty years,' he said. 'He has left you to get on with your life. There have been ample opportunities for my client to speak with reporters and investigators about the case. To give . . .' His pause was filled with the ripping sound of a cigarette burning down. There was some sort of commotion happening around him. People moving and speaking. He breathed out heavy over the receiver. Blowing smoke to keep me from hearing what was going on at his end. 'To give anyone interested in hearing it another version of what happened to Dean Gillespie. Of what *really* happened.'

I stood from my chair and walked to the far side of my desk. The phone line kept me from getting any farther. I looked sideways at the door. Looked to see if there was anything in the hall. Any shadows against the wall. Felt ridiculous for doing it. Still, I needed to check. To make certain my paranoia had not become a sick kind of reality.

'When is this taking place?' I asked.

'The hearing?'

'That's right.'

'It was in the letter you were issued by the state.' Waited for him to smoke some more. Waited 'cause I knew he was going to elaborate. 'The letter your wife brought with her when she met with your father.'

'Why would she do something like that?'

'To meet your father or to bring the letter?' He didn't pause long enough for me to respond. 'Your father told me she suspected that he wouldn't believe she was your wife. She wanted to bring a few things along that would verify her identity and her connection to you. So she brought the letter.'

'What else?' I asked.

'Photographs. A list of names.'

'What about this list of names?'

'I can't speak in too much detail about the list,' he said.

'Give me a name.'

He gave me more than one. He gave me all of the names I didn't want to hear. His voice was mellow. Matter-of-fact, but with a hint of sincerity too. Same as you would read the names from a list of dead soldiers. Reciting their names to a crowd gathered to mourn. Respect for each individual.

'Dean Gillespie. Oscar Lewiston. Charles Vincent McLean. Mick Sharpton.'

'My father told you she brought these names to him?' Came out like I was accusing him of lying. Maybe 'cause I was accusing him, but the only thing I was sure of was that I was scared. In a bad way. Like I hadn't been for a long time.

'No, Mister Pullman,' he said. 'He didn't have to tell me. He was good enough to present me with the list. It was written by your wife, and the interesting thing is that there are times and dates next to the names. She also left your father the letter from the state. Maybe that was a mistake, but it seems that the list was a gift.'

'Who is in the photographs?'

'Let's see,' he said. Sound of his breath came through the phone. Paper was getting moved. Voices in the background were growing louder. Laughter broke in the distance. 'A young boy with scars. You, I believe. Possibly when you were taken into custody on . . . There's no date on the photograph. And another of you, slightly older. Thinner in the face. I suppose this one is following the assault on the McLean boy.'

'What else?'

'You in recent years. A wedding photograph. Scars haven't faded much, I see. And your boy looks more like his mother. I hope you don't mind me saying so.'

'My father has seen a picture of my son?'

'Well, yes, Mister Pullman. He's seen all of the material your wife brought to the meeting.' He paused and I was trying to listen to him. Listened to the sounds in the background and tried to figure out where he was calling from. It didn't sound like an office. It sounded like a restaurant. Plates getting stacked and moved around. Groups of people moving in and out of range. Making noise as they passed this Muniz joker.

'Mister Pullman? Are you still with me?'

'I'm here,' I said. 'How can I arrange to see him?'

'You just said you would not be taking this any further . . .'

'How the fuck can I arrange to see him?'

'Phone the correction facility,' he said. Sounded like he was speaking with a smile on his face. Like he was trying to sell me a timeshare in Key West. He'd picked up the signals like I was real interested in what he had to offer. 'Make a request. It will be passed on to your father. Then a time for the meeting will be set.'

'How long does this take?' I asked.

'I can contact the facility to arrange a meeting on your behalf, if you feel it is urgent.'

'Done. How do I contact you?'

'No need, Mister Pullman. I have your number.'

Looked at my phone. Grabbed at the short-stack message pad I kept next to the pens. Pulled a pen and wrote the number on the caller ID. While I was writing I asked him again: 'In case there was a reason to speak with Carlos Muniz, attorney at law, how can I dial you?'

'There will be no need.'

'And where is your office?' I asked.

'I will make the arrangements necessary for you to meet with your father.'

'I'll wait for your call.'

Hung up the phone and walked to the door. Pulled it open and listened for the sound of something moving in the house. Floorboards shifting under a heavy weight. A hammer knocking against a nail. Drills screaming. Saws grinding through wood. But the house was silent. I waited. Breathing deep and wondering how far Carole had gone to learn what had happened to me as a boy. What had happened to those around me.

How much of a monster has she pulled from the shadows, Joe? How much of the boy has she seen already?

Walked back to my desk and sat down in the chair, looking at the number I'd scrawled on the message pad. Not an area code I was familiar with. Sat back in the chair and decided to wait for a while. Decided I needed to give it some time before I called Carlos Muniz to see who it was that was going to answer. I didn't have a lot of confidence that anyone picking up the phone would know him or work with him. I was getting played hard and it wasn't a good feeling. Trouble was I didn't know who it was that was playing me. Carole had left me a note. Important thing is she had left me. That's the stinger. Then my old man. One last try for a dying man to get over the walls that were holding him. He found my wife, maybe by chance. Maybe by design. Either way, he'd picked her at the perfect fucking time.

She'd been asking you for answers, Joey-boy. All this could have been put to bed. Avoided if you'd told her what she needed to hear.

The phone rang again. I was slow to answer it.

I lifted the handset.

'Hello,' I said. Nothing.

Silence.

'Hello. You there?'

I listened for a few seconds and could hear something more than a dead line. Something like wind blowing over a microphone. A kind of whoosh sound that came in and out. The ocean maybe. Too quiet to be the ocean, but that's what I was thinking.

'Carole?'

Something moved against the phone. Something scraped the receiver on the other end of the line.

'Who is this?' I yelled. 'Muniz. That you?'

Silence. A few seconds later and the line went dead.

Hit the button on the receiver and waited for the dial tone. With my hand shaking, it took two tries to press the numbers into the phone. I read them off the message pad where I'd written them down. I read them slow and took my time dialling. Listened while the number rang through. Counted the rings and got to eleven before the call was answered.

'Yeah, hello,' a woman shouted.

'I am trying to reach Carlos Muniz,' I said.

'A who?'

I repeated the name.

'Don't have anyone by that name.'

'Is this a law office?' I asked.

'Honey, you dialled a wrong number somewhere along the way. This is Stuckey's.'

'Where are you located?'

'About ten miles outside of Columbia. Off I95.'

'Someone just called me from this number. He told me he was a lawyer. Do you remember who made a call from this phone a few minutes ago.'

'I saw a little guy. May have been a lawyer for all I know. He was wearing a suit and he took the phone round the corner – far as the cord would let him. Said he needed to get a hold of his wife. Said she was in a lot of trouble with his father and that he wanted to warn her before it was too late.' She went silent for a second and added: 'You aint that girl's father, are you?'

'No,' I said. 'And that man doesn't have a wife. Not his own anyway.'

I sat back on the chair and waited. Gave me trouble thinking that Carole had got access to my father. Thought about it enough to get the acids going in my guts. After a while I decided I couldn't stay in the house. Grabbed my keys from the side table and took my coat off the hook in the foyer. I went out the door.

Chapter Six

I took the van up to the funeral home and saw Ted's car parked out front, so I passed on by. Figured he'd have the place under control. Gave thought to taking the long way round Henderson. Going out of town using the logger route and bringing the highway back in. Got as far as Darnell's and decided I didn't need to be sitting in a car. It was the way my hands were shaking while I was holding the wheel that made up my mind. Just couldn't calm myself down. So I pulled up in front of Darnell's and waited a while. Sat in the van and watched the customers sitting in the booths by the front window. Let some of the outsiders finish their meals and clear out before going in.

Went up to the counter and stood next to an old man. He was sitting on one of the stools eating an all-day breakfast and working on a coffee Sheila Hunter had set out for him. Looked over at the guy and didn't like how he was giving me more than a once-over. Figured he was slow in the head. Maybe too old to know any better than to stare at a fella. Things were all going crazy in my mind, and an old man with too much curiosity wasn't going to rattle me much. Not any more than I was already feeling.

Waved a hand at Sheila and ordered the usual. Coffee to go. Ordered it by pointing my finger at her and smiling with the side of my mouth. I'm a man of habit, so it's easy to know what it is that I'm after. She waved back with an order pad in her hand before turning to the coffee pot. I was feeling low after my conversations with Officer Leonard and the phone call with Muniz. I was glad Sheila wasn't close enough to start talking.

I put my boot up on the chrome foot bar and set my elbows on the red service counter. Then I waited like I always did for my order to arrive. Out of the corner of my eye I could see the old guy looking at me. He was really spending the time to see all there was to see. With Sheila down the counter, I tried to convince myself he wasn't giving all his attention to me. *Maybe he's looking past you, Joe. Maybe just had a thought so strong in his mind that he forgot what it was he was looking at when it first came to him. Staring at you, but he's only seeing that thing that's stuck in his head.*

Didn't make me feel all that much better with his eyes aimed in my direction. Still, I made like it didn't bother me and started scoping for folks I knew. Spun round away from the old man so he knew I wasn't interested in talking. Tables were mostly empty. It was midweek and evening time. Past the dinner rush, but too early to catch the drunks. They slipped down from Pin Kings or Thompson's Liquors round eleven, keeping a steady flow of custom until late and spending hours in the booths. Drinking black coffee and eating dollar burgers to soak up the booze. Get something in their guts, so they could get back in their cars and motor on home.

There were some outsiders and a few people I recognised from round town. Couldn't put names to their faces, but the couple of them that were looking my way got my nod. They did the same back. Then there was Mel Trainer off in the corner. Sitting all quiet in the far booth and looking anxious as ever. He was sitting there waiting for me to spot him. Poor fool almost jumped when I finally got round to him. He half-stood up from the bench and got caught in a real awkward way. His legs jammed in place between the table and the bench he was sitting on. Started fumbling with himself like a wrestler trying to get out of a hold. Stopped trying when I shook my head at him. Pointed a finger at my watch before I whipped a thumb towards the door.

He nodded his head real slow. Moved back down into the booth and turned his face to the window. He was wearing his heavy coat. Unzipped and the hood was pulled back off his head. With the way the shoulders were dry, I figured he'd been in the diner for a good long while. Mel's a simple man. He'll sit for hours and look out the window. Picking at the leftover tinsel that Sheila hadn't got round to clearing off the sill. He'd pick at the tinsel a while and then look out through the window again. Staring across Beaumont Avenue to where the iron gates of Potter's Cemetery cut up out of the ground like the opening to some kind of black fortress. Always looks worse in the winter months. Round here it's a long winter too. Sky goes grey one morning and stays that way for what feels like a decade.

Mel looked over at me again to see if I'd changed my mind. I do that sometimes. Change my mind and go over to sit with him. Let him talk for a while, so he can go back to that shack of his up there in the cemetery feeling some kind of relief. Maybe feeling like he could settle down for a while. He's always got a story to tell, but there aren't many people who want to hear him spin his yarn. Usually I don't mind, but not that day.

Behind me the old man started coughing. Not a deep cough like it was out of his control. More like a cough to get someone's attention. My attention. Made a slow twist of my head and came round to look at him. Damned if he didn't keep staring when I set eyes on him. Guy was bordering on ancient. Pockmarked skin with silver-yellow hair coming from every small hole in his head. Nose and ears sprouting the stuff. Long strands of it.

He stopped coughing and touched his lip with the side of

his finger. Dabbed at it in a gentle way. Something you'd expect a woman to do. Real delicate. I nodded to him 'cause it was what I'd learned to do. Then I looked forward and did my best to ignore him. He was looking at the side of my head for a long while. Sitting there all quiet with a white Darnell's Diner coffee mug held up to his mouth. He was sipping at it real slow while taking a hard look at my face.

I went to concentrating on the steel wheel up on the service window. A metal ring with hooks all round it. Hooks where Sheila sticks all her pink order slips. There were two pieces of paper on it and I was watching them blow in the breeze from the cook's fan. Tried to find some peace in the way they blew and bent. Tried to keep from getting annoyed at the old guy 'cause he wasn't letting up on checking me out. Slurping his coffee like it was too hot to drink. His eyes right on me, staring. Making too much noise for my liking. Sucking down his goddamned coffee.

The outsider lowered the mug and wrapped his knuckles on the counter top. Same as you do when you come up to a door of someone you know. Hit it hard and with some familiar kind of authority. No sense of hesitation about it. After that he went back to being quiet and leaned back on his stool. With him back so far, I couldn't tell if he was looking at me. Thought maybe he was trying to get Sheila's attention for something. Maybe leaning back and waving his hand round in the air to get her attention. Sheila had her back to us. Her wide ass topped off with the single bow she'd tied into her stained apron strings.

'That's some set of scars you've got,' the man said. I ignored him. Took in a heavy breath through my teeth and went back to watching the slips of paper moving on the order wheel. Blowing and bending. 'You deaf too?'

'No,' I said. 'It's just not all that polite to be so direct.'

'Well, I apologise, friend. It's just there's not many people with so much character on their face.'

'That's a new way of describing it.'

'Well, that's what it is. Mind if I ask how you got them?'

'Yeah,' I said. 'I mind.' Didn't look at him. Closed my hands up and dropped them so they were set on the counter. Kept them out in the open so he could see they were shaped into fists. Good and hard fists that were scarred up just as bad as my face. 'Let's just say it was an accident. A lot of accidents.'

He ate some of the eggs on his plate. Chewed with his eyes on me. Eggs falling out of his mouth and landing back on his plate – making sick wet sounds when they connected. He kept chewing what made it into his mouth. Kept going like he didn't notice anything other than the scars on my face. I made a sound that wasn't too far off from a growl. Seemed to come out of me without a thought. Sheila came over and I was so far gone I didn't even notice. She was there across the counter from me and set one of her hands down on mine. Squeezed it same as she always did when she caught me off-guard. When I wasn't able to get my hand away before she could take a hold of it.

'I'm real sorry, hun,' she said. 'Coffee's stale and I'm having to brew some fresh. Be ready for you in a jiff.'

'I'll take what you've got,' I said. Pulled my hand away and went for my wallet.

'Now, Joe, you just relax for once in your life,' she said. 'Sit yourself down on that stool and I'll bring you a fresh cup when it's ready.'

'Heard what the lady said.' The outsider used a long bent finger and pointed at the stool next to him. Same one I was standing over already. 'Take a load off.'

'Sure.' Took the stool and leaned my elbows up on the counter. It was wet from the rag Sheila had just dragged across it. It didn't matter to me. I sat there for a minute and breathed deep. Couldn't take the old guy looking at me. Didn't like Sheila standing so close. Even though she wasn't doing anything more than writing on her order pad.

Held my head in my hands and breathed deep.

'How're the boys?' Sheila asked.

Nodded my head without looking at her.

'Donald's playing basketball again, I see.' Touched my arm like she was checking to see if I was still alive. I nodded again and she started talking to the top of my head. 'Saw his name in the paper. Shame he didn't make the picture, though. Should really have been there for that. He's the best-looking boy on that team, you know.'

'That your son?' the outsider asked.

'It's his stepson, yeah,' Sheila said. 'He's got another boy too. Marty. A real firecracker that one. He's like a small man. Swear it. Comes out with some of the darnedest things.'

I dragged my fingers through my hair and hoped like hell Sheila was going to stop talking. The sound of the old man sucking his coffee again wasn't all that annoying any more. Dropped my head again and kept my fingers in my hair. Felt it was getting long. It was for me, anyway. It let me hide my eyes for a while.

'You're safer now, I take it,' the outsider said.

I laughed. It was more to keep me from getting angry with the guy, but I was laughing too 'cause it was so damned off-centre. Such a spit in the wind. See where it lands kind of thing. Sure, he was lonely and he was allowed to talk it out of his system. Find a bit of company and all of that, but I wasn't the guy to give it to him. Not when I was feeling so damned low. I just nodded and hoped he would leave it alone. Leave me alone.

'Was it trouble?' he asked.

Sheila looked up from her pad. Caught me staring at her through my hair. From the look on her face I could tell she wasn't too interested in staying around to hear what I had to say next. I waited while she walked down the counter and took her place at the coffee machine. Way down the end of the counter. Got under my skin the way she was standing there. Wasn't going to get that stale coffee, and the fresh wasn't going to taste any better. I'd have to wait for what I could have already had.

She was tapping her foot and scribbling something else on her order pad. Tucked her hand in the front pocket of her apron and pulled out some change. Counted it with her thumb. Moved the change round the palm of her hand. Dumped the change back in her pocket and wrote on her pad again. Foot kept tapping all the while.

'So what was it?'

'It was trouble.'

The outsider nodded. That much I got from the reflection in the wall clock behind the counter. He nodded his head and went on drinking his coffee. This time making less noise.

Thank Christ for that one.

'Comes blowing in like the wind sometimes, don't it?'

I didn't give him any more of a response than another nod of my head.

'You can't choose the things the wind brings you,' he said. 'Looks like your winds brought something heavy. Slapped it right down on you.'

Sure as hell did.

'If you're needing to talk you can go ahead, bud.' I turned to face him. Made a good long contact with him – eye to eye. Sonofabitch didn't flinch and he didn't blink either. Gave it to him with all I had. Malice. Menace. Everything. But the look didn't do the do. Maybe 'cause I was so tired. Maybe 'cause I had gone soft. It had been a long time since trouble had come my way. I was getting used to the easy life. Winds hadn't blown much trouble in my direction for a long time. Colin Lowell's antics in the past and the recent, but that was nothing to worry about. Then Carole going and doing whatever it was she was doing . . . Figured the winds had finally turned on me. I knew it could never last.

'Tell me your story if you need to. But, when my coffee comes, I'm gone.'

'No trouble,' he said. 'None at all. Like I tell you, I've been round a while and haven't seen many faces like yours.'

'I see it every day. Nothing special about it.'

He tried to put some more eggs in his mouth. Lost most of them to his plate. Still, he chewed on what he got in there and made a big deal of it too.

'I used to sit with my boy,' he said. He went on chewing and swallowed before finishing what he'd started. 'We'd go out to this place he used to like when he was real small. I'd lock the wheels on his chair so he wouldn't go rolling anywhere. Then I'd walk round and pick up leaves and sticks and pine cones. Everything. It was a big field. Real open.' He stretched his arms out. Moved one in front of me, and I got the feeling like he was really trying to get me going. Something he'd been doing a damned fine job of up to that point. 'I'd gather it all up and I'd put it in my shirt. Held the bottom out and load it up. Like half a sack. See?'

He was holding the bottom of his flannel shirt. Stretching it away from his waist – letting it droop like it was full of something.

'Just like that. Then I'd go back to him. I'd set all that stuff on the ground. I'd take each one of the things I'd found and I'd put them in his hand. I'd take his hand like this, see . . .' He reached for my arm, but I pulled it away. Got off my stool and stepped back from him. He went on like nothing strange had happened. 'It was a waiting game after that. Watching him after every new thing I put in his hand. Just waiting for him to make something out of it. Let me know somehow that he recognised something.'

'That's some story,' I said. Turned to look for Sheila. Not wanting the coffee any more. Just wanting to get the hell out.

'Oh, I'm not finished.' He smiled at me, but there wasn't too much that was friendly about the look he was giving me. His mouth was all bunched up and his eyes were crushed down real small. 'See, I kept at it for years. Wheeling him out there and putting things in his hand. Waiting. I didn't want to do it after the first few years. But there wasn't anybody else to do it for me. No one left to take him out and put something new in his hand, see. It's like everyone went away.'

'Listen, bud,' I said. 'No disrespect, but I'm real beat.'

He nodded his head. Breathed out in a slow, tired way that left his head drooping.

'Sure,' he said. 'I'll be heading back home soon anyhow. I'll thank you for your time,' he said. His face came up and he was back to being the old man again. Interested and ready to watch me for a spell. His hand reaching out to me, waiting for me to take it. I almost did. Almost reached my hand up and took hold of his, but I couldn't. Looked at his hand and saw the way it was shaking. Not a nervous kind. This was heavy. Uncontrolled. A palsy kind of shake. Couldn't bring myself to touch it. We both froze up for a while. Silent while we both looked down at his hand – watched it shaking between us.

Then he said something that I didn't want to hear.

'I stay in a place called Maritime. Nice town. Peaceful. Good people mainly. Always a bad seed now and again. But, like most things, the bad seeds get blown around. Them winds again. Never know where those bad seeds are going to find ground. Take root.'

Felt my mouth moving. Heat surfacing across my face. Heat creeping over me in a slow-motion wave. Finding its way down through my neck. My hands started burning, so I opened them. Turned so I could set them on the counter. Leaned my weight against it.

'You know anything about Maritime, Mister Pullman?'

Couldn't make a damned word come out of my mouth. My mind was locked on one thing. *Maritime.* I was watching the old man and all I could think about was the white colonial house my old man had bought there. My mother inside it going bad like rotting wood. The sounds my old man's tools made in the basement. Sounds that came up through the house – echoing up through the laundry chute. Sounds that rattled the place like it was a house made of bones. Kept thinking of the house while the outsider moved his mouth. Speaking again, but I couldn't hear him for the sound of my mother screaming. Couldn't stop the sound of my father's tools shaking inside the walls. My lungs filling so much they hurt. Same as they did when I ran into the forests. Into the open space that cut through Maritime. Ran to get away. Dean and me.

'Mister Pullman?' he said.

'How do you know my name?' I asked. Came out in a whisper. Cleared my throat and tried to say it again. Came out just as quiet – just as lame and affected. 'How do you know me?'

The old man smiled.

'So now you want to talk,' he said. Nodded his head at me and made his mouth crooked. Maybe a smile, but it looked pained.

He spun on the stool and faced his plate. Dug in his fork and this time got the eggs to his mouth. His head bouncing on his shoulders. Mouth chewing fast like he hadn't eaten in weeks. His eyes closed. He kept like that while I looked at the side of his face. Old bastard seemed almost peaceful – looked like he was really savouring the moment. Kept looking at the side of his head and waited for him to speak again.

'How do you know who I am?' I asked.

He nodded his head.

'That's not an answer.'

'That waitress said your name.' He looked at me as he chewed. Then he pointed his fork at my forehead and said: 'That's a dead giveaway.'

'She called me Joe.'

He dropped the fork on his plate and used the paper napkin to wipe his mouth.

'I'll check with folks back home and see if they remember you. Maybe some of them will come back here for a visit. Catch up on lost time.' He cocked his head to the side: 'How long ago was it you left again?'

'Who are you?'

He shook his head.

'You wouldn't know me, friend.' He smiled. Teeth grey as granite. Gums white as a trout's belly. 'Same as I don't know you. We're different people now.'

'Why are you here?'

'Passing through,' he said. 'Spent some time with friends in Meridian. They told me about a market here in town. Said I'd have to come by and check it out.' He looked past my shoulder and focused on something. 'There's a man in there selling jerky strips as wide as three fingers.'

I wanted to say something, but Sheila was coming back. She was walking and singing to herself. Low hum of a song like she was warning off the approach.

'Here's the coffee, Joe.' She pushed the large Styrofoam cup across the counter to me. I looked at it and nodded at her. She hung round. Kept her hands either side of my coffee. 'You two know each other?'

'Well,' the outsider said. He leaned forward on the counter like he was getting ready to tell Sheila a secret. She smiled in return, waiting for the old man to tell her a story she couldn't live without hearing. 'Can't really place him for sure. You think he can remember me?'

'No,' I said.

Sheila frowned at the old man. She kept her face aimed at him, but shifted her eyes so they were looking at me.

'What's your name?' she asked the old man.

He broke the smile he'd been aiming at Sheila. Turned it on me.

'Name's Jules, ma'am.' I was waiting for it and was damned sure I could take anything he was about to say after that.

I was wrong. 'My name is Jules Lewiston. But, like I say, Mister Pullman. You probably can't remember me. We're different people now.'

I tried to keep my eyes on him. I wasn't feeling anger any more. Everything inside me changed to a wild mix of breathing and panic. Familiar feelings of pain and fear started moving in. A feeling that had been left behind in another place. Left in the white colonial when I travelled away in the squad car. A fear that melted away while the officer drove up Westchester Drive in a slow crawl. The officer making his siren bark to clear the way. Fear drifting away while we passed the familiar faces of neighbours. Faces hanging round to catch a glimpse of the beaten boy. Westchester Drive fading away like paper burning. Fear falling to black ash and scattering, so no one could put it back together again.

This man can put it together, Joe. Every last shred of it. He can make it all real again. Not just memories and bad dreams. But real!

'What's the matter, friend?' Lewiston touched my leg. I moved back fast. He sat up like he was expecting me to lay one on him. Latch on his neck and keep squeezing until there was nothing left. His chin went heavy and pulled his face into a long expression. Almost fell off his stool – had to grab the counter to keep himself from going over. 'Hold on now,' he said. 'Hold on now, Mister.'

'Joe,' Sheila said. 'What's got into you?'

'I've got to go.'

'Your coffee,' she said.

I took it off the counter. Didn't slip any money out of my pocket. Didn't think about leaving anything behind for Sheila. Just needed to get out of there. Needed to move far away from Jules Lewiston. Get distance between us. Sure I remembered him. I remembered a younger man. Twenty years hadn't been kind to him. His hair had fallen out. Not much left when I last saw him, but what he had still stuck to his head had gone silver. His skin had sucked in close to his bones. But, he was still the same man.

What do you want? he'd asked when he opened the door. Really blowing out of his house like he'd been expecting someone else. Looked over my shoulder and out into the street.

I came for Oz. Wanting to see how he's been doing, I'd said while standing on his porch. Dean Gillespie lying on the ground behind me. Lying near the hedge in the Lewistons' front garden. Knocked over when Jules Lewiston had come crashing out of his front door. *We came, I mean. To see if he's okay and all.*

He's not okay.

Thing is, I already knew that. Hearing him say it didn't make me feel too good. Didn't take the edge off my nerves hearing him talk about Oz. Confirming that he was inside the house in a real bad way. Sure, I'd seen what Dean had done to him. Watched it happen and felt sick, deep inside my guts, for not stopping him. But, I didn't want to be round him any more. Right when we showed up. Right when I'd hit the door with my knuckles. When Jules Lewiston had thrown that door open with the wild look on his face. I didn't want to be there any more.

He'd known who I was. He'd called me back when I'd turned to leave. He'd said some things about Oz being on medications. Having been through a lot, but he wasn't telling us much. I'd stood there looking at him while he talked to me. He was running his hand over his head.

Right now he's not the kid you know. Or knew, even. Not my kid, either. He's someplace else.

Hit the front door of Darnell's with my hand and sent the bell ringing. Fumbled round in my pocket for the keys to the van. Felt like the old man was going to be out of the diner any second. Hollering for my attention again. Calling me to turn around so he could tell me something else about poor old Oz Lewiston. Something he hadn't told me when I was last standing in front of him. Something he'd learned from placing pine cones in Oz's hand. Something Oz had said while sitting in a wheelchair in the centre of his favourite open space.

Got to the van with the same feeling running right through me. Feeling like someone was behind me. Someone was real close and not too interested in letting me get back to the good life. Got the van door open and jumped inside. Slammed the door and locked myself in. Sat there with the key stuck between my shaking fingers. Had a feeling what Jules Lewiston would have said next. If he'd had the chance. He'd said enough to me inside the diner to paint the damned picture so well he'd never have to show it to me. Never have to say another word about it. Oz had lived a while with the damage Dean had delivered. Damage I never stopped from happening. Maybe I'd had the chance. Sometimes I'm not so sure.

He was always someplace else, Joe. Right up to the end. Right up to when I couldn't take his chair to the park any more. When I couldn't do it and there was no one else to take him . . .

Watched the front door of Darnell's. Watched the windows. Looked at all the people inside sitting under the too-bright lights and wondered what the old man was telling Sheila. She was leaning over the counter, biting at her lower lip and shaking her head. Same as she always did when she was listening real hard. Saving it all up inside her head for when she might need it later.

'It can't go bad again,' I said. 'Goddamn, it can't go bad.'

Carole and her note. Then Muniz. Your old man's got pictures of Marty. He's got a list for Christ sake, Joe! Don't let this get any worse. You can do something about this. He's right there. Do something!

Turned the engine over and let the van heat up. I sat with the hot air blowing against my legs. The snow clouds were moving and the sun was behind the thickest of them. I kept my headlights off and watched the window of the diner.

Old Lewiston didn't move from his stool. Stayed there propped against the bar. When he was finished he pulled something from his pocket and set it down next to his plate. Leaned over to Sheila and spoke a few more words about something. She smiled and touched his arm. Not much of a worry 'cause Sheila's that kind of a person. Always touching you to let you know she's there. Trouble was I didn't know what the old man was leaving her. She lifted it up. I couldn't make it out, but it was clear it wasn't money. Sheila covered her mouth and shook her head real slow. Lewiston bowed his head and nodded a few times. A mourner's nod. Then he left.

He got behind the wheel of a Jeep. It was covered in highway grit. He was parked off the side of the diner, off in the shadows. The windows of the Jeep were ash-covered except for the crescents where the wipers had knocked them clean. Even the headlights and the licence plate were covered in grit. The front grille was caked with grey icicles that looked like rock formations from a deep cave. They were thick and covered the gap where an accident had smashed the grille in. Filled the void where the left headlight had been.

Lewiston moved around inside the Jeep. He pulled the seatbelt over his shoulder and messed with some things on the dash. Finally started it up. White smoke came from the muffler. Built bigger clouds with each rev he gave the engine. I sat waiting for a while, watching him. When he pulled out he took Beaumont like he was heading out of town. It wasn't enough to hope.

I pulled the van into gear and followed him.

Chapter Seven

Pop shook me until I came round. Stood over me and showed me the same face he wore when I'd come home from parties stinking of beer. Years separated me from those moments, but the look he gave me sunk in the same feeling. Sat up on the sofa and wiped a hand across my face. Looked for my watch, but it wasn't on my wrist. Leaned my head back and closed my eyes. Hoped the hollow burn in my gut was going to fade.

'Joe,' Pop said, still moving his hand against my shoulder. Took hold of my shirt and gave a hearty yank. Almost pulled me off the sofa. 'It's late, son. You better get yourself upstairs. Have a good sleep in a real bed.'

Blinked my eyes for a while and Pop waited until I'd cleared my head. Until I was able to talk to him.

'Got yourself into a state,' he said. He was looking at the bottle I'd set at the foot of the sofa. He bent down and picked it up. Shook it and made a face at me when the bottle didn't make a sound. 'Marty's in bed. He'll probably be up to see you early tomorrow. Poor boy's drained with all his worrying.'

'What's going on?' I said. 'He's here?'

'Both of the boys are up in their rooms. Paul's been filling them with all sorts of nonsense. He's told them that Carole's left you, and then he tried to make out like they were going to have to live with him and Frances. Donald got all bothered about it and when he couldn't get a hold of you, he called me. So I went up there today and brought them back.'

'I didn't say anything to him about Carole.'

'You call him?'

'Yeah, I called him. But I didn't say anything about her leaving me. She's just gone to do some things. That's all I said. Told him she'll be back.'

'Kind of things she needing to do?'

'I don't know, Pop.'

'Sounds kind of screwy.' He scratched his fingers into his heavy white beard. Fingers got lost in all the fur. 'Screwy to me, and to Paul it must sound like a real conspiracy. Paul's not a man to sit easy on these things, Joe.'

'Well, he can suffer the same as the rest of us,' I said.

'Sure he can. Thing is, he's calling all kinds of people looking for his little girl. He's wanting some kind of update. He's got contacts and friends all over this part of the state. Some here in Henderson.'

'Well, he can use them. He can call them all he wants. She's not here.'

'She'll be back,' he said. He frowned as I shook my head.

'She left a note. Said she was going to be back too late to get the boys. Said she had some things to tell me.'

'So, she's got some things to clear with you. That's a good start.' Pop reached down and hooked an arm under mine. 'Get up. Go to your bed and get a rest. Boys will be up early and expecting you to follow their lead. Don't go moping round just 'cause Carole's decided she needs to search a few things out.'

Like a list of people from my past who came into some real unfortunate luck. She's looking for answers to questions I wish she'd never had the guts to ask. If she comes back I'm going to have some explaining to do . . .

And if she doesn't—

'What's the matter, Joe? You going to be sick or something?' Shook my head. 'Lay off the drink. Had your spell with the spirits, and now it's time you manned up and got the boys sorted out. Have this place in order for when Carole comes back.'

'I'll do that.' Pop pulled me towards the door. I leaned against him and held on to his shoulder. 'Sorry I didn't get the boys, Pop. That's a long drive up there.' Pop was nodding his head. 'I didn't get any calls.'

'Course you didn't.' He was looking at the bottle while he was talking to me. He was never good at hiding his disappointment.

'I'll speak with both of them tomorrow.'

'You're going to have to spend some time. They're both needing to let loose. They need someone they can open up to. They're good kids, Joe. Don't screw them up.' I nodded, but my head felt unsteady when Pop took his arm off me and moved away. Pop turned round and touched my shoulder again. 'Get some sleep. Then you take Marty out tomorrow and ask him what's on his mind.'

'How much does he know?'

'That's not for me to say.' He opened the front door and looked outside. Out into the late-night dark. He turned his head and caught me staring at his face. Caught me looking at the lines that hadn't been there a few years back before Mona died. 'Get yourself straightened out. Then you spend some time with Marty. Talk to Donald too. They need you. You'll know all about that.'

'Yeah,' I said.

'He's a thinker,' Pop said. 'Marty lets it all stew in there. And when it gets all jumbled he keeps on thinking.'

'Gets it from Carole.'

'I remember another young man who kept things to himself. Bottled it all up until he went off like a rocket.' Pop wasn't smiling and I knew he wasn't making light of the trouble I'd caused him. 'Brought some groceries for you. Filled up some of the necessities. Breakfast for the boys and all that.'

'Thanks, Pop.'

Nodded his head.

'Straighten yourself out, Joe. Can't keep messing up and relying on other people. We're not always going to be around for you.'

I waited in the doorway as Pop walked towards his truck. He slowed when he was passing the van. Stopped and ducked down. Ran his hand over the bumper. Stood up and looked at his gloves. Turned round to face me.

'You hit something?' he asked.

'Deer, I think. Wasn't big.'

'Good thing,' he said. He touched the paint on the side of the van. Ran his hand over it again. 'Should buff out okay.'

He walked to his truck and got in. Started it up and backed out of the driveway. Couldn't bring myself to wait for him to be gone before I shut the door and went upstairs to bed. Didn't make it under the covers. It seemed like too much of an effort to pull them back. Don't remember the position I fell asleep in, but it must have been close to the same one I woke up in. In my dreams I was driving on a mountain road. I was chasing something. What I was chasing was screaming and the more I gained on it, the louder it screamed. Before I reached it the screaming stopped. I looked around and saw the black trees and the empty road and a cliff that dropped down into nothing.

Chapter Eight

Henderson Crier January 12, 2009

MISSING MEMBER OF THE COMMUNITY

A request has been received from the family of Carole Quincy (Pullman) to assist in the search for her whereabouts. Mrs Pullman was reported missing on Thursday when her husband, Joe Pullman of Meaks & Pullman Funeral Directors, returned home to find the mother of two missing. Mrs Quincy-Pullman was last seen at Oswald Market at midday on Wednesday the 8th. Police searches have been unsuccessful in finding any clues to her disappearance.

The Quincy family thanks the citizens of Henderson for any assistance they can provide in locating their beloved daughter.

Sightings of Mrs Quincy-Pullman or information as to her possible whereabouts should be directed to Henderson Police on 652–4601.

Chapter Nine

Bones in my back creaked when I bent down for the mail. It was piled on the welcome mat inside the front door. Took it to the kitchen and dropped it on the table. Started to manoeuvre like I wanted the day to happen. But something inside wasn't right. Something in my gut was cramping up. In my head and in my body I just didn't feel right. I was slowing down. Making me wish like hell Carole would show up and relieve one of the problems I was facing – or at least was about to face.

I went to the cabinet and took out the paper filters and metal canister labelled 'high octane'. Filled the coffee pot. First water, then the coffee grounds. It was a race. The water was already bubbling. Starting to sputter and spit by the time the paper funnel was filled with fresh ground. A hot spray of steam caught my finger while I was shutting the flap. But I beat it. Somehow it mattered. Even something as small as beating the hot water with the ground beans. Some crazy coffee-pot game.

That's what you've been reduced to, Joe. Can you get any worse?

Carole laughed at my games. Years back, when times were still young between us. When Marty was just born. Before that too, but Marty came along and rejuvenated us. Our relationship started over when Carole fell pregnant. Made it new to be together. Life and marriage and us – all of us. Marty came before Donald. Gave me a hint about fatherhood. Marty changed things. He changed me. It helped that he was my kid. Ours. Donald was Carole's. Hers with some other dipshit guy named Kevin who shrugged off responsibility for the kid like most people shrug off rain.

The coffee pot finished brewing. Poured a mug full and sat down at the table. I set my coffee mug on the placemat. Moved it over the specks and stains of dried food. Lifted the cup and took a sip. Something inside wasn't balanced. As fast as the memories came they slipped away.

Opened the *Henderson Crier* and flipped the pages. Looked at the pictures and flipped to the next sheet. I was going through the paper more for the sound of the broadsheet pages turning. That sound was more important than the stories printed on the pages. It felt familiar. It filled in the gaps that were making the empty kitchen unbearable. Flipped to the next page and stopped. Eyes connected with a short headline. MISSING MEMBER OF THE COMMUNITY. Paul Quincy was the asshole of all assholes. Taking things into his own greasy hands and making them seem worse than they needed to seem. I stewed over the article for a while. Then I looked into my coffee mug and stared at the black liquid and wondered how much hassle this was going to bring my way. I was still watching the black coffee settle when Donald walked in.

Looked at him and gave him a smile.

'You alright, Joe?'

'Yeah, kid.' Handed over the paper to him. Page opened to the article. I figured he'd see it anyway, so it was best it came from me. Donald leaned against the table and read the piece. Shook his head as he passed down the column. 'Your grandpa say anything to you about putting something like that in the paper?'

'No. Jesus, this is getting crazy.'

'Getting,' I said. Looked out through the glass panel in the kitchen door. Snow had covered the cedars bordering our lawn, giving a good white barrier between us and Edith Krantz. An extra layer between me and the outside world.

Donald dropped his hair to cover half his face.

'Your eyes look red,' he told me.

I rubbed a hand across the bridge of my nose.

'I've been feeling allergies coming on,' I said. Made a laugh so the kid would understand. 'They really get me sometimes. Worst of all during the cold seasons. Heating in the house kicks up old dust.'

Donald looked real uncomfortable standing there. Like he was wanting to ask me something, but didn't know which word to start with. I figured I knew what was on his mind, but wasn't all that interested in getting his thoughts moving.

'What happened to you guys?' I asked. 'Thought you were up with your old folks until next week.'

'I needed to get away. Couldn't sleep. It's not my bed. You know what I mean? Grandma's place has that smell. That and I've got to share with Marty.'

'Why didn't you take the sofa?'

'They wouldn't let me. Grandpa wakes up early and he likes to read the paper and drink his orange juice without anybody around. So he wouldn't let me sleep on the sofa in case I disturbed him.'

'He's a loon,' I said.

Donald's head moved and I caught a sliver of the smile behind the hair covering his face.

'You want something to eat?' he asked.

'No, bud. Help yourself.'

'Cool.'

Donald pushed off the wall and opened the cabinet. He went through it without taking anything out. He finally pulled out a bag of donuts and held it up to his face. Turned it round and spent some time looking at it.

'You want something to drink?' I asked. 'I brewed some coffee.'

He shook his head.

'Hey, Joe.' He finished reading the donut bag. He opened the bag and took out a donut and held it close to his mouth. 'You know where my mom's at?'

I shook my head. Drank some of the coffee and rubbed at my eyes.

He took a bite of the donut and swallowed. Then he asked: 'You're still in your clothes from last night. You sleep on the sofa?' He hadn't turned his head round far enough to look at me. I used my foot to push the chair out across from me. He bit into the donut again and looked at the chair. Sat down.

'No, I went up to bed. Just didn't have the energy to change.' Put my hands out to kind of surrender to him. Feeling pitiful already. Feeling sick in a weird sort of way. Half-expected him to start picking me to pieces. Thing is, I felt like I deserved it. He'd lost his mom and that was down to me.

I'm rough, bud. I'm feeling it already and your mother's only been gone a few days. Real piece of work, huh?

'I'll get myself sorted out.'

Donald didn't take it as I hoped he would. At least he didn't look reassured.

'I came back down early this morning,' I said. 'Sat on the sofa and kept an eye on the clock for a while.' He frowned at me and reached round for the fridge door without looking away. 'I had a suspicion that time was going to stand still.' He stopped trying to tug the fridge door open. Had his eyes on me. They were looking tired.

'That's kind of a weird thing to say, Joe.'

'It's kind of a weird thing to admit,' I told him. 'I don't get what's happened with your mom. I don't get anything right now. So I sat on the sofa and waited for something to happen. For an idea to come into my head. For a place to maybe spring up. Some town that your mom was always talking about. Always wanted to go and visit. Someplace important. A place she maybe felt that I was holding her back from seeing. If I knew a place like that, I could go and look for her.'

Donald stared at me for a few seconds and for a moment I thought I'd hit the nail. He looked like he was going to spill everything all at once. Tell me how Carole had been talking up a storm about Maritime and Columbia. About some old man in a prison. How she wanted to see him before he died of the cancer that was turning his colon to stone. How she was going to travel up there and finish a story that had too many holes.

He went to the fridge. Took out the gallon of milk and set it on the counter. Took a glass from the cabinet and filled the glass halfway with milk and stood with his back to me. He drank the glass empty and filled it again. Stood with the gallon of milk still opened. The glass he'd poured still untouched. His head drooping and his shoulders rising and falling with a slow and heavy breath.

'Where is it you think my mom's gone?' He turned round and ran the sleeve of his shirt across his mouth. 'When Grandpa said she wasn't here, I figured she would show up at their place. That's what happens. Maybe she's just left for a couple days again.' He was looking at me through his hair. Staring at me to see how I was going to react. It wasn't easy to watch him, but I didn't want to stir up trouble. 'She hasn't called yet, right?'

I shook my head at him.

'You better sit for a minute,' I said. Pointed at the chair across from me. Felt like an asshole doing it, but it was just one of those gestures that happened without thought. Something a father does to a son when the kid's lost his way. Never did that kind of thing with Donald 'cause it wasn't my place to be acting like his father. But without any kind of warning there we were – in a house together. No one else to deal with him. To put him on the right path. So I made the gesture and he sat down. Watching him fall into the seat like that made me feel a sort of ease with him. Like somehow

I needed to help the kid along every way I could. I owed it to him to try and make things right. At least a little easier for him. I'd pointed out the chair he should drop ass in and took the look he gave me like I deserved it.

He sat on the edge, so I figured he wasn't planning to stay for long. Didn't even put the glass of milk on the table. Set it on his knee instead. No matter what it was I was about to tell him, he wasn't going to hang around. We looked at each other across the kitchen table. He pulled the hair away from his eyes. It fell back again, but he didn't move it away.

'Got any idea how Marty's feeling about this?' I asked.

'Nope.'

'Paul tell you anything about a note?'

Donald shook his head.

'Okay,' I said. Took a deep breath and lifted the coffee. Swirled it round for a couple of seconds and set it back on the table without taking a drink. 'I came back home the other night and found a note on the fridge. It was from your mom.' I looked at him for a few seconds. Trying to judge what was happening in his head through his reaction. He didn't make any expression. He sniffed, but he always sniffs. 'It says she's gone away. After I got the note . . . Well, that's when I called your grandparents.'

He'd lost interest in me and started looking at his hands. At the glass he was holding. Running the fingertips of his right hand over the glass he held on his knee. Knuckles were white. Fingers tightening their hold on the glass of milk. He stayed quiet for a while and then finally said: 'That sucks.'

'You're telling me.'

'Can I see the note?' he said.

I leaned to the side and pulled the paper from my pocket. It was wrinkled and damp and the ink was smudged. A handkerchief would look better after being passed round a Scout troop suffering from hay fever. I'd done a number on it. Before handing it across to Donald I set it on the table and used the edge of my hand to try and take some of the shape out of it. Make it flat again. Before passing out on the sofa I'd got so angry that I'd wanted to rip it up. Thought about finding the long matches we used to light the fireplace. Striking one and setting it up to the corner until the note caught fire and burned to nothing.

The anger wasn't directed at Carole. If she'd decided to leave me, I had myself to blame with all I had done to push her to a distance. My anger was aimed more at that note and what it had brought my way. It was aimed at the suspicions of Paul Quincy and his jumping the gun and putting an article in the *Crier*. My anger was centred on Jules Lewiston. He may not have been a part of Carole disappearing, but he sure as hell was adding fuel to my fire.

Sitting at the table, I knew why I'd kept the note. 'Cause it wasn't mine. Not entirely.

Spread the note flat one last time and slid it across the table. Donald sat with his hands in his lap and leaned forward to get a look at the note. His hands didn't move.

'Thanks,' he said, still not reaching for it. Just leaned over and blinked his eyes for a while. His hair had fallen over his eyes so I couldn't see what they were doing. Couldn't gauge what he was feeling. He finally lifted his left hand and hovered it over the note. His fingers moving like he was testing it for heat.

'She leaves notes in my room,' he said. 'Things she wants me to do.'

He lowered his hand and pulled the note to him. Slid it poker-style – not wanting to give anything away. Not wanting to see it until it was up close. Watched his expression while he made it through the words. His face didn't change. What I could see of it through his hair stayed the same as always. Long, pale and tight in the jaw. I could see his eyes only through the thin slit of his parted hair. His shoulders hung and he pulled his hair back with one hand and held it there, away from his brow. His eyes moving over the words – travelled one way in slow motion. Then they'd rocket back and start the next line.

He finished reading and cleared his throat. Lifted the note and turned it over. Lifted it close to his face and looked at it for a few seconds. Studied it like he was counting the chips left in the pulp. Dropped the note onto the table and slid it back towards the centre where I'd left it. He took his hand back and set it in his lap.

'Why would she leave a note? Why didn't she just call you?' he asked. I shook my head. Donald took it that I didn't understand the questions. 'Why didn't she just wait for you to come back so she could explain why she needed to go?'

'Same question I had.'

'Sucks.'

Nodded 'cause I didn't have anything else to give him.

'I know you're probably really angry about it,' he said. 'But, it doesn't mean anything . . .'

'I'm not blaming anybody, Don.' I sat there shaking my head. I had my stepson apologising for his disappearing mother. Like Houdini's children ever said sorry for their dad sneaking into his box. There have been few times in my life when I felt so pathetic. I felt a pang of guilt for what I'd told the cop when I was reporting Carole missing. *He's not my kid.*

'It's just . . .' Donald started again. He sat there in front of me shaking his head and running his fingers over the faint shade of hair he had coming through on his chin. 'I feel bad about it.'

'So do I, bud.' Gave him a smile that didn't make the plastic feeling go away. It was fake 'cause I didn't know how to smile at the kid. Not right then. Donald stood up and shook his head. With that he left and I finished drinking my coffee. Had two refills. Marty was still in bed. I was expecting him to come down the stairs, scratching himself like an old man. Carole would tell him to stop it. He'd look at her and frown. Without thinking he'd be at it again. Eleven years old with the manner-isms of an old-timer. Carole always said he took his bad habits from me. She said a lot of things that made me laugh. Things that made me think; consider the simple things that usually slip by unnoticed.

The coffee was still hot and it burned the roof of my mouth. Took another mouthful and held it. A small way of testing myself. Another stupid game. A sacrifice maybe. I needed to do something just so I could stop feeling lame. While the coffee burned at my mouth, I looked down at the note. Read the small words again.

'Where the fuck are you, Carole?'

'What's that?'

I looked up and saw a middle-aged midget in my doorway. His hair stuck up like an oil-slick duck. His face frowning at me. Eyes blinking against the bright lights of the kitchen. His hand down the front of his pyjama bottoms. Sound of fingers racking over skin muffled by the fabric.

'Hey, Marty,' I said. 'It's nothing. I'm just thinking out loud.'

'Dirty thought.'

Nodded my head.

'I'm full of them lately.'

The telephone started ringing. I looked at Marty and thought about going for it. Give him time to come to life. He turned his head and looked at the phone on the wall. Frowned like he didn't understand what was happening. Like the ringing was getting to him – really annoying the hell out of him. He was growing older by the second. Never looked so much like my father. A grumpy old man in a pair of Scooby-Doo pyjamas.

He turned and snapped his hand out. Pulled the phone from the carrier and slapped it to the side of his head. The plastic made a cracking sound when it connected. He looked more stunned than pained. Swapped ears and rubbed the side he'd just clattered with the phone.

'Yeah? Hello?'

'Marty,' I said. 'Be polite.'

'Sorry,' he said. 'This is the Pullman residence. Marty Pullman speaking.' He nodded his head a while. Looked up at the ceiling and breathed a big breath. 'Yeah, I'll get him for you.'

He reached his hand out, shaking the phone at me. I reached for it, but Marty let it go too soon. The phone hit the floor between us and made a sound like the plastic had cracked. I was getting up off the chair and lifted the phone from the floor and heard the sound of someone on the other end. A voice calling out the same words over and over again.

'Yeah, I'm here,' I said. 'This is Joe Pullman.'

'Joe, what's going on over there?'

'It's nothing. Just dropping phones and waking up to the day.' I touched Marty's shoulder and moved him towards the fridge so he could get himself started on breakfast. 'What can I do for you, Sheriff?'

'We've got a situation. It's probably best if you come down to the courthouse.'

'What's it about?' My chest was feeling tight. It was hard to keep pace with my breath. My lungs were working over-time.

'It's Daryl Evers. His daughter's been away for a few nights. And he came in to see me about it.'

Thought back to what I was doing a few nights back. Wondered how many people had seen me leaving Henderson with Evers' girl in the van. Lenny at the Trapper's Paradise could vouch for me coming home that night, but that was after I spoke with Carole. After she held me up at the house with her drunk talk. Lenny would still have my tab hidden up under the lounge bar. Maybe he'd remember me drinking beers and eating the rubber venison burgers he'd been cooking. Remember me going to my room *alone*.

'Yeah?' I said. 'Any idea of what's happened to her?' Nat made a few noises, but wasn't saying anything. 'Why are you gathering at the courthouse?'

'Well, the boys are down in the valley. Think maybe they've got something. We received a tip that she was seen out on Brevard. Close to the old Gulf Station. There's a bus stop out there, but it's kind of shady why she'd be that far out of town on her own.' *Well, I don't know, Sheriff. I dropped her off at the Meridian bus depot and that's the last I had to do with her.* 'I've got a few other boys over at Apple Mount. Seems they found Milton Berrill walking round over there. Told the officer he thinks he's seen something again. Could just be another tall tale, but I can't take the chance this time. Either way, I think you'll be needed. Daryl can use some support no matter what we find. I figured you'd be a good choice under the circumstances.'

'What circumstances are those?'

'Just come on down here, son.' Sheriff took a moment to cough. Moved his mouth away from the phone. Came back and said: 'The man's pretty broke up just now. Might have some questions about what happens next. Just to be prepared.'

'Sure,' I told him. Tried not to let my voice match the uneasy feeling I had rolling up in my guts. Daryl Evers was about as much a friend to me as a Republican is to a Democrat on election day. 'I'll be right down.'

I hung up.

'Somebody dead?' Marty asked.

He was sitting at the kitchen table with his chin cupped in his hands. Looking at me the same way he always does when he's waiting for breakfast. When he's between dreamland and Marty the eleven-year-old think tank.

'What'll it be, bud? It's got to be quick,' I told him. 'I've got to be someplace.'

'You doing a removal?' he asked. His chin came up from his hands and he wiped his eyes clear with the sleeve of his pyjama top. Looked aware of what was happening for the first time that morning.

'Don't know yet,' I said. 'I'm just heading down to the courthouse to lend some support to a friend.'

'Can I come?'

'Not this time,' I said. 'You hang out here. I'll get Donald to look after you until I'm back. We can see about taking a walk down by the river, if you're up for it.'

'That'll be good,' he said.

'So what'll it be?' I asked.

'Anything.' His chin fell back onto his hands. He looked at the tablecloth. 'Just make it quick. I'm starvin' Marvin.'

Chapter Ten

Nat Upshaw was standing at the window of his office when I arrived that morning. He didn't move much from that spot all the time I was there. He just stood and looked out over what we call the back of Henderson. It's woodland. There's probably quarter of a mile of paved paths, cutting off in all directions, ripping up the side of the hills. You can see them best in the autumn when the leaves have left the trees. In the summer they are hidden under great balls of green and blue. In the winter it's the snow that hides the paths. The rest of the back of Henderson has been left to nature. Streams cut through it and feed into three lakes. It's a part of town that's popular for family picnics and young people looking for privacy. It's quiet and it's peaceful. Once in a while you hear the sound of the sawmill coming through the valley, but it's never so bad it ruins the tranquillity. If the wind shifts just right you can smell the burned wood. Adds to the spirit of the place.

Nat nodded at me when I arrived and took his place at the window again, standing with his hands settled against the sill. Pleat running down the back of his police uniform puckered out whenever he went to stretch his shoulders. To that moment his shirt had puckered half a dozen times. He was getting stiff from all the standing. All the nothing he'd been doing. He'd been there for a long while. I'd been watching him for over an hour and felt like my guts were going to spill out the toast and coffee I'd forced down with Marty watching me. I just couldn't get settled. It's not easy to find solace under those kinds of circumstances. All the commotion down in the valley. Daryl Evers was sitting on the sofa across from me. He'd look over at me once in a while like he wanted to say something. Then there was the thing with my missing wife. It was a worry, sure. But it was also an embarrassment – now that the whole town knew about it.

Stood up and walked over to Nat's desk. Started shifting things round to pass the time. Lifted his name plaque and dusted it off and set it back down again. Flipped through the *Field & Stream* without lifting it off the desk. Whatever I could do to keep from sitting down. Keep from seeing Daryl Evers out the corner of my eye, looking at me.

Just get it out of your system for Christ's sake!

Nat was big on candy. Rock candy mainly. He had a glass jar on his desk. Sheriff's badge is etched on the side of the glass. Under the badge it reads: Big Man in Town. I reached in the jar and took a couple of the plastic-wrapped red balls and lifted one to my nose. Could smell the cinnamon before I had it to my chin. Real potent burn too. Took me back to the cinnamon gum I used to chew. Found myself running a tongue over the back of my teeth, remembering how Dean Gillespie called me out for making a sucking sound. The burn of the cinnamon cutting into the gashes my old man had punched through the inside of my cheeks.

I looked through the window where Nat was standing. I looked past him and I saw an emergency van pulling into view. It crawled round the curve in the path. Made it past the cluster of wooden skeletons. Oaks out of season, shaking against the cold wind without their leaves. Looking black and charred against the fresh white snow. Three hills rolled up between the rear windows of the Henderson Courthouse. One of them started at the edge of the lake. Two more swelled behind it. Made a steady incline from the back of the red-brick courthouse, ending in the valley where Jawnell Lake lay frozen. The surface of the lake was silver, with cloud-dulled sunlight flickering off the smooth gloss of ice.

A new storm was rolling in the distance. Clouds still a way off, but it was moving towards us with some strength. Clouds bringing the second coming of a heavy fall of snow. The earlier storm had moved through and dropped long shadows across the hills. Shadows that broke and took the falling snow away, but not before it locked up most of the roads with all that it had dropped. Now the sun was shining hard and it blazed yellow and skimmed off the surface of the hills in bright flashes.

Shadows were gliding in again, crossing over the hills like giants approaching. Moving closer. Edging towards the one long slope, ready to connect all the hills in a dull grey. The big slope was the backside of Apple Mount and it ended at the lake, where the emergency van drew up with flashing lights and skidded to a stop next to a police Jeep. Lights still spinning.

People started to move.

Daryl used the handkerchief to wipe his mouth. He looked at it for a second and then folded it a few times. His hands were shaking and it took some doing to get it back inside his jacket pocket. He stood up and watched his feet while he moved from side to side. Unsure if he wanted to dance. That's what he looked like. After a few seconds he sat back down on the leather sofa. Times like that were just about waiting. About getting your thoughts squared up for what comes next.

I started thinking about Marty. Wondering what was going through his head. Hoping he'd find somebody to talk to if he needed to get it out. Hoping he didn't need to clear his mind too much. Too much of the wrong things gets out into this town and people latch onto it. No matter if it's Nancy Lowell's crazy spirit talk or Marty's nattering on about a note his mother stuck to the fridge before leaving him behind, the more it goes round, the more stories start to pull together.

I stood up again and tried pacing. Pushed my arms through the sleeves of my leather jacket. Kept it on until I started to sweat, then I'd pull it off again. Folded it and draped it over the back of one of the chairs. Put it back on again just so I could take it off. To Daryl Evers I must have looked like a real prick. Here he was in a terrible state – all shook up about his missing daughter – and I was making a noise 'cause I couldn't get comfortable. That stopped me pacing.

'You okay, Daryl?' I finally asked.

He was perched on the centre cushion of the long sofa. On the wall behind him was a painting of a hunting scene. Two men in the background pointing long rifles at a blue sky. A boy up close walking forward. He is painted in detail. His head down while he makes his way forward. Ten more feet and he'd be stepping out of the painting. He's carrying two limp ducks by their legs. One in each hand. The ducks are dead and bending in an awful way. The boy looks like he might walk right out of the painting. It's big enough and he could've been real. It could have all been real, even the holes in the necks of the ducks with the veins hanging out. Blood leaking and running onto the high grass at the boy's feet. The boy is smiling.

Daryl was watching the window. I wasn't going to ask him again, but I kept watching him. When it got too tough looking at him, I looked at the boy behind him. Smiling away while he swung the dead birds by their skinny legs. Daryl pushed his square-framed glasses up the bridge of his nose – pushed them up until they were pressed into his thick eyebrows. He finally nodded his head, but kept his words inside.

We'd been in the room for two hours, maybe more. He'd watched the first clouds reach Apple Mount. Watched the snows start to fall again. Then I'd come and I'd watched the aftermath. I'd watched the sheriff chew through the lip of a Styrofoam cup. He took three good chews before realising it was something he didn't want to eat. He looked tired and embarrassed while he picked the small white balls off his tongue.

Daryl sat in silence for a while, nodding away. Nat turned his head round and looked at me – almost as a reminder that I was needed, but only in the shadows. No one wants me around, but there are circumstances that require my services. So I get the invite now and again. Most often I occupy my space well and keep quiet. I went back to doing what I do best. Kept myself hidden.

'I'm real scared, Joe,' Daryl finally said. I didn't raise my eyes to look at him. I just sat there and nodded to let him know I'd heard him alright. 'I suppose you don't need me to tell you that. This is not something that's new to you. Any of this really. But it helps me to say it out loud. I am scared.'

And you should be, Daryl. That precious little girl of yours lets people know how much you love your children, and Henderson's going to have a parade ploughing through. When all those people she's spoken with hear she's missing . . . That kind of story sells. I'm telling you, D, you're gonna be a star for all the wrong reasons.

'We know you're scared, Daryl,' Nat said. 'You telling us that doesn't change the way we see you.'

No, it doesn't change the way we look at you, Daryl. Little Miss Evers gone missing makes us feel sorry for you. Your shaking silence is normal under the circumstances. That is until you take into account it's probably the conscience of a closed-door kiddie-fiddler that's surfacing – not a doting father.

Daryl made a laugh that sounded like it wasn't meant to be heard. He coughed and took his glasses off his nose. Used a shaking hand to remove the white handkerchief from the inside pocket of his jacket. He sat there for a long while wiping his glasses. Clearing his throat now and again.

'Well, I suppose you're right, Daryl.' Had my eyes on him,

staring hard. He set his glasses back on his nose and his eyes caught mine and grew wide. 'It's nothing new to me.'

'Oh, not that,' he said. He showed me the palms of his hands. Held them out to me like he was trying to stop traffic. 'Not that way. Not at all. I was so sorry to hear about Carole. I hope she comes home soon,' he said. 'God, I can't tell you how much I hope that for you.'

My smile must have been enough to make him feel alright about things. It kept him talking anyway. As long as he was talking I could stay quiet, and that's just the way I wanted it.

'I meant in terms of your job,' he said. 'It must get you used to these kinds of things.'

'It's okay,' I said. 'I understand what you mean.' And I thought I did until he felt the need to clarify.

'I'm not talking about Carole. I read about that in the paper, but that's not . . .'

'Not what you meant,' I said. The smile felt loose on my face. Too difficult to keep from falling off. I'll credit myself with that one. I sure kept up the appearance. 'It's fine, Daryl. Don't get all worried about it.'

He stood and walked round in a circle. He went over to the ficus Nat Upshaw kept in his office. The thing had lost most of its leaves and was only starting to get some new growth. Daryl stood close and pulled two leaves off a branch. He looked at them and rubbed them between his fingers. He let them drop and watched them fall to the floor.

He walked back and took a seat on the sofa again.

'I'm glad you're here as a friend,' he said. It sounded like it was coming from a true politician. Someone up in Washington who was moving in on an election campaign. He must have felt like he was on a roll 'cause he added: 'I'm glad you're here as a good local man. That means a lot to me.'

I nodded my head and kept my face stern. Sombre and sober.

Daryl Evers was looking at me with his mouth moving like

he had a whole lot of words inside it. His eyes were watery. Small balls made of the blackest rock. Storm rolled and polished by a fast stream. They were shimmering behind the thick lenses of his glasses. He'd kept the tears from falling.

'If you're needing to leave for a while, Joe, I'll be here,' Nat said. I looked over and saw how his words had fogged up the glass. 'Take a breather if you're wanting one.'

I stood from the chair. My legs felt stiff and a bolt of pain in my forehead dug in deep. It had been there all morning, but it was gaining some added strength. Jabbing back in my head farther than it had before.

'If you could leave the radio,' Daryl said. His eyes watching the bulge in my black jacket. A weight pressing a shape from the inside pocket. 'I'd appreciate if you could leave the radio in here.'

'I'm not needing a long break. Just a breather.' I paused and looked at Daryl. 'I'm sorry, Daryl. I don't have a radio.' Feeling I needed to make it clear, I said: 'We use cellphones.'

'Is that so?' Daryl said. Eyes still on the shape in my jacket.

And the room froze again. Same as it had when I walked in first thing that morning. Shaking Nat's hand and then Daryl's. We stood there a while and watched the snows outside. It was cold then, and with the silence there was an awkward feeling about the room. The silence took control and seemed to hold everything in place. The heating kicked on and rumbled through the walls. Nat Upshaw jumped back and rubbed his hands together. Leaned against the windowsill again. Took his place at the window – close up and aimed his attention down to see what was happening at the lake. He was anxious, like he thought the heater was signalling that something was about to change.

I had that feeling too, that the signal was on the way and when it came Daryl Evers was going to be in a world of hurt. In a real bad way. Couldn't get my heart to stop thumping. My lungs needed more and more air. That's a bad sign. For me it's the sure indication that things were going bad. Lowered my head. Couldn't turn to leave while Daryl Evers was looking at me like that. Staring without expression. Lost in his mind the way he was – so I stayed and waited.

A knock came from the door. I turned my head and Nat Upshaw followed suit. He let the second round of knocks sound off before he called out.

'It's alright,' he said.

Anne Morris pushed her face through a narrow crack. She'd taken off her headphones. The impression they made was still dividing her head. Split her hair right down the middle – sideways.

'Sheriff,' she said. 'How are you fellas holding up?'

'We're doing fine, Anne,' he said. He straightened his back. Grimaced like he felt a harsh pull at the muscles. Down low in his back something must have stretched out of place. One of those thin, sharp burns. He held the position, awkward as it was.

'I get you guys another coffee?' Anne asked. 'Maybe something to eat?'

'No,' Nat said. 'You boys needing coffee?' He looked round the room. Then he looked at Anne and smiled. It wasn't long before the smile faded. Disappeared. 'I think I've had just about as much coffee as this body's gonna allow.'

His eyes trailed back to the window. There was a silence that took the room. A hard silence. No one knew what else to say. So the sheriff moved forward. Placed his hands against the windowsill. Then he leaned forward and breathed out.

'I'll be outside if you need me.' Anne moved her head from the door and pulled it shut.

'And I'm glad of that.' Nat turned his head without looking at the closed door. Outside the courthouse window darkness had sneaked in. Rushed up with a winter quiet. A calm that lulls. Eases. All the while the clouds came rolling. Clouds low in the sky, carried by the wind that cuts through skin and drills down into the bone. The same wind that pressed against the black skeletons of trees. Bending their branches and moving them to dance in the shadows. The white snow had turned silver. Interrupted by the sweeping red and blue lights of vehicles down by the lake.

Portable halogen lights were making circles in the snow around the banks of the lake. Figures moved where the lights made the snow a brilliant yellow. The figures followed the yellow circles. We watched them move. We watched in silence.

The room was quiet. I was looking at Daryl, who was folding his hands one into the other. He'd stop and would take a look at his palms. Searching for something. Maybe trying to tell his own future. Maybe trying to see if all his suffering had made his palms bleed. Only way it could get worse for him. After a while of looking at his palms he'd start folding his hands again.

The room was quiet for a while. Daryl started watching me and I was watching Nat. Then my cellphone started ringing. That's about when things went downhill. Like a damned train going over the side of a very steep mountain.

Chapter Eleven

I pulled the cellphone from my pocket and held it to my ear. Turned away from Daryl before speaking. Felt like I was in some kind of sideshow. Daryl was standing with his hands by his side. One of Nat Upshaw's deputies was on the line sounding real anxious about something. I shook my head at Daryl and Nat to get them to stop crowding me. The deputy was talking too fast. His words weren't coming together.

'Calm down, bud. You're breaking up,' I told him. 'Can you call me back on the landline?'

'Requesting your services, Mister Pullman,' he said. Sounded like he was trying to compose himself. I let the line go dead while he constructed the next sentence. 'We have a 415, sir. Requesting your presence for a 415. Over.'

'415,' I repeated. 'Copy that, Officer. What is your location?'

Turned round to see Nat standing behind his desk with a hand raised to his forehead. He pushed the white hair back from his brow.

The deputy gave me the address. Had to give it to me twice 'cause of all the interference on the line.

'That's in Fox Chapel?' I said. 'Officer?'

'Roger that, Mister Pullman.'

'On my way,' I said. 'ETA ten minutes.'

Snapped the phone shut. Slipped it back in my pocket.

'I'll need to head out now, Nat.'

'Sure thing,' he said.

'That about my daughter, Joe?'

'Not sure, Daryl. I don't think so, but I'll keep you both informed.'

'Can't be too sure, though. I guess you can't.'

'No, Daryl, I guess not.'

'You head on out, Joe. Call me on the line when you get word. Whatever it is.'

I nodded my head and went through the door and passed into the hall. The sound of Daryl Evers' slow-building moan muted as I closed the door behind me. Anne's small radio was playing some country song at the front desk. Walked towards her.

'You heading home, Joe?'

'No, Anne. I wish I was.'

'Well, I'm sure we'll see you real soon,' she said.

'Hate to say I believe you're right about that.'

Went past the desk and got to the front door of the court-house. Heard the music shut off before Anne Morris said: 'Henderson Police Department, what's your emergency?'

I passed the van through the Fox Chapel neighbourhood gates and past the police cruiser parked in front of a large home. The officer had the sense not to turn his lights on. The neighbours had yet to line the streets and show interest in what was happening. I edged the van up into the driveway and read the name on the mailbox. Romain. I'd heard Glenn had moved Tansy into the neighbourhood, but never expected to see his name on a house that size. I stopped the van behind a new Nissan pickup and shifted it into park. Looked up at the house and wondered how the hell a man working at the sawmill could afford that kind of place.

The young deputy came jogging towards the van from the side of the house. I started the usual ritual. Reached back and took hold of the blue coveralls hanging behind my seat. Pulled them off the hook and touched the breast pocket to see if there was still a mask folded up inside. Moved sideways and pushed my feet through the legs. Got my legs in while the kid made it to the van. He stopped before making it all the way. Turned his head to the side and started talking into the radio on his shoulder. I let him be and finished getting into the coveralls. Pulled on the latex gloves and watched the kid finish his call.

He made it up to the window of the van and stood there staring at me through the glass. I nodded my head at him while I struggled to get the second glove on. He frowned at me and knocked on the glass with his bare knuckles. Waved his hand at me. Rolling it in the air, mimicking the motion I needed to make to crank the window down. I lifted my hands to show him I was trying to get small gloves on big hands. He nodded, but didn't seem to understand. Still pointed at the window. Then at the door handle.

'What is it?' I asked.

'Mister Pullman,' he said. 'Can you roll your window down?'

'I can hear you fine, bud.' Still, I rolled the window down. Cold air cut in and blew round the warm cab. Gave me a sick feeling. 'What's the deal here?'

'The dog's found something.'

'Found what?'

'It's a glove. A woman's leather glove,' he said. 'Kind they wear in the holiday movies.'

'Kind of movies you watch?' I asked.

'Well, I'm not all that up on those movies, Mister Pullman, but I'm kind of seeing this girl and she's interested in culture. She's going through a black-and-white phase, I guess you could say. See, she rents anything that's not been coloured.' He looked off to the side of the house he'd just walked up. Breathed deep. Kind of like he was feeling the need to finish his explanation, he said: 'That's how it came to mind.'

'What about the girl?'

'My girl?' he said. Turned his head to me again. Was almost

proud for a moment. Poor bastard wasn't the shiniest peanut in the turd, that's for sure. The way he was looking at me I recognised his father in him. At least I guessed I saw his father in him. Couldn't remember the guy's name, but I'd seen an older man round town and in the pool hall that was pretty damned close to that kid-cop. Long, narrow face with teeth like a thoroughbred racehorse. Only in a skinny face those teeth looked wrong. The kid looked wrong – and the longer I took pulling my gloves on, the more he smiled at me. Showed just how many teeth had been fitted in that mouth of his. He wiped away snow from his forehead.

'Not your girl,' I said. 'The one you called me about.'

'I didn't say there was a girl, sir.'

'On the call you said there were remains of a female nature. Then something about a 415. Now you're talking about a glove . . .'

'It was a bad line. You got some of what I said.' He gave me a flash of teeth and went on: 'It's a woman's glove. Sure enough.' He looked up to the sky for a second. Squinted at the new flurry. Lowered his head to me and was still smiling his smile. I could have pulled those teeth out one at a time and his expression wouldn't have changed in the slightest. Probably could have felt good about it too. I wasn't all that pleased with being in the driveway of a house in Fox Chapel with a funeral-home van just to pick up a goddamned glove.

'Is that all we've got?' I asked.

'Well,' he said. He kept shaking his head in a slow way. The fool was savouring the moment. Getting me geared up for the big reveal. I watched him while he closed his lips tight. White bubbles had been collecting in the corners of his mouth. Those bubbles disappeared when he made a sucking sound. It wasn't a surprise to me when he smiled again.

Then he said: 'It's a glove, sir. But, thing is . . . It ain't empty.'

I got out of the van and the kid followed me to the side door. He was talking up a storm when I slid the door back and took out the cooler. I flipped a hand at him and he started walking and I followed the kid round the side of the house. He was moving fast in every sort of way. Legs going in short, quick bursts. Hands all wild while he talked. He couldn't stop himself from turning round to make sure I was still bringing up the rear. We were almost to the back of the house when he turned all the way around. He looked down at my right hand and gave me a look that didn't fit the moment.

'You think it's alright to put it in that?'

'It's a cooler,' I said. 'We don't want the ice around it to melt too soon. This will keep it all in one piece.'

'It's just I have one like that. Keep my lunch in it sometimes.'

'Well, it's not the same cooler. Now show me the glove.'

We got to the back yard. Came round the side of the house to see the Romains sitting on their wooden deck. Tansy stood when she saw me walking behind the deputy. She called something out, but I didn't catch it. Used my spare hand to wave at her. She moved to the edge of the deck and set her hands on the railings. Watched me until I stopped next to the deputy. I looked down at the glove. It was sitting next to the tree. Didn't look out of place, just somebody's glove left behind by accident.

'How are you doing, Joe?' Tansy yelled. I nodded my head, but didn't look at her. 'You recognise that glove?'

'No,' I said. 'It's nothing I've seen before.'

She let out a laugh that was too energised for my liking. I crouched down next to the glove and set the cooler in the snow beside it. Turned the glove over. Lifted it and was taken by the weight of the thing. Turned it round to have a look at what was filling it.

'Duke brought it back,' Tansy yelled. 'He brought it right up here on the deck. Then he tried to bring it in with him when I opened the door. Where you got it now is where it landed. I threw that thing as far as I could.'

'Nice arm,' I said. 'Real good distance.'

The deputy was hovering over me. He let out a laugh, but stopped when he saw I wasn't in the mood. I kept looking at the glove. Motioned to the cooler. Told him to fill it halfway with snow.

'What snow do you want?'

'Same snow you found it on. Dig up the stuff under where it was lying.'

He got to work. I got more comfortable on my haunches and kept turning the glove in my hand. I wanted to shout out that it wasn't Carole. It was a small hand. Short fingers. The glove was fake leather. Some kind of cheap-ass vinyl that didn't have a lining. Carole liked a fur lining. Some kind of wool. She had cold hands, so she was always paying extra for the good stuff. The stuff that was going to keep the cold off her.

'That's it ready, Mister Pullman.' The deputy was looking at me. I nodded my head at him and put the glove inside the cooler. Set it on top of the snow he'd collected.

We were halfway to the van when my phone rang. I took it out of my pocket and flipped it open. Looked at the number, worried it would be Upshaw or Daryl Evers. Recognised the number as the funeral home. I let out a long breath and cleared my lungs. Put the phone to my ear.

'Yeah, it's Joe.'

'Joe, you heard from Upshaw yet?' I told him no, so Ted kept talking. 'Well, he wants you to bring back whatever you've got from the Fox Chapel call. Said Maitland's on call tonight, so you need to drop it by the mortuary at the medical centre. Then you need to meet me over on Brestler Drive. We've got a bit of a situation.'

'Kind of a situation's that?'

'Seems there's been a sighting of a man and a woman heading up Apple Mount. They're getting a search team set up to head into the mount before the storm comes.'

'Nat told me about that already. The hell makes that such a situation?' I asked, pulling the side door open and setting the cooler on the floor of the van. Pulled the door shut. 'Sorry, Ted, I didn't catch what it was you just said there.'

'I said Milton claims the man was carrying the woman. Hauling her up the mountain fireman-style.'

'It's Milton Berrill,' I said. 'Who's going to believe that retard?'

'Seems a whole town full of people. Wasn't just Milton. Jody Verring was driving up that way and spoke with Milt. Claims he saw the prints in the snow too. Search parties are already gathering.'

'I'll see you down there.'

Hung up the phone and got behind the wheel of the van. The kid-cop was running up the side of the house again. He looked like he was interested in speaking with me about something else. I wasn't all that interested in hearing what it was he had to say. I pulled the van into reverse and skidded out to the road. He stopped in place and gave me a gormless look. Hat tilted back on his head made him seem better placed on an Iowa farm than a Maryland suburb. Honked the horn and made it up the road, heading for the mortuary with a bad feeling coming over me.

What the hell's Milton Berrill playing at now? He'll be getting folks riled up for nothing. Fool gets himself in the right places, Joe. He's seen things before. No telling what he's seen this time.

Chapter Twelve

Ted Hornby stood with his elbows propped up on the guardrail. He was holding a thermos flask in his arms like it was a sick child. Kept looking down at it and shaking his head. The more the cold winds blew, the more he shook his head and sucked in his cheeks. Chewed at what his teeth could catch hold of and lowered his head to shelter his eyes from the sandblasting snow. A long, howling wind came. Ted moved his head down fast like he was ducking punches.

Henderson winter is a harsh season. Heavy snow and mean winds cut right through you. Winds blow hard and come with cold teeth that bite. Trouble is it's just wind, so you have to take it. Find yourself talking to the wind and the cold. Calling them names. Make threats even. Just have to layer up and hope you didn't leave a slice of skin exposed. If you do, they'll get you. Both are just that hungry.

Ted had been out there a while and the wind had chewed him to the bone, from the looks of it. The wind must have sunk a good long fang in. He was shaking so hard white strands of hair had come loose from under his knitted cap. Steam clouds formed in the wind when he let out a long moan. A crazy, sick sound he didn't even know he was making. Lifted a hand from the flask long enough to swat at the loose hairs dangling over his eyes. Did it in this lazy sort of way. Same as he did in the summer months – trying to knock away flies when fishing for trout. Only then he would let his hand linger. Swatting slow, like he really didn't want the flies to go away. Like they were part of the atmosphere – keeping him company while he sat on his white bucket on the banks of Lowman Lake.

When he decided the hairs weren't worth the hassle, he dropped his hand back to the flask. Took a good hold of it again and moved his feet below him. An old dog trying to get comfortable before falling down for a rest. He looked up as I got close.

'Hey, Joe. You get the glove back alright?' I nodded and he did it back to me. 'Good. How are you and the boys doing?' I nodded at him again. 'Yeah, Pop told me he was heading up there to get them back the other night.' He waited a while 'cause he figured it was my turn to speak. 'Saw that bit in the paper. Anything I can do . . . Just say the word.'

We turned and propped our weight against the guardrail. Vultures on a hilltop waiting for a member of the herd to die.

'It's a damned cold night, Joe,' he said. 'Feel it down in my joints. Done sunk in so I can't hardly move for hurting. This old machine is rusting up by the second.' He pointed down into the valley and mumbled something. I didn't catch it all, but I'm sure that it had something to do with the commotion down there. He ended it with: 'Oh, shit, it's cold.'

'Hear you,' I told him. Thing is, the weather wasn't getting me down. Not like it usually did. I had other things on my mind and the cold winds were a distraction that wasn't all that painful. It was as welcome to me as Ted's suffering. I could look at him and see just how bad it could be. See what I had coming to me in another forty years. Watched him swat a slow hand at his hair, and listened to his words that lived a few seconds in the form of silver clouds. Clouds that came out of his mouth and floated round him. Scattered into the winds.

'Sure is a cold one,' I said.

'Damned, Joe. I bet when I get home I'll find Judy struggling to get up out of her chair. She'll be knitting and watching
her TV show. Asking me to help her up. Not even having to
say a word. She'll just be sitting there with that look on her
face.' He breathed out and said: 'Stuck.' Then he nodded his
head – one time fast.

I turned my attention to all the people gathering down in
the valley. Huddling in groups for warmth. Most of them
had been down there for the best part of an hour. Bracing
against the falling snow, like cows left out in a field during a
blizzard. Hopeless. Helpless. People were coming together
and shaking hands like they were meeting up for some kind
of a town fair.

*Look at that, Joe. All those folks down there in the valley. See
them smiling, Joe? You missing something here?*

'You don't look all that good,' Ted told me.

'Yeah,' I said. 'Well, I'm not feeling all that good, either.'

Was hoping he wasn't going to tell me to head on home.
To leave everything to him and whoever else showed up. But,
he didn't and that was a relief. He did look at me with this
questioning stare. It made me feel uneasy. So I took a deep
breath and felt the dusting of snow collide with my face.
Cold air getting inside – passing through and turning everything it touched to crystal. My lungs burned and I let the
breath out fast.

Ted was still watching me, so I made a half-smile and
reached an arm out and patted his back. Nothing too hard
'cause I didn't have the energy.

'I'll be alright,' I said.

'Sure you will.' Ted nodded and held tight to his thermos.
'They aren't doing anything down there. If they cross the
stream and head out for the forest, then we'll make our way
down.' He looked out over the valley. Moved his eyes up the
steep slope of Apple Mount and shook his head. 'I don't have
a good feeling about it happening tonight.'

'You never know,' I said. 'Things might not turn.'

Ted followed Apple Mount to its peak and looked up at the sky. I almost followed his lead, but had my attention snatched away when someone honked a horn behind us. Looked over my shoulder and watched Pop's red pickup truck drive past molasses-slow over the frozen road. Wheels making sounds like they were crunching shards of glass back into the sand it came from. Pushed away from the guardrail and took a couple of steps away from Ted. Pop pulled the truck over to the side and took his time guiding it between two of Henderson's blue police cruisers. He finished and sat in the cab a while.

His silhouette lifted the floppy cowboy hat onto his head. From across the road I watched the hat come off again. His big hand pressing his hair flat on his head before the hat took top once more. The silhouette was moving fast. Seemed kind of agitated. The door of his truck swung open. Pop hopped down and slipped up and almost fell on the seat of his blue-jeans. He righted himself and swatted at his legs like they were covered in something.

'Not a chance in hell,' Ted called out from the railing. 'Just can't see how they're going to get this search under way before those clouds break.'

I turned round and looked at Ted, still staring up into the sky. He reached a hand up and drew the outline of a cluster of clouds that looked the colour and weight of heavy stones. 'All those folks are going to get caught halfway up that damned hill. And then there's nothing to do but bring them all back down again.'

'I hear you,' I said. 'But it's the thing to do.'

'Sure it is,' he said. 'Trouble is we could lose a couple more of them while we're at it.'

Pop came up behind me and set his hand on my shoulder. I turned and looked at him. His white beard shining almost yellow under the street lights. The lights had started turning on about a quarter of an hour after Ted called me. First sign that things weren't going to kick off long before Henderson's finest had to start shutting it all down again. If they got it kicked off at all. Pop caught me looking at him and took his hand off my shoulder.

'What's happened that's got you so blurry-eyed?' he asked.

It took me a few seconds to speak. His breath wasn't minted and he didn't have a white ball of chewing gum dangling out the corner of his mouth when he spoke. The hot blast of fresh mouthwash didn't reach me with his words. There wasn't bourbon, either. No beer. No need to disguise what he'd been doing behind closed doors. It was just Pop, the smell of his musty hunting coat and the hint of old meat on his breath.

'Guess it's the weather,' I told him.

Pop screwed up his eyes and looked at the stone-clouds Ted had drawn in the sky. His lower lip disappeared under a row of white teeth. It reappeared and looked red and slick.

'How's things with you, Ted?' Pop asked.

'Yeah, things are fine. I'm getting on, you know.'

'Anything interesting down at the home?'

Ted was slow to answer and when he did it was nothing more than a quick shake of his head. His attention was on a group of teenagers. They had come in half a dozen cars that they took their time parking down in the shadows. Down where Brestler Drive intersects with Lincoln and Elm. They'd parked up and sat with the doors opened, with music playing loud. The teens left their cars and started the walk back up Brestler like a bunch of tailgaters heading for a football game. All smiles and laughs. Arms over shoulders. A few of them singing out of tune while the others walked along, shaking their heads. Took turns shoving each other down the road. They walked past where me and Ted were standing at the guardrail. Followed the lead of the other volunteers summoned by a young patrolman who was waving an orange glow-stick.

'Next group over here,' he called out. 'Gather round.'

He turned and checked the embankment. He looked worried about something and I couldn't blame him. The steps were narrow and the stones were slick in the cold weather. Two hundred and sixty steps in total, in a steep slope dropping down into the valley. Meeting a path leading to one of Henderson's four monuments. The patrolman turned to the group and raised the glow-stick. 'Follow me down. Take it slow. Keep a hold of the rail at all times. If you feel yourself falling, give some kind of warning. You could take us all down if you don't.' With that he turned to the opening in the fence and started down the steps.

'They're all smiling,' Ted whispered. 'Look at how those idiots are all smiling. It's like they don't even realise there could be a dead body up there.'

'They don't know any better.' White steam rose up from my mouth and moved in front of my eyes. 'And they don't know someone may be up there missing a hand, either.'

'They have any idea who it belongs to?'

'Nothing yet. I packed it up and dropped it off. It's not my responsibility now.'

'And all this,' Ted called out. 'Sure as hell will make for a jump in circulation for Partridge's newspaper.'

Volunteers followed the deputy's lead and filtered through the opening off the side of the road. Each one of them looking at the stone steps with a new sort of worry in their eyes. Some turning to look up at the rise of Apple Mount – maybe taking some kind of power and assurance from the mountain. Maybe wondering just what was bringing them out in the cold January storms. Not one of them stopped. Hesitations led to nods of acceptance for whatever the evening would muster. I saw Winston Kerr standing at the opening for a God-awful time. He looked down the steps and shook his head for a moment. Finally, he leaned back and stuck out his chest. Just before he went down the first few steps into the valley he looked up. Saw me watching him. His hand came up like he was saluting me. I nodded at him.

Pop was standing by Ted now. Two men who had been witness to these scenes over the years. Not always with so many people involved, but some kind of response just the same. Years had turned Pop into a pale man. His skin sagged while his body shrank. He grew a beard to hide what was happening. He grew it long and it turned white and it continued to grow. Pop grew old behind the mask.

Ted was different. He let the years have him, but did nothing to hide it. Sacrificed himself to age and decay. Kept his face bare for witnesses to take in what time was doing to him. Jowls slacking and falling heavy from the sides of his face. Veins breaking while his skin turned grey like it was slowly being reduced to ash.

'The boys alright?' Pop asked. I turned round and looked at his face. He frowned at me. Same way he did whenever he didn't understand the look on my face. When he was questioning my intentions and getting himself ready for something. I tried to change my expression, but I couldn't. Pop had a way of dropping the wrong question at the right time. Took my fingers away from the note I still had inside my pocket. Kept my hand down deep in my jeans, trying not to touch that note. I couldn't take my hand out. I didn't want to chance losing the only thing that connected me to my wife.

'They're fine, Pop.'

'You taken the time to speak with Marty yet?'

'We started.'

Pop nodded his head and looked down into the valley. The folks down there were moving towards a line of Henderson police officers. The officer in the middle of the line held a red megaphone to his mouth. He started speaking. What reached us wasn't anything more than an electric-drive-thru voice. Low and too mixed up to understand. They were less than a quarter-mile down in the valley, but the wind was heavy up on Brestler Drive. I leaned against the guardrail and turned my head. Cupped a hand round my ear.

'What's he saying?' Ted asked.

'Can't make out a goddamned word,' I said.

While the electric hum of the cop's voice scattered in the wind, more of the herd came together round him. Some of the people were turning round and pointing at us, up at Brestler Drive, and the long line of cars that had come in from town. Cars filled with people wanting to help find a woman lost in the snow. The police in the valley raised their hands and patted the air like they were pushing the crowd back. Shoving them away from Apple Mount and guiding them back to their cars.

'You seen Nat since you got here?' Pop asked.

'No,' I said without looking at him. I was watching Apple Mount, thinking it looked huge behind the crowd of volunteers. It looked the same as it did when Pop and Mona had first brought me to Henderson. Looked like it was reaching into the sky with large jagged blades peeling out of the white snow. Black trees almost motionless against the winds. Black trees that looked like shadows of skeletons – a whole army of them.

'There's no way a man carried a woman into that today.' Ted pulled his thermos flask to his chest and set his chin on the top of it. 'How the hell can that Milton Berrill believe it's even possible?'

'He must have seen something,' Mel Trainer said.

He appeared like a damned magic rabbit. Standing at my shoulder, out of breath and rubbing his hands together. If he had a couple of sticks he'd have made sparks. Set all of Henderson ablaze with the speed he was rubbing them together. His hands made the frantic gesture, but his face told a different story. He was looking pleased with himself.

'He's got all these people out there,' Mel said and moved his arm out like he was wanting to show us something we hadn't already seen. Like we hadn't noticed all the cars lining Brestler Drive. Hadn't taken in just how many people had walked past us and down the stone steps into the valley. Turned and looked at the street. Seemed like every police cruiser Henderson owned was present.

'Never would have thought Milton could get this many people out here. It's crazy,' Mel said. He sounded almost envious. 'He must have seen something this time, you know? For this kind of response, he must have seen something.'

'What do you think?' Ted asked.

I shook my head. My fingers touching the note in my pocket.

'He must have seen something,' I said.

'Where's Pop gone?'

Shook my head faster and turned away from the guardrail. Turned away from Apple Mount and still felt the pull of the thing while I started walking down Brestler Drive. Made my way towards the Henderson blue police Jeep. Heard a cop call out: 'They're coming back. Hey, Sheriff, they're all coming back up now.'

Followed the voice and watched a small fat cop come up from the head of the path leading down into the valley. He was holding the buckle of his belt with one hand and the handle of his pistol with the other. He took a few jogging steps before he stopped and turned to look down into the valley. When he turned back round he looked like he was about to start jogging again, and he wasn't too pleased with the prospect.

'Oh, hey there, Mister Pullman,' he said.

'How you doing, bud?'

'Fine, sir. I'm fine, I guess.' He turned his head like he was looking into the valley again. We were in the middle of the road and couldn't see anything more than the gravel shoulder of Brestler Drive. 'Man, I'd be better if it wasn't for all this.'

'They calling off the search already?' I asked.

'Looks like it,' the cop said.

He moved round like he was hopped up on something. Pretty damned sure it was nothing more than adrenaline, but still got me thinking. There's just no way to get ready for all that kind of excitement.

'Well, it'll be a long week of speculation,' I said.

He looked at me like he didn't understand. Then he said: 'Well, not really. We'll all be back out here tomorrow. Sun comes up, we'll come out again. Long as the snow holds off.'

Didn't want to look at the sky and I didn't want to look at the fat cop, either, but for some reason I couldn't pull my eyes away from him. Maybe it was the questioning look he was giving me. Maybe it was the fact that I hadn't had much luck with Henderson Police when it came to my missing wife. Maybe it was the wrinkled-up and sweaty scrap of paper I had sunk down deep in my pocket. It was a note that seemed less important on its own, but with the inclusion of the article about Carole in the *Crier* – it seemed real damned important. And now the entire town was preparing to search for someone. Couldn't help but imagine some of the conversations leading to speculation about the man and woman being me and my missus.

'You okay?' the fat-faced cop said.

I nodded.

According to Milton Berrill, there's a woman up that mountain. According to Milton Berrill, she was carried through the valley and up through the trees on Apple Mount. She was carried by a man. How about them apples, Joe?

'You alright, Mister Pullman?'

'Yeah,' I said. Swallowed hard and wiped sweat away from my brow. Sweat that had no place on my forehead, not with all the cold around me. 'I guess I'm just starting to feel the cold.'

'Joe,' Pop called out. He was standing on the other side of

the road. Nat Upshaw was standing with him. The two were leaning against the front of Nat's Bronco and Pop waved me over. I took my time making my way across the empty road.

'Sheriff,' I said.

'Afternoon, Joe,' Nat said. 'Thanks for coming out earlier and sticking it out for as long as you did. With all you've got going on, I suspect you'll be wanting to head on home and see the boys.'

'Yeah, that's about the gist of it.' I kicked at the snow and asked, 'Maitland figure out what's what with the glove?'

'He was cutting into it when I called back half-hour ago. Trying to figure out if it was human remains or if it was just some prank. Meat stuffed in and frozen.' He shrugged his shoulders like he didn't care either way.

I nodded my head, but didn't make out that I was eager to find out. Or that I was eager to leave and get back home. Nat must have picked up on it 'cause he looked at me and reached a hand out and tagged my arm.

'We'll break off here soon, Joe. If you need to head on home, go to it. Maybe come back out in the morning.'

'Your deputy seems to think it's a given,' I said. 'That the search is going ahead. Weather permitting.'

'We'll have to see.' Nat lifted his cowboy hat from his head and lowered it so he could look at the brim. He ran his hand round the lip, knocking away the crystals of ice and snow. He set the hat back on his head. 'I'm going to have to consider the source, Joe. Can't see how there's much possibility in Milton's story.' Nat looked up at Apple Mount. 'It's a stretch in my mind. But then again I've got a deputy who's real sure he saw footprints in the snow when he arrived. Hinges on Maitland's findings.'

'Prints could have been deer tracks,' Pop said, pointing out to Apple Mount.

'Or nothing at all. Just imagination.' Nat looked past me and frowned at the group of people making their way up through the opening in the fence. Moving in a slow line back up from the valley. Some of them making it known what they thought about the aborted search. About the weather. About the woman some of them feared was being left to freeze on the mountain.

'I'll see what I can find out from the two of them,' Nat said. 'Milt and my first on scene. Then I'll make a decision about tomorrow. It's a damned stretch, though.'

'Sure is,' I said.

'If I was sure that we had someone up there, I'd be moving in,' Nat said. 'I'd go up there myself. Search all night until I had satisfaction in the matter. But there's nothing to make me believe we have anyone to look for.' He shook his head at Apple Mount. I was nodding my head in response. Kept at it even after Nat stopped talking. 'Be ready for a meeting. Could be one tonight. Rumours will be floating heavy by now about the glove. No matter what Doc finds, we need to talk it through. So when he's finished with his business I'll call to get you and the others in.'

Looked at Nat and waited for him to look at me. He was focused on something on the hillside. Part of me wanted to look. The other half was afraid at what I might see. I turned and started to walk away.

'You heading home, Joe?' Pop asked.

'Yeah,' I said.

'Go right on then and spend some time with those boys.'

Pop moved off the front of the Bronco and reached out for my sleeve. He got hold of it and moved me round. I looked at him. Didn't like the way his eyes were searching me.

'You don't look right.'

'So you keep telling me, Pop.'

'If you need some time, I'll come round to your place and take the boys out for you,' he said. 'You can use the time to get caught up on sleep. Whatever it is you've got to do. Just go home and rest.'

Nodded my head at him. He squeezed my arm, then let me go.

With my head down and the energy sucked out of my shoulders, I went back to the van. Got in and sat behind the wheel for a long time. Got the engine running and waited there with the hot air blowing against my legs. The radio played low like voices whispering. Closed my eyes and leaned back. I stayed like that for a long while. Thinking about Carole. About the boys and about the trouble that was about to come calling my number.

It's only a matter of time, Joe. Remember what happened after Dean. You remember waiting for them to come and get you? How long were those hours, Joe?

Feeling in my guts was about the same back then. Easy to remember a feeling like that. Listening to the radio. Music and the news. Holding the handle of a pocketknife under my pillow and waiting for my old man to come home. Waiting for someone to knock on the door. Music was playing, but what songs I can't remember. Then the DJ came on with some news. Talking in a voice that was more for entertainment than to deliver word that the body of a schoolboy had been found. I had hated him for that. Hated the sound of him talking.

Voices on the radio kept whispering. Soft voices make it easier to deliver tough news that people don't want to hear. To give an update on the unlucky events in the life of Joseph Reginald Pullman.

I shifted the van into gear and drove onto Brestler from the soft shoulder. Passed cop cars and pickup trucks. Looked at the people sitting in vehicles. They were all staring up at the Mount, searching all the trees for a sign of that woman. Searching the skies above for a break in the clouds. Hoping a search was still possible.

I checked the rear-view mirror and saw the shape of an old man moving along with the marching group. The old man moved under the light. I turned the van round and made my way back towards the line of pedestrians. Moved towards the crowd as they walked up the road towards me. I kept my eye on the old man. He wasn't looking too steady. I pulled the van to the soft shoulder. Waited for the crowd to pass. Called out to the old man and watched as he made his way over.

'Thought you'd gone already.' Ted was out of breath. His hands were shaking.

'Yeah, well, I'm taking the van back to the home.' I watched Ted as he wiped his hand across his mouth. He turned and eyed the crowd that had already passed him. They were getting in cars and starting engines. Ted turned back to me. He looked weaker somehow. 'How about you?' I asked.

'I'll get back and check on Judy. We'll hunker down tonight with the electric blanket on and probably stay under it till late in the morning.' He shook his head at the sky and said: 'Don't expect me in the funeral home too early tomorrow.'

'I won't. Now, I better get back and check on Marty.'

Ted nodded. I reached my hand out and touched Ted's shoulder. He was looking at the side of the van. Same look he gave the thing when we were heading out for a removal: with the eyes of a man who didn't want to see inside the thing. Not even for one last time. Ted turned and started towards his Datsun pickup. He went away in a slow walk. Really making a show of it.

My phone started ringing while I watched him. Figured it was Marty wanting to know when I'd be heading home. Telling me he was hungry or that Donald had a date and wanted to leave. Maybe had already left. I pulled the phone out of my pocket. Flipped it open and looked at the number. Put the phone to my ear with less energy. Less enthusiasm.

'Joe speaking,' I said.

'Joe, it's Nat. Sorry to throw this on you. You far off already?'

'I haven't left Brestler yet. What's going on?'

'Maitland's ready to talk. We'll see you at City Hall in fifteen?'

'Sure.'

Snapped the phone closed and pulled the van into gear. Drove off the soft shoulder again. The move from the crunch of the gravel shoulder to the hum of asphalt was less inviting. Made my way through the people walking along the road. They were all moving away from the search zone.

I found Ted's number and listened to the phone ring. Waited for him to pick it up. He took his time.

'Ted, it's me. I just got a call from Nat. We're getting together to talk about the glove.'

'Tonight?'

'Yeah,' I said. 'I'm heading over to the City Hall now. You able to stop by the house? Check in on Marty. Maybe take him back to yours if he's on his own?'

'I can do that,' he said. 'You expecting to be long?'

'No,' I said. 'How much can Maitland say about a glove?'

'That man can speak.'

'Well, whatever you can do for Marty I appreciate.'

'Don't stay out too long. If it gets late I'll have him take the back room. You can pick him up in the morning.'

'Sounds like a plan.'

Found my way through the pedestrians and off Brestler. Drove into the empty streets of Henderson. A storm was coming and folks that weren't at Apple Mount had the sense to stay inside. Hunker down in the warmth and let it pass over. I was taking my time. The snow was falling and adding layers to the layers. Burying deeper what was already hidden and waiting to be found.

'Keep on coming,' I said.

I drove on and I thought about the glove and the Romains' dog carrying it back to the house. From there my mind worked in reverse until I saw the glove fall from the dog's mouth and settle into a hole. He scrapes snow back over it. Sniffs. Circles the spot and backs away. Before I play the scene back again I think about the German shepherd. About the tendency for a dog to return to important places. Where it found the hand will be the most important place that dog knows.

He would be going back.

I tried not to think about the hand and all the other parts still hidden under the snow. I kept driving and watched the ghosts of snow moving into the funnels of my headlights. They were moving towards me. They were dancing right up to the van. It was like they were returning home.

Chapter Thirteen

Roland Nisbet was a hundred and fifty pounds heavier than his five-and-a-half-foot frame could handle. He'd start sweating if he lifted his arms too high. Simple things like tying his shoes were out of the question. So he paid people to do things for him. He got a clean shave down at Polson's every other day. He went to Polson's instead of Bob's Barbers because he was able to use the reserved parking space that was just outside the shop door. Bob's is two hundred yards away from Roland's personal space at the bank, but that's just too far to shake his fat ass. He would get Moira Bilston at Solomon's to deliver groceries to his house. Even paid her extra to stack his shelves. Didn't even cook his own food. Three local women took turns on a private rota. They'd go round and make him meals, and when he was finished – Christ knows how long it took him to eat all that food – they'd clean up. He ordered specially made dress shoes with Velcro fasteners. It was an amazing thing seeing this trick he did to flip off the strap with the toe of his other shoe. He put his shoes on with no hands. Without ever seeing what the hell was happening down there.

Roland didn't give much thought at all to dropping a few pounds. For a man his size, it probably would have been easy. Eat a carrot instead of a Twinkie. Maybe set down the donut and pick up a grapefruit. Instead he pulled the Lincoln Continental he purchased from a dealer in Baltimore out of his driveway and drove it two blocks up the street and parked it again. Less than a minute's drive at twenty miles an hour. He'd stick that big boat on wheels up in front of the Henderson Savings and Loans. Fitted it in his personal parking space listed: RESERVED FOR BANK MANAGER. The space is slap bang between two handicapped spaces to give him extra room to manoeuvre.

He sat directly across from me at the council meetings. With each member vacating a seat on the council, a space is created and that space is filled immediately. My chair was in the middle of the table and had been occupied by my aching derrière for six years. I fell into the contours dented in by Pop's backside when he upped and left for the last time – after twenty-six years of debating, planning, bitching and moaning about the town's business. That's the way we worked on the town council. Henderson's a place of controlled habit.

The council meets to discuss budgets. We are called together when funding is needing to be allocated for festivals, public utilities and that sort of stuff. Grievances are few and far between, however they need our attention just the same. So we come together and talk it all out. Then there are moments like these. No one had ever found a severed hand before. We didn't know what to do about it, but Nat Upshaw thought a meeting was going to help.

Doc Cliff Maitland's chair was at the head of the table, and on the wall behind him was an old painting. It showed the founding fathers of America leaning over a table that's not all too different from our old slab of wood. In the painting the men in wigs were signing a document. All of those men were looking at the paper to show it was of some great import-ance. It's not a famous painting, but it was something that each one of Henderson's council members had taken a long look at. Not just because it's a symbol we all took pride in. It's the only painting in the room – and there was always someone late to the meetings.

Nat Upshaw walked through the double doors and made a swift line for Cliff Maitland's chair. He leaned down to Maitland and whispered something in his ear. Maitland nodded and stood up, then he paused for a second. Seemed to deflate almost. His shoulders sank and his hands lowered down to his sides. His smile wasn't convincing.

He scraped back his chair and dropped his hat on the table. It was more a dog marking his favourite spot than a man trying to be casual. Head-of-the-class type thing. From my spot it's at the other end of the room.

'I appreciate you all coming this evening on such short notice,' Maitland said. I spent my time looking at the reactions of the other council members. Watching their faces to see if there were as many suspicious looks flashing my way as I suspected there were going to be. Instead what I saw were nine faces all looking at Maitland. All waiting for him to finish what he'd started to say. All looking just like they were expecting to hear what they needed to do next.

'We have a situation in town,' Maitland said. 'It's a situation that needs leadership. We all need to come together and form some kind of a united bond. We need our efforts to keep the town calm.' He was now behind Roland Nesbit.

'Did you bring it with you?' Nesbit asked. His round face was smiling inside the circle of fat. He wiped his brow with a yellow napkin. His jowls fell heavy on the sides of his face and hung over the tight-buttoned collar of his grey shirt. He guided the yellow napkin over his forehead again and wiped the sweat away.

'No,' Maitland said. 'With issues of hygiene, and respect for those members of the council lacking interest and the stomach for viewing the item, I decided to leave it in the freezer in my office. It will remain there until we find out who it belongs to.'

'Any ideas, Cliff?'

'No, Vincent,' Maitland said. He was shaking his head and pursing up his lips like he needed us to believe he was thinking hard about something. 'That's the biggest mystery of them all, and there are a few to go along with it. We just don't know who it belongs to.'

'Is it local?' Vincent Partridge asked. He waited for Maitland to answer – sitting there with wide eyes. His hands open in front of him with his elbows on the table. His pen lying across the palm of one open hand. The large legal pad of paper sitting on top of his placemat. The long yellow pages already scratched with words. Vincent's sheet of paper was already half-filled with words. I couldn't see what all those small words said, but he had four lines of thick, bold letters. One line read:

Hand in Snow Points to Missing Person Mystery

'Again,' Maitland said. 'This is something we haven't had to deal with before. We are new at this type of a crime . . .'

'If a crime has even been committed,' Nat Upshaw called out. His voice sounded loud, but there was the usual jovial sing-song to his words. He sounded like he was telling a joke. Filling in the punch-lines to aid a stuttering comedian. Not a heckler, but a saviour. Trouble was the smile he had on his face – it seemed to fit too easily into the mix.

'Are you implying this could have been an accident?' Vincent asked.

'Well, what I'm saying, Vincent, is that this could be any number of things.' Nat sat there nodding his head. His hands out in front of his chest like he was ready to hold Vincent back if he decided to charge him. He turned to the window and looked out for a moment. We waited for his eyes and attention to return to the room. He turned round to the table and sat silent and smiling while the rest of us waited for him to continue. His eyes ended up on me.

'It could be an accident,' he said. 'Could have been a crime. Hell, I can't tell at this stage.'

'What's your gut feeling, Sheriff?' Bert Kennedy asked.

Nat Upshaw took his eyes off me and aimed them at Bert. Then he moved his attention back to Vincent Partridge.

'My opinions don't get published on this occasion,' Nat said.

Vincent clicked his pen. The small tip extended and then disappeared. A groundhog without a shadow. It was going to be cold a while longer. He put the pen in his pocket.

Nat nodded his head and continued: 'I'd say it's from some accident. Possibly I'm wrong and there's some outsider some-where that got involved in something criminal. They come passing through Henderson on the way out of the big city. Happens more often than we'd like to consider.' Nat put his hands up like we should be living on his every word. 'A piece gets left here in town. That's my thought.' He looked at the faces surrounding him at the table. In the silence, I took the time to study the same faces and I can tell you they looked confused. Seemed to me like they wanted to question what they'd just heard. But it isn't always easy to question a man like Nat Upshaw. Not when he was as certain as he seemed to be that his ideas were bullet-proof.

'I wouldn't be surprised at all if that's just what all this comes down to,' Maitland said.

All heads shifted from one end of the table to the other end. Maitland had got back there without me noticing, and I don't like that kind of thing happening. Makes me feel uncom-fortable when people go sneaking around.

'I can't give you facts just now,' Maitland said. 'What I can tell you is my belief. My theory. If that's any good to you.' He moved his eyes round the room. There were no protests, so he went on. 'My belief is that this glove belonged to an outsider. That is what we are dealing with. An outsider.'

'And what makes you believe that?'

'Vincent,' Maitland said, smiling and using his hands to scratch his beard into shape. 'I can't be certain at this point in time. What I can do is give you my opinion about what's happened so far. The hand has been cut by a saw. Possibly electric. Skin around the wound is ragged, indicating a rough blade. Maybe some hesitation. Possibly indicating an accident of some kind. I can't identify the hand by sight, but I can tell you that I have seen no patient missing such an appendage.' He raised his own hand as if indicating that it was the hand he was discussing. 'Not one of my patients is missing a hand . . . or a glove for that matter!'

He laughed into the back of his hand. We watched him and waited until he saw the joke had not been received well. He showed his hand and nodded his head.

'So, we need to discuss risk management,' Nat said. 'We will have people out there right now calling their friends and loved ones. Handing out bits and pieces of information that will change and alter each time they're passed on. So, when we wake up tomorrow we'll all hear a strange version of what happened. Of how that hand came to be in the snow.'

'So what are we supposed to do, Sheriff?' Bert Kennedy called out.

'Don't let this hand grow arms and legs,' Nat said.

Maitland let out a laugh and a few others joined in. I watched as the other council members looked around the table and made small noises. That need to laugh didn't reach me. The sense that things were going to be okay. That Henderson and all the people living in it were going to return to normal. They laughed and I wanted to go around the table and tell them all to shut up. I wanted to bounce each of their heads on the table, same as I'd done to Colin Lowell. Bounce them off the wood and shout at their stupid faces that it wasn't going to be okay.

My wife is missing, you idiots!

'Vincent,' Maitland said. Laughter slowed. Simmered. 'I suggest you run a story angling part of what was found. We can give the perspective that it is not unheard of that Tansy and Glenn Romain thought it was more than a glove. Write it up with their quotes. Put it all in. Only, finish it off with my quote.'

'I agree, Doc,' Nat said. 'Can we have a show of hands here? All those in favour of taking the sensation out of this one, raise them high.'

Hands were raised and from the looks of things there was no need to count. Vincent Partridge was the only one without his hand raised in the air. He sat across the table staring at me. So I focused on the headlines he'd written on his legal pad. Upside down and still I could imagine the impact those words would have on the town. I could hear the sound of voices in the morning. While the snow was freezing to the streets, faces would be moving over the folds of the morning paper – some reading it aloud. Big and black on the front of the *Henderson Crier*:

HUMAN REMAINS FOUND INSIDE GLOVE

'Joe,' Nat Upshaw called out. I leaned out over the table so I could see him. He was making himself visible past Les Knowles, who was holding his chin in his hands. Nat was looking at me with one eyebrow raised.

'Yeah, Sheriff,' I said.

'I didn't see your hand in the air.'

'Nope,' I said. 'I kind of expected you knew my thoughts on all this anyhow.'

'I do, Joe,' he said. 'So we're all in agreement.' He smiled and kept his eyes on me.

Nat finished by saying to Vincent: 'Spin it slow and make it an empty glove, Mister Editor.'

'Alright, Sheriff,' Vincent Partridge replied. I looked at Vincent and found him still staring at me.

'We're adjourned then!' Nat called out. He stood with his arms folded in front of his chest. Watching everyone from the top of the table. As folks started moving, he lowered his arms and hooked his thumbs in his belt. He caught my eye and nodded his head. I did the same in return, only without the smile. Then I turned and made my way for the door, hoping Vincent Partridge wasn't going to try and catch up with me.

I got out of the parking lot before any of the others had even made it to the front porch of the building. I wanted to feel good about it, but there was just too much that was bringing me down. A weight of uncertainty about how the silent softly approach was going to work when more of the woman was brought up from the snow. I thought about going home and leaving Marty with Ted, but the kid hadn't been in his own bed many nights of late and I figured it would be best to wake up in our house. So I drove to Ted's place and he met me at the door. Marty was asleep on the sofa. I went in and shook him. He looked up at me with wet eyes. I told him we were heading home. He blinked a few times and I told him he needed to get up and go to the van. He moved slow and made a lot of noise about it, but he finally got out there. He lay on the gurney in the back and I strapped him in. He blinked his eyes at me, but didn't make out like he was waking up. I shut the door and got into the driver's seat.

'Thanks for looking after him, Ted.' Went to shift into reverse and get out of there, but Ted stepped up and put his hand on the door.

'You're in a hurry tonight. Something happen over there at the meeting?'

'No. Just the usual.' I didn't want to tell him about it. But he wasn't moving away from the van. Took his hand out and shook a lighter like it was going to make the flame stronger on the next strike. Somehow giving it an ability to beat the forces of nature. He flicked it and it lit. A wind came calling and, like a magic trick, the flame disappeared. Ted grunted and pushed his hands inside his pockets. He blew hot air between his lips. Steam bellowed from the thin slice between them. His unlit cigarette looked like it was doing the business after all.

'I'm moving to Florida,' he said. 'Swear it to you, Joe. One of these days I'll pack up and go.'

'Aching again, old man?' I asked.

'Always aching,' he said. He looked round behind us, then he turned forward and moved his hands round in his pockets. Digging them deeper where the wind couldn't get to them. I felt bad for him standing out in the cold. He was only doing it to get the rundown of what was going on in the meeting, so I gave him the rundown and he stood there nodding his head. Unlit cigarette in his lips.

When I was through he said: 'You've got to be more careful with these things, Joe.'

'Why's that?' I asked.

'There's a level of expectation you've got to maintain. As a council member you are bound by the expectation of the people of Henderson and they expect that everything's going to remain the same. People want this place to keep being the way it is. Just as it is now. Same as it was when I was a young man. Me and your Pop,' he said.

'Places change, Ted. It's the way of the world.'

'No,' he said. He was anxious. Enough emotion was running through him to risk taking his hand out of his jacket pocket. He used the hand to pull the cigarette from his lips. 'Some places change. Some places need to change. But we've got no problems here, Joe. Only time we ever find we've got a problem to deal with, it's usually brought in by some outsider. We keep to our own. We tend to our own. What we have left, Joe, is the last real small town.'

'We can't always halt progress,' I said.

'The heck are you talking about? Progress is when we put a new soda machine in the town hall. Progress is setting up the newspaper dispensers outside the post office when Eugene got too old to man the stall.' He pointed the cigarette close to my face. 'That is progress.'

'I'll level with you, Ted.' He looked behind us again. Felt like the close of our conversation, and that was alright by me. He put the cigarette back in his mouth. 'I've never questioned this place,' I said. 'The authority in town. Powers that be and the decisions they make. Now, I'm not sure about the authority or the people that give up that authority. I'm not so sure about the place even. We've got something happening in this town and they are wanting to brush it under the carpet.'

'Don't make trouble, Joe. You'll get yourself all wound up and in a bunch of mess. It's an outsider. So brushing it under the carpet's the best place for it. Things turn out to be different and we can deal with that too.' He stepped away from the side of the van. 'Right now we're going to take a stand by keeping it low-key.'

'Low-key,' I repeated.

I revved the engine and watched smoke rise in the mirror. Ted patted at the side of the van. I saw his mouth moving and I revved the engine again. He shook his head.

'Keep it low-key,' I said.

Knowing it wasn't really an option. Not knowing it was all going to get much worse before the winter was through. I drove home with my window down. My face and hands were numb when I pulled into the driveway and cut the engine. I rolled up the window and went to the side door, pulled it open. Marty was still asleep. I unclipped the straps and shook his shoulders hard. He opened his eyes and said something about the cold. Then he slid out of the gurney and shuffled out of the van. We went into the house and Marty slumped through the family room and up the stairs to his bed. I watched him pass out of sight before moving to the study. Moving down the hallway, I found a red light on the answering machine. There was a note stuck to the table:

Some guy called for mom. Left the message on the machine for you to hear. Can't make it out. Had to go out for something. Back in morning.
— Donald

Pressed the flashing button and waited. Sound of movement was all I got. Then a man speaking. He sounded out of breath. Sounded agitated and anxious. He stuttered a few times and then knocked something over. Glass shattering and more movement followed. He spoke, but it was muted. Still I heard what he said. I listened to him and found my hand clasping into a fist. Not in anger. It clasped at the cloth of my shirt. Tugged at it as if I was trying to hold myself back. Only I had nothing in me. When the movement stopped, the phone clicked dead. I watched the red button flash for a few seconds. On. Off. On. I watched the light blink and my eyes dried. As I hit the button again, my hand grasped my shirt harder than before. Movement on the line. Muttering.

'Carole,' he whispered. 'Are you still . . .' Feedback. Something making a sound in the background. Something passing by. 'Are you . . .'

Listened to the message half a dozen times. Tried to make out the voice. Tried to decide if it was someone I knew. Listened close to figure out what the hell the sound was that blocked out the voice. A truck maybe. Something passing on the road. Caller must have been outside. I went into the study and sat in the chair behind my desk. Looked around for anything Carole might have left behind. Anything to tell me where she had gone. Went through the drawers of my desk that Carole had been going through. Maybe she had taken something, and maybe I'd know it. So I started looking for something that wasn't there. *Story of your life, Joe.* Still, I was hopeful. I spent too much of the night at the desk and finally, when I was certain there was no hope, I sat back in my chair and closed my eyes. I felt a weight inside my head. Took deep breaths and let my shoulders hang on the memories. They fell down. They felt heavy. Same way they felt when Carole would stand behind my chair and push at my muscles with her strong fingers. Digging in until I couldn't stand the pain. She would lower her mouth to my ear and speak to me.

Breathe, Joe. Relax.

I took that deep breath and waited for Carole's hand to fall against my shoulders. Push down hard and then pull all of that bad energy away from me.

Let it go. Breathe and let it out.

'I'm trying, Carole.'

I breathed and my shoulders still hung heavy.

The house was silent. I listened to my own breath and I wished Carole was there to match it. Somewhere in the night I fell into a deep sleep and Carole was waiting for me.

Chapter Fourteen

– Joe? Joe Pullman?

  – Huh?

  – You there, Joe. It's Jim. Jim Shiels. Down at the tavern. We've talked before.

  – Yeah. I remember. You're breaking up . . .

  – Sorry. Is that any better? (Pause.) I've been asked to call you. You need to be here before people start coming round.

  – Where's here?

  – 223 Deaver Street. That's at the bottom of Apple Mount. North side. You know where?

  – I know it. Polstons live that way. What is it?

  – A house.

  I grunt.

  – What is the call for? Who is it?

  – You're breaking up. This is a terrible line.

  – Who is it? Who are we picking up?

  – It's for the Knowles family. Do you hear me?

  – I know them. Which one?

  – Theodore.

  – Damn.

Chapter Fifteen

The phone felt heavy in my hand. I blinked and still my eyes felt hot and sticky. Trying to pull closed every time I opened them. The wider I made them go, the heavier they felt. Like lifting something heavy over your head. More times you try it, the less strength you have to keep it up there. Ended up letting them close without much of a fight. I faded and slipped off into another sleep. Dreams moved aside the warmth of my study and placed me in the conversation I'd just had. Only I was in the snow to my waist and it was a woman's voice on the phone. I looked round and I saw her. She was stretched out in the snow. She was in the ice. Her arms and legs were trapped in the ice and it was only her head that was free. She kept talking to me and telling me there was a pickup to be made on Deaver Street.

'Get out there and do your job!'

I tried to move, but my legs were cold and numb. The ice was filling in around me and the woman kept talking as I screamed. I was trying to get free and she was telling me about the removal. *Don't forget Deaver Street.* Her voice was so familiar. I turned to see her, but she was facing the other way. I could only see the block of ice and the pale of her legs stuck inside it.

'I can't move!' I yelled. 'The ice is too thick.'

She started laughing and I couldn't move my head to look at her again.

I jolted awake and sat forward on the chair. Rolled my head and let my neck crack itself loose. Sat there for a moment and looked at the phone. The handset was down on the cradle, but it was all screwed up. Sitting the wrong way round. Cable kinked and wrapped up on itself. I leaned forward and tried to stretch my body. Tried to take some of the ache out of my back. Enough to bring me to life again. It didn't help and I was angry as hell at myself for not being able to get things moving.

Turned the chair to the side and sat with my head hanging down. Assumed an uncomfortable kind of hunch – same as the position on a fast-falling plane. Ran a hand over the right leg of my jeans. Tried to smooth the creases away, but there wasn't real effort in it. My clothes were the same as when I'd left Apple Mount. Still smelled of the damp of new snow.

I pulled my ass off the chair and the smell of my clothes got stronger. Like the rub of cloth against my skin was bringing it all out. I'd somehow stirred it up with the slow motion. Went out to the kitchen and looked up at the cabinet doors, hoping Carole had come back to leave me something. Hoped to find another Joseph Pullman note waiting for me – something to keep me going. There was nothing on the cabinets, so I walked into the family room and sat on the recliner. Sat in the dark and watched the black television screen. Waited. Before long I fell asleep.

'Joe.' My shoulder was moving. 'Joe.' Ted's voice was mixing with a hazy scene. Carole walking through the snow. She was wearing her blue sweater. She'd seen it in a magazine and had torn out the picture. Kept that picture on the dresser in our room for weeks. So, I'd called round and found it in Baltimore. I'd gone into the city for that sweater. There she was walking through the trees and calling out to me. I called back, but my voice was too weak. I couldn't yell. I couldn't breathe. And then she called out to me again. The sound of her voice echoed in my head. It echoed through the hills and the cold winds moved in. And her voice faded.

My shoulders moved.

Ted's voice was louder than Carole's.

'Joe,' he said. My shoulder shaking. Opened my eyes and found him standing over me. 'You need to get up and move, Joe. I got a call from Jim Shiels down at the tavern. Said he'd spoken with you half-hour ago. He called me thinking something was wrong. Damned good thing he did, too.'

'Yeah,' I said. 'I'm moving.'

Ted gave me a hand getting up off the sofa. Then he gave me a push towards the stairs and set me free. My head was not working. Felt like I'd been drinking the night away.

'You see Donald's car outside?' I asked.

'Nope. Just the van,' he said. He came to the bottom of the stairs and looked up at me. 'You hurry up and get showered. We need to get this removal sorted out quick-style, Joe. It's already been too long. I'll get the coffee going.'

Ted left me standing there looking down at him with a dumb expression. Wondering how I was going to conduct a removal with Marty in the back of the van. Kept running versions of the scene through my head as I climbed the stairs. At the top I waited for a few seconds, listening out for Marty. He sleeps on his stomach. Makes a heavy snoring sound when he's out. Standing there, I couldn't hear anything. Went down the hall and into his room. He was on his back with his mouth open. Arms out wide.

I wiped the spit and sweat off my face with the back of my hand and tried to work out what it was I was going to tell Marty. Any other day I'd leave him to sleep. But, with Donald gone, I didn't want to chance leaving Marty on his own. Hated the idea of him waking up in an empty house. So I started forming stories. Tried to come up with some kind of a way of making it easy to deliver it to Marty. Make it easy for him to understand without spilling all the details.

Don't think the kid can handle a dead child, Joe? You worried seeing that Knowles baby will change him? Give him some of his own scars?

Like Mona used to do to me. Standing in the kitchen while she was cooking steaks for me and Pop.

You don't want to get mixed up in what Pop's doing down there, Joe.

Mona had a raspy voice in the end. When I first came to live with them she had a different voice. Young and inviting. I'd sit with her while she cooked and ask her questions that would keep her talking. She'd say just enough to get me to respond. I always kept it short, so she could talk. So I could listen to the way her voice would rattle. Sometimes I wasn't interested in hearing what it was she was telling me. I just wanted to hear her voice say the words.

Make yourself useful, Joe. Peel some of those potatoes if you're just going to sit there. What are you gawking at? You should be a chef. Use your mind to create something special. Don't waste yourself and become a mortician. Working with the . . . Deceased people give you no opportunity for progress, Joe.

And I did what she told me to do. She gave me a small, dull knife. It was when she was still uncertain about me. When she would look at me from across the room. Stare at me 'cause she didn't think I knew she was looking. She'd touch her face while she looked at me, trying to decide if there was a connection between us after all. She'd look away if I turned to her. She was still piecing me together. Right up to the end, I think. Trying to decide what I had been through. Trying to decide just how much it had all affected me.

You don't have to stand here, Joe. You can take them back to the table. If we're so close, I won't be able to get all this prepared. So I peeled and she spoke. *Do you like working with Pop? Do you find it disturbing in any way? I would prefer if you didn't smile that way. Talk to me. Tell me what you are thinking. I can't interpret your smiles.*

And when Pop came up from the basement he was always rubbing his hands together. They were always wet and he always smelled like chemicals. Deodorant. Preservants. Disinfectants.

Joe's been a real help. That's what Mona thought. *He's been telling me all about helping with the business.* Her voice was different. It was distant, but it was also assured in a strange way. Assured that I was able to deal with the routine. With the emotions attached to the business. Most importantly, I was able to deal with the bodies.

He almost ready? Pop was standing next to me. The potatoes sitting in a pile between me and Mona. The knife I'd used sticking up from a potato in the middle of the pile. *About time to get him involved?*

I believe he is as ready as he will ever be. Mona patted her hands against her apron. Stood looking at me. Her head to the side. Same feeling came to my belly as when Maureen Gillespie had moved close to me. When we were out looking for Dean the day he went missing. The same ache in my belly that made me want to be close to her. *I think he is almost there.*

With my half-dream head still on and with Mona strong in my thoughts, I leaned up against the wall and tried to catch my breath. Tried to get my mind sorted out before waking Marty. Standing there, I decided Marty was a smart kid and he'd understand whatever I had to tell him. Decided that I'd never have a problem with Marty learning about the dead – or what it was that I did with them. Trouble was, Carole had a problem with the business. She had a hell of a problem about it.

Marty was pressed down into the bed like he'd fallen from a big height. He didn't come to when I called out to him. No response when I was standing over him with a hand on the bed. First shake and he was making a noise. Took hold of him under his skinny arms and turned him onto his side. His head flopped and his eyelids fluttered. Set him down on the pillow and watched him blink a few times. He looked at me for a second, then his eyes rolled. Lids shut. He was out cold again.

'Marty,' I said. 'Come on, I need you to get up.'

'Huh?' He didn't open his eyes. 'Time's it?'

'Doesn't matter. Get up. You need to come with me.'

'Time's it, Dad?'

'Just get dressed.'

Heard Ted down in the kitchen. Coffee pot brewing. He'd be pushing a few frozen waffles down into the toaster. I went to my room and tossed fresh clothes on the bed. Had a shower and decided against a shave. Dried and dressed and headed down the stairs.

Ted was pouring coffee into my travel mug. While he was working on it I picked through the fruit from the bowl on the table and chucked the worst of it in the trash can. Tied up the trash bag when I was finished. Rotten fruit can make a place go bad. The smell is infectious, just moving the fruit from the bowl to the bag had broken it free. It goes from room to room and I didn't know how long we were going to be gone. Didn't want to come back to find another stink in the kitchen.

'We about ready?' Ted asked.

'I got to get Marty first.'

'Well, I'll be out in the van.'

I went up to get the boy moving. Felt bad for having to put a spur in him – especially when I have the same trouble waking up. But we had to go and I couldn't leave him on his own. Not while all the shit was kicking off in town.

'Marty, you okay, bud?'

'Yeah, Dad.' He let out a yawn that was too loud to be anything but show. 'You can come in. I'm decent.'

I opened his door and walked in. He was sitting on the edge of his bed tying up the laces on his sneakers. He had his chin resting against one knee. He finished tying the shoe and put it on the floor. Lifted the other and took his time tying it.

He set his chin on the other knee and watched his shoe with half-closed eyes.

'Donnie's not home this morning,' I said. Marty nodded his head to show me he understood. 'Meet me downstairs when you're finished. We better get going.'

Marty nodded again. I went back to the kitchen and lifted the coffee Ted had poured. Took a few drinks. It was strong enough to keep me going, and that's what I needed. I didn't want to go to the Knowles' removal tired. Needed to be aware and ready for a tough show. There's protocol. There's professionalism. I drank the coffee to give me an edge. To get my brain working. Started going through the procedure, visualised how I was going to approach the Knowles family. Speculated who would be present. Figured the asshole brothers would be in attendance. The sister – very dramatic, but harmless. Grandmother. She was a rock. I'd need to seek her out in case anything went sour. I pulled the bag free from the garbage can and made sure it was tied tight. Then I set it outside the back door.

'Dad?' Marty said.

I turned round to see Marty standing in the doorway. His shirt was inside out. He stood with his shoulder pressed against the wall, rubbing his eyes like a slapstick comedian. All show.

'You taking me fishing or something?' he asked.

'Nope,' I said. 'Man, I wish we were going fishing, bud. We'll do that soon.'

'What are we doing then?'

He tried looking at me, but couldn't stand the light. Screwed his eyes up and raised his hand. Held it flat to his brow and kept blinking while he struggled to keep me in his sights.

'I've got to be someplace. So, I need you to come with me,' I said. 'You'll be one of my co-pilots for the morning.'

Marty perked up. His eyes opened wider. They were red.

'You're going on a removal?' he said.

'Huh-uh. I got a call this morning telling me I need to make

180

a delivery. So you're coming with me. Just dropping stuff off. That's all.'

'Oh,' he said. Looked disappointed. Fell back into the slumped-shoulder kid who hates waking from a deep sleep. 'So why can't I stay here?'

''Cause Donnie's not here, bud. Or else I'd say that was fine.'

'Where's he gone?'

'Told you already. He didn't make it home last night.'

'Oh,' Marty said, looking confused. 'Think Mom came back for him?'

'No,' I said. 'Why would you think that?'

It was easy to see what his head was working on. Mom's come back and left the kid behind. Picked up the son she needed most and disappeared again. He went back to rubbing his eye. Just the left one this time. His lips swelled up. Jaw moved out to the side.

'You're mom hasn't been back, Marty. If she had, you'd be the first person she'd come to see. I can guarantee that.'

'Okay,' he said.

Ted had set out a plate on the counter. Two waffles were sticking up from the toaster. Burned my fingers pulling them out.

'You've got to butter these up yourself,' I said. 'I've got to get some things together.'

'Yeah.' Marty got up and went to the fridge and lifted the butter off the shelf. 'How long before we leave?'

'Soon as you get those things in your belly,' I said.

'Not long then.' Marty looked at the tub of butter and hovered the knife over it. 'You get the message on the machine last night? Some guy called for Mom. He sounded sad.'

'Yeah, I got it. You know who it was?'

'Who?' he said.

'Kind of the answer I was looking for.' I poured a refill on my coffee and left the kitchen. In the den, I pulled out a clear plastic bag. Inside the bag was a red collapsible container. I unwrapped it and built the thing. Unzipped the small plastic envelope that was inside and found the invoice. Read the wording and didn't like the sound of it. The feel of it. The look of it.

I set the new red container by the front door and went back into the kitchen. Marty was chewing on the last of his waffles, staring out at the far wall. Seeing something in the pattern of the curtains. Thinking so hard it made everything else disappear for him.

'Okay, bud?' I asked.

He nodded. Chewed faster. Swallowed hard.

'I was dreaming something when you woke me up. It's almost there where I can see it again. You know when that happens? When you wake up and you're not supposed to. Like when you're falling and right before you hit the ground you kind of jerk. Then you're awake and the fall is finished.'

'But you remember the falling dreams,' I said.

'Yeah.' He looked confused. 'Yeah, I do. I remember the falling dreams. That's really weird.'

'Maybe it's the way you're woken up. Someone else does the waking for you and you lose it. The dream's gone 'cause it was interrupted. Not like when you're saving your own skin from falling.'

'I got to pee,' he said. 'Then I'm ready to go.'

I loaded the container into the back of the van. Sat in the driver's seat and looked over at Ted. I didn't say anything and he didn't try to make small talk. The way he was looking at his watch said it all. I revved the engine, waiting for Marty to show. He came to the front door and waved. I rolled down the window and called out to him. Didn't know what he was saying. His mouth was moving and his hands were darting round in front of his face. Shook my head.

'You have the key?' he yelled louder.

'Don't worry about it. Just come on.'

He shut the door and high-stepped through the low snow, went to the side, got in and slammed the door shut behind him.

'It's really cold today,' he said.

'Still early hours. Should warm up some later.'

'We taking this to the meeting?' Marty asked. He had his hand on the red container.

'Yeah.'

'Can I ride on the gurney?'

'Not just now,' I said. 'We're in a hurry, so we better get a move on.'

'Howdy there, partner,' Ted called out.

'Hey, Ted.'

'Why're you out with us this fine morning?' he asked.

'I'm the co-pilot. Dad needs me to come along. That and Donald is nowhere to be found again. I didn't have anyone to watch over me.'

Marty was touching the case in the back. I asked him to hand it over to Ted so he could make sure it was ready to give away. Ted looked at the container for a while. He unzipped it and opened the flap, then he looked inside and shook his head.

'Man, this is tough, Joe,' he said.

'What's in that bag?' Marty asked.

'Nothing, son,' Ted said.

'What's it for?' Marty asked. When Ted didn't answer, Marty tried again. 'It's like what Donald uses when he's taking his stuff to basketball.'

'It's nothing, Marty. I just have some stuff in the bag that I need to drop off this morning. So I'll take it in the house with me. Then we'll leave.'

'You want me to stay in the van with Marty?' Ted asked.

I shook my head.

'I'm pretty certain I'll need you in the house.'

'Settle into the corner there,' Ted called back to Marty.

183

'Sit yourself down in the jump seat. Fold it down. Against the wall. See?'

Marty found it.

'Pull it down and settle in. Strap up. This van's a slider.'

Marty was sitting in the jump seat in the back of the van. He was checking the runners on the floor and sifting through the yellow boxes of disposable rubber gloves. Masks. Shoe shields. It kept him from understanding what we were going to do. Kept him innocent.

I took the back roads to try and keep the attention of the locals down. News would spread fast enough. There was no need for twenty cars to follow us down the road. Clog the lane at the Knowles' house so we couldn't make an easy getaway. Took the roads I knew Moses Detroit had salted with the gritter. He'd been up that morning. A fresh peppering of grit made it easy to choose the roads. We got to the house just after five in the morning. An ambulance and police cruiser were parked on the street. The windows of the cruiser were fogged. The curtains were drawn in the windows of the house and ice was hanging from the eves of the place like glass daggers.

'Marty,' I said. 'You stay put. We're just going in for a minute or two. Have a look round the van. Don't take anything out that's got a skull on the box. Okay?'

'I'm cool, Dad. You go ahead and give them what they need.'

'Huh?' I asked.

'From your bag,' he said. 'Give them what you brought.'

Ted needed to be there. It's never easy to deal with the people that are left behind. There was the usual empty feeling creeping in, the closer we got to the door. With it was a nervy feeling. I'd never been all that easy with the Knowles boys. They'd been troubled by my celebrity early on. A young kid with scars and inches in the columns of national papers. Some folks didn't like the notoriety. The

Knowles had a problem with it when I first came to Henderson and that feeling never left them. After high school I'd hooked up with the girlfriend of one of the brothers. Didn't know it was his girl, though it probably wouldn't have stopped me anyway. He'd found out and brought a beating my way, courtesy of his overweight siblings. Kind of figured we were through after that, but some people can't let their insecurities die.

'You speak with the family,' I said. 'I'll go back and make the removal. You can spend all the time you want inside. Just meet me in the van when you're through.'

Ted had the paperwork in a leather portfolio. He held it with both hands, up tight against his waist. Looked more like he was going to deliver the eulogy than hand out the papers binding the family to our funeral services.

'You think Verring's going to be hanging around the place?'

'No,' Ted said. 'He'll be part of the mourning, but that's only after the body has been removed. Jody's got the stomach to deliver pain, but he's got a weak tear gland when it comes to dying friends and family. Regular Henderson waterworks.'

We went along the path to the house. Shapes in the snow where the shrubs lay frozen. I felt like an intruder walking up on a place that didn't want me. For good reason too. We are body-snatchers. Faces in the houses we visit don't look at us. When they do look, it's with eyes that don't see much more than thieves. Part of the death process. We take away the physical remains. Folks don't always find it easy to discern physical remains from the spiritual and emotional. You can't tell them the reality of it all. The decaying of flesh. Liquefaction of the internal tissues. Trapped gases that keep swelling inside until they find a way out. They don't want to hear that the physical remains are dirt. Easily discarded. Human skin and rotten banana peels. It's just about the same thing. However, people hold memories. Bodies hold memories – and we come to take them away. Walking in unannounced with a red gym bag needing to be filled with the remains of the youngest family member.

We are unwelcome visitors. We come without warning.

I knocked on the door and waited for a few seconds. Heard someone moving on the other side. Bolt slid back and the door went in. A tired-looking woman eyed me and then Ted. She stepped aside and let us past. Walked in to the smell of cigarettes, grey ghosts making the smell pass along the ceiling, snaking through the blades of the ceiling fan. I nodded at the family members gathered in the front room. Counted ten, but with some sitting and others standing it was hard to tell. Only looked at each of them once. Gave the smile of commiseration rather than the smile of friendship. Leanna Knowles stood from her chair and touched my arm. She held a dry tissue to her mouth and pointed to the end of the room. She guided me by the arm into the hall and past three closed doors, looking at the bag in my hand.

'Is that what you're putting him in?' she asked.

'Yes, ma'am,' I said. 'We use these containers when tending to smaller remains.'

'It looks like . . .' She didn't finish. I waited while she put the dry tissue to her mouth. Her shoulders heaved for a moment. When she took the tissue away from her mouth it was limp and frail. She folded it and crushed it in her hand.

It was dark in the room. A cot sat against the far wall. The mobile that had once been connected to the rails was on the floor, on top of a furry blue rug. One side of the rug had a small bear's head sewn into it. The walls held a framed clipping from the *Crier* announcing the child's birth. I moved to the cot without turning on the light. Looked down and took in the sight of him.

Theodore Knowles had been the biggest baby of the year. Born to a small mother and father, he was an anomaly. When the story appeared in the paper it ignited speculation about the father. Suggestions as to the reality of who made the child began to pop up and feed the rumour mill. The more gossip was fed into the mill the more speculations were churned out. Soon enough the stories were all over town and David Knowles started showing signs that the rumours were taking a toll on him. Was seen seldom in town and, when he was, he didn't speak. Hung his head down in permanent shame.

I reached into the cot and pulled the small arms down from where they'd been reaching over the boy's head. Set them at the side of his heavy, round body. Wrapped the blue blanket round him. Made it tight. Swaddle-style, the way Carole used to do to get Marty to sleep. Before I lifted the bag into the cot I looked round again. Considered how the place was set. Considered the peaceful look of the boy. The rocking chair in the corner and the pillow leaning against it.

I unzipped the bag and spread open the plastic lining. With a hand under his head and one supporting his legs, I picked Theodore up from his cot. Took him away from the mattress and set him inside the red container. He was no longer a child. He was cargo. Pulled the plastic round him and sealed the zip. Gave a last look at the pillow on the rocking chair and wondered how long I'd be able to keep my own suspicions quiet. Figured it was safe to stay hidden a while.

A suspicious man is allowed no suspicions of his own, Joe. You bite your tongue until the blood runs thick. This town is about keeping everything the same. Brush that baby under the carpet along with that hand you found . . .

I walked out of the room and shut the door behind me.

Ted was out in the main room with the family. He'd completed the papers, had the portfolio closed and was holding it eulogy-style over his groin. One of the Knowles women had his pen in her hand. She was twisting it, but her eyes were on Ted. He was speaking in a low voice. His effort to calm them seemed to be working. I passed through the room while he continued to offer condolences. While he assured the family that we would do everything possible to assist in their time of need. Before Ted was finished I had headed through the front door. Faces of the people in the room aimed at me as I went. An older woman sitting in the corner tried to stand. She got up from the sofa, but struggled against the arms of a young man who went to pull her back down. He held her and spoke in whispers against her ear. I looked away and kept walking.

'You all finished, Dad?' Marty asked. He was wearing disposable white coveralls. Wrinkled and baggy against his narrow frame. Wrists and ankles bulging up. Fabric inflated in places where his limbs couldn't stretch to fit.

'All done, bud. You sit tight. Just do what you're doing . . .'

'Thought you were leaving that with the family,' he said, pointing at the bag.

'Well, I needed—'

A scream came from the house. The old woman, from the sound of it. It was the wildest scream I'd heard in a long time. The front door was swinging shut and I was glad for that. At least there had been something to mute the scream. I had a moment's flash where I saw a woman standing behind me. Pulling at my shoulders while she tried to get to the red bag. Tried to pull it open for one last look at fat little Theo.

'Who's that?' Marty asked. He moved to look past me. He had a new excitement in his eyes, hoping the screamer would be there in the snow and moving towards the van.

'Just stay in where you are. Settle down.'

'You about to have trouble?' He stepped towards the door. I put a hand out and touched his chest. Shoved him so he moved back. Tried to get to the other side of the van, but he wouldn't go. I didn't want to push him harder.

'No, Marty. No trouble. Now, just do what you're doing.' I dropped a hand on top of the red bag and felt a small arm. Pulled my hand back. Took the straps and gave them a tug to take away the shape. Worried Marty would see the outline

188

of an arm. A leg. The baby's head. He looked at my hands while I tugged on the bag's straps. A line appeared on his forehead. 'Do not touch this. Understand?' Another scream came from inside the house. This one muted, but full of the same pain as the last. 'Listen to me, son. Don't touch the bag. This is off-limits to you. Tell me you understand me.'

'I understand.'

It wasn't enough and I knew that much. Standing there, looking at Marty's face, I knew it wasn't enough. *You can't trust Marty to fight his curiosity, Joe. Take him in the house with you or take the bag back inside.* That was out of the question. I looked at Marty for a second longer. He looked back at me. Knew I didn't trust him – not all the way. But he wasn't ready to witness a scene like the one happening inside. He didn't need to see people in that state.

'I'm cool, Dad. It's off-limits.'

'Okay,' I said.

This time I went fast. Moved across the lawn and up to the porch. Didn't mess with the pathway. Got to the door and went in. Everyone was standing. Ted was in the middle of them all. Moving round the circle the Knowles family had made. Had his portfolio raised and was speaking in his preacher voice. Sounded like he was delivering some kind of sermon about faith and eternity and forgiveness.

The Knowles were a big family and they all lived round that one part of Henderson. So when Jolene got up and checked on her baby boy early in the morning, she had family with her in a moment. Happened in old-style telegraph. Called her father, who called her mother. She called her other sons 'cause she lived a few streets over and didn't drive. By the time we got there the whole family had been back to the little man's room and had a good look down at him. There wasn't a single one of them that looked better for it. Human nature makes you look at the deceased, but it doesn't prepare you for what you see. That one last look can change a person.

I went between two of the women and stood next to Ted. He had just finished speaking and was crouching next to the oldest Missus Knowles. Speaking with her about taking the time and stopping by the funeral home over the coming days. I listened to Ted speak and finally stood back and looked at the family. Some were sitting. Others standing. Men in the Knowles family are bred big, except for David. He's the runt and, looking round for him, I didn't see the grieving father. All I saw were high foreheads, crooked noses and dental problems. All that in a bunch of big faces.

'I would like to express my condolences to you for the loss,' I said. I was looking at Jolene at the time. She was sitting on the sofa with her head pressed into the shoulder of her most obese cousin. She moved her head away from the man's shoulder and nodded a brief nod. Then she went back to a silent kind of moan.

'Well, my condolences to you for your loss too,' Keith Knowles said. He was standing beside Ted with his arms crossed over his wide chest. I looked at him and didn't see a single seed of sincerity in his eyes. 'Strange how you don't have the look of a man who's grieving,' he said.

'I grieve for the families,' I started. Seemed useless. Figured Keith has decided to split his tension by crossing paths with me. Jody Verring may not have been in the room but he was still able to speak his words through the dimwit brother of a devastated woman.

'The hell you don't,' he said. He pointed a finger at Ted and drove it into his back. Ted stood straight and frowned. His face twisted to me. 'Him I'll accept. I'll take his grieving. I don't want you grieving for my family.'

'Keith,' Missus Knowles called out. 'That's enough. Mister Pullman . . .'

'He done disappeared his wife,' he said. 'Only reason he's getting away with it is 'cause he's part of the council. Take away his family name and he'd be up there in Baltimore. Next in line for the freakin' injection. Either that or sharing a damned cell with his daddy.'

'Enough!'

I moved back towards the door. Watched Ted's face and kept moving. I'd started breathing heavy. Lungs filling and emptying. My body was getting ready for a fight. Wasn't willing to be part of it, but the body has a way of getting you ready just the same. Keith said something else, but I couldn't catch it. Wish like hell I hadn't let it get to me. But things had been building. A town full of whispers had been chipping away at me since Paul Quincy had placed the article in the paper. Since he'd started a new product in the Henderson rumour mill. Those rumours had ground down same as the ones about the father of Theodore Knowles. They'd ground down to other rumours. Small rumours drift on whispers and, when they collect over time, it can get to be too much to hold. Right then I had a weight of whispers I could carry no farther. So I unloaded. Standing at the entryway of the Knowles' family room – looking round at all the faces – I unloaded.

'I didn't kill my wife,' I said. Standing with my hands pumping at my sides. 'Never would lay a finger on her.' I had the door open and felt the cold air pressing against my face. I muttered the last sentence not even thinking it was going to reach Keith Knowles' ears. 'If I was a weaker man, it might have been different.'

My foot made the snow when something hit the back of my head. It was hard and when it hit me it gave way. Shattered and sprayed on the door and walls round me. My head didn't go down straight off. I saw the spray of something fan out either side of my head before I ducked and staggered out into the front yard. I looked up at the van and thought about Marty. Not wanting him to see me rolling round in the front yard of a house. So I reached a hand up to the back of my head to check for a hole. Thinking that the skin would be open.

Thinking there was going to be a mouth in the back of my head, with something that felt like a hot tongue wagging out of it.

My hand found wet hair, but there wasn't anything hanging down that felt like meat. Took two steps towards the van, expecting Keith Knowles to come running through the door. What I was going to do next hadn't been decided. I just knew there wasn't a chance in hell I could get back in the van without resolving this.

I turned and stepped back towards the house. Got to the door. It was still open and the horseshoe of people had re-formed in the room. A few more were standing now. They weren't standing with their arms folded and their heads down. Now they were dangling fists and staring straight at me. Looking half-angry and entirely perplexed at the sight of me coming back.

'What did you just throw at me?' I called out. 'The hell was that?'

Keith was blinking. His teeth were closed together and his lip was peeling back. Through the gap left in his mad-smile I saw his tongue moving. With each deep breath he took it moved again.

'He's sorry for that, Mister Pullman,' Missus Knowles said. 'Are you hurt?'

'No, ma'am,' I said, looking at her. She was still sitting on the sofa. 'And I apologise to you for playing into the moment. I regret it deeply.' She nodded her head at me. 'I will do everything I can to make it up to your family.'

At that I left again. I made a slow walk back to the van. Expecting something else to come flying towards me. Connecting with my back. Maybe getting that lucky shot again and opening the mouth in the back of my head after all. But nothing flew my way. I opened the door to the van and sat in the driver's seat. Ted hopped in the passenger side a few seconds later. The engine hesitated when I tried to pull away.

Then we took off with the wheels sliding in the snow – pitching the van to the side. I corrected it and turned round in the cul-de-sac and set the course for the hill.

'What a family,' Ted said. 'How's your noggin?'

'Head's fine,' I said.

'You sure don't want to make a friend on the job, do you?' He laughed, but I didn't join in.

'I'll tell you what. That's not a bunch I'd like to deal with again,' I said. 'Not anytime soon.'

'Tough clan for sure.'

We drove a while. Radio playing away. Just enough to give us background noise. Turned it up so I could hear the song. Then I looked in the back. Quick turn of the head. With all the excitement, I'd got into the van without saying anything to Marty. Coming back to the van was like entering the old world. Me and Ted on a job together. Only us. Working a removal and setting on back to the office. Ready to unload the cargo and start the processing of papers and body.

Marty wasn't talking . . . That's not a good sign.

'Ted, you see Marty back there?' I asked.

Ted looked back. He nodded his head.

'Sitting in the jump seat. Same as before.' Ted leaned out of his seat and stretched the belt. Reached out a hand and grabbed for Marty. 'You alright there, partner?'

There was no response.

'He sleeping?' I asked. Hopeful.

'Nope. Looks tired. You tired, Marty?'

There was nothing. All the way back to the home there was nothing but silence coming from the back of the van. The occasional soft rattle of something in the boxes on the shelves. There was nothing from Marty. I parked in the space at the back of the funeral home. Ted looked at me and nodded his head towards Marty. I tossed a thumb over my shoulder. Ted got out and opened the sliding door.

'Come on, partner,' he said. 'I've got to head over to Darnell's to pick up some grub for me and your old man. What do you say you come with me?'

Again Marty didn't say anything. He got out of the van still wearing the white coveralls. Rubber fingers of rubber gloves looking empty on his hands. He followed Ted to his truck. Got in and buckled the seatbelt and kept his head down. I watched them leave, thinking maybe he was going to give me a smile. Toss me a glance even. Anything to let me know he was alright. Some kind of signal. There was nothing.

I looked into the back of the van and had a mixed feeling about what I saw. Marty had almost been able to get the zipper closed. Not all the way. Probably didn't have the energy to get it all back in place. Part of the plastic lining was poking out. Part of a knitted blanket had come out with it. Through the puckered zipper and below a thin layer of plastic sheet I could see the small features of Theodore Knowles. A wide, pale nose above ashen grey lips.

You stupid boy. Why didn't you listen to me when I told you? Stupid little boy, Marty. You will suffer for this. Let me tell you this is going play in your head for a long, long time.

Chapter Sixteen

Ted and Marty came into my office. Ted had two white paper bags in his left hand and was using his right hand to push Marty along. Marty came in and fell into a chair on the other side of my desk. Ted followed and stood beside him. He looked down with the same concern I was feeling.

'You alright, bud?' I asked.

'Kind of.'

'I got you both ham on rye. Sheila wrapped the fries up in foil to keep them warm.' Ted set the white bags down on the corner of my desk. 'You two eat up while it's still hot.'

'Thanks, Ted.'

He left and I made like I was doing something important. Moved papers round while I waited for Marty to start talking. He was busy picking at his fingers.

'Let's get home with this stuff,' I said. 'How about it?'

Marty stood and left the office. I was slow to follow him. We got into the van and drove back home in silence. He didn't go for the radio and I wasn't pressing for anything more than the numbing hum of the heater. We got back to the house and Marty went for the sofa. Sat there in the white overalls, zipped right up to his chin.

The television was off. Poor kid looked real alone sitting there. An empty bowl Donald must have left was still on the coffee table, next to the glass he'd used. I knew it was Donald's 'cause of the chalky white of his protein-shake coating the inside of it.

'You alright?' I asked.

'Not really.'

He sounded tired, but there was no harm in that. He didn't sound like anything was really eating at him. Not like he was going to break down. Start crying. But then he'd only said two words. It's easy to hold your nerves when saying two words. Marty's a good kid. Tough enough to bottle up what needs bottling. Release it in the right way. I trusted him to suffer.

'How long you planning to sit here?'

Shrugged his shoulders.

'Couple hours. Maybe. I don't know.'

'Couple of hours is a long time, bud. Maybe you should talk about it. All the stuff that's been happening.'

'Yeah,' he said. 'I didn't want to disturb you.'

'Let's get some of this food down our necks, huh?'

He followed me into the kitchen. Opened the bag and took out the foil wrappers. Put one on the placemat in front of his favourite chair. Set the other on my side of the table. Did the same with the sandwiches. While Marty put the food out, I went to the fridge and pulled out a couple of cans of soda and set them on the counter top.

'So what's going on, Marty?'

'Nothing, I guess.'

'That doesn't give me much to work with,' I said. I gave him a minute. Hoped he would come out with more on his own. Tell me what it was that was on his mind. When he didn't speak, I turned with the sodas and set one in front of him. Cracked the other open and sat down. Tried to figure out what the hell I was supposed to do next.

'You want some help?' I asked.

'No.' He worked the foil of the sandwich and spread it out wide. Dumped the fries on top and looked at it. Muscles in his jaw making a small mound appear and disappear. He was chewing on some tough thoughts.

I nodded.

'Glad to see you making a start.'

'Guess I have to.'

He wasn't saying anything else. Didn't seem to have anything left to say. Even when Marty's thinking or withdrawn he's still playing with his hands. Stretching his fingers or tracing the lines on his palm with his index finger. Testing the bend of his thumbs. Always doing something. But right then he was just looking at the mountain of fries and the sandwich below it.

I smiled, but that's not what I was feeling. I felt like I was losing something again. Only this was more painful. I had a chance to do something about it – but was becoming more confused the more I tried to figure it out. Still, I was hopeful that I could prevent things from getting worse. So I shook my head and kept the smile on my face. Pulled my chair back from the table and I sat back, wiping a hand across my mouth.

'Shoot me straight, bud. I'm here now. There's nothing to stop you from making all the noise you need. Nothing to worry about.'

'I know that, Dad.'

'Okay, then. What's eating you?'

He took a breath. Wiped his hand over his mouth. Looked at me like he wanted to see if he was doing it right. Matching movements. Motions. Being the same man his old man was. And that made me feel good. Better anyway. Then he spoke.

'I'm pretty sure I'm cursed,' he said.

'Kind of a curse do you think you've got?'

He looked worried.

'How many kinds are there?' he asked.

'Couldn't tell you, Marty. I just know some people feel they've got a . . . Well, something specific. Like a personal curse.'

'That's the one I got,' he said.

I nodded 'cause I understood where he was coming from. We had this connection. Not that I was cursed. Not that I even believed in the curse thing. It's just he was feeling unlucky and something was causing the unlucky feeling to be real intense. Only he had it pinpointed. He knew what had started the whole thing.

'So how'd you get it? The curse, I mean.'

'I don't know,' he said.

'How do you know you have it?'

'That's another problem.' He lowered his head. Wrinkled up the bridge of his nose. When he looked at me I thought he was going to cry. His face was turning red. I reached a hand out and set it down on his shoulder. His nose smoothed out. Face went pale again. He closed his eyes a while, then looked up again. His eyes turned clear.

'I got the curse of the dead baby.'

I nodded.

'That one in the red bag,' he said. 'You took it out of the house and left it in the van with me.'

'Marty,' I said. 'I'm sorry, bud. I swear it's not something I wanted to do. The situation was bad. Circumstances were . . . They were shitty for everyone.'

I couldn't explain it to him. Not so he would understand. So I let it all hang there for a while. It was quiet. Dead silent. We were looking at one another and the sound of the soda bubbles were all that could be heard. Small popping sounds that were echoing inside the cans.

'It would've been bad to take it back in the house,' he said. 'I know that. So you left it with me. Told me not to look, and I gave you my word.'

'It's my fault, Marty.'

'Nope. It's mine. That's part of the curse. 'Cause I went to open the bag. First time I stopped. Remembered what you'd told me. Thought about that story you told me once. A while ago.

The one about the boy who was curious and went into the woods to find the noise.'

'That was a real long time ago.'

'Yeah, but I remembered it. 'Cause it scared me. So I went away from the bag. But then I went back and unzipped it. All I saw was that clear plastic bag, all wrinkled up on top.' He looked at me. Wiped the back of his hand across his mouth. 'So I zipped it up again. But it was too much. I couldn't stop from going back. So I opened it and pulled back the plastic. And the dead baby was looking at me. Not like it was putting the curse on me. But it was looking at me like it was reminding me that the curse was there already.'

I didn't know what to tell him. While I was thinking to myself that the whole curse thing was crazy and I should be telling him so, I was thinking he had a point. All the trouble we were having wasn't normal. I didn't put it down to a curse or the baby, but he did. He had something to focus on and something to try and remedy. I had a missing wife and a town that was getting more and more suspicious about what I was capable of doing. That's about as bad a curse as you can get.

'Why would it do a thing like that?' I asked. 'Why would the baby remind you of a curse that already exists?'

''Cause curious boys always get killed in the end.'

'What makes you say that?'

'You told me.' He took a fry from the top of his plate and looked at it for a moment. He set it down on the table, away from the rest of the fries. 'I asked you why the darkness killed the boy. The one in that story. You said the boy shouldn't have been in the woods. It didn't make sense to me. So you said it was because the darkness was angry. And I told you it didn't make sense. So you said curious boys always get killed in the end.'

'I said that because you wouldn't give up, Marty. You were a persistent little fella. I needed something that would stop the questions.'

'That makes sense.'

We smiled at one another for a while. Things seemed to almost fit back together again.

'I'm pretty sure Mom won't ever be able to come back now,' he said. "Cause of the dead baby curse.'

'I don't know of any reason for Mom not to come back, Marty. But I can tell you that if she doesn't come back, it's got more to do with me than it does with you. People have problems some times. Adults especially, and it gets complicated. Me and Mom had things we needed to work out.'

Marty looked at his hands. They were small – all balled up under the light. He sat there folding them into one another. He watched his hands while he meshed them together. It must have helped him think 'cause after a while he started shaking his head.

'Mom could be dead. I don't think she's coming back.'

'Marty, she's not dead. Don't think that, and don't let me hear you saying it again. She went away for a while. That's all. Nothing to get all hyped up about. She'll be back. It's not healthy for you to think all crazy like that.'

'Okay,' he said. His hands came apart and fell flat on the table. 'You know something else, Dad?' I raised my eyebrow. He didn't look up, but he knew to continue anyway: 'I did everything I could to keep Mom from going away.'

'What do you mean?'

'In my head. Closed my eyes and tried real hard to get her to stop. The night before she left. The day she was going. All the drive up to meet Grandpa. I really tried to keep her here.'

'How long have you thought she was ready to go?'

'When you two had the fight. The last big one, I mean.'

It was tough to look at him. His eyes looking at me with an innocence in his round face. But there was something in the tone of his words that made me uncomfortable. I couldn't get angry 'cause he had a right to tell me his thoughts. I'd asked him to start talking for Christ's sake. And he was right, we had fights. Me and Carole had some real shouters. But I had a feeling he had a couple of those fights on his mind. Recent moments that had more heat than the others.

'You want to talk about that big fight?' I asked. 'One you think made her go away?'

'No,' he said. 'It just happened. You guys just . . . yelled.'

'Which one are you worried about most?'

'You came home and Mom was asking you about when you were a kid. She was asking about my other Grandpa. She wanted to know about a boy named Dean. She kept asking you questions and, when you wouldn't answer her, she kept yelling.' His hands went together again. He was creating a puzzle to keep his hands occupied. 'I wasn't trying to listen, but Mom was really . . .' Marty stopped talking and looked past me. He looked over my shoulder and focused on something else for a second. 'She was really scared about what you did. She was so scared she got louder and louder. Mom was always loud when she was scared. When you two had fights.'

Didn't want to look at him with mean eyes, but right then I couldn't control how I looked. I was only able to consider the next question to ask. Something that would draw it out of him so we could move on.

'How much of that conversation do you remember, Marty?'

'I don't want you to be angry with me. But, I remember most of it. Pretty much all of it really.'

'Good,' I said. 'That's a good thing. The reason it's good is because I don't remember much of it.' I reached out and touched a finger to his hand puzzle. It was a magic touch 'cause the puzzle fell open again. 'Maybe you can help me remember.'

'You came home and Mom was waiting for you,' he said. 'She had been talking with someone on the phone. She kept calling whoever it was and, when they didn't answer, she'd hang up and call back again. When she got them on the phone she told me I had to go upstairs and listen to my music. I went upstairs, but I sat in the hallway and I listened to her talk.

'They talked about it too. Same thing Mom was asking you about. She kept saying she didn't believe it. That she couldn't see you doing something so horrible. She got really angry with that person too. She kept telling them that she was going to get Sheriff Upshaw involved. Then she started to cry, and when I was coming down the stairs she yelled at me. She yelled more than she ever had before. After a while she started talking again. But she was different. She went quiet . . . That's the same way she went on the phone.'

'Did she say a name when she was on the phone?'

He shook his head.

'After that you came in and Mom was ready. She was waiting up and she didn't like you keeping quiet about all the secrets. She called Nancy and I heard that conversation too. She said that she didn't know what to do. That she loved you and that she would do anything to protect you, and that she would even let you go away. You pulled up when she was on that call. And she got off the phone and started yelling at you when you came in. I remember 'cause she was getting louder and louder. And I couldn't understand you. Your voice was low. The sound, I mean. Mom kept asking you what you did to Dean. That's the boy she was talking about on the phone. Then she was yelling a lot.'

'Do you remember what she was yelling?'

He nodded his head. He looked at me like he didn't want to say it. I gave him a half-smile and tried to show him that whatever it was he was about to say didn't matter. Not between me and him. It wasn't going to change how we were together. How we'd be alright, no matter what. He deserved that much reassurance – and I needed him to keep talking.

'She was yelling about your father. She kept asking you what really happened,' he said. 'She wanted to know who had really killed that boy.'

We sat at the table for a while without talking. I kept a hold of the smile, even though I didn't really feel like holding on to it any more. Didn't like the idea of Marty having the conversation in his thoughts for all that time. Didn't like him feeling he should hide it from me. I understood why he kept quiet, but I didn't like him holding onto something that damning.

'I'll tell you about it, if you want to hear,' I said. He nodded at me. Figured I owed him that much. 'When I was a boy I was friends with a kid named Dean. He went missing one day and I helped his mother look for him. When we couldn't find him we called the police, and they came out and searched the woods around our neighbourhood. It went on and on and it didn't seem like they would ever find him. Then one day they did find him. My father – your grandfather – had killed him. Somehow your mom got it in her head that it wasn't only my father that did it.' I pushed my hands towards him. Moved across the table. Kept my hands palms up so he could see them under the light. So he could see they were clean and didn't have a mark on them. 'I have had to live with those kinds of questions all of my life. I still live with them.'

'Mom always said your scars were deeper inside than they were on the outside.'

'She told you that?'

'No, she always told that to Missus Lowell. When they had coffee and would sit around and talk about things, Mom would always tell her how good a man you were under all the scars.'

He tapped his finger on the table and started playing with the fry he'd separated from the plate.

He looked at my hands for a while. Then he said: 'When the fights got louder I got more worried. Every time she went out I thought that was it. After that last fight, I was pretty sure she was going. Leaving for good, I mean.'

I sat there and nodded my head. Almost relieved and feeling like I'd defused a bomb. His face was down – he looked helpless. It made me feel better, 'cause Marty didn't want to get away from me. He was alright to sit across from me at the table, even after talking about what was eating him up, he was okay to stick around. It made me feel better that he didn't have anything worse to tell me.

He looked up and said: 'When she took the Jeep I thought things were going wrong.'

I went cold.

'Why were you worried about the Jeep?'

His eyes were still on me. Now they were filling up with water. Really welling up in a hurry and looking close to spilling over.

''Cause that's where she put all of her things.'

'What things would those be, Marty?'

'All of the things she'd been collecting.' He didn't look so helpless any more. He looked like he was in control. 'Things about who you were before Pop and Grandma Mona brought you here. She had it in a big suitcase. She kept it in the back of the Jeep.'

We went quiet. We stayed that way a good long while.

Chapter Seventeen

I spent the day in the study. Sat on the chair for a long while and finally called into the funeral home and spoke with Ted. I reminded him that his Datsun was in my driveway, and I offered to pick him up and bring him back here so he could get it. He told me it was no big deal, that he would find a ride and get it back. I was looking for a way out of the house. I didn't have any other ideas. I ended up falling asleep in my chair and when I woke up it was dark outside.

Went through to the family room and found Marty on the sofa.

'The cupboards are bare,' I said. Marty's eyes closed halfway and he nodded his head at me. Seemed to be considering what he should say next. I didn't give him the chance. 'Let's get out of here and do something useful.'

Marty nodded his head again and stood up from the sofa.

Got the keys and handed Marty his coat. Walked him out to the van and drove out to Solomon's, the biggest grocery store Henderson's got. Town's got small shops and butchers and the market's good too, but Solomon's has it all in one place. Best of all, it's open mortician's hours. Every damned minute of every damned day.

We pulled into the parking lot. Marty was mumbling away about some photographs he'd snapped of icicles and sun sparkles on frozen bushes. Told me how he'd taken the camera from my study and walked round the outside of the house. Seems he'd been doing it for a while. A kind of hobby. Something I didn't know anything about. Must have been sharing his pictures with Carole. He hadn't made it as far as telling me he had an interest in snapping shots until she decided to remove herself from the mix. Marty was making up for lost time. Talking away and using his hands to describe the photographs he'd taken. His fingers flared out when he was talking about the light reflecting off the ice. I kept nodding my head to keep him going. When he was talking I could stay quiet. Could think and try to get my stories straight. Seemed that's what I needed to do. So he kept speaking. I kept nodding while I motored through Solomon's parking lot.

Crawled towards the front of the store. Passed all the empty spaces and kept moving forward. Always hopeful of something up front. I drove on and Marty was getting really animated about one of his photographs. I nodded my head and said something to him. Wasn't much, but it was enough to keep his enthusiasm high. We'd talked out the curse already and I was hoping he would talk out any suspicions he'd come to have about me. Marty was talking and laughing and I was feeling calm and thinking life was finding the rails again. Turned my head to show Marty I was listening to him. He stopped talking and looked at me.

'What's the matter?' he asked. 'Why are you making that sound?'

I stopped looking past him. I didn't want him to see it too. Shook my head.

'Nothing, bud. Keep talking. Tell me all about the photographs.'

He started talking again. I was looking at Marty, but it was the car travelling behind him that had my attention. I watched it move up alongside us, up the next row of spaces. It was keeping pace with us. Same slow crawl. The car was familiar and it got my attention straight off. Felt a block of something form in my throat.

I kept watching Marty and he was looking straight ahead, talking and moving his hands. Icicles and light. Glares and flashes. And while he spoke I watched Paul Quincy hold the wheel of his Cadillac Eldorado with one hand. His other hand was hanging outside his car door. The window was down and he was talking, but I couldn't hear what it was he was saying. It was a cold night, so the windows of the van were up. All the fools driving round Henderson that night had their windows up and the heaters on full blast. All of them except for Paul Quincy.

Pop warned you, Joe. Paul's a desperate man, and a desperate man can do dangerous things.

I was starting to feel my own desperation building. The steam coming out of his mouth told me he was saying a lot. The look in his eyes told me he wasn't reciting poetry. His hand pounding at the side of his Cadillac wasn't tapping out the tunes of his radio.

Considered leaving the parking lot. Driving away and forgetting the evening grocery shop. Thought about taking Marty to dinner someplace instead. Come back to Solomon's in the morning and see if Paul Quincy was still on the prowl. Looked back over at Paul's car to see if he was still shouting. He'd stopped and was looking forward. Then I caught sight of something. Hair. Lots of it. Long hair blowing in the seat next to Paul. Frances didn't have long hair and Paul wouldn't be so damned crazy if he had Carole in the car with him.

'It's cold, bud,' I said. 'So I'll drop you up at the door. You go in and get a cart ready.'

'What difference does it make?' Marty said. He made a laugh the same way he does with his friends. Same sound he makes when he wants them to know he thinks they're stupid as a weed. He looked at me like he wanted to finish what he was saying about the photograph. Some picture he'd taken of the cedar trees in the back yard.

'Didn't mean to interrupt you, Marty,' I said. 'But, I just remembered that I've got a call to make.' Even lifted my cell-phone out of the carrier on the dash for effect. 'You run in and get that cart for us. By the time I'm finished you'll be ready to go.'

'Fine,' he said.

I dropped him at the front door and waited for him to go inside. Then I took the van to an empty space and parked under a light. I sat there looking round the parking lot. Expected to see Paul's Eldorado facing me head-on. Pitching from side to side while he revved the engine. Only thing I had in front of me was a beat-up old VW Beetle with a head-light missing. I checked the rest of the cars in the lot. Paul's road-boat was nowhere to be seen.

Shut off the van's engine and got out. Wind cutting into me hard. Shoved the keys in my coat pocket. Stuffed my hands in my jeans and started a pained jog towards the store. Looked round as I went. Paul had disappeared. Him and his passenger with all the hair. Hoped he'd seen that I wasn't alone. Got second thoughts about messing with me. Maybe he'd figured how far I would go to keep things quiet with Marty. Either way, he wasn't around any more and it was a relief to me. Got to the doors. Stepped on the rubber mat and the door pulled open. A heavy breath of hot air blew down on me. Took all the moisture from my eyes. Marty was waiting with the cart. He was standing on the back of it, making circles near the service desk. Some young girl with a farm of pimples on her forehead was watching him. She leaned on the counter of the service desk, chin in her hand, chewing slow on a piece of pink gum. When I walked towards Marty she straightened her back. Stopped chewing. Used a short finger to push the glasses up the bridge of her crooked nose.

I took the cart from him and pushed it from aisle to aisle. Not feeling like shopping. My mind was on Paul and the trip he must have taken to come out here and see me. *What's he planning to do now, Joe? The hell's that old fool up to? You saw what he put in the paper. He's got some serious plans. Can't like the idea of that. Not one bit.*

Marty was talking to me, something about a guy who was picking on him. I started to take notice of his story when he said the kid had swung a few punches his way. It was the kind of problem I could help the boy get through. Show him how I'd been in the same shoes once. I'd tell him how I had made those shoes more useful than something to keep my feet warm. He told me he didn't think it was all that big a deal 'cause this kid picked on everybody.

'I got shoved a few times, then the swing. But it was nothing. It didn't even get me. He wasn't even trying really.' Marty looked at me and I was shaking my head. 'It's nothing too heavy, Dad. Nothing to draw blood.'

'He hits you, hit him back. Swing for the fences and don't stop until someone pulls you off him.'

'Sure, Dad.' He went quiet and moved up the aisle. 'Thing is, I don't really want to fight.'

'You don't always have a choice, Marty. Sometimes these things just come after you. They chase you until you have to do things you're not comfortable doing. Things you don't want to do, just so they can't chase you any more.'

After that Marty spoke about the other suckers. Kids who had got the hard side of this bully. I listened for a while. Connected on both sides of his characters. The bully and the bullied. There's a fine line between the two. A line that can be crossed too easily. When the bullied steps over that line it can get nasty. Things can change and never go back.

My attention had started to fade, but Marty didn't realise I wasn't with him. He spoke a bunch of names I'd heard in passing. Surnames I recognised from invoices at the funeral home. People he trusted and liked as friends. People he was now concerned for – because he saw them in trouble.

That kid of yours is always thinking about other people. All the mess his family is facing and he's worried about a bunch of children and the bully who's after them. Fairytale horrors. A wolf amongst the flock of sheep. A lion in with the lambs.

Marty was still talking to me, but I was only getting pieces of what he was saying. School bells. Teachers on the lookout. Principals who cared. It was all tame. What I was catching told me he had it easy and this bully was no real thug. So I cut off and allowed myself to worry about other things. Consider the more pressing stuff, like when Paul Quincy was going to stick his head round a corner and make a scene about his missing daughter. If Marty needed me, he would come calling. Right then he was just chattering and what was coming out of his mouth was soft noise.

'What would you do?' Marty asked.

'About what?'

'You're not even listening to me.' He started walking off. Stomped his feet even as he went away from the cart and down the aisle. Got me riled 'cause he didn't know the half of what I was dealing with.

You want to hear a story, Marty? A real story about real boys? Well, here goes. A long time back there were these two boys. They hung out in the woods behind one of their father's houses. They buried animals under the Killing Tree and they walked the forest like they owned the place. It was sacred place to them 'cause the bullies couldn't find them back there. It was a place where the sun fell through the trees in sharp yellow blades of light. There was never any trouble until one of the boys decided that the Killing Tree wasn't enough. He decided that the animals they had given it weren't filling the need.

Then this boy comes along and starts following them around. He has this goddamned limp and he wants to keep up with those two boys. He wanted to be part of what had already been created. But the more he slowed them down, the more frustrated those boys became. And then something happened. A thunderstorm on a calm day. An earthquake on the most stable land. No warning, and one of the boys started beating the new kid. And he was yelling and screaming. But the energy was in the air. The storms were on him. On all of them, and the hands fell and the legs kicked and the screaming grew louder and louder until there was only silence. And they tied the boy to a pole and they left him there in the forest. They left him and they didn't care if he ever found his way home.

'Dad!' Marty said. 'Where are you going?'

I looked at him. He was standing at the end of an aisle, shaking his head at me. I'd made it to the end of the aisle and was almost to the double doors leading to Solomon's loading bay. I looked up at Solomon's sign on the door and wondered how I could lose myself so easily. How the world of here and now can disappear completely into a world long dead.

Marty came to the cart and was staring at my hands. I looked at them and saw how they were shaking. Saw how white my knuckles had turned as I'd pulled a hard grip on the handle.

You did nothing, Joe. You did nothing but watch it happen. You watched the storm build in Dean until he had to release it on something. It couldn't be you. And when Oz came along, it was only a matter of time. But you didn't know when. Dean didn't tell you when it would happen. He just broke open and when he spilled out he made a mess of poor limping Oz.

'I'm sorry, Marty. I guess you caught me daydreaming there.'

He knew there was more to it. He didn't start talking from where he left off. He didn't talk at all when we started walking with the cart again. He led the way and I followed after him. Slower than before. Marty was taking things off the shelves and putting them in the cart and I kept pushing, not looking at what he was taking. It didn't interest me any more. He would look at me when he put something else in the cart and I knew he was testing me, looking to see if I was paying attention. I may have been working towards giving him some of that attention when I spotted Paul Quincy's long figure slump by the end of the aisle. I pulled a bag of rice off the shelf and tossed it into the cart and wondered what he was planning.

Shoved the cart into the next aisle. Acted like I was looking at the potato chips. Probably looked pathetic, taking so much interest in the wall of plastic bags. *Ridges or regular? Barbecue or Sour Cream and Onion? This one's new and improved, Joe!* Made a show of it. Marty headed up the aisle and stopped. Turned round and came back. He looked at the bags of potato chips along with me. When he looked at me, I shook my head and chewed on my lip. Did my best to look like I was trying to make a decision.

'Get the Ruffles, Dad.'

'Yeah,' I said. 'That's what I was thinking. Was also thinking we need some more soda. I think we passed it already.'

Marty shrugged. He said, 'We can go back.'

'How about you go back to get it for me? Save us some time.'

He headed off and I pushed the cart into the next aisle. Waited. Not for Marty. I waited and hoped Marty would take his time. Knew damned well he wouldn't, but still I had hope.

'Joe,' the voice called out. Loud. Gruff. Direct.

'Yep?' I called back, like I didn't know.

'Thought you'd have been in contact by now,' Paul said.

'How's that?' Turned round and watched the old man move up the aisle towards me. His right leg working better than the left. His cane looked like it was more flexible than his bad side. Still, he came at me fast. Must have wanted to intimidate me from the start. His face was worked up with anger. His free hand swinging up and grasping, before moving back down with his next stride. Up and reaching. Grabbing with the next step. Pulling himself towards me even faster.

'My daughter goes missing and I get a phone call from you, Joe. A single phone call and then nothing.'

'I don't have anything else to tell you, Paul.'

'Well, there's enough to fill the papers.'

'I saw that.'

'Good. It's good that you can see there are people looking for her. People who care enough about her to be looking for her.'

I stared at him and wondered what it was he wanted me to say. Wondered how deep the suspicions had rooted in his mind. If it had only gone so deep to fear that I wouldn't look for his little girl, or if it had sunk down to where he figured I had done something to her. Watched his eyes for a sign of that depth.

He stood there, willing me to move round the cart and let the confrontation begin. Maybe if Marty hadn't been with me I'd have humoured him. I'd have gone right up to him and let the old fucker ramble and get it off his chest. Whatever he had to say to me didn't really matter any more. I'd been living for almost a week without a wife, and I kind of figured I deserved more than him standing under the fluorescent lights of a grocery store showing how pissed off he was that I hadn't called him with updates as to the whereabouts of his daughter. Under the lights of a grocery store his accusations didn't sit right with me. I kept to my side of the cart and I was hoping like hell he'd stay propped up on his cane at the other side.

'Must have had my mind on other things,' I told him.

He dropped a large hand on the end of the cart and gave it a shove. It connected with my hip. It was more painful than I let on.

'Bet you got a lot going on in that head of yours.'

'Listen, Paul. I meant to come out and see you. Sit down with Fran and you and have a long talk. It's been a tough week . . .'

'Tough week?'

Paul leaned against his cane. Stepped away from the cart and looked like he was going to fall. Teetered for a moment, and all at once looked too relaxed to regain himself. Then he was up and almost straight. Almost strong again. He used one long finger to point at my chest. Held that shaking hand out – pointing it at me without saying a word.

'You can't get away with this. Since my girl picked up things with you, I have feared for her safety. I know what you're all about. She talks to me. She tells her mother all the things you hoped to hell would stay quiet. But you know that already. You know damned well that my daughter talks. There's no secrets in the Quincy family. That must eat a man like you to pieces.'

'This is not the place to pick a fight, Paul.'

'You stole my daughter from me,' he said.

'This is not the place.'

'No?' he called out. 'Where do you want to go? What kind of a place should we do this then? Same place you took my daughter? You've torn my family apart. Why should I make this easier for you? Why would I do what you want?'

'I'd have welcomed a conversation at my office, Paul. You could have come to the house.'

'That's your place, Joe. You don't tread on my land, so I don't tread on yours. Don't take it as a matter of respect either. It's nothing of the sort.'

'Listen, Paul. I've got—'

'I don't give a damn what you got. Not the slightest care in the world. What I care about is my daughter, and it appears she's gone. No trace. Not a word from her and not a hint to where I might start looking for her. That's what troubles me. So what I want is an answer,' he said. He shoved the cart again. It hit my hip. I tried pushing it back. He had his hand on it. I couldn't get the thing to move. 'I read about her in a letter I received, Joe. A letter that was mailed to me from here in Henderson. See, I open an envelope the other morning and

I find a handwritten letter. Someone took the time to write me, Joe. More than a small note. I read the letter and came across some interesting information. Information about you. You fighting with my daughter. Her leaving the house in the late evening and returning the following morning. It happened several times in recent weeks.'

I tried to keep a strong face on, but hearing Paul talk was making it tough to keep control. Listening to his story about a letter wasn't making me feel any easier. I wanted him to shove the cart into me again. Needed that jab of pain to stop my head from spinning. Too many images rushing through my mind. Tried pushing on the cart. He held steady and didn't shove back.

'How long have you been living at the boarding house, Joe?' He smiled and started nodding his head like he was real pleased with himself. Must have seen in my eyes that I wasn't comfortable. Seen that he'd broken into me the way he'd planned. Hoped. 'Strange thing you living in another place. Renting a cheap room, surrounded by other drunks. Seems a good place for you. Tell you the truth, it seems like the perfect place for you, Joe Pullman. Trouble is, I didn't know anything about it. My daughter didn't tell me anything about it. That's a problem for me.'

'Because in the Quincy family there are no secrets,' I said.

'No, you asshole! Because the moment you move back in, my daughter goes missing!'

'She was missing before I came back, Paul. It's the reason why I came back. I need to take care of Marty.' Stepped away and tried to turn the cart. This time Paul shoved it. Rammed my hip again and the pain cut in. I was pressed up against the shelf. Paul shoved again and hit me with force. Something fell off the shelves behind me. It hit the floor with a crack. Glass breaking.

'I understand you're angry.'

'Well, sure you do. You're a smart man, Joe. You've kept

all this to yourself. For good reason too. That's what I think. So I'll be speaking with the sheriff and seeing how much more they know. And I'll be passing on that letter and some of the stories I've been keeping over the years.'

'Don't make this something it's not, Paul. She left and she stuck a note to the fridge door.' I turned and looked down the aisle. Expected to see Marty. Half-hoped he would show up. Expected he was too smart to come down the aisle if he heard what Paul was saying. An old woman was passing down the far end of the aisle with a basket in her hand. She slowed, but kept moving when she caught me looking at her.

'One question's floating round in my mind, Joe. I'm sure, as hell is hot, that you know just what that question is.'

'Paul, I've got no idea where Carole's gone off to.'

His cane came up. I wasn't ready for it. It took a diagonal motion. Floor to my chin. Then it was back to the floor again. My head snapped to the side. Found myself looking at the line of salsa dips. Smelling the tang of salsa rise to my nose. I moved my foot and slipped in a spilled mess. Tried to gain my footing. Concentrated on the pain swelling in my jaw. My neck seizing up, with the quick way my head snapped to the side. A shock more than a crushing blow.

'Goddamn,' I breathed. Grabbed for my mouth. Moved my jaw to see if it was still working. See if it had come unhinged.

'I got more,' Paul said. 'This is a side I keep to my own, Joe. A side of me I don't like. So I'm asking you to tell me what's what. Give me what I need so I don't have to use this again.' He lifted the cane from the floor. I flinched and Paul saw it. He shook the cane at my face.

'Just hold it, Paul. Take it easy now.'

I swallowed and took down some blood. Put my fingers in my mouth and touched the ridge that my teeth had imprinted in my tongue. Paul watched while I closed my mouth and looked at my fingers. Red lines cutting and spreading through the saliva. Small trails of blood running over the lines of my knuckles. Sucked at my tongue and watched Paul's cane. Waiting for it to move. Considering the possibility I might finally get the chance to punch my father-in-law. Feeling guilty about the prospect. About the eager anticipation of the step before the punch. The dull collision of hard knuckles against his fresh-shaved face.

'What happened?' Paul asked. 'What did you do to her?'

Shook my head.

'I'll use this if I have to, Joe.'

'Use what?' Marty asked.

Paul looked past me. Marty was back there. Somewhere on my left. I relaxed for a second. Paul looked like he was going to fall to the side. Seemed destined to knock down the Pringles display on his way to the ground.

'Marty,' he said. 'I didn't see you there.'

'What do you mean, Grandpa?' Marty walked past me and set a twelve-pack of soda cans in the cart. I looked at Paul and he returned me a new expression – this time more child-like. Less threatening. I shook my head.

'Just mean I didn't see you there. That's all. Your dad was just telling me some things.'

Marty shrugged. 'So what's going on with you two?' he asked.

'Nothing,' Paul said. 'I saw your dad and wanted to check up on him. Haven't seen him or heard from him in a while. Your grandma's wanting to know how you're doing. Wants to know when you're coming back up to stay with us.'

'So what are you doing in Henderson?' Marty asked.

I could've smiled, but my mouth hurt too damned bad.

'Came over to see a friend of mine. He's not been well. So I wanted to come along and see if there was something I could do. Something to help get him back on his feet quicker.'

'And Grandma?'

'She's keeping fine, Marty. I'll tell her you're asking for her.'

'She didn't come with you?'

'No, son. She's been busy with other things. In the middle of organising some important things.'

'Who's your friend?' Marty asked.

'Well, I'm not sure you've ever met Fisher,' Paul said.

'Don't know. What's his whole name?'

Paul laughed. It was a struggle, but he got it out. He kept at it for a while, like he was practising the laugh for the first time. When he was finished Marty was looking at me. His forehead cut with lines. He looked at Paul while the laugh died off to nothing.

'You're a bright boy, Marty. A real bright young man.'

'Been good seeing you,' I said. My words were weak. Slurred. Marty was looking at me. I pulled at the shopping cart. Had to pull it a few times before Paul looked down and realised he was holding on to it. Had his fingers through the metal grille of the cart and was squeezing it with all he had. I pulled again while he was looking at his hand. He let go and I turned away from him. Started walking too fast. Had to slow the pace before I gave Paul the satisfaction and Marty something to worry about. Marty came along with me and looked over his shoulder. He reached out to take hold of the side of the cart.

'I best finish up here,' I called out. 'See ya later, Paul.'

'You do that,' Paul said. 'Finish up and get on home. It'll be storming again later. Big storm by morning. I'll tell Fran you both were asking after her.'

'Do that,' I said.

I pushed the cart hard and picked up the pace. Got to the end of the aisle and started to turn. Marty kept at my side, pulled up close to me when Paul called out one last goodbye. Pushed into my side and turned to look over his shoulder again. We made it to the end of the aisle. I turned and went down the next.

'What just happened?' Marty asked.

'Nothing,' I said.

'So why are you talking funny?' he asked.

'Bit my tongue.'

'Doing what?' he asked.

'Just bit it,' I said. Gave a smile without looking down at him.

'Grandpa was standing different when I came up the aisle. Like he was mad.'

'Wasn't all that happy, I guess.'

'So he hit you with his cane?' Marty asked.

'No.' I laughed out loud. Shook my head and stopped the cart. Looked at the cans on the shelf the same as I had looked at the potato chips. Pulled one of the jars of instant coffee from the shelf and set it in the cart. Started moving again.

'Man, no,' I said.

'So what was he angry about?' Marty asked.

'Nothing.'

'He's mad 'cause of Mom.'

'Sure he is,' I said.

'Thinks maybe you did something to her,' Marty said.

I stopped the cart and this time I looked down at him. Didn't feel angry, but I felt I had lost something. Another piece had fallen off and tumbled off into the shadows where I might never find it. Things didn't feel right. It wasn't anger I was feeling. It was fear. Anxiety. Marty was old for his years. He could read people. See what made others false. And while I looked at him I wondered what he saw in me. If what he was looking at was a lie. Some asshole pretending to be a father. An unfit joker with no idea what he was supposed to do and who he was supposed to be. Maybe he saw a failed husband. Or worse.

'Why would he think that?' I asked.

''Cause people have been talking,' he said. 'It really gets on my nerves too. But people think it's weird Mom just left. Without me or Donald especially. More about Donald, I think, 'cause he's different.'

I nodded and said: 'Just *her* son.'

'Yeah,' Marty said. 'So she should have taken him. That's what I've got from it all. From what people are saying, you know? I get that people think she would have taken him.'

'Taken him if what?'

'If she left on her own,' he said. 'If she was just trying to get away.'

'Why would she want to do that, Marty?' I asked.

'I don't know.'

We walked to the end of the aisle. He put his hands in his pockets and his head slumped down to his chest, his shoes started dragging against the glossy supermarket floor. Made a squeaking sound.

'What have you heard?'

'You've got a bad history in the town,' he said. 'That's the thing that's going round now. That you have a secret. Maybe a few. Things you don't want people to know about.'

'Yeah,' I said. 'That can get a guy in trouble.'

We walked the next two aisles in silence. We didn't put anything else in the cart.

'Dad?' Marty asked.

My nerves were raw. I hadn't felt that much on edge for a real long time.

'Yeah?' I asked.

'You got a handkerchief on you?'

'Yeah,' I said. Went for my back pocket and pulled out the white kerchief I keep back there. No telling when I'll meet up with a grieving widow. A best friend. A long-time neighbour. There's always people who know someone I've buried. My conversations can end in tears. I handed the kerchief to Marty.

He shook his head and looked past me. He stared at a woman who was pushing her cart by us. She looked at me and looked away quickly. Marty waited until she went by.

'Use it to wipe your mouth,' he said.

'Why?'

'You've got blood on your chin.'

Chapter Eighteen

Came home and unloaded the groceries with Marty. He stuck close and kept leaning in. Touching me when he emptied another bag out on the kitchen table. Brought the stuff to me and set it on the counter top. He'd touch me like he was wanting to make sure I was real. Like he was worried I was going to dissolve right there when he turned his back. We set everything in the cabinets and left the kitchen, then Marty went up to bed. I waited on the sofa for a long time. Looked up at the painting over the fireplace. It was a painting Carole had picked out.

She'd found it when we took a trip to Georgia a few years back. We'd dropped the kids off with her parents and drove down without sleep. Stayed two nights looking out over the ocean. We ate seafood and walked along the beaches. She found a gallery when we got caught in a storm. We went inside and Carole started talking to the woman who ran the place. She told Carole about the artists and where they came from and what inspired the works. Carole had asked me what we needed for the house. She'd been in a good mood – all smiles and laughs. She was beautiful when she smiled, and I went along with it and let her lead me. She found the painting and listened to the story about the artist. Some woman who had lost her husband to a car accident. The artist had found comfort in the waves and so she painted a beach scene with high grasses bending. The clouds off in the distance were rolling in a storm. I'd asked Carole why she wanted the painting. I asked if it was for the story behind it or if it was the painting itself.

It's not just the scene, Joe. It's the feel of it. Look at the sand dunes and the grasses. Waves just over the sand. You can barely see them. That's inviting. Can't you feel that? It's the ease of it. But there's a storm coming. Out there on the horizon. I could sit on that beach and watch the storm coming in, Joe. Could watch it for hours. I could sit on that beach and watch that storm come in all my life.

'What storm are you watching now, Carole?

I went to the study with a half-interest in checking my emails. Hit the button on the computer and listened to the thing power up. Engine whirling away. I leaned back and put my hands behind my head. Spotted something on the back of the door leading from the hall. Sat forward and walked round the desk. Touched the door closed and waited for it to slow-swing shut before pulling away the note:

Joseph Reginald Pullman

The hell are you playing at? Using the full name now . . .

It was a half-sheet of white paper. Nothing special about it. Basic plain white. The kind loaded in any household computer. Sitting in the storage cabinets of any company. Filling the copier at the local convenience store. It's from anywhere.

I flipped the note open:

Joseph Reginald Pullman

Bet you didn't think it would go this far. I'm doing better than you may think. Finding out what new things people are capable of every day. Things you wouldn't expect. I see you are taking care of the boys to the best of your capability. Keep at it. It may get

easier with time. You will know when I find something meaningful. I'll send someone for you.
  Carole Felicity Quincy

I walked back to the desk and sat down. Opened the drawer
and took out the original note. Still wrinkled and smudged.
I pulled the note out and set it on the table. Opened it up and
looked at the words. Nodded my head as I read it. Nodded
and smiled because the words were different. Different in
meaning and different in writing.

'This is going to end,' I said. I lifted the new note and put
it under my nose. Smelled the stale whiff of smoke on the
page. Not a cigarette. Not a pipe. Smelled of cigar smoke,
and one that was not entirely unfamiliar. 'Damned right, it's
going to end.'

I went through the house and checked all the doors. Pulled
on the windows, and when I was sure the place was locked
up tight I went upstairs. Laid on Carole's side of the bed and
listened out for Marty. He'd been playing music. Something
he'd taken from Donald's room. I'd told him it was alright to
take what he wanted when Donald wasn't in. He'd skipped
out on us for the night, so I figured it wasn't any harm. Marty
wanted music and Donald had a good stash of it. I listened
for the music and heard the low, dull sound of Marty's snoring.

Laid still on the bed and watched the ceiling. Made shapes
out of the swirling patterns of the plaster. Things I'd missed
all the other times I'd looked up at them. Thousands of
them. What had I missed? While I looked at those patterns
I thought about Carole. How she would watch me looking
up at the patterns. Asking me if I'd spotted anything new.
I'd tell her what I saw, and she would laugh and tell me how
strange I was and how warped my eyes made the world. We
would lie there, my arms around her and she'd point at the
ceiling. Sometimes she'd point and draw the shape and not
say a word. Other times she wouldn't move, and when she

223

didn't move and she didn't speak, I would hold her and we would both watch the ceiling. After a while I would see something in the pattern and I would point it out and tell her what it was.

You are an odd one, Joe Pullman.

That was the last time we had lain together that way.

You never had a chance to see it any other way.

It was a good memory. The smell of her hair and the smooth softness of her naked shoulders pressed against my chest. She had cried then and I'd held her until she'd struggled to get away from me. Then she'd sat on the edge of the bed and she'd stared at my clothes draped over the chair in the corner of the room.

You never had a chance.

I guess I didn't.

You don't have to go. Listen to me. Joe, listen.

I went anyway and I regret that now.

Marty snored again. I listened to him and I wondered how much he dreamed of his mother. I feared he was dreaming of the last fight he'd witnessed or any of the other fights between me and Carole.

I'd walked over and lifted her glass from the coffee table. Took it to the cabinet where we kept the spirits. An antique hutch she'd received as a gift for her first marriage. I pulled up a half-empty Smirnoff and poured it into her glass. Dashed in some cola to change the colour for her. With the drink in hand, I tried to gather myself. Tried to plan out what I was going to say. How I was going to get out of the conversation before it even started. *It always ends ugly, Joe. She's going to press you until you leave. The story she wants to hear is the only thing that's going to stop her from trying. Meeting you at the goddamned door.*

I set the drink on the coffee table. She looked at her hands between her knees. Hair pulled back behind her ears. Her eyes were wet and I put it down to her being drunk. It didn't happen that often, so when I found Carole drunk I knew something was really troubling her. Knew that it was most likely caused by me. So I hung my head and let her stare me down. She'd kept her eyes on me. Watched like she was expecting to see something incredible.

At first she was content to listen to what little I gave her. She allowed me the time to pour out the story at my own speed. We'd lie in bed and she would trace the scars on my face. Run her finger over the lines one at a time. Trace it from beginning to an end. *Where did this one come from?* And I would tell her. Sometimes it would be the true story. And she would go to another. *You were a fighter in your day. How did you become so soft?* The more stories I told her, the harder she pressed for details. Didn't know what was spurring it on – all the extra attention she was giving it.

But, whatever it was had dug into her deep.

She stared at me and I tried to stare back. Wanted to look into her eyes and tell her everything. It's something I'd planned to do. Eventually, and in my own time, I would have told her. Sitting in front of her like that, I almost made up my mind to do it. A sharp surge of adrenaline travelling through me. Muscles and joints aching with the burning of extra energy. Real sharp inside my fingers and knees. That's where I remember the pain the most. When the fight is about to happen. Just before the blood begins to fly.

Do it, Joe. Tell her what she wants to hear. See the look on her face when she finds out you . . .

Got as far as clearing my throat. Felt the sweat starting to slick my palms. Chest ached. Breathed in deep and let it out slow. I'd almost made up my mind to tell her. Was so close to giving it all to her – delivering it moment by moment from the beginning. Starting from the first scar. Telling her how I met Dean Gillespie at the creek bed and how we buried animals we found on our walks in the forest. I would convince her that they were all dead when we found then, because it was important for Carole to know that. Worried, even as I prepared to tell her my story, that she would understand none of it.

I looked up and took a breath. The way Carole was looking at me made me change my mind. Made the thought of telling her the story slip away fast as snow-ghosts in headlights. And we sat in silence, and I thought of the story I needed to tell her and I thought about how the story would sound like a confession. There was so much she needed to know if she was going to understand what happened. If she was going to believe that I had no choice.

I sat and watched while she drank. It was hard to see her like that, but there wasn't anything I could do. Concentrated on her, and when it was too much I got up and went to the kitchen. Took a bottle of beer from the fridge and dropped in my seat for the rest of the show. Figured that's the way the night was going.

I drank and I waited. Looked up once in a while and wiped the palms of my hand across my thighs. Looked up to see if she was going to speak. Say something to start things off. Her eyes were wet.

'What did you do?' she finally asked me.

She said a lot more. Trouble was it wasn't coming out. Not so I could hear it anyway. Her mouth was moving and there was something happening. Something behind the moving lips that I was supposed to be hearing. Watched close, but I couldn't make out what it was she was trying to tell me. What it was she was wanting me to know. Understand. She was blowing words at me, but I couldn't catch any of them. Not a damned one. Something about the way she was looking at me – all direct – and accusing. That made it hard to look at her.

I looked away. Looked at the painting above the fireplace. Looked at the front door. Judged how long it would take me to get to it. Get through it. Get back to TP's before Lenny rented my room out to some idiot tramp. I wanted to get away, but I couldn't go. The way she was looking at me made me feel responsible. She was in a state and I was the cause. So I drank my beer and I gave her time. Let her keep talking. Speaking to me without making a sound. I tried to let her storm blow itself out, hoping the alcohol was going to kick in more and drop her off in a slow sleep like it always did. Eventually. I just needed it to work a little faster.

'Who's that boy you talk about?'

Her mouth stopped moving. Now it was her hands. Fingers tapping out something on her knees. Playing a fast song on a piano. Tapping out a suicide note on a typewriter. One that tells the masses why you can't wait to end it all. Fingers moving and making mistakes *'cause it just don't matter no more!*

'What was that you said?' I asked her. Playing stupid 'cause I'd heard her fine. Not much sense in denying it now. Watched her fingers pick up tempo. Tapping faster. 'What boy?'

'You talk about a boy.'

'I can't remember that,' I said. Held the bottle up to my mouth. Hovered it like I was holding back, giving myself a chance to think. Like I was really concentrating hard.

'You wake me when you talk about him.'

'Okay,' I said. Kept real calm about it. It's not something that was hard to do. We'd had the conversation before. Start of it anyway. I'd get questioned about the woods. About my old man and the way he beat seven shades of shit out of me. She'd want to hear about my mother and about my school. About the foster families who came later and my time at St Martin's home for the unwanted. *Give her a story, Joe. Tell her about Pop and Mona. Tell her how they came and took you away.* This time it was about Dean Gillespie. She was specific in what she wanted. I figured I'd give her the same story as before. Maybe add a few things to it. Get all wet in the eye while I spoke, and when she was softening up I'd tell her I couldn't finish. That's the way it would end when Carole's conscience would weigh in – like all the other times. *Poor Joe can't finish the memory. Don't make him go back to that place, Carole.*

'It's just some dream, Carole.'

She moved back on the sofa. Pushed herself up on it like she was trying to get as far away from me as possible. She sat there, perched like a gargoyle on the side of an old church. She watched me and balled up her fingers into fists so she wouldn't keep tapping away at her knees. Then she got up off the sofa. Stepped up so her shins were pressed against the coffee table. Stood looking down at me. Long hair wild over her shoulders. Tangled on the side where she'd been spinning it in her fingers.

'Who is . . . Who is Oz?' she asked.

I'll admit there was almost a moment of relief. She hadn't used names before. Not for *the boy*. If there was a name coming from my dreams, it was best being Oz. Breathed out and shook my head slow. Doing my best to keep her from seeing just how glad I was.

'Oz was a friend of mine,' I told her. My voice was calm. Mellow. Paced my words so she would listen to me without interrupting. Looked up to judge how she was taking it in. To see how much more she would be expecting me to say. Sat up so my back was straight. So she wasn't towering so high over me. 'You know him. Of him, I mean.' It wasn't enough. She shook her head at me to keep me going. 'Oscar. One of the kids my old man . . .' Made a kind of cranking gesture with my hand. It was easier than having to say what she had already heard before.

'The first boy your father kidnapped,' she said.

'Yeah.'

'Then why did you tie him to the pole?'

There was no keeping breath in my lungs. No easy way to make Carole think I was in control. I didn't know how much she listened to my dreams and how much she'd pieced together on her own. My dreams come and go. Some nights they're worse than others. For a good long while Carole had been waking me before I could say too much. I'd wake to her holding my head, wiping her hand across my face. I'd come to and she'd have her arms round me. Rocking and pulling me hard against her chest. Then something changed.

She had contact with my father and with that contact came a new version of events. My old man had found a sympathetic ear and it just happened to belong to my wife. And her curiosity had drawn her in, just like the boy in the story I'd told Marty all those years ago. And Marty knows what happened to him . . . *The darkness killed the boy.* Why? *Because the curious boy always dies in the end.*

'Carole, I don't know what you're talking about.'

'Tell me why you tied Oscar Lewiston to the pole.'

'I can't help what I dream about.'

'What did you do to him?' she asked again.

'I didn't do anything to Oz.' It came out right. Came out just like I'd expected it would. Her eyes opened and her face moved up and I saw that she was coming to life. And something inside me wanted her to keep coming to the surface. 'It really wasn't my fault what happened to him. He was always following us around. Me and Dean let him come along and we never gave him hassle about it. We just let him stick close 'cause there wasn't any reason to make him go away.'

Carole wanted more. She was always wanting more. I wanted to give it to her. I wanted to . . .

You've got to believe me, Carole, with everything happening that summer, Oz just kind of got in the way. My mother getting taken away, and my old man and his beatings. That was enough for me. Dean had his interest in pushing the thrill. The rush he was finding in all the things we did in the forest was growing intense. He found a primal impulse that summer, and he explored it and it went too far. What happened wasn't planned.

Dean lost control.

I stared at Carole and shook my head.

'I didn't do anything to him.'

She was holding her arms. Elbows cupped in her hands,

keeping them close to her sides. Trying to hide from me while I was looking at her. Keeping warm maybe. *Protecting herself. That's the worst thing, Joe. She's protecting herself.* Her mouth was moving again. I looked away and listened to her breathing. It was loud. She was struggling. So I knew what was coming was going to be hard to hear.

'What about Dean?' she said.

'He was a friend of mine.' Nodded my head and kept my eyes away from her. 'The one my old man . . . We don't need to speak about Dean.'

'You need to tell me what happened to him.'

'Everybody knows what happened to Dean Gillespie!' I yelled.

'About your father and Dean!' she screamed back at me. 'Everyone knows the story. I want the truth.'

Nodded my head again and wiped the cloth of my shirt across the back of my hand. Kept doing it while the pulsing in my forehead picked up tempo. Concentrated on the back of my hand. Tried to focus on something. My lungs weren't working. There didn't seem to be any air left in the room.

'Your father was in a hotel in Washington. He went to meet with a man named Jeff Moon.' I looked up at her and shifted my weight. Wasn't going to get up, but Carole didn't know that. She moved back. Let go of her elbows. Reached behind her and fell hard onto the sofa.

'What are you . . .'

'Your father was making plans, Joe!'

'The hell are you talking about, Carole?'

'He was going to leave.' Raised a hand to her mouth. She was shaking. Fingers touching her lip for a second – still playing away at some silent tune. Then she pushed the heel of her palm to her eye. Held it there while her shoulders heaved. She stayed silent. I moved on the sofa and she stood up.

'Where are you getting this, Carole?'

'It's nothing you don't already know.' Her hand fell. Both

hands fell. She kept them at her side. Shoulders hunched. Head falling forward on a weak neck. 'You need to tell me what happened to those boys.'

'I can't do that,' I said.

'You were with him.' She breathed in deep. Shoulders raised back up and her arms had life again. Her eyes weren't looking at me, but she was controlling things. Controlling me. 'You were with Dean Gillespie when he died and I need to hear what happened.'

'It won't make sense to you. You don't know what happened that summer.'

'Then tell me what happened!'

'You think it's that simple?'

'You've never lied to me, Joe.' She pointed a finger at my chest. 'You have never lied to me.'

I shook my head.

'So tell me.' She paused. 'What happened?'

I got off the chair. Walked round the table and stood in front of her. She moved away from me. I moved with her and reached out. Held her shoulders in my hands. Squeezed just enough so she had to look at me. Eyes wet. Mouth closed, but still moving.

'He was a bad kid,' I said. 'Dean Gillespie was a very bad kid. You've got to know that.'

'What happened?'

I held her shoulders. Pulled her to me. Squeezed. She went limp in my hands.

Chapter Nineteen

It was two minutes before the brick came through the front window of my funeral parlour. I was sitting in the back office. Hunkered down in the office chair Carole and Marty had bought me for turning thirty-four. A year on and the thing was pretty well worn. Dust-covered on the high back. Scratches marking the seat where my lazy ass dragged off it a few thousand times. In that chair behind the big oak desk I usually feel like I'm in control of something. Usually it feels good sitting there. But I had a problem. So many problems I was starting to lose count.

I'd been sitting there for two hours. Shuffling papers. Calculating debts. Writing invoices and drinking coffee. Refilling and slow sipping until that coffee turned cold. All the while I was watching the phone. Waiting for Donald to call and tell me he'd busted up the car. Expected Edith Krantz to call and tell me that the house was on fire. Maybe the school to call and tell me Marty had got into a fight with that bully. Had his teeth knocked through and needed me to pick him up. Expected something bad to happen and was certain it would be my fault, no matter what the problem might be.

I needed a phone call or a visit from someone that told me things were back on track. But the chances of that kind of thing happening were a million to one. I'm not much of a gambling man, but I've been around long enough to know my odds weren't good. When you aren't a lucky person, there's no reason to start hoping it's going to change in an instant.

I was wasting time, reading the names from the top of invoices and flicking through them. Looking for something to catch my eye, but not all that interested in searching for anything in particular. I'd look up at the clock and see another five minutes had passed. Maybe ten if I was lucky.

And then the sound came. A good hard crack followed by a weird sort of hollow sound. Next thing was the sound of a hundred buckets of nails being pitched out and scattered on the floor. The sound lasted a long while – felt like minutes more than seconds. I watched the door of my office. Wondering what the hell was happening on the other side.

There was a pause after all the sound. Almost a dead quiet except for the sound of wind rushing in. Cars driving by in the distance. Then Ted hollering, a woman's scream. Sounded like she was in a lot of pain.

I got round the desk and to the door and spun the handle. All the excitement to get out there, I didn't turn it far enough. Cracked the hell out of my shoulder trying to get through it. Turned the handle again and pushed and this time I went tumbling out and kept my balance, had to trot into the show-room just to keep from falling down.

First thing that got me was the traffic on the street. It sounded loud. All the time I'd worked in the parlour, first with Pop and now with Ted, that sound hadn't been there. It was a quiet room. Peaceful. Something to keep desperate people calm. It was chaos with the cars. Engines drumming past. A heavy wind whistling through. More car horns honking. Voices of people yelling from across the road. A crowd had formed. Folks parked at Dairy Queen were pointing at me. They stood like idiots – gawking at my windowless window. Taking it all in. Watching and waiting to see how we were going to react.

They're about to get a show.

233

The parlour was cold. Snow kicked up off the fresh bank of drift that Moses Detroit's plough had left on the sidewalk. It swept up and moved through the gap where the window had been. Scattered across the floor like smoke over water. It came in through the oversized square where I was standing with my hands at my side. The snow danced on the floor along with the shards of a million diamonds. Blew round in big circles that were carried by a wind. The circles bobbed round like they were searching the place. I watched them move. Blowing round and round.

'Joe,' Ted called out. 'Holy Christ, Joe.'

I followed Ted's voice. Sometimes he could sound like a young man. Not lately, but he had it in him. When times got rough he always sounded old. Slow and tired. Glass crunched under my boots while I made it round the display of fake carnations. I came round to find Ted on his knees. He had his handkerchief out and was holding it in two hands. He was using it to fan a woman. Same as they do to boxers in the corner after a heavy round. He was whipping the hanky, and the older woman in front of him had her head back up against one of the casket displays. Mouth open and eyes closed. If it had been the coffin she was buying, I'd have lifted her into it then and there. She didn't look any better than dead.

I couldn't tell who she was. She was whimpering now and again and letting out an odd kind of holler. A call for attention more than pain. Ted stopped waving his hanky at her and leaned down. Hushed her same as you do a baby when it's cried so much it forgets to breathe. After he'd hushed her enough, he lifted back up and started waving the kerchief again.

'The hell's going on?' I asked.

'Some kid just came by and tossed that brick there through the window,' he said. He let go of the handkerchief with one hand. Used it to point out what had knocked the window

234

through. I slid my feet through the shards of glass and came to a red brick that wasn't any more than a couple of feet from the front door. It had a piece of yellowed paper on it, tied with a piece of parcel string. Whoever tied it had done a good job. Spun it round all the sides and finished it off in a double bow. Some people don't even take that kind of time when wrapping a gift. I didn't like the surprise waiting inside. Wasn't all that interested in opening it to find out. I kicked the brick with my boot.

'Think they got the wrong place?' I asked.

'Can't say, Joe. I didn't get a good look at him. Little bastard just dashed up and chucked that thing through the window. Didn't even slow down when he did it. Seemed pretty certain to me.'

'And you didn't see who it was?' I asked.

'I saw him alright, but with his hood up like it was, I couldn't see a face. Small guy,' he said. 'That's the best I can tell you.'

I looked across the street. More people had gathered on the sidewalk. They looked at me and I kind of felt like an ass standing there. Hands in the pockets of my jeans. Feet apart and sucking at my lower lip. Shifted my eyes down to the brick. Couldn't find the motivation to pick it up. Didn't know if I had the energy any more to deal with what was inside that yellow note. Bundled up nice and neat. Special delivery.

All those people across the street were waiting for something. What they were expecting me to do was a complete mystery. Come running out of the shop looking for the kid? How was I going to know who threw the brick? And if I saw the wrong kid walking up the road, I didn't know how I would react. I was tense. Didn't know how objective I could be when deciding on a guilty face. What to do with it when I decided it was part of the problem. I didn't have much faith in personal restraint when I was decided on guilt. At that moment, I was really feeling a good heat building up inside me. A strong rage pulsing. So I was better to leave off standing in the parlour. It had been a bad season for mistakes already.

I stepped out through the new opening that once held the name of my funeral home. And when I stood on the sidewalk I looked across the street at the folks standing next to their cars and trucks. Taking up space in the parking lot. They were all giving me their full attention. I watched them right back. Contemplating the next move and feeling awkward and angry and cold.

'Where you going, Joe?' Ted called out.

The woman on the floor moaned again. She whimpered for a while and I stood there and listened. Seemed like the right thing to do. Like I owed her that much at least. When she finished I looked both ways, up and down Martin's Drive. Listened to Ted try to calm the old woman down by talking a lot of soft words to her. I couldn't catch what he was saying 'cause of the wind. It was whistling past and finding a way to shoot a cold breath right inside my flannel. Making me shake. It was telling me to get back. Go back into the office and quit being a lame dick and call the police. The crowd across the street was getting anxious about something. A few of them were taking steps towards the road. Towards me. This one little fat guy was jumping and waving. Dancing in place and yelling something he thought I'd find real important. With all the wind I couldn't make out what they were saying. And with all of them yelling at the same time, it confused things even more.

So I raised my hand. Waved to let them know things were under control. Then I followed the hand of the little fat guy. He was in a puffed-out jacket that made him look extra round. He was pointing down Martin's Drive and yelling out to me. I followed his hand and saw what all the commotion was about. Saw what had got them so excited.

'Ted?' I called over my shoulder.

'Yeah,' he said.

'What colour was the kid wearing?'

'Something dark. It was a black hood anyway. Maybe a—'

'He have a denim jacket on over the hood?' I asked.

'You see him?' Ted was all excited.

The woman he was looking after moaned again. Louder than before. I turned to find out what was going on. Ted came up to my side and looked out across the road at the people lining the sidewalk. There wasn't any traffic moving up the street between us, but something was stopping them from crossing. They just stood there looking at us. One of the guys was pointing up the street. Ted followed the gesture and he laughed out like he was real pleased at what he was seeing.

'You go see to that woman, Ted. I'll check this kid out.'

Ted muttered something at me. If it was a protest, he didn't have much force behind it. I walked the sidewalk, down Martin's Drive. Took my time making my way up there too. My boots had good grips, but the snow had started to ice over. The cold morning had turned anything slush to uneven ice. Walking on a greased tightrope would take less concentration. But it didn't matter how long it took. From the look of things, the kid wasn't going to be moving away from his resting spot.

Blood was coming from his mouth and nose. It was streaming out of him pretty quick. Flowing faster with every breath he was taking. It collected in a pool under his face. Small clouds of steam puffed out of his mouth. His arms and legs were straight and looked stiff as rods. His hood had only come down partway. I still didn't know the kid. Couldn't make any connections to him. I tried. Something to make it clear why he would feel the need to knock the front of my parlour in with a heavy message. I leaned down and patted the kid's shoulder. Nothing.

'Oh, man,' I heard someone say. 'He really took a shot.'

I turned my head and saw the fat guy who had been standing across the street. He had his hands stuffed deep in the pockets of his black puffed jacket. He was walking towards me with a schoolboy swagger. He stopped when he was standing over me and leaned down to get a better view. There was a skinny woman making her way along the path behind him. She was speaking into a cellphone and judging the ice like she was touching hot coals to bare feet. She got close and kept talking into her phone. I couldn't make out what she was saying 'cause she was using a hand to cover her mouth while she spoke.

'You see what happened?' I asked the guy.

'Oh, man,' he said. 'We was about to go in DQ. And Sally, that's my girlfriend,' he tossed his hand over his shoulder. I looked up and saw the woman who was struggling along the path. 'She needed me to help her out of the car 'cause she's pregnant and can't walk all that good. Especially on this stuff.' He tapped his foot against the path. He must have decided that her chances on the ice had improved 'cause he watched her swing her arms out and back while she was moving towards us. He didn't move to give her a hand. 'So I was helping her out of the car and I heard the glass smash. And that guy was running like a motherfucker.'

'Okay,' I said. 'What happened here?'

'That pole, man. That's what I'm saying.'

I turned and looked up. A few feet up Martin's Drive stood a lamp post. It was just past me and the kid.

'What about it?' I asked.

'That's what happened, man. That guy looked back and when he turned around again he slipped. Not just slipped, but just went. Know what I'm saying? He went and – bam! Next thing is he's clocked his face on that pole.'

'Right.'

I wanted to laugh. I was looking at the lamp post, thinking how ridiculous it was that the kid's luck was worse than mine. I hovered over him and, from the way he was breathing, I could tell he was out. It was cold and the snow flurries were due before long. So I bent down close and patted his shoulder. Leaned down to his face and did my best to revive him.

'Hey, asshole,' I said. 'Wake the fuck up.'

'I wouldn't turn him over,' the skinny woman said. She'd put the phone away, but was still holding a hand over her mouth when she spoke. Figured it was bad breath or crooked teeth. Either way, she didn't want to share. I didn't feel the need to press her.

'He'll be frozen to the ice if I don't move him,' I said.

'Well, he could have a neck injury,' she said. She moved her hand away and made an awkward expression. A kind of smile, only she did it without showing her teeth somehow. Just stretched her lips wide until it looked painful, for her and everyone watching. Maybe it wasn't a smile, but something to question what I thought of her advice.

'He hit it that hard?' I asked. I let out a laugh. The fat guy joined in.

'Knocked his ass cold, man.' The fat guy looked at his girl-friend. He kept laughing and she raised a hand to her mouth and bounced her shoulders. 'Really bashed his face, man.'

Sirens started wailing in the distance. I looked at the kid. Made sure the steam was still coming out of his mouth. Then I looked up at the skinny woman with the bad teeth. Nodded my head and thanked her for calling the paramedics.

'I didn't call for help,' she said to her hand. 'I called my mom to tell her what happened. She says it's crazy.'

'Yeah, man,' her fat boyfriend said. 'It's real crazy.'

'It's just nuts,' I told them.

They talked and laughed and stood close together and looked like they were having the best of times. After watching the kid freeze some more, they'd go over the street and fill their guts with grease and laugh it up about the dipshit vandal. Take some memories away to share with their kid. Poor thing wasn't coming into the world with a lot of hope. One ugly parent and it might have had a chance.

I kept my hand on the kid's shoulder. Half-expecting him to wake up. If he did he'd either try to jump up and leg it or he'd need someone to let him know what had happened to him. I wanted to be there either way. Kneeling down there close to him, after he'd just smashed my window, was like being part of a joke. All of a sudden I was the punch-line.

An ambulance pulled up and skidded to a stop. Didn't even hear it coming along. No sirens wailing. The first paramedic jumped down from the cab. Looked back at the front of my funeral parlour and then turned round. Looked down at the kid. I recognised the paramedic, but couldn't place him with a name. He smiled and shook his head.

'This a crime scene, Mr Pullman?' he asked.

'Kid hit the lamp post,' I said. 'My window's a crime scene. No sense spreading any more rumours.'

'What happened to your shop?' he asked.

'He did,' I said.

Stood and rubbed at my arms. The flannel shirt I was wearing wasn't doing much to keep the cold off. I turned and brushed past the girl as she talked into her hand. Her fat boyfriend hit me on the back and said something I didn't catch. I skidded over the path and stepped through the hole and into my funeral home. Ted had the old woman sitting up. Used his hand to rub her back. She was holding the handkerchief now. Dabbed at her forehead like she was sweating. She kept on whimpering and sounded more pathetic than I could handle.

'How's the kid?' Ted asked.

'Out cold. Paramedics are looking him over.'

'I need help,' the woman said.

'They'll see you next, I'm sure.' Ted rubbed her shoulders.

'I'm a wreck,' she said. 'Such a mess.'

'Should see the kid who did this,' I told her. 'Must've slid four feet. Ended face-flush with a metal pole. He'll be spitting teeth for weeks.'

She whimpered.

I couldn't take the sound. But then I didn't think it was a good idea to turn her screws any tighter. She was a victim as much as me. She wasn't dripping blood and didn't have a dent the shape of a lamp post in the middle of her forehead. But she was hollering up a storm. That kind of thing sings lawsuit. Internal pain. Psychological and skeletal. Just 'cause you can't see it don't mean they can't make you pay.

She kept making her noise, so I occupied myself studying the brick. Looked down at the thing and wondered what the hell I should do next. Waiting for Nat Upshaw to arrive was an option. But he could be off somewhere. Interrupting an ice-fishing trip or digging into breakfast at Darnell's wouldn't make me any friends. Right then I needed all the friends I could get. So I lifted the brick and took it to the back office. Sat down at my desk and twisted the lamp until the brick was lit up nice.

More people speaking close by. People must have stepped into the showroom. Voices coming into the parlour. Paramedics talking to the old lady. The more attention she got, the more noise she was making. Before I had the bow untied and the string sitting loose on the desk she was a wreck. I peeled the paper away from the brick.

It was a hard piece of yellow paper. More like the weight of paper that kids use to cut and paste shapes at school. Had that hairy kind of feel to it. It was a single piece, folded up a few times. I unfolded it half-open so I could see what it said. Read the word that was written in fat letters:

Murderer

It got me breathing heavy for a second. But it's not like I was expecting things to go easy for ever. Things had been getting worse for a while. Not everyone has the ability to think for themselves. Some people take truth in the thoughts of others. And in Henderson, a usually fine and peaceful Maryland town, there seem to be a lot of people taking part in this surrogate thinking process.

I opened the paper wider. Flipped the last fold and inside there was another message. It confirmed that the note and that brick were meant for me. For a long while I sat there looking at the card. Flipped it back and forward. Opened the card and looked at the single word on the front. Flipped it back again so I could read that message underneath:

Was one killing not enough, Mister Pullman?

Sucked in a heavy breath. Sucked so hard and deep my lungs burned. I held it inside and I closed my eyes and tried to keep the rage from flowing. Tried to dilute the anger by holding it in. Ten. Nine. Eight. The old woman was screaming again. Seven. Six. Five . . .

'You little shit!'

I lifted the brick from the desk and threw it. It hit the glass barrel Ted used to hold his spare change. Ten years of pennies and nickels flooded to the floor. Spilling out like water. Copper and silver flashing all over the place. They spread far and wide. Dropped my head into my hands to hold the rage in. To try and contain it. Ted hit the door and rushed in.

'What the hell's going on in here, Joe?'

He looked at the floor. Saw the coins. He followed my hands as I removed them from my mouth and set them down on the desk. Between my fists was the piece of yellow paper. I watched his face as he started to work things out.

'What's that brick have to say?' Ted asked.

I shook my head.

'Something else to do with Carole?' he asked.

I slammed the side of my fist down on top of the paper. Pulled my hand away and the paper rocked back and forward. Ted stepped up to the desk and lifted the paper.

His mouth made the words while he read it in silence. I watched him.

Murderer.

He flipped the card open.

Was one killing not enough, Mister Pullman?

'Can't see that kid doing this on his own,' I said.

'Now, Joe. There's no big conspiracy happening here. That kid's just some dumb punk who had too much time on his hands.'

I tried moving, but the chair got in my way. So I kicked it to the side. It slid back and banged up against the wall. Shook something off the shelves, only I didn't look to see what it was that was falling. Stepped forward and grabbed the paper from Ted's hand. Read it like I expected the words had changed. Altered somehow. The same feeling swelling up in my guts. Burning and powerful. Rage spiralling like the snow coming into the shop for the first time. Searching for something. Only this wasn't going to settle. My rage wasn't going to fall and die and dissolve into nothing.

'Where are you going, Joe?' Ted asked.

I didn't know. But I went.

Chapter Twenty

Ted came up next to me, talking at the side of my face while I made my way towards the front of my funeral parlour. Broken glass diamonds crunching under the soles of my boots. Grinding to smaller crystals with each step. Ted was grabbing for my arm. Really trying to pull me back. The more I pulled away, the more he tried to latch on.

'Joe. You don't want to go out there,' he kept saying. His voice all high and wild. 'Not like this. Calm down. You don't want all that stuff coming back.'

'All of it coming back?' I said. 'Jesus, Ted. It's back. It's been back. I'm sick of this shit.'

I was shaking a fist at him. He looked at my hand and couldn't seem to focus on anything else. I shook it out in front of his face like I was trying to get my fingers unstuck. I kept at it to make sure he knew I couldn't take any more hassle. He looked me in the eye again. His face loose.

'These notes are killing me,' I said.

'Don't do this, Joe. You don't want the trouble.'

I didn't, but I went anyway.

I stepped out into the cold air and started moving up Martin's Drive – right for the kid. Where he'd slapped up against the lamp post and where he'd made a stiff-armed angel in the snow below it. Went straight towards the pole and towards the ambulance. I walked fast and I stared at all the people surrounding the little bastard. He was already loaded up on the gurney and that was fine by me. *You won't even have to bend down to shake the mess out of him! Maybe roll him out in front of a car before anyone could stop you.*

I heard my name being called out and I kept on moving. It came again and something clicked inside my head. A small voice, but one that was loud enough to slow my pace.

'Why don't you stop where you're at and think about what you're doing,' the voice said. 'Then you can come over here and talk to me about it.'

I turned my head. Kept walking, but there was more taken out of my step. I tried to fight it, but I couldn't keep going on with the same gusto – not after the sheriff made his presence known. Nat Upshaw was leaning against the wall of the Spinning Pennies Laundromat. His arms crossed over his chest. A hunting coat replacing his usual star-embroidered leather jacket. Wool round the collar made him look like a cowboy from one of those cigarette advertisements they used to run in magazines.

'You don't need to go down there,' he said. 'The kid's all strapped in and ready for his ride.'

'I need to know who he is.'

'Well, that's not necessarily true.'

He let his arms fall from his chest and he kicked off the wall. He looked down Martin's Drive to see if they'd got the kid in the back of the ambulance yet. It was a Merrimont Ambulance Service vehicle. I couldn't figure out how it had got to the kid so quick. With the roads bad as they were, it usually takes a quarter of an hour before they show. Kid must not have had such an unlucky day after all 'cause they had him bundled and ready to go in half that time.

'You want to know who that kid is,' Nat said. He turned his face back to me again. His thumb and index finger were wiping at the corners of his mouth. 'I can understand that. All the hassle you've been getting. Colin up at the Trapper's and the letter from Carole. This . . . You're doing a fine job keeping that temper under wraps and I applaud you for that, Joe. I really do.' He waited for me to look at him before he finished. 'But you don't need to know anything more than this: the kid's been caught and I'll be dealing with him from here on out.'

I was hot with anger and wanting to let everything out in some kind of eruption. Hands. Word. It didn't matter how I did it, but it needed doing. Nat was keeping me from getting my hands on one of *them*. Finally taking hold of one of the pricks screwing my life.

'I get notes in my house, Nat. I've got more of them. They show up like the damned spooks who are leaving them. Someone's been playing a game and I haven't been able to see who it is until now. I've got a kid over there who's just tossed a brick through my window and it's my turn to make a play. I should get the chance to roll on him.'

'Yep. You're right about the kid. He's got answers to some of your questions, that's for sure. And I will get the answers for you. Until then you need to go back inside and leave the dirty work to me.'

Nat nodded his head. He was looking past me. Must have been even more of a crowd gathering over at the Dairy Queen parking lot. Right then I couldn't give a shit if I had a stadium full of people behind me. I needed things to get back to normal again and I didn't see that happening if Nat Upshaw took care of things.

'You do what you need to do, Nat,' I said.

He pushed his Stetson up on his head. Exposed his silver hair and stood there nodding his head and looking past me. He kept at it until his hat had fallen back into place. Cast a shadow over his eyes and made me wonder what it was he was hiding.

'I'll do what I need to do,' I said.

'You start playing judge and jury and it's liable to get real damned messy.' Nat wasn't looking past me any more. 'Messy for you and everyone else. So I'm asking you to leave this to me.'

'Sure,' I said. I turned to walk back to the funeral home. The wailing woman wasn't wailing so much now. I wasn't planning on staying for long. I'd have to go down to the hardware store to buy some plywood. Saw myself spending just enough of the morning tacking up pieces of wood to keep the snow from filling up the place – then I'd go and see what I could find out about the kid with the dented face.

Nat must have been watching me close. Saw me looking at the gap in the front of my store. He said: 'You need me to have a couple of the boys stay back to help you get this cleaned up, Joe?'

'Nope. I'll fill the gap and Ted'll sweep the glass away.'

I walked to the empty window and looked inside. Lines cut through the debris on the floor where Ted had followed me out. They trailed off where he went back in to check on the woman. I stepped inside and started back towards the office. Glass crunching under the soles of my boots.

'Joe,' Nat said.

'Yeah.'

'Don't get involved in anything else.'

'I've never been involved in this, Nat. I've been targeted by it,' I said. Turned round and felt a flush of rage come up inside. 'I'm affected by it. Tarred and feathered by it. People you're protecting are *involved* in it. Now I'm cleaning up their mess. It's taking up all my damned time. All my damned patience!'

'I'll get to the bottom of this and I'm going to start right now. I'm heading over to see what that boy has to say for himself.' Nat pushed on my shoulder and it was enough to set me off again. Caught the look he was giving me and I was able to hold back. Was able to take that breath that kept me from making a bad decision. 'Other than this incident, I wasn't aware of trouble.'

'I've had people following me. They're calling the house. Leaving notes on my doors. They are getting inside my life, Nat.'

'Well, then we need to discuss that too. But right now I need to deal with this. I need to see what this boy has to say for himself.'

Ted was kneeling beside a paramedic. The woman must have screamed herself into exhaustion. A steamed-up oxygen mask round her red face. Ted was looking at me like he wanted to say something. His eyes real wide.

'Anything I can do for you, Joe?' Nat asked. 'Before I go.'

'I got holes need filling,' I said. Waved Nat off. Swatted a hand in his direction. 'Suppose it's best I do it myself.'

Went back into the office and sat down in the chair.

Chapter Twenty-One

I made a call to Jamison's Hardware and Lumber Yard and had sheets of plywood arriving at the front of the funeral home before I'd taken a sip of my fresh-brewed coffee. It came in the back of a beat-up truck with Nails'n'Stuff painted on the side. Kevin Richards was driving the truck and I paid him cash like I'd agreed over the phone. Kevin put the money in his shirt pocket without counting it. He reached in his cab and pulled out a paper bag full of nails. Handed it to me and reached in his cab again. Came out with a hammer and handed it over. It still had a price tag on the handle.

'Harry said you probably don't have one here at the parlour, so he told me to leave this one with you.' Kevin Richards took off his hat and scratched himself like he was really needing it. 'He's not in a rush to get it back. Just whenever.'

'I appreciate the thought,' I told him. 'Probably a good thing I didn't have one here. I might have used it already.'

He nodded at me and said: 'So it was some kid who did it?'

'Yeah,' I said. 'Smashed this and went running off down there. Ended real quick at that pole. He's probably over in Meridian getting his jaw put together again.'

'Not the one that did this,' he said. 'That kid's over at the medical centre. He's still here in Henderson, from what I heard. I was loading up the truck when Jody Verring stopped by for some attic insulation. You know Jody?' he said. I nodded.

'Yeah, I figured. He's off-duty, but he's always listening into the scanner. Born to be a cop, right?'

'So what's he saying about it?'

'He told Harry that the kid's up there at the medical centre getting checked over. But they don't think he's going to need anything they can't handle here in town. Broken nose and all that. Jaw's may be busted too, if he hit it hard as you say.'

'You heading back into the store?' I asked him.

'Nah, I'm off for the day,' he said. 'Probably just go back to the trailer and watch some television until Jennie gets home.'

'How about knocking these boards up for me? Here,' I said. Handed over some extra cash to him. Gave him all that was left in my pocket 'cause I needed to keep him sweet. Needed him to fix my shop while I fixed something more pressing. Don't know how much it was that I gave him, but he took it quick. Slipped it in his shirt pocket with the other bundle he was supposed to take back to Harry.

'Yeah, sure,' he said. 'You needing to be somewhere?'

'Yeah, bud,' I told him. 'There's someplace I need to be.'

I didn't go back in for my coat. I walked down Martin's Drive. Past the Spinning Pennies Laundromat and past the lamp post that took the kid out. Hung a left down the alley and found my van in the parking space next to the funeral parlour's shutter door. I didn't want to go inside 'cause Ted was still in there. He'd ask questions and want to know where it was I was heading off to.

Got in the van and started it. Didn't give it the usual few minutes to warm up. Had it backed out and ready to drive through the alley when the delivery shutters came up. Ted was standing inside waving at me. Moving his arms all over the place like he was trying to stop an accident. I suppose he was too.

I honked the horn and drove off. I was still upset, but not so much that I couldn't control it. Probably just 'cause I had something to aim at. Someone to focus it all on. When it's not blind rage it's easier to control. Sometimes anyway. All I know is there was a kid sitting in a hospital bed. Before he got himself too comfortable, I wanted to see how much he could tell me about the people behind my broken glass. I wanted him talking before the dope kicked in.

Took the back roads and came round Apple Mount. Took Brestler and then Gamer's Lane to bypass Beaumont and all the lunchtime traffic. Came up to the back of the medical centre and had my hopes of meeting with the kid crushed by three Henderson police cruisers. If that wasn't enough, Nat Upshaw's Bronco was parked in the ambulance bay. Stuck to the sidewalk near the emergency entrance.

I decided I'd take my chances anyhow and meet up with them all. Speak with the cops and see if any of them knew just what the hell was on the kid's mind. What had got him so hot he chucked a brick through my window. So I put the van in a space and started to walk towards the entrance. Pulled on a denim jacket I'd left in the van a few months back. It stank of mould but it was enough to keep the cold winds from blowing right through my skin.

Sal Pulver was heading back to his cruiser, carrying a Styrofoam cup in one hand and a plastic-wrapped sandwich in the other. He took his steps in a bouncing sort of way and stopped to put his cup on the roof of his car. He went for his pocket with his free hand, got the door open and looked up in time to see me passing.

'Oh, hey there, Mister Pullman,' he said.

'How you doing, Sal?'

'Fine, sir. I'm fine, I guess.' He turned his head like he was looking for something or someone. Where we were, we couldn't see anything more than the dark windows of patient rooms. 'Man, I'd be better if it wasn't for all this.'

'There been some trouble?' I asked. Felt stupid for saying it. But the fat cop didn't make out like he found it all that strange.

'Looks like it,' he said.

'That kid they brought in, you mean?'

'Huh?' he said. 'No. Colin Lowell getting shot.'

'When did that happen?'

'About half-hour ago. Seems he got into it with someone behind the market. No witnesses yet. I'm heading back over there now to ask around and see if anybody saw anything. We all figure he's mouthed off to the wrong person. Said the wrong thing one too many times and they decided to send him away on a permanent vacation.'

'Where?'

'They got him once in the shoulder and then again in the stomach,' he said. He used his hands to give me a better idea of the exact location.

'Okay, but where did it happen?'

'Like I said, right there behind the market,' he said. 'We don't know how long he'd been there, but he bled a lot. We got a call after a delivery driver spotted Colin lying across some crates. Driver thought he was drunk, so he told Bernie Stewart who called it in to us. We showed up and . . .' He motioned with his hand towards the hospital, same way the models show off a prize refrigerator on a game show. 'Nat's not happy about it 'cause no one in the market heard a thing.'

'Colin in there now?' I asked.

'They're going to transfer him to Union Memorial when they get him stable.'

Sal Pulver moved round like he was hopped up on something.

'Well, it'll set some new rumours in motion,' I said.

He looked at me like he didn't understand. Then he said: 'Well, we hope not. Colin came to long enough to ramble about a few things. Gives us something to go on.'

'What did he say?' I asked.

He shook his head and looked off into the distance, hoping to find a hole to escape through.

'Oh, I can't tell you anything like that. We're still working on the case.'

'Any idea what kicked it all off?' I asked. Starting to feel a new wave of problems about to come crashing down on me. I didn't like my chances in this one. 'Well, I hope you find the guy who did it.'

'You okay?' Sal asked.

'Yeah,' I said. Swallowed hard and wiped sweat away from my brow. 'I'm just feeling the start of something.'

'Well, you take some vitamins and get some rest. This winter's only just started.' He went like he was going to get into his cruiser. Then he popped his head out again. 'You find out anything else about your wife?'

'Not yet. I'm still looking.'

Sal grabbed his Styrofoam cup from the top of his car and made a lot of noise when he went to sit behind the wheel. I walked away and headed for the entrance of the medical centre. I wanted to see the kid, but now I had to check on Colin Lowell. Hadn't spoken to the guy since I'd knocked his nose out of shape, and I kind of figured it was best to keep up appearances. I didn't want anyone thinking I'd put a slug in him on my way to the funeral home that morning. I didn't know the timeline, but I knew that a dead man wouldn't be able to convince anyone that I hadn't fired the shots.

Just hope he's awake, Joe. And hope he doesn't freak out when he sees you for what you did the last time you met. That could give the wrong impression.

I walked past two more patrol cars and looked in the back seats. Had a real weird feeling that I was meant to be inside one of them. Not sitting and talking and smoking a cigarette, like some of the patrolmen did with local folks. But sitting in there all anxious and bound up.

I saw Pop standing with Nat Upshaw. The two were leaning against the front of Nat's Bronco, looking at the building and taking shelter from the winds. Looked like a good trap to catch me before I got into the hospital. Pop was waving his hand at one of the nurses who was outside having a smoke. She waved back to him and pulled open her heavy coat to show her scrubs. Did it in a flasher sort of way. She laughed and so did Pop. Nat turned to get a look at her too. While they shouted their conversation I slipped across the other end of the parking lot and headed for the mortuary.

I went in through the back door and the kid at the desk looked up at me. I dropped my head down and walked past him. He didn't try to make conversation and I moved faster while I had the chance. The mortuary leads to a service elevator that could be seen from the main entrance. I figured Nat would be keeping an eye on the lobby from where he'd parked, so I took the stairs. Scaled them two at a time and made the first floor breathing hard. Turned the corner and pushed through double doors leading to the ER and did a half-walk, half-jog down the hall.

A group of people in yellow jumpsuits were wheeling a gurney towards me. Looked first at the medical staff and then at their patient. It was Colin Lowell and he wasn't looking all that good. Face white against his dark stubble. I stepped back and let them past. Colin had his eyes closed and that was fine by me. At least that way he couldn't make a reaction towards me that started more rumours.

With the hall cleared, I went through the door and entered into a large room filled with blue curtains. Nurses were walking round carrying clipboards and cardboard bedpans. Took a couple steps towards the first curtain. A young nurse with dark hair grabbed for my arm.

'Excuse me, sir. Can I ask what you're doing?'

'Yeah, I'm looking for a kid that was brought in earlier,' I said. Made a motion with my hand. Circled it in front of my nose. 'He's got a mashed-up face. Took a pretty nasty spill.'

'Are you friend or family?'

'Friend,' I said, but the look on her face told me she wasn't convinced.

'Have a seat in the waiting room and I'll have someone come out to see you.'

'Sure.'

She walked away and I went towards the blue curtains. Behind the open curtains were empty beds. People moved behind the closed curtains, so I went close to each one and listened in. From that I could tell what was happening back there.

Behind Curtain Number One: 'Just hold on,' this guy was saying. 'Doctor says you'll be fine. Just keep breathing. Relax now. That's my girl.'

Curtain Number Two: 'It's that medicine. I told you that medicine would be the death of you, Harry.'

Came to a curtain that didn't have people talking. What it had was a weird kind of bubbling sound. Air getting pushed through something soft and wet. Something that wasn't working like it should. I pulled the curtain back. There was a stiff figure. Pillow-propped and high-up on the bed with his eyes swollen shut. White wrap all round his head, like he'd just come out of a desert somewhere. I went through the curtains and closed them behind me. Got to the side of the bed before the kid cracked a slit in his swollen eyes. He took a look at me and made like he'd seen the Grim Reaper.

Dropped a hand onto his chest. Really brought it down hard on him and he made another kind of sound with his breathing. This time it had pain in it. Some kind of sucking sound followed. Pushed hard and made sure he knew he wasn't going anywhere. There wasn't much left in me to ask him nice. He was looking at me and moving his mouth in a real odd way.

'Busted your jaw, bud?' I whispered. 'That why you can't open up?'

He kept moving his mouth and it was making me sick in

my gut. Each time his jaw went, more blood leaked from his nose. It was old blood. Black and clotted and mixed with a yellow worm of mucus.

'Don't talk too loud,' I told him. 'Get too much attention and I'll fix your jaw for you. I'll put it straight again. All it needs is a good crack on the other side.'

He leaned his head back against the pillow. His eyes went glossy and water lines started to appear at the sides of his face. Lines that ran from his eyes down to his peach-fuzz sideburns. He was soft and I figured that was going to be the case. Trouble was I needed him to talk fast. I didn't have the time to go easy on him. I pushed on his chest again and listened to him wheeze. Leaned down to his face and spoke into his ear.

'Who told you to throw the brick through my window?' I asked.

He shook his head.

'That's not doing much for me. Tell me who gave you that note. That busted jaw's not enough of an excuse to keep from talking.'

'A woman,' he said. Came out all screwy, but it was clear enough for me to understand.

'A woman?' I asked. He nodded. 'What did she look like?'

He said something else, but I couldn't make it out. Sounded like he was saying something about a knife. He was crying some more. Poor fool was crying up a damned river and wasn't even making a sound. It was all coming out of him. Out of his eyes. Fresh flow of something nasty was slipping out of his nose too. Mouth was all slanted and open, but there wasn't a damned thing coming out of him. I let my hand up so he could take a breath. It wasn't making me feel any more sorry for him. Pitied him for his pain. But that wasn't enough to keep me from getting what I needed.

Stayed there close to him and tried to work it out. What it was he kept saying. Over and over. He finished sucking in his breath and started saying it again. All quiet. So no one was going to come in and stop him from telling me. So I wasn't going to get angry with him and drop another heavy hand down on his chest.

I gave the kid a few seconds. Leaned down to him, trying to pick up on just what it was he was telling me. Each time he spoke I'd look down at him and shake my head. He'd close his eyes. More water would run down the lines at the sides of his head. He'd take a quiet breath and say it again.

'You're wasting my time, kid. I've got about—'

Holy shit, Joe! You catch that? Did you hear him? What the hell is this kid talking about?

Leaned down and put my mouth to his ear. Watched his eyes when I spoke.

'You trying to tell me my wife gave you the brick to throw through the window of my funeral parlour?' I asked. His head nodded. His eyes didn't open. 'You heard any rumours going round about my wife?' He nodded again.

Still, I couldn't accept that the kid was telling me the truth. He was laid out and looking a real mess, so I couldn't figure why he would be making something like that up. I stood straight and watched the kid do his best to move away from me. Kind of crab-crawling over to the other side of the narrow mattress. I went for my back pocket and he watched my hand all the way. When I brought it back he relaxed.

'Nothing but a wallet, kid.'

I opened it and took out a picture of me, Carole and Marty. Marty was just a small fry, but Carole looked the same as the day I saw her last. Held out the picture to the kid. Before I could say anything he was nodding his head. Kept saying 'her' the best his jaw would let him.

Was putting the photograph back in my wallet when the curtain came sliding back. Turned to see Nat Upshaw standing with his angry face shaking red. Before he could start talking, I raised my hand at him and talked him down from the balling he was planning to deliver.

'I didn't come here to do the kid any harm, Nat,' I said. Sheriff Upshaw stepped towards me and made his hand like he was going to grab hold of me. I shook my head at him and his hands hovered where they were. 'I asked him what I needed to know and he gave it to me.'

Some kind of noise came from behind me. It was the kid trying to talk. Maybe he was just nodding his head. But the sound he made wasn't pleasant.

'Get outside, Joe.'

'I'll do that, Sheriff. But first I want you to hear who gave him the brick,' I said. 'Go on, kid, tell the sheriff here who it was that had you smash through my window.'

'This is not the time or the place.'

'The hell it's not!' I slapped a hand down on the side of the bed. Grabbed hold of the metal rail. 'This is the only place. Ask him, Nat. Ask him who gave him the brick he chucked through my window.'

Nat shifted his eyes to the kid. We listened while he choked on his fluids for a while. Then we watched him vomit a mix of blood and mucus over his bed sheets. When he was done I asked him again.

'Was it the woman in this picture who gave you the brick? Is she the one who told you to throw that brick through my window?'

'Joe,' Nat said, pushing me back.

'Look at him, Nat. Look!'

The kid was nodding his head. He kept nodding until his body lurched and another gush came rolling from his mouth.

Chapter Twenty-Two

Pop didn't knock.

He walked in and took off his coat. Shook it over the rug and tossed it at the wall. Somehow it stuck on one of the pegs and stayed up. With all the weight of the double lining and the snow-soaked shoulders, it still found enough peg to stay up. He walked into the family room and clapped his hands and rubbed them while looking at Marty.

'So, my man, you ready for a day of fishin'?'

'It's kind of cold, Pop. Maybe we could shoot some pool. Maybe bowl a few frames.'

Pop shook his head. Stopped after a couple of seconds and frowned. Looked at me and raised an eyebrow.

'Seems your son's got a problem with the winter months.' He looked back at Marty and said: 'Bit of a chill in the air. Mix in a bit of snow and you've got a hard chill. Still, it's nothing but a chill.'

'Effects us all in different ways, Pop,' I said.

'He's got your blood. Thin as a Bahama Blonde,' he said. I laughed. Pop joined in. Marty tried to hold on, but ended up letting it out just the same. He kept his head down so we wouldn't see his face. His shoulders bounced and his laugh escaped him in the end. Pop looked at him and decided to clarify. 'That's a beer, son. I'm not talking ladies.'

'It's cool, Pop,' Marty said.

'Why don't you go and get your stuff. Pack clothes for fishing, and dress for pool. We'll decide what's what later. Half the fun of a day like this is not knowing. Now, collect your duds and we'll roll.'

Marty left. Pop came over and dropped onto the sofa. Leaned back and clasped his hands together. Bounced them between his legs. He was watching me. Nothing more difficult than reading a newspaper with eyes on you. Pop knew he was making it difficult. Being a stubborn old asshole, he was doing it for a reason – and not just because of the circumstances. I tried to concentrate on the words. Hoping like hell he'd leave and forget about me. But that's just not Pop's style. All through my teens Pop had something he wanted to say. Add a piece of his wisdom to flesh out whatever I was experiencing. Edgerton Meaks' world of life's knowledge. Drugs. Crime. Girls. Sex. He'd wait like a leopard and, when the magazine or newspaper fell, he'd pounce.

'What's on your mind, Pop?' I didn't look up.

'What were you playing at with the hospital fiasco?'

'Just happened in on the kid when I was looking for accounting.'

'Bullshit,' he said.

'It's like a maze in there. Honest mistake.'

'You're not making things any easier on yourself. Nat's all fired up.' Pop's hands came up like he was ready to catch something falling. He shook them at me. I lowered the newspaper and looked at him. 'If that kid says you assaulted him, there can be trouble. He can press charges.'

'I didn't touch him.'

'Well, he can still say you did. There wasn't anyone around to say otherwise. Damn it, son, that was a stupid thing to do.'

'Well, it's over now.'

'You hope like hell it's over.'

I folded the paper and leaned forward. Set it down on the coffee table.

'I had a visitor this morning,' he said. 'Not all that welcome. I hate folks dropping in all unexpected.'

'Who was it?' I asked.

'No need to get snappy, Joe. I'm just letting you know it all happened kind of crazy. I was off-guard and didn't have my head on straight.'

'I'm feeling even less like I want to hear this.'

'Well, you were involved. That's for damned sure.'

'Upshaw?' I asked.

'Paul Quincy. He had someone else in the car with him. Couldn't make out who it was, couldn't see through the windows. Paul was right up close. Tried to edge in to make himself more of a man than he is.'

'What was he after?'

'Keys.' Kept rubbing my hands together. Pop was nodding his head. Felt my expression matched his feelings. 'Came by to get keys to the funeral home.'

'The hell he want the keys for?'

'Thinks he'll find something that will confirm his fears about Carole. Kept shouting at me about the keys. Give me the keys, Edge. Give me my daughter back. Had this stare, like he was planning to go through me. No matter what I did, he had intentions.'

'This is getting out of control, Pop. The hell does Paul think happened at the funeral home?'

'Like I said, son, that man is dumb with grief. Sounded like he was on something, but I couldn't smell a thing on his breath. Jabbering away about all kinds of things. Making no sense. Waving his hands all round the place.'

Marty came back into the room. We went quiet. Marty had a bag over his shoulder. Looked stuffed with enough equipment to do him for a week in the wilderness.

'You okay to go out, Pop?' he asked.

'Damned right, boy. Got your goods?' Pop called out. He stood up and nodded his head at me. 'We're off.'

I walked them to the front door. Pop stayed behind and we watched Marty struggle to get into the cab of Pop's truck without taking the bag off his shoulder. He sat in the seat and swung the bag round. Set it on his lap. Wrapped both his arms round it.

'You watch your back tonight, Joe.'

'That old sonofabitch can't hurt me, Pop.'

'He's gaining the interest of other people. He's got a lot of stories and he's quick to spread them around. Influences the right people and it may not be Paul Quincy you need to look out for.'

'I'll be fine, Pop. You get out of here.'

After Pop left with Marty I sat down on the sofa and closed my eyes. There was work I could be doing. I should have been going through the invoices down at the funeral home. Maybe checking with Mel Trainer to see if the ground was thawed enough for him to dig the Osmonds' graves by hand. Not that I felt like I had the energy, but I was almost interested in offering to help him throw soil, just to have something to do. Something to take the energy out of me.

I leaned my head back against the cushions and closed my eyes. Tried to get Carole's face to float into view, but it wasn't happening. Gave it a while, but I knew she was going to stay away. Let the weight of my head sink further into the cushions. Before long I was off into a deep sleep.

Somewhere in a dream I can't remember there was a knock coming from my front door. I turned my head and looked and the door was far away. I couldn't tell if I was still in the dream or if I was coming out of it. Must have sat there for a long while just watching the door and waiting for the sound of the knocking to happen again. I watched the door handle – half-expecting it to turn. And when it did I couldn't move.

She's come back, Joe.

'Joe,' Ted called through the opening. 'You in there?'

'Yeah,' I said. 'On the sofa.'

Ted pushed his face in through the gap and looked round. He nodded his head at me, narrowing his eyes.

'You waiting on somebody?' he asked.

'Carole,' I said.

He stepped into the house and stomped his feet on the mat. He took the time to scrape the snow off his boots. Really looked like he was digging the soles in. Doing it in a bull-mad kind of way.

'You been in here all day?' he asked.

'Time is it?'

'Past the dinner rush anyway,' he said.

'Then, yeah. I've been here all day.'

'Let's get you out of here,' he said. 'This kind of thing's not doing you a bit of good, Joe. I'm worried for you. About you. Whatever. It's just not right.'

'I feel fine.' I looked round the place. Empty and quiet. 'Seems right to me.'

'Get your shoes.'

'Why?' I asked.

''Cause I'm gonna get you drunk. Then I'm going to kick your ass.'

So I pulled on my boots and shoved my arms into a coat. It all felt pointless. It felt like I was spending energy for no good reason and it was getting me worked up. Still, I pulled on a coat and locked the door behind me. Got in Ted's truck. He did all the talking and I just watched out the window. We passed the funeral home on the way 'cause Ted wanted to make sure he'd shut the lights off. Then we passed the hardware store to see if Archie had got the new shipment of snow shovels yet. Ted saw them displayed in the front window. You would have thought a red plastic snow shovel could cure Judy's cancer, from the way Ted hollered out.

'That's just about the saddest thing I've ever heard,' I said.

'Well, you're not a bundle of joy anyhow.'

He went quiet for a while. I felt like I should say some-

263

thing, but when Ted sulks it's easier to let him get it out of his system. It never takes long.

An hour later I was hanging over a pool table in Spade's. Started to feel better for draining a couple of beers. I was shooting half-decent pool and was finding something to laugh at now and again. It was all shaping out. Ted came out of his funk with a new energy. He stood with a limp cigarette in the corner of his mouth and held the cue with both hands in front of his chest. He looked like a caricature of a medieval knight. One who had passed through time and taken up heavy drinking – and grown fat in the jowls. I leaned over the table looking for another shot. He shook his head, laughing his noiseless laugh. A motion in his shoulders to let folks know he was amused.

'You didn't leave me much' I said.

'That's a fact.' He smiled. The limp cigarette almost came free from his mouth. He corralled it in with his upper lip, and took a hand off his cue. He held the cigarette between two fingers. 'Pick a shot. We're paying by the hour.'

'I'll get it,' I said. 'Just give me a second to look it all over.'

'Just finish it off, kid. I don't need another shot.'

I nodded and looked at what was left on the table. He'd put all his colours down. He was high-ball. There was something about Ted when he played the high-balls. Almost never lost those frames. Whatever it was, he came through in a big way. I took aim on the red. Looked down my cue and was ready to shoot when Ted caught me off-guard. I thought he was joking. Ribbing me in his usual bad-sportsmanship way. He was calling for my attention in a hushed-up voice. Same as he did when a good-looking woman came round and he didn't feel like he could tell me about her in a normal voice. I wasn't paying attention – hoping he'd quit it after a while. He elbowed me again. So I got with the joke and laughed to give him some satisfaction and to get him to quit nudging. Came up off my shot and looked at him. Only he wasn't looking at me. His eyes were on the door. So I followed them and still didn't get what he was on about.

'Sonofabitch,' he said.

Eugene Duffy was walking towards us, navigating his way through the tables. Waiting when he needed and giving people time to play their shots. Pool-hall etiquette. Something you get taught in Spade's with a slap to the head or a shove to the chest. It gets worse from there, depending on how long it takes you to learn. Eugene knew all about waiting on shots. As the local alcoholic, he'd been taught the lesson more than a few times. He'd eyed Ted on his way in, but he was looking at me while he waded his way towards us. Coming on slow with an anxious look about him.

He made it to the table. I held my cue same as Ted. Two hands, with the butt of the thing centred between my legs. I felt in control. It was my table to play. I'd stopped my round and so it was my place and my time. Eugene wanted me for something – that much was obvious. He looked almost sober, which made me remember him the day he came into the funeral home to request that I bury his sister. It was the only other time I'd ever seen him unaffected by alcohol.

He came closer. I stood with my pool cue in hand and gave him my attention. Something to tell him he was alright by me. Even though I knew he'd been dipping into the register behind his wife's back. The till at Darnell's was coming up short every night and Sheila was sure upset by that. But she was a bright one. Only thing she ever did that clipped her wings was marrying good old Eugene Duffy. A handsome man in his day – but the drink had made his insides go hard and the cigarettes had turned his skin to stone.

'Hey, Joe.' He showed me teeth that had turned a thick yellow. They were layered with something that would take more than a brush and paste to remove. 'I need you a minute. It's real urgent.'

'I'm listening, bud.'

'Well . . .' Eugene looked at Ted and he lost the easy expression he'd had. Nodded his head and then he turned back to me. 'I got something to say that maybe you want to hear on your own.'

'I think I can hear it just fine. Right here with the music on. With Ted listening in just the same as me.' I looked over at Ted, trying to convince myself that it wasn't anything to be worried about. Didn't take much. The alcohol had given me a good buzz. *He's just a drunk, Joe. Let him speak his piece and move on down the road.* Eugene Duffy's a waste of space, but I kind of felt bad for him. He'd taken the time to come down. Had stayed off the drink for it too. At least I figured he had, with the way he'd made it through the tables without getting smacked around.

'He's like family, you know,' I said. 'Ted here's the man I've known second longest in all my life. If I can't trust him, there's no one I can trust.'

'Well, that's about right,' Eugene said. He looked down at the table. Nodded his head and brought his face up kind of fast. Made me think something was about to be declared about my situation. Damned if he delivered too.

He shifted his eyes from Ted and met me. Square-on. Wanted to see that I took him as sincere. That I saw him as honest. Then he said: 'I saw her today.'

'Who'd you see?'

Eugene closed his lips. His Adam's apple looked like a tennis ball in the centre of his thin neck. He swallowed hard. The ball bounced up and held for a second. Then it fell down. Dropped what seemed like a hundred feet. It wobbled when he cleared his throat.

'I seen her down near the market,' he said.

'Got yourself a love interest?' Ted asked.

Ted laughed and I tried to join in. Eugene kept his hands on the table and shook his head. Looked like he didn't want to be round any more. Could see he was thinking about leaving.

And that was fine by me. I could get back to my game. Back to my beer. Forget all the shit that was happening in town. But when I looked at Eugene and he caught my eye, I didn't feel all that anxious for him to go. There was more he needed to say and more I needed to hear. The way his mouth moved real slow, like he was whispering, made it that much more urgent.

'Eugene's a real lady's man,' Ted called out. Then he leaned his head back and laughed some more. Still no sound. Not enough to make it over the music. His shoulders bounced. And when he levelled his face off to me, I was laughing with him. Only for show. Then I made my face like I remembered something.

I turned back to Eugene. His eyes hadn't left me.

'Why don't I take you outside and get you a ride home?' I said. Eugene nodded his head at me, but his mouth was slack. Didn't seem all that certain about what I was planning to do to him once we got outside.

'Don't think you'd be right to walk all the way home in this kind of weather, Eugene.' I set my cue against the table and pushed off. 'Man, Sheila would be one upset lady if she knew you were walking from here to home.'

'Oh,' Eugene said. 'She really wouldn't like that, I guess.'

'I tell you what,' I said. Looked over at Ted and pointed towards the front door. 'I'm gonna take Casanova here outside. You get yourself to the little boys' room. The amount of beer you're drinking . . .'

'I could drain it,' Ted laughed. This time I heard it. 'I'll do my duty and you get yourself back in. This is the longest damned shot.'

'You'll be damned impressed with what I've got in the making,' I said.

I moved round the table and took Eugene's shoulder. Spun him round and pushed him towards the door. Pool ethics were out the window. Eugene bumped into a young fella who was going for black. The guy came up and put his arms out to his sides. Looked like the angriest Christ you had ever seen.

'Fuck's your problem?' Christ asked.

'Cool it, bud,' I said. 'He's had too much already. I'm getting him out before he ruins somebody's evening.'

'Ruin his fucking night,' he said and dropped his hands.

I never stopped moving. Eugene hit the door and I pushed his back. He staggered out, kicking up snow along the way. He righted himself and turned round. Wiped a hand over his face. Pulled a knitted cap from his back pocket and slipped it on his head. He patted it down like he was trying to mould a piece of clay.

'You don't have to be angry with me, Joe,' he said.

'I'm not angry with you. It's just I don't really understand what you're on about. That's all. You saw someone.'

'I did, Joe.' He was walking again. This time he was heading away from me like he was ready to give it up. I wasn't in a mood to stop him either, but I wasn't ready to go back inside. I watched his back and heard the door swing open behind me. Commotion of pool balls banging together and music rushed out. Felt someone hit my arm and looked to the side to see some guy staggering out past me. He moved down the path and got tangled up in his own feet. He fell fast, wrecked his leg on the ground. I watched him roll off the path and into the snow. A woman came out of Spade's and moved up against my shoulder. She leaned into me and laughed like there was no tomorrow.

'You alright there, bud?' I asked.

I don't know what the guy said. It was something mumbled up and mixed with profanity. He got off the snow and tried dusting himself with wild hands. A brown slush covered his left side. He swiped and swiped and somehow missed the whole damned thing. The more he swung at himself, the more he went off-balance. I let go of his woman. She swayed and went forward down the path and managed to hook her arm through his.

'There, now. You're all good to go.'

Guy nodded his head. Then he leaned into his girl and they made off for a blue pickup. I let them get into the cab before lowering my hand. Chances were good I'd be seeing them again real soon. Stiff and cold, most likely.

Eugene watched the couple while he made his way back to me. Must have felt safer seeing me being helpful to the woman.

'That guy shouldn't be driving,' he said. 'He'll end up same as me when they catch him. Having to walk every place he's got to be.'

'You were about to tell me something important,' I said.

'Yeah, I was . . .' He turned his eyes to me. 'I saw her this morning. Down by the market.'

'Who did you see, Eugene?'

'Carole,' he said. Then he made his face like I should have known. Like he'd asked the simplest damned question and I'd drawn a blank. And he held that expression for a long time. All the while I stood watching his face. Waiting for anything in his expression to change. Something to tell me he was yanking my crank.

'Okay,' I said. 'You saw my wife.'

'That's right,' he said. 'Me and Sheila was down at the market. She went in to pay Darnell's vegetable invoice. We had plans to go into Baltimore and buy her some new clothes. I'd been in the car for a while waiting for Sheila. When it got too long a wait, I got out and went to find her. She loses time in all that yapping. So I was walking towards the first stall and I heard someone yelling. Kind of got my attention. It wasn't an angry kind of yell, but it was loud, so I looked over. That's when I saw Carole. She was right there crossing the street and heading out towards Cedar Road.'

Felt an urge to grab hold of his shoulders and sling him

around. Sling him until he told me why he'd taken so long to find me and tell me about it. Tried to keep myself on track. Tried to give myself the feeling that it wasn't a big deal. I said: 'All of the people in this town and it's just you who saw her.'

Don't forget the kid with the flat face, Joe. Sure, we're not spreading that one around, but there's more than this drunk who's spotting your missus.

'I'm telling you I saw her. She was right there, no more than fifty feet away, crossing the road. I know Carole. Known her a good long time, Joe. It was her. I swear on a stack of danged bibles.'

'Henderson's not some big place, Eugene. If I wanted to get lost – to stay lost – I'd sure as hell get out of town. And you're telling me that Carole's still here, and no one has seen her but you?'

'I can't explain it, Joe.'

'Sure you can't,' I said. 'Why the hell would you need to explain it? I'm trying to get things straightened out since she took a hike. I'm trying to make sure people know I didn't do anything to her. And now you're telling me she's running round town. She's crossing streets in broad daylight, and no one sees her do it. I'm not a bad man. You see, I'm needing a witness to prove she's not missing. That's what I need to get all these other assholes off my back. So they can be sure that I didn't do anything to her. Now I have that witness.' In mock excitement, I reached for him and grabbed his shoulders. 'I have a witness!' I yelled. 'Just happens to be the town drunk. No one's going to believe you, Eugene. No one!'

Eugene threw his hands up. A child fearing the falling hands of an angry father.

'Then ask Herman Dorlund,' he shouted. 'He was yelling out to her. Standing up there on the balcony of his place. Standing up there calling out to her to come back to him or she would be sorry.'

'Dorlund?'

I pushed on Eugene's shoulders. They felt fragile. Felt small and brittle. He was breakable. I didn't want him to be a victim. I wanted him to get away from me.

Herman Dorlund has been listening to Nancy's stories about the boy in the bog. He's heard a lot about a lot of bad things. No telling what else Nancy's been spouting about you. A bunch of damned crazies with a pile of damaging information. You need to sort that out.

'Ask him, Joe. Go ask Herman what he was doing with Carole. Hell, I know I've got problems, and that's causing you more trouble. You can't believe the drunk, right? Even if you want to. You don't know what to believe and what to toss aside, but if you can speak with Herman and get him to tell you . . .' Eugene put his hand up to his face. Held it there, then dropped it and shook his head. 'It's a danged shame, Joe.'

'You're not fucking kidding.'

I turned to go back into the pool hall. Was needing to leave Eugene behind. What were the odds that a drunk would spot my wife? And spot her with Nancy Lowell's goddamned psychic friend? I was feeling the need to pay Herman Dorlund a visit and kick my boot right through him. Goddamned psychic, my ass! He won't see this one coming . . .

It's not smelling too sweet, Joe. All the hours between seeing Carole and finding you . . . Where's Eugene been? Why didn't he just show up at the house? What about the funeral parlour? And Paul finding you at Solomon's. How'd he know you were going to be way out here at Spade's? It's a long walk, Joe. Think about that.

'How'd you know I was going to be here?'

'Sheila called me. Said Ted had stopped by the diner. Told her he was taking you out to blow off some steam. She said I better come up when I had the chance. Be a man, she told me. Do it so you would believe me.' He touched a hand to a bulge in his jacket pocket. A bulge shaped like a short bottle of spirits. 'Her way of telling me to keep off the faithful.'

'This is shit.' He nodded at my sentiment. 'I'm not about

to believe Carole's still here. I'm not giving in to this one.'
He just stared at me with eyes that told me he didn't have a
game to play. He was upright and truthful and it just happened
that his story was incredible.

'What was she wearing?'

'A red knitted hat and jeans. She had her jeans tucked into
riding boots.' He must have seen something in my face. He
looked down at the snow. 'Well,' he said, 'they looked like
riding boots anyway.'

'You always so sure about clothes, Eugene? Always able to
remember things so well? Such detail?'

'No,' he said. 'But I knew I needed to remember that. Had
a feeling it would come in handy, in case anyone wanted to
confirm it was her. Took a real hard look and remembered
what she had on, so I could tell you what I saw. Tell anyone
who asked me.'

'Go home, Eugene.'

'Look, Joe. I'm real sorry for any pain it brings you.'

'What the hell did you think it would bring me?'

'Relief,' he said. 'Just some kind of relief. Peace even.'

'Well, I don't feel much of that.'

Eugene kept talking as I walked away from him. I went
back into Spade's. Took my time getting between the tables.
Angry Christ was leaning over, taking another shot. I decided
at the last second to stop and let him finish the shot. I was in
the mood for a fight and he looked willing. Only thing that
stopped me was having to explain it to Marty later. That and
I was saving myself for another of Henderson's finest. I got
back to the table and found Ted leaning against the side with
his arms crossed.

'You been gone a while,' he said. I nodded. 'You wait for
the cab to arrive?'

'No,' I said. 'Just gave him a minute to talk at me. Then I
left the poor fool out there in the cold.'

'You think he saw her?' Ted asked.

'Who's that?'

There was a pause. A long moment while I listened to the music and hoped Ted would disappear. Dissolve in some mist and fog sort of way. I lifted the cue and leaned over the table. Looked at the red. Thought it was strange how a pool table can stay the same for years if there is no one around to disturb it. But, we pick up sticks and change it all with one big push.

'Carole,' he said.

'What about her?' I asked.

'Where'd he see her?'

'Near the market,' I said, ready to shoot.

'Judy saw her down by Potter's Field.'

I shot. Missed the mark. Watched the cue ball hit three sides and come to a stop without hitting a single colour.

'When was this?' I asked.

'Few days back. I didn't say anything at the time. Thought she was just getting mixed up. Meds she's on can cause that sort of thing. Hallucinations. Voices. Always had it, but it's getting worse. She's for ever telling me she saw someone when it wasn't them at all. Has a problem with faces.'

'She'd know Carole,' I said.

'Yeah, but it didn't seem right.'

'Nothing seems right, Ted. It's all fucked up.'

Ted stood straight and took his cue from where he'd leaned it against the table. He took the shot without looking. He wasn't interested in playing any more, but shooting the ball kept him from speaking with me. Gave him a moment away from my eyes. I took my cue and leaned over the table. Didn't want to think about Carole walking round town. What made it worse was that other people were seeing her. Everybody except for me. For some reason it was easier to think she'd gone off for good.

She's not missing if you know she's gone, Mister Pullman.

'If she's in town, where the hell's she been staying?'

I took the shot. Two of my balls went down. Dropped in

273

the pockets without touching the knuckles. Watched it happen and didn't have the usual good feeling that was supposed to follow. I stood up and looked at Ted. His eyes went back to the table. They stayed with the balls that were waiting to be knocked down.

'Judy didn't see her going in any place?'

'She saw her in Potter's Field and that was it.'

'And you didn't tell me.'

'She's a sick woman, Joe. She sees things all the time. I don't know what is real. She doesn't know.'

'Well, I know that I need more beer,' I said.

He moved for the bar and I stayed put.

The music was louder. It kept getting louder through the night. Ted kept the drinks coming and I kept making them disappear. It was an assembly line that was going to produce the biggest hangover. We didn't talk unless it was to remind ourselves whose shot was next. What balls we were shooting. I kept my mind on one thing and tried to decide how to do it without hurting anyone. I wasn't good at figuring those things out.

Spade's was slowing down and so was I. The room felt like it was tilting and I tried stretching my back to even out the lay of the land. My muscles burned and when I stopped stretching I looked at the front door. I'd been watching it all night. Expected Eugene Duffy to come walking in again. Asking me to sport him money for that cab ride. But it wasn't Eugene I saw in the doorway. Wasn't Herman Dorlund, either, and I was wanting him in a different kind of way.

I saw one of Nat Upshaw's men. He was by the door with his arms crossed. He was watching me. I started watching him and I wondered what the hell had happened that brought them here. How do they all keep finding me?

Chapter Twenty-Three

Nat Upshaw stood like a ghost at the end of the room. A haze of smoke mixed in the air between me and him. He was slow to move the hat from his right hand to his left. The thumb of his right hand dropped down and hooked inside his belt. He stood between two of the tables near the entrance to Spade's. From where I was standing he had a clear line on me. To walk or shoot – whatever he was planning. Couldn't tell his intentions from his face. Not through the smoke. Not with the ragged feel of my head with all the drink I'd put in it.

Behind Nat, Jody Verring was standing with another deputy. Surrounding Nat and his dynamic duo were a couple of dozen locals. I can't remember that many people being in the pool hall before the sheriff came along. They just seemed to appear. White rabbits from a dusty magician's hat. Figured they'd all followed Nat and his men in from the parking lot, expecting some kind of confrontation. Some kind of cheap weekend entertainment. I set the pool cue down and kept my hand on the edge of the table.

Nat came walking towards me. Lifted the right hand from his belt and started flipping his fingers at me like he was wanting me to follow him. Got up closer before I saw he wasn't too pleased that he was coming to get me in such a public place. I wasn't too pleased that he'd brought so many of his men. Not the way he usually called on me when we were heading off for a job.

'What's happening, Nat?' I asked him.

'You come away from the table, Joe.' Nat said. 'Come on so we can have a talk.'

'Sure,' I said. Thing is, I didn't move. The beer had set in good and easy. I'd counted plenty of hours in bottles and I'd moved on to spirits. The more I moved, the more they mixed in my belly. Started to churn up a real unpleasant feeling.

'Come with me, son.' Nat pushed his hat back up on his head and used his free hand to wave me over. Not being nasty about it, but telling me I better start moving. 'There's something we need to talk about.'

'What's going on?' I asked. I wasn't looking at him. Still hadn't taken my hands away from the edge of the pool table. Something comforting in wood and felt. Comforting in the way it held me upright. Looked down at the balls still left on the table. Three of Ted's and two of mine. Reached out and pulled the black into the side pocket.

'Your van,' Nat said. 'And a Jeep down in the ravine.'

I nodded my head.

'You know something about it, Joe?'

'No,' I said. 'I know about my van. About a Jeep . . .' Shook my head. Looked up and considered telling him just what it meant to me. But Nat wasn't looking at me like he was interested in hearing a story. He was looking at me like he was worried. His right thumb wasn't in the front of his belly any more. It was still looped in the belt, but was closer to the handle of his pistol. I watched his hand for a while, then I looked at his eyes. Didn't like the way he was staring at me. The way his left foot was farther forward than his right. The way Pop had taught me to stand when I was getting ready to shoot his pistol.

'I'll come with you,' I said. 'No need to get excited about this.'

'That's good, Joe. You just come on. Easy now.'

All credit to Nat Upshaw. He wasn't giving much away. Not in his eyes and not in the tone of his voice. I was itching to know what they'd found. How much they could tell from a Jeep in a ditch. I wanted to hear him talk about it. I'd take it all in and wait until the end to see how it was going to effect me and Marty. Thing is, I didn't want the locals to hear about it. Didn't want all the magic-rabbit people standing behind the sheriff to hear what Nat had to say.

I stepped forward. Nat backed away and scooted himself between two tables. Passed by him and was aiming for the door when Jody Verring stepped forward. Had his hands away from his belt. Nowhere near his gun, but he didn't make me feel any easier about the whole thing. I took the steps and had to hold the side of a pool table while I passed Verring. Started to feel off again. Balance leaving me all of a sudden. The shots of whiskey me and Ted had downed were sinking into the blood. Mingling with parts of me that set the ground moving.

'Where did you find it?' I asked.

'Get going, Pullman,' Verring said. He took hold of my arm. Things started spinning. Someone screamed. I think it was a woman. Direction left me. I left all direction.

Felt like I was spinning for a long, long time.

Chapter Twenty-Four

Verring had a good hold on me. Handful of the hair on the back of my head. I yelped at the pain and saw the faces of people – stunned and uncaring. Like they were all falling from some high building, only they'd made the decision to jump all on their own. Uncertain, but nothing they could do to stop what was about to happen. I heard the sound of Ted's voice coming from my right side. Something sounded like a prayer rattling off in a need-to-save-a-soul-double-quick kind of way. On my left was Nat Upshaw talking slow and steady.

'Now, you just back up, gentlemen. We'll be out of here in a minute,' he was saying. 'Go on back now. Finish your games.'

Then I'm spinning. Looking up and seeing a blur of ceiling lights. Coloured lights over the pool tables. I'm coming round again. Catch the neon blaze over the bar. My legs find a stool and knock it out of the way. Maybe I go round again before my face meets up with the wet bar. Jody's out of breath. He pulls hard on my head. Punches his hand into my lower back. I yell out and we go faster. More ceiling lights. More neon. Getting bigger. No stool to slow my motion. I make a deep kind of sound when I hit the bar. Sound comes up from my guts the same moment my face hits the wood surface.

Came to in the back seat of Nat's Bronco. We were on the road. Put a hand to my face and pressed where it hurt the least.

Followed a path of pain and discomfort to a lump. A small ball that had formed between my teeth and cheek. Rubbed it for a few seconds. Pressed it until it moved. Pain cut through my face. Ran the length of my neck and sent my stomach turning.

Watched out the window. Pushed the fog away when my breath misted the view. We were passing through the town. Taking a creeping entrance to the courthouse. Not something that caused me too much concern. Nat Upshaw was driving and Jody Verring was riding shotgun. Figured he'd be wired to go another round. A long drive gave me time to recover.

'You with us, Joe?' Nat asked.

'Yeah, I'm with you.'

'Things got out of hand, son. You hang in there and we'll get you cleaned up.'

We'd turned onto Summerset and before long the cars parked against the side of the road were two deep. Saw the crowds starting a block before the courthouse. A gathering of folks huddled together. Some holding flashlights. Some holding themselves. Everyone looking real expectant.

Don't think the search party is planning to go up Apple Mount tonight, Joe. They seem to know what they are looking for. They're just waiting for it to arrive.

They'd gathered to see me hauled in by the sheriff. Clusters of folks waiting for the cruiser to pull up with me inside it. All of them in front of the courthouse – watching out for Sheriff Nat Upshaw's police truck to arrive, so they could get a look inside.

'The hell is so important about the goddamned Jeep?' I asked.

'Shut the hell up, Joe.'

'Keep it calm, Jody.'

We passed and all eyes in the crowd stared. Half of them had never met me before. Most only knew of me through stories. Only knew me 'cause I'd buried their dead. But in their eyes I saw a mean kind of hope. Even in my drunkenness I could see there was a sinister glint in the way they looked at me. Something in their eyes that travelled through the late-winter evening dull. Something that was just too damned big for them to hide. Fear. They were all scared as hell. On that night – at that moment – they had a right to be. Every last one of them.

Nat Upshaw slowed the police truck down as we passed. All those people watched me as we went. Looking hard to see if I was going to become a new kind of monster. Out of man and into beast. With all the attention, I was getting anxious. Not all that able to defend myself. Hands in cuffs and alcohol still heavy in my gut. My head was still lazy and the sound of the pool balls clacking and the music playing was still ringing in my ears. Wished like hell I could have given them what they wanted. Put on a show. Become the kind of man they expected me to be . . . kind of man I am.

Can't ever get away too far, boy. Once a monster always a monster.

Henderson sure did come to life, there's no doubt about that. Sleeping dogs may lie, but hit them with a big stick and they come round quick. Some may even bite.

Nat Upshaw drove towards the courthouse in slow motion. Sonofabitch turned on the light inside his Bronco just so the folks outside could see in. The light was bright and it cut out all the faces I'd been looking at. My head pulsed while I tried to keep my eyes on the people surrounding the courthouse. All standing in line and pointing. Men taking steps towards us – towards the road.

Upshaw made noises while he watched them coming. He hit a switch that made the white snow spin in blue and red. Swipes of one colour and then the other reached out and stroked the crowd. He pulled a receiver from the dash and put it to his mouth. His voice boomed outside. He called out a warning that made the men stop. I screwed up my eyes to get a look at their faces. Tried to place them. In the dark it wasn't much use. Not with the light burning inside the truck.

I wanted to believe I didn't know those men. The women with their hands covering their mouths. If it all blew over, I'd have to pass them on the streets some other day.

Nat called back over his shoulder, 'You may want to lower your head, son. I'm about to pull up in front of the courthouse.'

Jody Verring turned to me and smiled through the grate separating me from them. He shook his head and pulled at the tip of his nose.

'He's wanting to see a show, Sheriff.'

'Damned if we aren't the centre of that show, Jody. Sonofagun, they are out tonight.'

All those people were prepped and ready for you, Joe. Whatever they found in that Jeep, they must have spread the word out far and wide. Look at all those people. More than what gathered after Milton spotted the trouble on the Mount. It's all for you . . .

My face pressed against the glass of the rear window. Only way I could keep from passing out again. Sheriff was sitting behind the wheel, steering through the snow while he was looking at the crowd, swearing under his breath and shaking his head so hard his Stetson almost slipped off. He said something to Jody Verring, and Jody gave him a thumbs up. He was smiling like he'd seen the entrance hall leading to some slick new world.

'You got yourself some fans, Joe Pullman,' Jody said. 'I'll be damned if the whole town's not out for you tonight.'

I looked at Jody's face and saw a man I almost didn't recognise. He had changed into someone new. Primitive and worked up about something he couldn't truly handle. I looked at his face and saw the way he was almost excited to see the people in front of the courthouse. He was not the man who shot bad pool and couldn't handle his beer. He wasn't the lanky, self-conscious fool who refused to partner with me on the Henderson High wrestling team back in the day. The man sitting in the front seat of the truck was dangerous. He had failed at a lot of things and everyone had seen him fail, but he's not falling behind any more. He was in the front seat and he was dragging someone behind.

Turned my eyes from him and watched the crowd and the courthouse drift away and come back again. Nat took the side road towards the back of the building. Used the radio while he kept the Bronco from sliding off the road. Held on to the receiver with one hand and the wheel with the other. He had a lot of things to say in the radio. Some about the snow and the ice and some about the backup being nowhere in sight. He kept talking in a lot of police code. After a while I stopped listening and closed my eyes. Breathed through my nose. Acid was bubbling up in my stomach. I found a rhythm that helped settle it back down. *Swallow and breathe. Swallow and breathe.* Not all that confident that I was going to keep from coming up what I'd put down.

Eleven bottles of beer, a couple of Benny King's chilli dogs and all those shots could leave a mark, Joe. You're not going to make any friends with that, buddy.

Swallow and breathe.

Finally looked up as Nat was navigating the Bronco through the electronic gates. The fence opened with a sound like a roller-coaster chain. Clinking along in a dragging and snagging sort of way. The jerking motion made it tough to watch, so I looked at the back of Nat's seat. When my stomach settled again I looked out the window at the boxwood shrubs creating long white shapes. There were perfect holes where icicles had fallen from the gutters. Slipped down through it like thick knives.

'You going to be sick, Pullman?' Jody Verring asked.

I shook my head.

'Sounds like you're going to be sick,' he said. He looked at Nat. 'Think he's going to let go, Sheriff.'

I didn't catch what Nat said. Maybe he didn't say anything at all.

Shook my head again, knowing that I was lying. Watched Jody's profile while he looked at Nat. Waited until he looked at me and tried to keep my eyes on him for a few seconds. It was a tough thing to do. *Swallow and breathe*. It was coming up, but the rhythm I had going was keeping it down. *Swallow and breathe*. Feeling the dull throb on the side of my face made it hard to concentrate. Was losing the rhythm. Wondering where the pain came from. Remembering the waltz Jody had led me in. Hard wood and my face connecting.

'I asked if you're going to be sick,' Verring said. 'Oh, Jesus Christ, Nat. Stop the truck. He's going to do it.'

Next thing I'm leaning against Nat's truck. Looking up and seeing we'd made it into a secured parking space. Fence all round us. Razor wire circling the top of the fence. Nat had pulled the Bronco up to a neat square sign right up near the building. 'Sheriff,' it read. I started coughing and my neck started burning and my guts felt hot and empty. Bent over and kept at it. Held my knees in my hands for a while. Kept like that and breathed deep breaths. Looked up to see Nat standing behind Verring. Verring was twisting his lower lip between thumb and forefinger. Nat looking down at his shoes. Jody reached out a hand and pushed it up under my face. He kept reaching and found my chest. I looked up to see his other hand cocked into a fist. He held the fist at his hip.

'Asshole,' Verring said and opened up his fist. Used the hand to take my shoulder. Raised me to standing and spun me up against the side of the Bronco. I slipped and had to keep my feet moving so I wouldn't go down. The smell of vomit was rising up and it was enough to keep my legs going, until Verring took my arm. Pulled me towards the path leading to the rear entrance of the courthouse.

Smell of vomit following us. Looked down and saw a red stain on my shirt. *That's not puke, Joe. That's blood. Hot, fresh blood.* The stain reached down to my waist. I started to worry

283

how bad I was hurt. How much had happened since I'd been out. If I'd been talking like I did with Carole.

'The hell you say, Pullman?'

'That's enough, Jody.' Nat turned and looked at me. Turned again and kept walking. We followed. Jody pulling me along. I staggered as best I could and made a survey of the situation.

Could've been a lot worse. That's the way I figured it. Not like my old man, and the way Maritime lit up with national cameras. Tragedy tourists coming to photograph the white colonial we'd lived in. All the faces of the people from Westchester Drive watching us. Looking at the house and waiting for the broken child to be taken away. It wasn't like that in Henderson. The grapevine was strong. It had good, deep roots and long-reaching branches, so enough people heard. Enough curiosity was tweaked to get people moving down Main Street to catch a bit of the show. Sure, I felt uncomfortable about the whole thing. But it didn't feel so bad this time around.

Jody Verring took a good strong hold of my arm and tugged me up the path. He'd already made up his mind that I was guilty. I just wished I knew what the hell I'd been accused of doing. With the way Jody was pulling me along, I knew it was something bad. He tried to rough me up every chance he got. So I went along with him. While he pulled I tried to work it all out. *Just what the hell has got this guy so fucking nuts, Joe? What Jeep did they find? Carole's? Well, then they've got no beef with you. She's walking around the damned market.*

'Nat,' I said. 'Listen to me. You need to speak with Eugene Duffy. He saw Carole down at the market. I swear to Christ, Nat.' *Swallow and breathe.* 'You heard that kid who threw the brick into the funeral home. That was Carole too. You saw him.'

I started to get angry.

284

Even with my hands behind my back I was giving thought to taking a shot at Verring. Blowing my usual cover of cool and kicking at his legs. Something to stir him up as much as he was rousing me. But I kept my rhythm *swallow and breathe* and thought about Marty and Donald. They were enough to make my slack mind perk up. Enough to remind me that I needed to act like a man. A real man and see if there was a way out of this.

'Take it easy on him,' Nat called out. 'There's eyes watching what you're doing there.'

Verring pulled me up straight and used his shoulder to knock me into the side of the fence. We were leading up the path towards the rear of the courthouse. 'Be steady, Pullman,' he said. 'Go crazy at all and I'll knock you to the ground. You understand me?'

'Sure, I do.'

So we went up the path to the courthouse with Nat Upshaw leading the way. Two inches of powder-white covering the ground and the sky was speckled with another fresh flurry. Silver clouds hovering. Verring was pulling at my arm like he was real interested to get me to the cell. Almost told him to be nice and I'd make it worth his while. But he started grunting and pulling at me even harder, so I didn't want to give him any more fuel to blow his fire. My feet slipped on the snow and I let him take my weight. He grunted more and pulled harder.

'Listen up,' Nat said. He'd made it to the back entrance to the courthouse. Verring pulled me up the two steps so we were level with Nat and the door. I looked at Nat and almost felt as sorry for him as I was feeling for myself. Old bastard was really looking lost. 'Inside there's going to be a lot of people with a lot of questions,' he said. 'I'd rather you didn't try to answer any of them right now, Joe. This is a God-awful situation we're all in. It's no thanks to you, but I'll give you this advice just the same. What you say in there will get out

285

in the town. It'll be all over the place before you wake up in the morning, and there's only so much I can do to keep it from reaching your boys.'

'Go see Eugene Duffy. Ask him what he saw at the market,' I said. Nat shook his head at me and made his face like he was tasting something sour. 'Carole's not gone, Nat. She's still . . .'

My arm went back and Verring lifted me off the ground. My shoulder pulled out of shape and I felt something tear.

'Enough!' Nat yelled. Verring set me down. 'Don't say another word, Joe. Do you understand?'

'I don't have anything to say,' I told him.

'That's good.' Nat turned his face to Verring. 'We're going in and past the desk. I'll lead the way and you just keep moving him through. You're not going to stop and you're not going to talk. Just follow my lead and get him into the back.'

'I've got you, Sheriff.'

Nat turned to the door and touched his short, broad index finger to numbers on the keypad. One small red light turned off. A green one came on. He pushed the door open and it sounded like another world was alive inside the building. One full of real excited people.

We walked in and Nat kicked the heels of his boots against the rug and shook snow from his shoulders. Straightened his cowboy hat and went round the first corner. There was a quick silence followed by a louder, crowded conversation. Voices of a hundred people all talking at once. It was hard to focus on what any single voice was saying. I kept my rhythm going. *Swallow and breathe.* Jody Verring took a tighter hold on my arm. He started dragging me and I didn't try to stop him.

'Pick it up, Pullman,' he said. Worried Nat Upshaw was going to get all the good attention for himself.

Upshaw wasn't saying much of anything. He walked fast and pushed his arms out. We followed and all the voices called to him and he just kept walking as best he could. Slowing down when people got in his way. Put his hands up in the air and shook his head, and the crowd moved aside so he could get past. We caught up to him and Nat kept wading through with his hands raised in the air. He was shouting: 'Back! Move back, folks.'

When we slowed he gave angry looks at the people circling round us – and there were plenty of them. Cameras flashed. I was hit in the side of the head and looked over and saw a voice recorder. It was hovering a couple of inches from my eye. Jabbed out again and caught my brow. Lowered and moved at me again and connected with my swollen cheek. Sent a jolt-pain into my temple. I recovered and looked to see who the hell was on the other end of the recorder. Vincent Partridge swung it at me again. Reaching the thing out, the way you'd reach out a gun to keep a killer at a distance.

'Joe,' he said. 'Can you tell me what's going on?'

I shook my head at him. He pushed the voice recorder at me again. Caught the side of my face – this time over the left eye.

'Quit hitting me, Vince.'

'Back off,' Verring shouted. 'Everybody just get the hell back.'

Anne Morris was working the phones in between looking at me and the sheriff. She'd sneak a look at Jody Verring now and again. Her eyes were wide open. I caught Jody showing her a wink. Real proud of being the big man in town. Getting to hold the monster in chains.

Both of the courthouse front doors swung open and half a dozen police officers came moving into the room. Looked like all of Henderson's finest had scrubbed up to be present for the evening show. The crowd started to shift, but didn't have room to get out of the way. The whole room moved en masse and started turning round in a circle. A whirlpool of bodies and they were sucking me in. Only no one was really wanting to be near me. It was frantic and sudden, and the crowd drew into a panic. All at once they realised they couldn't get out of the way of danger. Couldn't escape some terrible thing that was about to happen.

Doc Maitland came through the crowd along with the deputies. Took up a space in the chaos made by two officers. Maitland waded in and sidestepped his way towards me. Got that far before the crowd stopped moving. When it stopped, so did Maitland. He waited a few moments and looked like he was expecting the swirling to start again. It was calm and he took the lead of the new wave of officers who wrestled with the crowd to make his way forward. He found a place where I could see him clear. He gave me a look that eased my mind. Raised his hand and nodded his head forward.

It was only for a second, but it was something that told me he knew I wasn't as bad as some people were thinking. It helped, but after that second was up – when our eyes broke – I was back to being pulled along. Starting to feel nervous. Ready to fight, but certain I didn't have a chance of keeping from getting torn to pieces. Only a chance to draw some blood to mix with my own.

'I need a word with him first, Sheriff,' Vincent Partridge called out. He was walking alongside me. Verring reached across me and swatted at Partridge. Vince moved out of Verring's reach and barked over the rest of the fools.

'I think it's the right of the people,' Vince called out. 'The right of Mister Pullman.'

'The right of the people, Vince,' Nat Upshaw said while he kept walking, 'is justice. The right of Mister Pullman is to have a phone call to get a lawyer. And to have some kind of peace from the rest of you.'

'So, Sheriff, does this mean Mister Pullman is being formally charged? If so, what is the crime? Is it in connection with the disappearance of his wife or Miss Evers?'

'No comment.'

'Have you found something? A body? Do you have the rest of the remains?'

Swallow and breathe. Swallow and breathe.

'We received word that you located a Jeep in a ravine. Has the recovery of that Jeep led to this arrest?'

A sharp pain opened up inside my guts, pulling me forward. Bent me so hard and fast I couldn't control it. I went down. It took me by surprise, and Jody Verring too. He pulled hard on my arm and twisted it back farther than it was supposed to go. I tried to come back up to compensate for the bend. My stomach wouldn't let off and Jody pulled hard again. I called out.

'You're hurting him,' Vince yelled.

'He's resisting,' Jody said. He pulled again and this time I came back up. 'No crazy stuff, Pullman.' His mouth up close to my ear. Words poured into my head. Heated and wet with his spit. 'I warned you.'

Vince held the Dictaphone to my face again. This time it didn't hit me, but I wished it had. Something to take my mind off the pain opening up in my shoulder. Something to take me away from all the faces we were passing. Take my mind off my wife. *Swallow and breathe.* All the voices talking at the same damned time. Mouths moving and not one of them to focus on. Some kind of carnival ride with the freaks lined up. Spin kicking up faster and the noise building.

'Are you being charged, Joe? Have you been told why you are being arrested?'

'No comment,' Nat called back over his shoulder.

'I'll have representation for you, Joe,' Vince said. He leaned in close and repeated himself, like maybe I hadn't heard him. I didn't care either way 'cause I wasn't going to take help from a small-town hack. Not a chance in hell I was going to be indebted to Vince Partridge. 'I'll arrange representation. Just give me five minutes of your time and I'll get on the horn and find the best attorney in the state.'

'Back off,' Verring said and reached a hand across my chest. This time he connected with Vince Partridge and pushed him away. The reporter came back with a new energy.

'What do you say, Joe?'

Swallow and breathe.

'I don't need an attorney,' I said.

'And how did you figure that one?' Jody Verring called out.

'Innocent,' I said. 'Of whatever it is you think I've done. There's no need for an attorney until I think I'm in trouble. You haven't told me what's going on. This is a damned big show. It's nothing but a show.'

'It is a damned big show,' Nat Upshaw said, still moving towards the door to the cells. Still with his hands out, only he was moving backwards and still pushing people out of his way. 'You're right about that. Now if you all will excuse us.'

With that the sheriff took my other arm and pulled me towards a metal door. Vince Partridge came close again and tried to whisper something to me. I didn't get a good listen. Before he could try again he made a pained sort of moan. I turned my head and saw him on the floor, holding a hand across his gut. Someone called out in the crowd – a man's voice from the back of the freak-show. A flash poured overhead before I was through the door. Someone called out again. This time it was a scream. Nat was quick to shut the door.

'I got that on film, Sheriff,' a man yelled. 'The whole thing.'

'Doggone it!' the sheriff shouted at my face. His eyes were staring at me, but he was distant. He pushed me up against the bars of the first cell. Shoved his hand hard against my chest and dropped his eyes to the floor between my feet. He was breathing heavy. The door opened and Jody Verring came through, lowering his head like he was tall enough to crack it on the jamb if he didn't shrink himself to fit. *Feeling like a big man, now.* He had a smile splitting his thin lips all the way across his face. Showed just how much he enjoyed the circus.

Jody looked up just about the time Nat met him with an awkward step. Nat swung a leg out and was more like a child taking a frustrated swipe at a football. Not a man kicking with the aim for pain. But he connected. Boot landed solid against Verring's leg and Jody hopped in place and tried to hold back a howl. It was just too big to keep inside.

'Shut the hell up, Verring!' Nat called out. 'Jesus H Christ!'

'That for, Sheriff?'

'Don't go knocking folks round in this town!' The sheriff looked at me. Same as he always had – any other time before today. It was good to see that look come back. Something of understanding and compassion in his eyes. He turned his eyes back to Jody. They changed. 'Specially not when it's a reporter,' Nat said. 'Not when the cameras are around. When people can go back to the page day after day and see what you did.'

'He was too close to the prisoner, Sheriff.'

'It's Joe Pullman, Jody. He's not just some prisoner. He's Joe Pullman.'

'I thought we was arresting him, Sheriff.'

Swallow and breathe.

'I haven't decided on all that yet,' Nat said.

'What about the Jeep? All that was . . .'

Swallow and breathe.

I could only manage to swallow. The breathing part wasn't happening. Not just 'cause of the way Nat Upshaw was pushing his hand against my chest. Not 'cause the bars of the holding cell pushing into my back. I started working on the story, trying to piece together what I'd been hearing since the moment Nat Upshaw walked into Spade's. Someone had found a Jeep in a ravine. It was hard to breathe 'cause I was about to go into a holding cell and I didn't know when I was going to be coming back out. I started sliding along the bars of the cell. Moving towards the cement floor.

'Feeling the weight, Pullman?' Verring said.

Nat Upshaw took his hand off my chest and threw a punch at Verring. It landed solid on Jody's head and knocked his hat clean off. Jody covered up with both hands and it sounded like he was humming. Waiting for the next shot. But the sheriff was just hovering. Hands down by his side and breathing heavy again. He looked at me, where I was slumped against the cell bars.

'That's enough of that, Verring.'

Nat pulled me up. He grunted and moaned while he pulled. I came up and leaned against the bars. My legs felt like they weren't going to hold me. Like I was just going to drop down again. Nat put his hand back on my chest. Pushed it against me hard. One good shove and then he kept it there. It caught me off-guard. Nat eased up and took his hand away again. It didn't make it any easier to stand strong. I kept trying. I was underwater somewhere. Far off, but still able to see a fading light overhead. Felt like I was down in cold water and not able to swim up to the surface.

Swallow and breathe, Joe.

Nat patted me on the shoulder without looking at my face. Trying to keep a distance from me – even while his hand was sliding down my arm.

'I'm going to have to put you in this here cell,' he said. 'You'll get fed in about two hours. I think it's chicken. Maybe meatloaf. All depends what Thelma is getting ready at the church next door. Always makes an extra helping for folks visiting us in here. It'll be here if you want it.'

I felt sick and I felt sober. Clear, but shaking.

'I suggest you eat something, Joe. You'll need to get all your thoughts together before we can talk this thing through.'

'So you're arresting me?' I asked. My words slurred. Mouth dry. Tongue sticking to the roof of my mouth. Feeling like it was three times as big as it was supposed to be. 'This is all wrong, Nat. You're going to regret this. You need to talk to Eugene. He was with Sheila and saw Carole at the market. Go and talk to him. Talk to that kid who tossed the brick through my window. He'll tell you it was Carole. He *told* you, Nat.'

'Hold on now, Joe. You don't want to talk too much. Not until you get your ideas in order. We're not talking yet. When we do talk, it's not going to all be about Carole, either.' He backed away from me and put his hand up between us. Held it the way he did for a handshake. Only he wasn't interested in touching me. He was wanting to make a point. He was wanting me to take that point. 'I'm not calling this an arrest just yet, son. It's something I'm looking into. With this preliminary investigation I've got too many questions to have you out of sight. I've got pressure from Paul Quincy coming in, and all the folks he's got convinced that you're up to no good. I've got to do it by the book. Probably best for you to be in here. State you're in especially, you need to be kept safe.'

'Christ,' I said. 'This is all wrong.'

'Settle down, Joe. Take it easy now,' he said. 'You're turning blue on me. Take some air.'

'I can expect it then?'

'Expect what?'

'To be arrested.'

'I've known you a long time. Since you were a skinny thing. First brought to town. So damned sad and quiet. There's history between us, Joe. I played ball with your Pop. I've got fond memories of Mona too. You come from good people. Good people brought you here.' He paused. Must have been thinking the same thing as me. *Good people took this boy in. Brought him to a good town. Gave him a chance to change. But that's not his people. He comes from a different kind of people.* 'Mona was a real fine lady,' he said. 'Real sorry when she took ill.' He cleared his throat and patted my shoulder again. 'So I'm giving you a whole lot of benefit of my doubt. If you had a hand in this, I'll know soon enough. If you didn't, I'll know that too.'

'I didn't do anything to Carole.'

293

Nat Upshaw nodded his head.

'What makes you so sure this is all about Carole?'

'Well, I . . . I haven't done anything to anyone . . .'

'Before all this can get sorted out, I'm real hopeful I can see you innocent. I don't want to see you any other way.' He pulled me away from the cell bars. Turned me to the side. 'Folks expect me to find the answers to tough questions. Don't go taking this the wrong way.'

'It's crazy,' I said.

Upshaw walked away and left me leaning against the bars. Jody Verring stepped in front of me and screwed up his eyes. I looked down to see he was balling his hands into fists. His arms were moving up and down. Pumping the blood through his veins and getting ready for me to do something stupid. Nat used a small round key in a metal lock on the wall. Something unhinged in the ceiling and he pulled the cell door open. I slid down towards the floor again.

Jody Verring reached his arms under my arms and pulled me to standing. I let him turn me and move me towards Nat and the waiting cell. I made it past Nat's outstretched arm and walked through the cell door without Verring's help. Nat spent a long time unlocking the cuffs. They'd cut hard red lines into my wrists. After a few minutes free, my hands ached as the blood came flowing in again. It came like hot trains and left a blaze wherever they ran new tracks.

'We'll make sure supper comes in when it's ready,' Nat said. 'I'll be back to check in. When that sauce drains out of you, we'll have a talk.'

I nodded my head.

'Start thinking about what's happened, Joe.'

Nat watched me for a few minutes and then he left.

I sat and waited. Looked at the small sink and took deep breaths of the lemon smell coming from the toilet. Stood and walked to the wall and put my hand on the oversized cement blocks. Pushed hard, hoping they would fall away. Hoping I would fall through to the good life that was waiting on the other side. I pushed and I went nowhere. Spent a good long time at it. Pushing and walking round. Looking at the cracks. Putting my face to the walls, hoping to feel a breeze coming through.

I went back to the cot. Fell into a long-lying position with my arm under the back of my head. I watched the ceiling and before long I was heading off into a drunk-spin. I let it take me, knowing the lemon-fresh toilet was close by if the spinning grew too heavy. I went along for the ride. Before sleep came I was already thinking about the beginning of the whole mess.

About the trouble with Carole. How keeping it quiet hadn't helped me. The acids in my guts were rolling up in high waves. Looking for a way out. Listened for the sounds of someone laughing. My old man, maybe. Slipped out of the state pen's medical centre. Made his move while some half-assed doctor left him alone to die in silence.

He hadn't finished with me yet.

How about that, Pullman? Your old man never gave up on you . . . He's up there giving it to you hard, boy. Ain't nothing stopping him now.

'I believe it,' I whispered.

Then, like Dorothy and her wet rat Toto, I'm spinning off to some far-off land. Only the world I fell into looked a lot like Henderson. Looked identical to the small place in the middle of nowhere. Only difference was it was in the past tense. Ten unlucky days can make a difference. I wasn't feeling too confident that things would ever find a way back to normal. People who once shook my hand in the streets were crossing the road when they saw me coming. So, maybe that's why I went back. Lying on the cot with the acid bubble bursting inside my gut, I dreamed of better times than these.

Swallow and breathe.

I kept spinning.

Swallow and breathe.

Chapter Twenty-Five

'Pullman,' the voice calls.

It is an excited voice. Some kind of electricity in the words – anticipation of danger. Like the voices from the night before. They'd all been hopped up and agitated, but that's just to be expected. It wouldn't last. At least I had some kind of solace in knowing that the frenzy I had caused in Henderson during the night was about to turn. I had that going for me.

'Pullman, sit up,' the voice said. 'Your breakfast is coming through.'

It was the kid-cop with all the teeth. He moved up to the bars holding a tray. I went to stand and he shook his head and stepped away from the cell. He kept stumbling over his words, telling me to settle back. He was standing there frozen, like he'd been out in the blizzard too long. Maybe he was one of the idiots in the crowd who was cheering the whole night through. His eyes were too wide for his skinny head. I sat back on the cot. He waited a few seconds, then lowered to a crouch and tipped the carton of milk on its side. He pushed the tray under the bars.

Stood up fast. I stayed seated, but reached out and hooked a finger over the lip of the tray and pulled it towards me. There was a plate of cold toast. A plastic bowl with a small box of cereal inside it. Carton of milk he'd tipped over and a clear plastic tub of apple juice. It looked like a specimen cup full of piss.

'Can I ask you something, Mister Pullman?'

He was closer to my cell door than he was to the door leading back to the safety of the courthouse lobby. He didn't feel protected. But that wasn't stopping him sharing his curiosity. Maybe he didn't feel he needed to put on a show. There wasn't the same urgency in him as his fellow deputies felt the night before. I wasn't just Pullman the suspect. I was a human again. I was Mister Pullman. Mister Pullman in a cage.

'Shoot, bud.'

'That glove Tansy Romain found. The one with the hand in it,' he said. He was waiting for me to look up at him. I lifted the specimen cup and looked through it at the bar-bulb overhead. Things were floating round in there. Lots of things. 'That wasn't part of your wife, was it?'

'No,' I said.

The kid showed that excitement again. His hands dangling at his sides started moving round. When I answered, his hands rose up and took hold of his belt buckle. He ran his fingers back and forward on the belt. Moving them from the buckle to the holster on one side and the handcuffs on the other. They slid back to the buckle again.

'So you know that wasn't your wife's hand for sure?'

'Of course I know it wasn't Carole's hand.'

'How can you be so sure?'

I kept the cup of apple juice raised in the air, but turned my head so I was looking at the young cop. His hands stopped moving over his belt. His lips peeled back as he sucked at his empty mouth. White teeth got the slow reveal.

'How can you be so sure, Mister Pullman?'

'Carole's got long fingers,' I said. My voice was calm. It sounded loud in the cell. Everything sounded loud inside my cell. 'The hand from that glove didn't have long fingers.'

'Right.'

'Is my wife missing her hands, Officer?'

'No,' he said. 'I mean, I'm not supposed to give you any information about the investigation.'

'Are you investigating my wife's missing hand?'

Swallowed hard and took a breath. My heart was pounding heavy. Pulse was picking up tempo all over my body. Felt it up in my throat. I kept staring at the kid-cop, trying not to show him I was breaking down. Didn't want to fall to pieces inside a damned cage. Become the animal spectators come to see for pity and giggles.

'So you found her,' I said. If nothing else, I wanted to use the kid to work out how deep my hole already was and how much I could keep from digging it any deeper.

The kid looked confused. He sucked at his mouth, and his lips pulled up high enough for me to see his yellow gums. His hands left his belt. One fell loose to his side and the other reached for the top of his head. His fingers ran over his short-crop of hair. He scratched while he sucked his mouth.

'Where did you find her?' I asked. 'Was she in this Jeep the sheriff keeps talking about? Or was she sitting down at the market just waiting to be found?'

'I can't tell you anything.'

'But you found her,' I said. 'You wrangled her in, like good cops.'

He shook his head.

'Tell me about my wife!' I yelled, jumping from the cot. I grabbed the bars of the cell and for a moment the kid was in striking distance. I could have reached out and taken hold of him. Pulled him in and squeezed the information out of him. The kid was white and shaking. 'What about my wife?'

The door behind the kid-cop shot open. It's hidden down a short hall and I couldn't see who it was that was pushing it open. Could hear heels scratching on the cement floor. Shoes moving in place. Shoes of someone trying to make up their mind to come or go. I decided to make up their mind for them.

'Don't be a fucking coward,' I yelled. 'Come out here! Get your ass out here and tell me what the hell is going on!'

Heels scratched a last time before they dug in with louder steps. Heels cutting against the cement floor. I watched the corner and the wall beyond and waited for the figure to show. Watched the wall until the shadow grew long. Nat Upshaw twisted himself military-style, so he was aimed at me. Looked as upset as he did when he'd pulled me in at Spade's. Still wrinkled round his eyes, and his mouth was shorter than usual. Pursed up from thinking all his nasty little thoughts.

'You do not have that right,' he said. Heels moved him to me. Short clicking sound of his heels connecting echoed through the room. His hand came up with a finger pointing at my chest. 'You have no right to speak that way to anyone in my jail.'

'Where did you find her?'

'I'll be asking the questions.'

'Let's have them, Sheriff. I've been here all night and there's been nothing.'

'I'm letting you sober up.' Nat Upshaw turned and patted his kid-cop on the arm. Nodded his head towards the door, but the kid didn't go. 'Get on out of here. I've got this covered.'

Got tired of holding the apple-juice container, so I let it go. It hit the floor. Flat on flat. Made a sharp snap-sound. That kid looked like he'd filled his shorts. Poor fool of a cop, lifted off the ground with his hands coming up to his cheek like he was expecting to take one to the chops.

'Bit jumpy,' I said. 'The hell you expecting me to do from in here?'

Leaned down for the bowl of cereal and milk. I wasn't feeling hungry. Or I was feeling so hungry it had turned into a pain. Either way I didn't feel like eating with the angry sheriff holding on to my cell door. Looking in at me with the eyes of a zoo keeper who knows he's going to have to put down his star beast.

'You about ready to talk?' he asked. 'Head cleared?'

'I'm always ready to talk, Nat.'

'Well,' he said. 'Let's talk then.'

I lifted the bowl and the milk and sat for a few seconds. It felt strange holding something like that. Something domestic. Picnic-plastic white bowl with a generic box of cornflakes from Solomon's Grocery. It was local milk. All familiar. But it seemed wrong having it in my hand while sitting inside a jail cell. Sitting behind bars when the world was still happening outside. I leaned over and set it all back on the tray and stood up. Turned so I was facing Nat Upshaw.

'What about Donald and Marty?' I asked.

'They're both fine,' Upshaw says. 'Ted went back with an officer. Went by Pop's and told him what was happening. Pop went and stayed at your place last night.'

'What'd he tell them?'

'Last I heard, Pop had told the boys that me and you took a trip. If they ask, he'll say we're fishing. Seemed to me the best option. Pop knows you and he knows the boys. I'm sure he'll figure out what lie works. He'll keep them away from the radio and television in case the story gets out.'

'Donald's going to hear about it,' I said. 'He'll have people calling him on his cellphone. Kids stopping by the house. It's not going to stop word getting to them.'

'Well,' Nat said. 'I guess we'll have to hope that doesn't happen too soon.'

Wasn't all that sure why timing mattered. If it happened sooner or later, it was still a big deal to me. I didn't want Donald and Marty hearing about my arrest from a gloating kid. Some asshole with a grudge and a bit of nasty news to deliver. I didn't want them to hear about their mother, either

– whatever they had about her anyway – but it was going to happen. I wanted to be there with Marty when the news came in. No matter what that news was . . .

'I didn't kill Carole,' I said.

'Good.'

'Don't think you have to keep me company either, Nat.' Walked over and touched the wall with the palm of my hand. It was still cold and hard. Pushed off and came back to him. 'Go do what you need to do, and come back when you know it wasn't me.'

'May take some time, Joe.'

Walked to the cot and tossed the single fleece-sheet aside. Nat leaned in and took a better hold of the bars of the cell door. Gripped them and pulled. Jerked hard until the metal clicked in place. Confirmation that I was nice and secure. I wasn't going anywhere.

'I can't be sure about anything right now.' Nat shook his head. 'Like I told you, son. I'm giving you more leeway than I probably should. 'Cause of your folks, that is. The way you've been acting lately makes me think there's a possibility that I shouldn't be cutting you slack.'

'This is slack?' I called. Tossed my arms out to the sides. Showed off my cell. My small corner of the big bad world. Lemon-fucking-fresh.

'Yeah, Joe, this is slack. And I'm cutting it for you and I hope like hell I'm not wrong for doing it, either. But my gut feeling's got me questioning what my head is telling me.'

'Well, you can trust your gut, Nat. I'm innocent.'

'Sure you are,' he said.

He stayed there. Hanging on to the bars. Watching me while I watched the floor. We both stayed quiet and listened to the water drip in the cistern. Experienced the growing scent of the disinfectant bubbling away in the tank. Had a smell that caught in the back of my throat. Made me want to spit. I couldn't stand any longer, so I sat down on the cot. Breathed through my nose. Put my hand over my mouth and smelled the cigarette-stink coming from my fingers. Spade's cologne on my hands. Picked up from the felt on the pool tables. Lay down all the way. The springs creaked and the coil went to chewing my hurt back again.

'Do me a favour, Joe?' Nat asked. 'Make my life easier and do this for me . . .'

I nodded and looked up from where I was lying.

'Tell me about what we found inside Carole's Jeep,' he said.

Stayed still with my eyes wide. Smelling my fingers and staring at the cracks in the ceiling of the cell. Imagined the Jeep and the suitcase Marty had been talking about. Carole's collection of the Joe Pullman of yesteryear. Pictures. Documents. My old man's ideas. I had no idea what was in there, but I knew it would make me into something that I wasn't. Not any more.

Nat made a noise. A low sort of groan.

I stood from the cot and shook the image out of my eyes. Walked over to where Nat was standing at the cell door. Maybe I did it too fast. Felt a wild urgency. Wanted to get it all cleared up so I could get on out of there. Carole was in her Jeep and I was about to get the news from Nat. Straight from the man who had seen her. Wanted to hear it from him so we could move it to a finish. Nat moved back a step and watched me. I knocked my head against the bar. Pain jolted and my mind started working. Spilling out a sort of inventory. Contents of the Jeep last time I'd been in it.

'Carole had it in the shed. I went to empty it out. She'd been going on about it for a while. She said I'd been trashing it,' I said. 'That's a few weeks before Carole took it. She had a load of shit in there. Cassettes. A couple of pairs of gloves. Gas receipts. Maps. Notes. A lot of papers. Magazines. All kinds of . . .'

'What's the smile for?' Nat asked me. He was looking at me through the bars. Keeping his distance now. Hands together. Hands wringing back and forth. One going over the other.

I shook my head.

''Cause I didn't leave anything in the Jeep. I cleared it out 'cause Carole would have given me a world of shit if I'd left any of my stuff in it.'

'Carole would have,' Nat said. 'Why would your stuff be in the Jeep?'

'I'd driven it a few times. Had it when Ted's truck was getting serviced and he took the van. I used Carole's Jeep at the Trapper's a while. Check with Leonard if you need to. Carole had more things in the glove box, but I'd cleared my stuff out.'

'Nothing else in the car?' Nat asked. 'When you last *saw* it.'

'No,' I said. Didn't like the way he was emphasizing *saw*, like I'd been and should have seen something important in the Jeep – something incriminating. 'Look, the Jeep is Carole's car. I don't have anything to do with it. I drove it a few days. Don't have anything to do with anything you found in it.'

Nat's face was turning a new shade of red. Making his jaw clench and his hands ball up. Veins in his neck swell, even. This time I didn't figure it was the wind that was turning him.

'Nothing to do with you?' he asked.

'What are you getting so worked up about, Nat?'

'Think about the last time you looked at that Jeep. Last time you were close to that Jeep. Tell me what was inside it, Joe.'

My mind wasn't working like I needed it to work. His question needed an answer straight off. Nat wasn't waiting round for me to come to my senses. He was trying to throw me off. He was trying to get me to slip up. Maybe already heard what he was after. He was angry as hell. I figured someone had gone through it.

'Look, Sheriff . . . Nat . . . I don't know what you're asking me. Like I told you, I cleaned up my stuff from it. Then Carole took it with her. So, I don't know what you found in there. If that's why I'm in here . . .'

'If that's why you're in here . . .'

'Help me out, Nat,' I said. 'Whatever's going on, I've had nothing to do with it.' Nat took hold of the bars. He grabbed them so his hands were over mine. 'Nat. Sheriff. Damn it.' I shook my head. I was getting confused. 'Carole took it and she left. Wherever it is . . . Hell, whatever it is you found is something Carole—'

'This is not about Carole!' he yelled. His voice echoed across the cement walls. Did a bullet-ricochet all round the place and hit me a hundred times. Rattled round in my head. Brought the hangover pain back. Spiked it in deep. 'This has nothing to do with Carole!'

'Then whatever you found has nothing to do with me.'

His skin was red. His eyes wide and white and accusing.

'*She* put a man inside her Jeep? She set an old man behind the wheel and pushed it down into Tanbark Ravine?' He squeezed on my hands. 'She put a man named Jules Lewiston behind the wheel of her Jeep? That's what she did, Joe? You're putting the blame on your wife?'

'What are you talking about?'

'I'm talking about an old man. That's what I'm talking about. That's *who* I'm talking about. A familiar face. A person from your past. We're talking, Joe, about a man you were speaking with at Darnell's. Sheila's already told me all about that. Filled me in completely, and she's got a way of recalling every last detail. I went into Darnell's with a photograph of our driver. Handed over his licence to Sheila on the off-chance that he'd eaten at the diner on his way through town. She told me about your conversation. Then about the conversation she had with the man once you'd left. Seems you left in a hurry. Kind of suspicious that we find him in a ravine a few days later. Frozen and wrapped up in Carole's wrecked Jeep!'

304

'He wasn't in Carole's Jeep,' I said.

'No?' Nat took his hands away from the bars. My hands felt cold without his hands covering them. 'Kind of vehicle was Jules Lewiston in, Joe? Kind of car was he driving?'

'I don't know, Nat. But, that wasn't her car . . .'

Oh, Jesus, Joe. You are fucked, son. Just following him out of town. Just making sure he's gone . . . Didn't even realise he was in your wife's car.

'How do you know it wasn't Carole's Jeep? Not the same colour? Well, you're wrong there. It's white. Covered in road grit, but under it all it's still the same white Jeep. Same factory-white that's marking up the front corner of your van. Strange coincidence. All these coincidences.'

'There was a dent on the front grille. It was smashed in. Carole's Jeep didn't have any damage on it. Not like that . . .'

I was blinking. I was watching Nat's face, waiting for it to move. Waiting for something that would correct what it was he'd just said. His face moved, but not to speak. He came closer to the bars. His nose moved up to my nose. He looked into my eyes. Smelled cigar on his breath.

'Tell me how Lewiston got into Carole's Jeep. Tell me why the Jeep hit your van. Then tell me how it ended up in the ravine.'

'Carole took the Jeep,' I said.

'Sure she did.'

'Those scratches happened a while back.' My voice came out calm. Real convincing. 'Ran into the Jeep when I was pulling the van into the drive a few weeks ago, Nat. It was a minor thing.'

Nat pushed off the bars of the cell. He turned and started for the hallway. I called out to him, but he didn't turn round. He got to the hall and stopped, straightened his back, and clicked his heels all the way down the hall. Opened the door and the sound of the people in the courthouse came rushing in to me. It was a powerful noise. It pushed me back. It moved me to the cot where I sat down. Then I laid down. Pulled my knees up to my stomach and I waited. Thinking about Carole. Thinking about the last time I'd seen her.

Stop, Joe, she said to me. *You can stop now.*

I can fix this, I'd said.

No. Stop it.

Carole. I'll fix it.

Chapter Twenty-Six

It was early the following morning when Nat came in and unlocked the cell door. He wasn't looking as angry as before. I sat straight and moved my head round to try and get the stiffness to go away. Pillow smelled like sweat. It held the yellow grease from the last inmate's head. I'd tossed it on the floor and slept flat. Henderson Courthouse gives you the appearance of comfort. After that, it's below basic.

Nat moved his hard heels against the cement floor. Sound made my guts start to roll. Made me feel sick, so I took a deep breath. The sharp lemon stink from the toilet caught me in the back of the throat. Burned at my insides and got me swallowing hard. Tongue so dry and heavy that swallowing wasn't all that easy. First dry-heave came when Nat Upshaw changed the direction of his pacing outside my cell. He'd just started coming back when I folded up. Second heave came when he was a few feet away from the cell door.

Lurched across the cell and crawled the last few feet to the toilet. My guts folded again. What came out was hot liquid that burned every piece of my insides. I finished and held on to the toilet. Breathed in deep. Thick stink of lemon and vomit filling my nose. Tilted my head back and a fresh wave of dizziness came rolling in. Turned away from the bowl and looked at Nat. My mouth hot and wet. Something was hanging from my lip.

'Joe,' Nat said, nodding his head at me. 'You sleep well?'

I wiped my mouth with the back of my hand. What was hanging came off and made my hand feel cold. Steadied myself and put a hand on the floor.

'Can't say that I did.'

Nat was chewing on something. He had a red stain on his tie, so I guessed he'd just finished breakfast before coming through to see me. Probably stopped by Darnell's and took his time answering a load of questions about the murderous mortician that was living in their quiet community. Somehow it was the idea he'd eaten that got me angered the most. It was alright to let him be a celebrity for once in his life, but thinking about him sitting in front of a plate piled with a Darnell's Roadmaster Breakfast made me want to unlock my grip on the toilet and take hold of good old Nat Upshaw's neck. Shake him until his insides came spilling out.

He said: 'Follow me down the hall, son.'

We were alone, so I kind of figured it was a good sign. Maybe they decided during the past few hours that they'd got it wrong. Spied Carole's car down in a canyon somewhere, but found it was empty after all. Maybe the shape they'd thought looked human turned out to be a bent-up seat. Maybe it wasn't anything at all. Stood up from the floor, my legs tight and full of needles. Pain shooting through every part of me. Tested the cell door and it slid open. Looked at it for a few seconds. Confused and suspicious. Got up the nerve and followed him down the hall and into a small room. There was a desk with a radio recorder on it. I took a seat in the chair farthest away from the door. Took the chair 'cause that's where the microphone was aimed.

Nat shut the door and dropped into the chair like he'd been hoping to occupy it for hours. It all seemed rehearsed. When he was seated he seemed to enjoy the feel of the thing. He slumped when he breathed out and ran a hand down the length of his face. He was a man ready to finish with some heavy business. Chuck aside a burden he didn't need to carry any longer.

'We've got to clear up a few things,' he said. He started nodding his head. Didn't stop until I matched him with a nod of my own. At that he finally looked at me. 'Bet you could use a coffee. Maybe something to eat.'

I nodded again.

'Anne's going to bring it in. Coffee first. I'll have the folks next door cook up a big breakfast.'

'Same people that forgot to bring my dinner last night?' I asked.

Nat wasn't looking at me right then, but I knew from the slow shaking of his head that he was embarrassed. Not just by the meal, but by the circus he'd started. His hands moved round the table. Where they moved they left fogged prints on the black surface. Good Ole' Nat Upshaw was sweating this one. Gave me a real good feeling to see him that way. He was feeling small for all the clowns he'd rounded up. Felt a prick for the way his performing deputies had cracked their whips. Ringmaster Nat had lost control of the big top. Now he was looking shy and frail. Must have been playing over in his mind the way they all had tried and convicted me in a single evening. It was good to see the sheriff go all sheepish like that. Told me he was a man who could see error in his ways. More important, it told me that Nat Upshaw saw me as an innocent man again.

'I believe you,' he said. It was enough to get me to forget about the food. Forget about the burn the sickness had left in my throat. 'We can start there.'

'That's a relief,' I said. It wasn't a tone that was meant to convince either of us.

'I understand what you're going through, Joe. Thing is, I'm under pressure here.' His eyes were wet and tired. I looked away from him and made out like I was checking my hands for something. 'I've had Paul Quincy calling me all hours of the day and night. He's on the phone every time it rings. Asking me to check out the funeral home. Search your house. Dig up all the graves Mel Trainer's dug since Carole went missing. Even asked me to check the crematorium in Meridian. He thinks maybe . . .' He swiped a finger below his nose and checked his hand. 'Thinks maybe you passed her off for some other deceased.'

'Paul and I have never had a strong relationship.'

Nat let out a laugh that he didn't expect. He tried to play it off with a weird sort of humming sound. Finally cleared it out of his throat. 'I guessed that, Joe. When he mailed me a list of possible scenarios, I took it that you two were at odds.'

'Did you tell him this exercise didn't work?' I asked. 'You call him this morning to say that your arresting me was a mistake? You tell him it's done nothing more than 'cause me to wade deeper through the shit? You tell him about the crowd that gathered last night? He'll be glad to know that the harassment I'm getting will double. He'll be thanking you for that one, Nat. Hell, that shouldn't be a concern for you. Job done well, in Paul Quincy's eyes.'

Nat nodded his head. 'I told him. Only I didn't have to call him. He's staying at The Lodge on Beaumont. Been there a few days.'

'How'd he take it? All this good news you had for him.'

'Like a bear with his nuts on fire. Excited and angry.'

Expected that laugh to cloud up in Nat's throat again. But the room stayed quiet. His nails rolled on the desk once and then it went back to silent.

'What happens next? Jules Lewiston in the Jeep . . . What did that turn up?' I said.

'Turned up a lot more questions. I'm sifting through all the documents we found in and around the Jeep. All the photographs and papers.' Nat looked me in the eye and this time it wasn't difficult to give it back to him. He was genuine. Back to old times. 'I need you to help with the sifting.'

'Let's get started,' I said. Using my hand to indicate that he could turn on the recorder without offending me. He looked at it and frowned. Shook his head and waved a hand between us.

'No need for that, Joe.' He balled his hands up under his chin. Bounced his chin against his knuckles for a few seconds and said: 'I think you need to tell me something about Maritime. About when you lived there. Not the stuff you've given us over the years, but the secrets. Things that may give me an idea about what we are dealing with here.'

'Not something I want to go into really.'

'Well, I can understand that. Thing is, I've got even more witnesses that place you with Jules Lewiston at Darnell's the night before we found him in the ravine. You can imagine the state we found him in. Busted up and frozen through.'

'Sorry to hear about him, but I didn't do anything to cause the accident. He was in Darnell's like he'd been waiting for me. I came in, he just started to talk. Real straightforward kind of questions that made me uncomfortable. Told me he was from Maritime and then he made out like he wasn't sure he knew me.' With that out in the air, I spread my hands. Shrugged my shoulders. 'He made out like I should have known him.'

'Sheila says he knew you. Says he told her how you had been friends with two boys who came to some unfortunate ends. One of them was his son. A boy named Oscar. Sheila knew about the two boys in Maritime. These friends of yours that Lewiston was speaking about – his boy Oscar and a Dean Gillespie. Sheila told me she'd made connections between you and the Lewiston man through your father. Says she remembered reading about your father's crimes some years back. What he did to the Gillespie boy and what happened to Oscar Lewiston before that. She'd been real caught up in the stories coming out of Maritime when they happened. Kind of hit close to home for most of us. Even more after you came to live here in Henderson.'

'What's this have to do with Carole?' Sat forward and tapped at the desk between us. Hit it hard with two fingers. Aimed them into the grain and hit the desk between me and Nat. 'He was in Carole's car and I don't have a reason for that. So, what else did you find, Nat?'

'When I hear that a man from Maritime was confronting you in Darnell's, and he ends up dead a few days later, I perk up. I get suspicious. That could have been enough. Just the body and the confrontation. But we get down and check out the Jeep he's in. We run the plates and registration and find out it's Carole's. That causes more concern. Right then it's building up. The case is building and it's got one name attached to it. You see where I am? Then we pull out the man's belongings and open up a new kind of concern. A Pandora's box of your past.'

'What'd he have?'

'An old-style briefcase,' he said. 'Fake leather grain. Lock was busted and when my deputy pulled it out of the vehicle, it fell open and the papers scattered. My boys chased them round in the wind for the better part of half an hour. Made them go and catch them all before we made our way back to the courthouse. They came back with the papers and the case and handed them over to me. Thing is, they were already talking about what they'd found. No way I could have stopped that.'

'What were they talking about?' I asked. 'What was in the case?'

'Evidence,' he said. 'Evidence against a very young Joseph Reginald Pullman. It was like a case file from a prosecutor. Someone ready to go to trial against this boy.'

Swallow and breathe.

'Kind of evidence are you talking, Nat?'

'Photographs. You at the hospital after your father's arrest. Close-ups of the bruising on your face and neck. Reports from the arresting officers about the final attack you suffered at the hands of your father. There were other reports. Interviews with neighbours. Teachers from your school. Some interviews are about Dean Gillespie and others about you. Maureen Gillespie, the boy's mother, gave a long statement.'

Nat stopped talking then. I'd been looking at my hands. Listened to the silence and wanted him to keep talking. Wondered how much the idiot deputies had read about me. How much information had Jules Lewiston compiled over the years? Every time he'd wheeled Oz out to that field and placed another goddamned pine cone in his hands, he must have found a reason to keep searching. And all of his efforts were sitting right there in a plastic briefcase.

'You alright, Joe?'

'What did Maureen say?' I remembered walking with her the morning Dean went missing. Following her lead. All of her frantic calls. She moved round the path and called out. Over and over. She was tireless. I followed her. Watched what she was doing. Got up close to her – fascinated. A mother looking for her boy. Desperate and searching. We found his raincoat. A piece of it anyway, and that's when she turned on me. No longer the kind woman who had shown me pity. Taken me in when my mother had been sent to the institution in Virginia to die. It was just me and my old man, and she'd taken me in. Then we found the raincoat and she didn't see me as that pitiful little boy any more.

Where is my son!

'Missus Gillespie claims you visited their house the morning Dean went missing,' Nat said. Nodded my head and he continued. 'She went out to search for him. She said you followed her into the woods. Said you were watching *her* more than you were searching. There is a moment when she claims you looked . . . excited.'

'I don't know what she could mean by that.'

'Aroused is the word she uses. When asked to clarify, she said you seemed aroused.'

'At fourteen?' I asked.

'I'm just giving you an idea of some of the items in the case, Joe.'

We sat for a while. Silence was broken by a knock at the door. It opened behind Nat, and Anne Morris walked in. She was carrying a tray. There were two white mugs and a plate wrapped in tin foil. Anne walked into the room and set the tray down between me and Nat. She looked at me and straightened her lips.

'How you doing, Joe?' she asked.

'I'm fine, Anne. Thanks for asking.'

She walked out of the room and closed the door, the way you do when leaving a baby that has just been settled. She barely made a sound. Nat lifted the mugs from the tray and set one in front of me. I took a sip of the coffee. It was at room temperature. I was glad of that. Downed the cup like it was water and felt the effects straight off.

'There were other reports. Photographs. Receipts. A list of witnesses . . .'

'Witnesses to what?' Maybe I called out too quick. Maybe my voice was too loud. Nat snapped his head up and his mouth sucked in. I settled back into my seat. Nat rolled his head and touched the back of his hand to his lips.

'Witnesses that placed your father at a hotel the night before Dean Gillespie disappeared. Receipts to show he'd paid for parking the morning the Gillespie boy was killed. The hotel was fifty miles from Maritime.' Nat shrugged his shoulders. 'Not impossible for him to go back and kill the boy, but it does raise questions.'

'Where did Lewiston get all of this information?'

'Well, Joe, that's the trouble. It wasn't his suitcase.' Sat looking at Nat and he sat looking at me. We sat there like a couple of damned porcelain dolls, collecting dust. 'It was your father's suitcase. It is inscribed "Property of Richard Pullman. Maryland Correctional Adjustment Center, Baltimore, Maryland". How it got into Mister Lewiston's possession is beyond me.'

'I didn't know anything about this, Nat.' *Sure you do, Joe. That fake lawyer Carlos Muniz told you all about it. Carole handed over those snaps of Marty, and your old man gave her a briefcase of all his goodies. No wonder she was all over you to start talking. Your father got in her head, Joe.*

'Nat, whatever you have taken from this . . . Whatever you believe, I wasn't responsible for what happened to Oscar Lewiston. Or his father.' Lifted my mug and looked in it and wished like hell I had more. I held on to the mug to give my hands something to do. I watched the cup and its emptiness and I willed my hands to stop shaking. 'And Dean Gillespie.'

'What about Dean?' Nat asked.

'He was a troubled kid.'

I stopped talking when Nat put his hand in the air. He leaned forward and lowered his hand as he came towards me.

'Look, Joe, you need to bring yourself together. You've been going through more than any man can handle. That's no thanks to what we put you through, and I will do all I can to make amends for that. But you need to settle down and listen to me very carefully.

'We checked the damage on the van and it doesn't match the damage on the Jeep. The Jeep was mangled pretty good, but we believe it was hit on the rear of the driver's side. The damage to the van is on the driver's side. So you couldn't have hit it on that part of Tanbark Pass. The road's too narrow. Matches up with your story about hitting the Jeep coming into your driveway. Still, that was a thing I needed to make sure about.' His hand swiped across the air between us. Cleared that part of the mess away. Trouble is he had more to move on to. 'The suitcase in the car tells me Lewiston was here with an agenda. Seems he was on an agenda set and controlled by your father. That's still puzzling me.'

Nat sat back and made a long, high-pitched whistling sound. I looked up at him, hoping he'd finish soon. Hoping he'd decided things had come to a close a long time ago. That he was too busy with town drunks and vandals to reopen a can of worms that didn't belong to Henderson soil.

'Now, this last thing is the most troubling,' he said. 'Hardest to hit you with, knowing all you've been going through.'

'I'm ready.'

'Well, I called over to Maritime to tell the sheriff that we had one of theirs in the morgue at Henderson Medical Center. He asked for all the information on the deceased, and I gave him Jules Lewiston's name and told him he was in a car that didn't belong to him. I told him how Lewiston had been found in a Jeep owned by one of our locals.' Nat rubbed a hand down his face and sat forward again. 'Well, this sheriff, a man named Wilcox, he went all quiet and told me Lewiston's car had been found in Maritime. Said it had been abandoned at a place called Wild Lake.'

Felt my face turning a deep red. Burn of it was trailing down into my neck. Heading in a free fall towards my chest. Couldn't stop it. Nat stared at me while he considered the last of what he had to say.

'Wilcox told me Lewiston's car was in a public parking lot and that they had found blood inside,' he said. 'The keys were still in the car along with one other item of interest. A handbag. Maritime police checked the bag for identification and the sheriff was about to call us when I called him.'

I was shaking my head. It's all I could do.

'I kind of hoped you'd be able to clear that up.' Nat drew circles in the palm of his hand. He used the index finger of one hand to draw the circle in the other. He kept at it for a while without stopping. Finally said: 'There wasn't a lot of

blood in the car, but enough to make them think someone
had been injured. Not enough to be life-threatening.'

'What happens now?'

'Well, I went to Maritime yesterday and looked at the car,'
Nat said. 'It's in good condition. No sign that it's been tampered
with. I spent a good bit of time with Wilcox. He remembers
you. All that happened with your father and those two boys
still haunts that town. Since it was you, he gave me some help
in talking with folks. We met with a woman who works in a
dry cleaner's who claimed she spoke with Carole a few days
back. According to this woman, Carole was in Maritime the
same day you dropped the boys off with Paul Quincy.'

'Now, Sheriff . . .'

'Hold on, Joe.' Nat had his hand in the air. This time he
didn't look angry. He wasn't even looking at me. Not in the
face. Had his eyes on my hands. Looked concerned at how
I'd balled them into fists. Used them to crack down on the
table. 'This woman says Carole was asking about the Gillespie
kid. She was asking about you too.'

'I'm not following,' I said.

'It seems Carole was going around Maritime claiming that
she was a reporter working on a story about your father.
Said she was writing a piece that would capture the monster
of the man. Had everyone believing it would get printed after
he died. Maritime has been on a countdown since news broke
of your father's illness. Woman in the dry cleaner's was sold
on the idea of the article. Told me how they are all cheering
for the cancer. She said, "We hope it feasts on that sonofagun
with hungry teeth."'

'What about Carole?'

'She went into the police station and asked round for information. Wilcox told me his deputies kept giving her a cold
shoulder. Told her that she wasn't welcome, snooping round
like she had been. Told her she should leave it all alone. But
she persisted and she went out and spoke with locals. She

317

found the woman at the dry cleaner's and they spoke between customers. Carole was making notes in a leather journal.' Nat used his fingers to draw a rectangle on the table between us. 'This woman was specific about that because it had the words "Funeral Services" etched onto the front of it.'

'So she was there for a day,' I said. 'It doesn't explain . . .'

'Carole stayed for more than a day, Joe. And that wasn't her first visit to Maritime. She's been there on several occasions. Now this might trouble you, but . . . she hasn't always been alone.'

'What are you telling me?'

'She had a man with her.'

'That's great news, Nat. Bring me into a cell and shatter all my credibility and then throw into the mix that I've been a sucker all my married life. You're breaking me down.'

'Well, I'm not entirely finished.' He rubbed at the rectangle with the palm of his hand. He was fogging up the surface of the table again. 'Marty told me he heard a fight between you and Carole.' Nat held his hand up. He must have anticipated my reaction. Never gave me chance to get a word out. He knew I didn't want Marty involved and he'd gone over to the house to speak with him anyway. I didn't say a word, but it's not 'cause there was nothing to say. He continued.

'First thing this morning I went to see him. Pulled a long night over in Maritime and stayed over with Wilcox and his daughter. I came back from there and went over to your place. Marty was up watching the news. That boy's a fire-cracker, Joe. I swear he's about the smartest child I've ever met. He listened in while I told Pop about my trip. Knowing Marty was listening, I didn't give anything away about the car or the blood. Just that I had been up there and met with Wilcox. But Marty wasn't leaving the room. He asked me if we found something, and so I told him we didn't. He asks me what the hell we're holding you for.' Nat let out a laugh and looked at the ceiling. He made a Marty face, brow down low over his eyes, lower lip hanging: '"What the hell are you holding him for?"' Nat let out a laugh and found his own face again.

'How is he doing?' I asked.

'He's good, Joe. We talked a while and he told me about the fight between you and Carole. One he overheard a few nights before she disappeared.' Nat gave me a few seconds to take that one down. 'He told me about it because he said it was important that he was honest. Marty said you two had gone all quiet towards the end of the fight and that he'd come halfway down the stairs to see what was happening. He told me you fought, but that you finished the fight by hugging onto her. She was holding you back.'

'Sounds about right,' I said.

'He also told me that you went back to your room at the TP, but it wasn't until late in the night. Said Carole was still at home and that he'd found her asleep on the sofa the next morning. Ted confirms you were working on the Osmonds' funeral that day. Said you both spent the morning and through to lunchtime together. You working on Edmund and him working on Bernice.'

Nat took a drink from his coffee mug and curled his lips in at the taste. He looked inside the cup while he set it back down on the table.

'And what does this mean exactly?'

'It means Carole was around when you came back to get the boys. Marty said she was up in her room doing something when you picked them up and drove them to the restaurant where you met Paul. It also tells me that Carole left before you got to the meeting with Paul that afternoon. You dropped the boys off at two-thirty and were back in Henderson for four-thirty. Leonard is sure you were back in before four-thirty, 'cause he never misses *The Price is Right*. Your van needs a new muffler, Joe. Leonard tells me when you drive down the street, he always has to look to make sure it's not a natural disaster coming his way. So he knew when you pulled into the parking lot that day.'

'And?'

'Seems Carole's in Maritime and Lewiston got a hold of her Jeep.' Nat clasped his hands together and opened them up again. Made like he was trying to squeeze out pins and needles from cold fingers. 'I'm clearing you from the Lewiston crash and from his abandoned car in Maritime.'

I didn't want to ask him for any more information about Carole. About what they've turned up there. I didn't want to know if they'd come up with anything about my past, either. Figured he'd read through the contents of the briefcase and pieced some of the puzzle together. Didn't want to talk so much that I put a few more pieces in place for him. Something told me they didn't have an idea about where to begin. I felt like it would incriminate me somehow if I showed too much interest in my father's suitcase and the stuff inside it. Might change Nat's mind and alter his theory about the entire thing. But I knew the night before hadn't been a dream or a drunken blackout gone wrong. It had been real and Nat Upshaw had been an angry man. He'd stood up close to me and that look in his eyes was the look of a man who believed that I'd killed some people. Past and present – he saw me as a murderer. And now he was sitting across from me telling me breakfast was going to get cold. He was even taking off the damned foil and moving the tray towards me like he was looking out for my interests.

'Tell me what you found in Lewiston's car,' I said. Looked down at the cold bacon and eggs. Moved them round with a plastic fork. Feeling no appetite. 'Everything. I need to hear about it. How did it look?'

Nat nodded his head.

'It was clean,' he said. 'The glove box had all the registration documents. Lewiston's identification from the agency where he worked. A pack of tissues and a flashlight. In the

320

back seat was an empty plastic bottle. Carole's handbag was on the floor of the front passenger side. Other than that, the car was clean.'

'And the blood?'

'Not enough for Carole to be in danger,' he said. 'That's if it's even her blood, Joe. There's not enough there to be a concern. Maybe jammed her finger in the door. Had a nose-bleed.'

'What else? Who is this other person, Nat?' Stopped moving the food round the plate. Pushed the plate to the side. 'The one Carole's been taking to Maritime?'

Nat looked at me for a long while and shook his head. I wanted to press him. Grab the collar of his shirt and hold him against the table. Keep him down until he was ready to talk to me. But I also wanted out. I needed to get out and make sure what he was telling me about Marty was true. Wanted to test life in Henderson again. Sitting in the chair, it almost felt safe with the brick walls round me. There was no telling what was awaiting me outside.

'I can't give you anything else, Joe. I'm sorry, son, but that's all I've got.' He was smiling and he knew it was working on my nerves. He knew how Pop had taught me restraint. Taught me to bottle up before I blew apart.

'A local,' I said.

Nat's smile faded.

'Not from Henderson,' he said. 'What I gather, he wasn't from Maritime, either.'

'Where's he from then?'

Nat shook his head.

'Give me a few minutes, son,' he said. 'I'll get things sorted out up front. Then I'll take you home.'

Chapter Twenty-Seven

Half hour later I walked out of the courthouse and fell into the snow. Slipped up on the third step and crashed my shoulder against the flag post on the way down. It was too cold for people to be wandering round, so the town was empty. It didn't make it any easier being outside. Getting up from the snow was a struggle. Boots slipping on the frozen crust. Felt like a fucking idiot climbing back up the stairs again. Rubbing at my shoulder under the canopy of the courthouse porch. Waited there for Nat Upshaw to finish his piss so he could drive me home.

Over to the west, the sky was a mix of grey and black. Storm clouds were rolling our way. It was supposed to be heavy, according to Anne Morris. Chances were good that I'd be seeing at least one victim of a crash in the morning. They'd look a shade pasty, with skin cold as the snow. They'd be followed by their relatives – either in person or on the phone. Standing on the porch of the courthouse, I didn't think I could handle speaking with relatives of the dead. It takes patience to comfort people. I didn't have patience and I was sure that I was as hurt and lost as they would be.

The door opened behind me and Nat Upshaw came out, hollering over his shoulder, asking Anne to clean up the office when she got a minute. She yelled back that she never got a minute. Nat shook his head and came up behind me and smacked a glove-clad hand on my shoulder.

'You holding up, partner?' he asked.

I nodded my head.

He looked out at the clouds rolling in. Black and churning. Between the clouds and the trees covering the hills outside of town there were streaks in the sky. Charcoal scratchings connecting the two.

'That's a hell of a storm brewing,' he said.

'I'd appreciate you getting me home before it hits.'

'Sure, Joe. Pop's already taken Marty back. He's waiting for you.'

Nat stepped off the porch and took the steps without care. I wished he'd go down. Take the fall that saw me sprawled in a lump. But he knew where to step. This was his house. His town. Ice didn't get to him here. He was up the path when I joined him. Followed him to his Bronco without speaking. Inside he listened to the scanner. Reports of accidents in Clinton and Waldorf. The storm was all around us and was already disrupting things.

'If it's bad in the city, it'll be tenfold for us here in Henderson,' he said.

'Yeah.'

He pulled the Bronco onto Beaumont Avenue. Took the left and had to ease up on the accelerator. He let the truck move into the far lane, then accelerated and we moved off again.

'Look, Joe. I hope you don't have any hard feelings about what's going on. Me and your Pop have known each other a long while. Really does get me thinking that this thing could tarnish a lot of good years. Memories I'd like to hang on to.'

'I've got a lot to think about, Sheriff. Until I get the time to go through it all, I guess I'll be keeping quiet.'

'That's a truism, Joe. I'll be gosh-danged.' He tapped the steering wheel with the palm of his hand. 'A truism indeed!'

'One thing you could do, Nat,' I said, 'is take some time

and look into the sightings people are talking about. Seems everybody's seeing Carole round town. It's a hard fact.'

'Yes, it is. I have plans to speak with a number of people about that. I'm sure Vince Partridge is on the case too. He'll probably have something for you before you can snap your fingers.'

'That doesn't put my mind at ease. If you found your-self accused of a crime and the evidence is floating round town, who would you rather sort it all out? A man who specialises in sensationalism, or a man who is investigating the crime?'

'Again, I hear you loud and clear, son. And like I'm telling you, it's something I'll be looking into. Only trouble is, folks usually clam up when they're speaking with me. Unless they're a hundred and ten per cent sure as the day is long that what they saw is what they saw.'

'That's what I need to square up.'

'Now, see here, Joe. That tone of voice is what's been getting people suspicious of you. A man short of patience and hot on temper can get a reputation. Don't matter a spit how unfounded it is. And when a man's wife goes missing under suspicious circumstances, people will remember all the bad traits. Rumours pick up speed fast as white in a blizzard.'

I grunted.

'A word of advice for you, Joe. Get in contact with Carole's folks. I'll be getting another visit from Paul and I'll try to smooth some of the rougher edges. You can have my word that I'll do all I can to make Paul believe you're not guilty in all this. It probably won't be something that gets ironed out overnight. But it would make both our lives easier if Carole's folks believed in you.'

'They're not interested in closing off what history we have.'

'Yeah, boy.' Nat tapped at the wheel like he was needing to be distracted. 'I've heard about the history. I've been out to Cumberland and sat with both Frances and Paul. They've told me some stories about one angry fella. Now Paul's out here all loaded up with even more stories.'

'They've got stories alright.'

'Now, Joe, I have to admit some of the stories are troubling. For a man in my position, I can't just let these things pass through my ears. Like you say, I've got to register it all. File it away. And once in a while it's these kinds of stories that cloud good judgement.'

'This your way of telling me why I was arrested?' I asked. 'Why you thought I was capable?'

'Just detained. And no. I took you aside for a while 'cause rumours can get people hurt.' Nat concentrated on the road. It was empty of cars and covered in snow.

'I take it you know they're just rumours,' I said.

'Got a pretty good idea of what people are capable of, Joe. Most of the folks in this town I've known all their years. So when you hear stories you know they're stories. Separating fact from fiction is a big part of my job, son. Most of my time is spent listening to folks ramble. Good, concerned citizens with heads full of trouble. And you know how I deal with them?'

'With an iron fist,' I said.

'Never in this town.' He paused a long while, like he was considering towns where he had employed that iron fist. 'I just let them finish. Sometimes they talk a while. I've got patience to spare. They finish spewing and then I sit and think about it. Ask them to do the same. And after a while I offer a new spin. And you know what the effect of that process is?'

'I suppose you turn people around, Sheriff.'

'Well, now.' Nat took a deep breath. Took a hand away from the wheel. Shifted his weight in the seat and breathed out. 'You're right,' he said. 'I turn folks around. Sometimes people can think themselves into trouble. You understand what I'm getting at?'

'I understand what you're saying.' I was looking out the

window. We were passing Potter's Field and the gates were closed. Over the crest of the hill the clouds were starting to reach the edges of Henderson. A single line of dark smoke was funnelling into the cold air from somewhere over the hill. Back up over the rise and over the skeleton arms of black trees, Mel Trainer was tossing more wood into his fire. Stoking his small metal stove, trying to keep warm.

'That's a good thing,' Nat said. 'Glad we understand one another.'

'I understand what you're saying, but I think you're implying something too.'

'You're a smart man, Joe Pullman.' He was nodding his head. I watched his reflection in the passenger side window. Couldn't bring myself to look at him. All the attention he brought last night. Only thing missing was a Russian on a trapeze. Now he was giving me advice and trying to talk me down. 'Sure are a smart man,' he said again in a low voice almost like he was amusing himself. 'A real tight whip. More like Mona than your Pop. I'll be straight with you, Joe. Doc Maitland suggested your interest in Carole's appearances – the sightings, I mean – are going to cause problems later.'

'He never said anything to me,' I said.

'Well, I asked him for an opinion. I've been thinking about it. More than I'd like to, if the truth be told. Even with all the stuff happening round town. Colin Lowell getting shot up and the Romains' German shepherd digging up the hand. Hell, Daryl Evers' daughter running off to meet up with some Mexican. It's been a real crazy winter so far. And in all that mix I'm thinking about Carole. Even now, I've got a strong gut feeling that she's still in Maritime or thereabouts. Alive and alright, but staying away for some reason that I can't understand.'

We drove the last few miles in silence. He pulled up into my driveway, manoeuvring the Bronco around the circular path. Pop's truck wasn't in the drive, so I figured he'd changed

plans and kept Marty at his place until I was home. I got out
and went for the front door. Was glad Marty wasn't around.
He'd be leaning against the windowsill in his bedroom, looking
out through the curtains. He was always expecting things to
be right. It was best he wasn't around to see me then. I couldn't
give him what he needed. Couldn't give him reassurance. I
couldn't give him anything.

'You take care of yourself, Joe.' Nat was leaning out of his
window. 'If there's anything comes up, I'll drop you a line.'

'Yeah,' I said and turned on my heels. 'Maybe she'll show
up in town in the middle of a crowd of witnesses. Maybe one
of them will see her . . .'

Made a fast jog to the front door. Slid in the key and turned
the lock. Pushed the door in and threw a hand up at Nat. He
did the same and backed out of the driveway. I went inside and
watched him through the window. Waited until he'd made it
to the road. Wheel straightened out and then he was gone. I
went out through the door, almost running to the van.

Chapter Twenty-Eight

I started up the van and let the engine heat before I backed out. Drove the long way round town. Went out past the riding stables and up to Town Hill before heading back into Henderson. Hooked up with Beaumont and found it deserted. The threat of the storm was keeping folks inside. The occasional semi came rumbling down, but mainly it was just the van. I came up to Market Street and pulled round the stalls. Found a place out back and parked.

Sat in the van and looked up at the two salmon-coloured buildings behind the market. One was a lopsided thing three storeys high. It'd been painted pink over an earlier baby-blue. A section of pink had peeled back like a giant piece of bark from a redwood tree. Part of it had broken free. Fallen into the boxwoods below. The pieces still clinging to the building blew in a wind. Dark shapes grew on the blue underneath. A single raw brick was exposed under a broken slat of wood. Harsh weather had softened it over the years. Rust-coloured smears drained from the building and bled down into the soft foundations.

I'd been waiting in the van a long while before I decided to make a move. With all that had happened I was feeling cautious. Still, I had a conviction moving in me. I'd put off what I should have done after Nancy came by. She'd spouted off in my front room and I should have made a move. Too many years of lying low had turned my muscles weak. I sat in the van and looked up at the building and decided it was a good day to change. Lifted the cellphone from my pocket. Punched a number in and listened to the electronic voice of the operator. I gave the details I was looking for and asked for the call to be connected. There was a pause before the phone rang. Three fast electric rings. Another pause. Then a voice answered.

'Thank you for calling DRS. This is Herman speaking. How may I help you?'

'Mister Dorlund,' I said. Surprised myself at how right my voice sounded. How much it was not my own. Not a weak man at all. A new kind of man was behind the voice. Solid and in control. 'I'm not certain you'll remember, but my wife called you some time ago. You've been calling our house about a debt she owes.'

'Oh, right. Well, I would need to speak with your wife if it is her debt. I cannot disclose information about accounts unless I'm speaking with—'

'Well, I don't see it being a problem. You called us requesting a payment and I received that call. The message at least. You asked for payment to be made immediately or else action would be taken. Am I right, Mister Dorlund?' I listened while he made a few strained noises. Looked up at the buildings to see if any of the curtains were moving. If his face was up close to one of the windows. He sounded like he was choking. 'The calls you made were to my house, not just to my wife.' He laughed, but it wasn't convincing. 'It wasn't just a couple of calls, Herman. It was a dozen at least. Jesus, you must really want this money.'

'I think I'm going to hang up, sir.'

'But you want your money. Your clients will want the money. Hanging up will get you nothing. You are Dorlund Recovery Services. Is that right?' I asked him. 'If you don't recover, you're not living up to your name. You are in the business to recover, aren't you, Herman?'

'It is your wife I need to speak with. If I could take a note of *her* name . . .' He must have decided against it. Decided against reasoning with me. 'I cannot give you any information . . . I can't speak with you about the case.'

'I am only trying to get this money to you.' God, my face was aching holding on to that stupid smile. *Smile while you dial*, I kept thinking. 'Look, Herman. The reason for my call—'

'I would prefer you didn't call me that, sir.'

'What? Herman?' I waited. 'Okay, look, Herman, the reason I'm calling is to find out how I'm supposed to get this cash to you.'

'You can send a personal cheque, cashier's cheque or money order made payable to DRS.'

'To?'

'I will send an envelope. Self-addressed. Pre-paid. Cashier's cheque would be preferred, however we can accept personal cheques.'

I got out of the van and shut the door without a noise.

'That sounds fine, Herman.' I walked towards the pink building. Went up the path leading to the wooden steps, wondering which of the three storeys he was on. Which of the rooms he was sitting in, sweating through the call. 'That sounds like a grand old deal.'

'Good then,' he said. 'I will have that envelope sent today.'

'And I would appreciate an invoice stating the name of the company filing for your services.'

'Absolutely, Mister . . .'

'Gillespie,' I said.

'Mister Gillespie.' He sounded out the words like he was writing them down. He took his time with each letter. 'Your wife's first name?'

'How many Gillespies have you been calling for debt collection?' I asked.

'Sir . . .'

330

'Herman,' I almost yelled into the phone. 'I'm sorry, I thought you were going there.'

'Is there something else you need?'

'Are you a local business?' I got to the first floor and stood in front of the white door. Pushed the round buzzer to the right of the door. Listened as the sound of the electric chime came through the door. 'Are you located in Clarkesville?'

'No,' he laughed. It was strained. 'We are out of Baltimore.'

'Oh, what a coincidence. I do a lot of work in Baltimore. Are you at the harbour or are you up towards Druid Hill?' I went up the steps two at a time and made the second landing. Reached out and buzzed the bell. It sounded through the door. Hit it again and listened for the same sound to come through the phone. Nothing.

'No. Um, we are on the other side of town. Closer to Johns Hopkins.'

'Right. Eastside?' Ran up the next flight of stairs. Took them two at a time and made the third landing before Herman had a chance to respond.

'Mister Gillespie. I am not certain where you are going with this.'

'Well, Herman, my wife skipped out on me. She owes some money.'

'You sound hostile, Mister Gillespie.'

'I sound troubled to you, Herman?' Buzzed the bell. Heard it in the telephone. Sound came through the door same as it came through the phone. I buzzed again. Heard it in stereo. 'Do I sound troubled to you, Herman Dorlund?'

'Mister Gillespie . . .' he stopped. 'I have someone at the door. So, regrettably I will have to go. Your name has been noted and I will find your address through our records. You can expect the envelope to arrive at your home within a few days.'

The phone went dead. The door swung in.

'Hello, Herman,' I said, snapped the phone shut.

'Oh, shit!'

I grabbed hold of Herman's shoulders and pushed him to the floor. He went down fast and hard. I wasn't expecting him to be such a pussy. Stepped into the apartment and swung an arm round and hooked the door closed. Twisted and was back on Herman, who was crab-walking away from me. Making like he was planning to do that crazy walk right through the far wall. He stopped when he hit the sofa. Made a sound like he'd winded himself in the collision. Stepped up so my legs were either side of his feet.

'Debtor's spouses don't call you. From the look on your face, Herman, I'd say even fewer have come to visit your fine place of business.' Looked round the room for a second. Scanned the empty pizza boxes and torn porno mags on the sofa. Picture of a green Chinese-looking woman in a crooked frame on the wall. Smell of marijuana creeping into the air. A thin blue line of smoke rising up from a bent cigarette in a Budweiser ashtray on the coffee table.

'You're trespassing.' He sounded pathetic. It didn't stop him from trying again. 'Joseph Pullman.' He didn't like the sound of my name. I didn't like the sound of his voice saying it. 'You need to get out of here before you get yourself into some serious fucking trouble.'

'What is real trouble to you, Herman?'

'You better leave.'

'Convince me.' Twisted my head so I was looking straight at him. Looking down at him with a new anger brewing up in my guts. Herman Dorlund is a man with an odd body. Broad shoulders, but an otherwise slight build. Belly shaped out a perfect circle of jelly. Swelled up good and plenty under his stained shirt. His dry black hair was moving in all directions. 'Stand up and speak to me the way you did on the phone.'

'Look, Mister Pullman.'

'Joe.'

'Sorry?'

'I hate this "Mister Pullman" shit. No one calls me Mister Pullman unless they are trying to make something sound sweet.'

'Joe.'

'Yes, Herman?'

'Can you back away from me?'

'Sure I can.'

Stepped back a few paces. Watched while Herman struggled to gain his feet. He leaned against the sofa for a few seconds before pushing off. Took a step towards a side table, then stopped. He looked at me for a moment and made the whole situation seem dangerous. His hand was moving up, making a slow rise to the drawer in the table. Coming up like a hand in water. Smooth and even on the rise.

'Hold it!' I yelled. He stopped and held his hand where it was. 'Come over here, Herman.' I was talking through that smile again. 'Take a seat.'

'I was going to get a beer.'

'Let me get one for you.'

'I know where they are . . .'

'Herman.' Made my face to show him I wasn't interested in making funny any more. Showed him he should stop messing around and get himself on the sofa. 'Chances are they'll be in the kitchen.'

'Yeah,' he said. He took a few steps and dropped down next to the mags and pizza boxes. The cushions came up round his weight. 'They're in the fridge.'

'Best place for them.'

Passed Herman on the sofa. Kept an eye on him while I moved by. Figured he was the kind of guy who would jump on your back if he was feeling it was his last chance. Maybe take a sucker shot at your head when you weren't looking. I couldn't help but figure he would do some kind of damage. Get all that weight behind a shot – even a pussy kind of windmill punch – and he'd stun you at least. Knock your damned lights out at best. I didn't want to give him the chance.

'Start talking while I'm walking, Herman. Where's my wife?'

'I thought she would be at home,' he said. Made a sound like he wanted to keep talking, but got caught up on a word. 'Your home. With you.'

'I've been in jail.' Slammed my hand down on the table and watched him come up off those cushions. 'You heard anything about that? Whole damned town knows about me, Herman. Can't see a bright fella like you being out of the loop. You missed a show last night!'

'Heard something about it, I guess.'

'Sure you did. So, what you thought doesn't make any sense. Carole wouldn't be home with me and she wouldn't be with me in jail, either. All the shit that's happening is 'cause she's not with me. There's a lot of talk going round town. A lot of people with ideas about where Carole is right now. None of them believe she's with me. So, I ask you again, Herman.' Hit the table hard. Stung my hand. 'Where is my wife?'

'Please. I don't know anything.'

'Well, I hope you have more to say to your spirit friend, 'cause right now you're sounding real fucking useless. Figure if you can contact ghosts you'd be able to tell me exactly where my wife is at this very moment.' Looked at Herman and saw how his eyes were still on the table. He looked at me and his eyes opened big and showed all kinds of uncertainty. 'I'm a desperate guy, Herman. I need answers.'

'Mister Pullman, I'm telling you I don't know where Carole is.'

'Well, she's not in this desk, Herman!' I reached for the handle to the drawer and started to pull it open.

Herman sank back into the sofa. Covered his face with his hands and made a sucking sound. Trying to take in a breath through his closed fingers. He let out what he was able to get in. 'Oh, my God.'

'I'm opening up this drawer, Herman. What will I find?'

'Jesus.'

'He's a ways off, Herman. Of course he could be real fucking close, for all we know.'

'It's a gun,' he said. 'There's a gun in that drawer. I wasn't going for it. I swear to you I wasn't going for it. The desk's in the way. I was just going for a beer. That's all. Swear to God. I was trying to get through to the kitchen. I had to get close to that desk. You see?'

'How's the desk in the way, Herman?' My voice was even. Calm and even flow. Really got Herman worked up. 'I'm standing right here and it's not in the way.'

He sat up and turned. Stuck his arm out and jabbed like a wild man behind the sofa.

'It's halfway. I was going for a beer. It was in the way.'

'In the way.'

'Yeah, in the way. See. That's what I mean.'

'And you stopped going for that beer.'

'You said something.'

'What did I say, Herman?'

'I can't remember. You've got me all screwed up. I'm really freaked out.'

'Where is my wife?'

'She went away for a while. All I know about it for sure is that she and Nancy Lowell came here before they left town. Then they went away together. That's all I know. Last week some time. I don't remember exactly.'

'Where did they go, Herman?'

'Up north someplace.'

'Name of the place, Herman.'

Shook his head.

'Maritime?' I asked.

He nodded at me and said: 'Yeah. I think that was it.'

335

'See, Herman, that was painless. Now why the fuck are they in Maritime?'

'I don't know. They went to see someone. Your wife had a suitcase with her. She kept talking about it, but she didn't bring it up here. But they were taking it to make a trade for something. Carole had things she wanted to talk to someone about. She kept saying she needed to find out what had happened.'

'Who was she going to see?'

'I don't know.'

'So, why did Carole come back here? Why did she come to see you, Herman?'

'What? I haven't seen her. Man, I swear to you it's been a week since they came by. Maybe more than that. She came by with Nancy that one last time. She was right there.' He pointed to the front door. 'Wouldn't even come in the place. Nancy came in and asked me for something. She wanted me to test some of the stuff she had in the case. That and see about getting my gun.'

'Test what stuff from what case?'

'Just stuff. It was nothing,' he said. Head shook from side to side. Had a lot of motion and not much meaning. 'Nancy just told your wife to give her the stuff from the case so I could get a feel of it.'

'So why was Carole here the other day?' His head moved faster. Hand came up boxer-style. 'Listen up, Herman, I've got people telling me that Carole was here two days ago. They tell me you were calling down to her while she was crossing the street. You were standing out on the porch, calling out to her while she was walking towards Cedar Road.'

'That wasn't Carole. That was just some . . .' He looked down at his feet. Gave them a real good stare, like he was hoping they'd turn into something fast. Must have worried he wasn't going to be able to high-tail it out of range in a pair of house slippers. Goddamned fake Indian moccasins.

'Look, man. I went out to yell at some bitch who put an envelope under my door.'

'What envelope?'

'I don't want any trouble.'

'Well, you already got it. Now tell me about the envelope.'

'There was some money in it. A couple of hundred and a
letter telling me I needed to make a few calls.'

'And why did you go after her?'

'Look, I hadn't opened the letter when I went out there. I
only knew there was an envelope that came under my door.
I'd had a few of them already and I didn't like what was inside
the other ones.' He kept his eyes off me. Tried to move, but
he was stuck where he was. Moved from side to side, but
didn't leave his spot. 'I saw the envelope and I got spooked.'
I didn't take my eyes off him. Slid back the drawer and put
my hand inside. He watched me and started talking again.
'Listen . . . Colin Lowell put an envelope under my door a few
days before that one, alright? He stuck some pictures of Nancy
coming in here in an envelope and he slid it under my door.
He'd put a note in it saying to leave her alone or he was going
to kill me.'

'What's that have to do with Carole?'

'Nothing. I mean, that's why I went out when I saw that
new envelope. I figured it was him again and I wanted to stop
it happening. I saw her running off and kind of thought Colin
had put her up to it. So I yelled out to her. It wasn't until she
was gone and I came back in here and opened it up that I saw
the money and what they wanted me to do.'

'What did they want you to do?'

'Nothing . . . just call a number and leave some messages.'

'My number and my answering machine.'

'I'm sorry, man. I swear to you, if I didn't need the
money . . .'

'And Colin?'

'I'd been smoking, man.' He pointed to the ashtray and the

bent home-roll he had burning in it. 'Had a hot head on. I kept looking down to see if he'd moved. I needed to go down to the market for some supplies. Some food. I was starving and he was just standing there.' Herman stood up and walked to the window. Pointed down at the market below. 'I waited until he was gone, and then I go down there and I'm doing my thing. He jumps me and he's wrestling on me and I wrestle him back. He falls into the boxes and shit. I get up and he's starting to come at me again. So I did the thing and came back up here.'

'What thing did you do?'

'The thing.' He made his hand into a gun. Looked a real idiot with his thumb up and index finger out. Billy the Kid hopped up on fruit juice and weed.

'You shot him.'

'He came after me, man. Kept telling me to leave Nancy alone. Kept telling me to keep away from her and Carole. Tried to get away from him, but he kept going on about it. Kept saying that I didn't know enough to get involved. Said I needed to keep clear of them two.'

'What did he mean, you don't know enough?'

He stopped looking out the window and went back to looking at his shoes. Shook his head and showed me his face. It looked tired and worn. He was feeling the strain of things. But as long as he kept talking it suited me just fine.

'All of this is about you. Getting arrested like you did. People all getting together in that mob. Jody Verring and the rest of them are spreading word that you killed some kid and got your old man locked up for it. Verring's been talking to people. Telling them stuff about when you were a kid. He's got newspapers showing you when you were in Maritime. He's telling everybody who'll listen that you killed the kid.' I felt my head nodding. Moving on its own. 'Well, Verring was talking about what they found in that car. The one down in the ravine. He said it was Carole's and I didn't believe it, but when they talked about the briefcase I knew it was hers.'

'Why the hell would Verring tell you this?'

'Not just me. He's telling *everybody*. We were at Kobi's drinking and throwing darts when Verring came in with a posse of his deputy friends. All plain clothes and smiles. He gathered us round. Not just me and Lou and Red, but everyone in the bar. Made a roll call and had the place stop for him. Then he started the story. Started passing round pictures while he talked.'

'He only talking about the thing with my old man?'

'Said something about Carole's Jeep getting found down in a ravine. Said it had a dead guy in it and then he went on about you killing people.'

'He say anything about how the man got in Carole's car?'

'The dead guy?' he asked.

'Yeah, Herman. The dead guy.'

'He didn't say. I just figured he's the one she was meeting.' He shook his head. Shook it hard enough for the hair to move over his eyes. He brushed it to the side. 'I don't know for sure. She only told me that she was after some kind of end. That's all she kept saying. While she was standing over there at the door she said it a few times. When I told her I couldn't contact that Gillespie kid, she looked at Nancy and said, "This is going to end."'

'She leave anything here? Nancy or Carole. They leave anything behind?'

'No.'

'I want a name, Herman. I want to know everything you've got in your greasy head about this trip my wife took. A name. A person, Herman. Who am I looking for?' His head was moving. Kept my eyes on him and stepped away from the desk. Moved towards him. He slumped back. 'Muniz. That sound familiar?'

'No. Nancy didn't give me any names. Carole was only here

a few times and she didn't talk much. I don't know any names. Your dad gave Carole a lot of stuff and it was causing her a lot of trouble. So she decided to go and see someone about it. That's it. That's everything I've got. She went out to find this guy who knew your dad. See if anyone in Maritime had the same problems with you that he had. If they were still suspicious about you in Maritime. She kept saying it's got to end. It's got to end with Richard.'

It's got to end with your old man, Joe. Carole said so. If she's wanting it to end, then why the hell was she giving up a suitcase to a man like Jules Lewiston?

'How much of the information in that suitcase did you read?'

'Nothing. Of what Carole got from your dad? Nothing. I swear. Nancy told me a few things. Nothing that was a major deal.'

'Last thing Nancy said to you before they left?'

'She wanted to contact the Gillespie kid.' His face blanked out for a few seconds. The penny dropped at my use of the name during the calls. His mind played a game of catch-up. He snapped out of it – came to and said: 'Nancy wanted a gun. I told her there was no way I was going to let her take mine.'

'So you gave them nothing. No weapon. No psychic reading . . .'

'I can't do that stuff. I don't even believe in it. I was just in it 'cause of Nancy. She needed a friend and I thought it sounded interesting. She thought I had an ability. Some kind of aura was all she kept saying. I told her a few things, but it was just out of the blue. Off the top of my head kind of stuff, and she thought I had something. She had herself convinced.'

'How often did you meet here?'

'Now and then. Whenever she tried to contact him.'

I lifted the gun in my hand. Lifted it and was surprised at the weight. Hefted it a few times before looking at Herman. 'Did you give her a false lead?'

'I told her that the kid was talking about water,' he said. 'Told her he was around a lot of water.'

'The hell made you say that?'

'Nancy told me about Maritime. I was always listening to her and acting like it wasn't making it inside my head. Then I'd come back out with it and she'd go wild. She thought I was talking to the dead. Got all excited about it too.' He looked at me and saw I wasn't impressed with his psychic Casanova routine. 'When she said she was trying to get that Gillespie kid, I kind of went with it. Maritime sounded like a place with a lot of water.'

'I'm going now, Herman.'

'Mister Pullman, I swear I didn't know this was going to go so far.'

'Shut up.' I walked over and stood next to him. He stepped back and watched my hand. Watched the gun I had aimed at his chest. 'I'm going to leave you with this, Herman.' He shook his head. 'My wife is still missing and I'm real broke up over that. I think that you had a lot to do with keeping me from getting to her. That's the big problem I'm having with you.' I raised the gun and stopped when it was pointed at his face. He cupped his hands round his mouth. Pushed farther back against the wall. 'Do you see how much of a problem I have with you?' He nodded his head. 'Good. If you hear from Nancy or Carole again, you are going to call me. Use the number in the phone book. It comes through to my cell. Anything from them, you call me. If I find out that you didn't . . .'

I took a step towards the door. Herman's eyes were red. Long silver lines fell from the corners. They ran down his face and left glistening snail tracks down to his chin. I went through the door. Slipped the gun into the waist of my jeans and headed down the steps.

Herman Dorlund slammed the door between us.

Chapter Twenty-Nine

Marty met me at the busted screen door. He grabbed my waist and held on to me so hard I couldn't bring myself to push him away. I moved with him still holding tight. Moved inside Pop's house and got the door shut. Dropped my keys on the windowsill beside the door and gave Marty a minute. Put my hands on his shoulders and told him things were going to be alright.

'Some kind of misunderstanding. It's no big deal. No matter what you've heard, Marty. It's all good.' I pushed his head back away from me, turned it so he could look at me. He fought against my hands and got his head free. He drove it into my gut. 'No matter what any idiot in this town's been saying. Understand?' Figured he kept holding on because he needed more than I'd been giving him. He knew I'd be leaving again. I tried pushing him back, but he wouldn't budge. Turned to get a look at him in the mirror so he could see me and know I was back. That I was alright. Then I caught sight of his face and from the look of him I could tell he wasn't just holding on to keep me from going. He was holding on so I wouldn't see his face.

'What happened to your eye, Marty?'

'I got into it with somebody,' he said.

'Who?' I asked.

'Doesn't matter.'

'Does to me,' I said. 'Where's Donald?'

'He left. Both me and Pop tried to stop him, but he said he was leaving. He called his dad and told him you got arrested and that Mom's disappeared. Pop tried to cut him off, but Donald shoved him away.'

'Pop alright?' I asked. 'Donald didn't hurt him?'

'No. Pop was angry. He was yelling and cussing, but Donald didn't stop. He went and told his dad everything.' Marty backed away from me and ran his fingers over the lump on his cheek. Kept running his fingers up his face until they rested on his swollen eye. 'I told him to hang up the phone. To stop telling lies. He kept talking and I tried to get the phone off him.' His hand kept rubbing the lump. 'I don't think he meant it. It was just a thing.'

'A thing,' I said.

He shrugged and moved away until his back was against the wall. He crossed his arms over his chest and moved his jaw in a round motion. Kept at it while I looked down at him. Tested it to make sure it was still working. Kind of figured at first that he was making a show of it. Then he shifted and the light caught his face. The shiner on his swollen cheek glistened. He'd taken a good hit. Maybe a couple.

'Tell you what,' I said. 'I've got nothing to do. Nowhere to be. Was planning a walk somewhere to clear my head. Wouldn't mind some company if you're up for it.'

'Where you going?' he asked. I shook my head. 'Down by Cedar Creek's alright when the snow's fresh.'

'Doesn't get much more fresh than it is now,' I said. 'Been at it an hour. Probably will get going again before evening sets in. But if we head off, we'll get a good long walk before the next fall.'

'That'd be good,' Martin said. 'You want to wait for Pop?'

'Where's he at?'

'He went out. I think he was looking for you. Said he was only going a few places. I wanted to stay here just in case you came back. I'll write him a note to let him know where we'll be.'

'You do that. I'll brew some coffee and throw some snacks in a bag.'

He moved away from the door and went down the hall to the guest room. I watched him and had a weird feeling as he passed out of sight. Half-hoped he'd tell me the whole story about what happened with Donald. About what it was he'd been telling his asshole dad. About what he thought I'd done. I wanted to know if Donald hitting Marty was really some kind of an accident. *Just a thing.* Expected there was more to it.

I went into the kitchen and lifted the phone. Dialled a number and listened until Ted picked up. I didn't let him get through his usual greeting. Just cut him off and told him I needed a big favour. He must have had someone with him in the parlour 'cause he cut me short. Told me to hold the line, like he told all the other people who phoned in. Held quiet and listened to a few voices in the background. They faded. Ted came back on.

'Yeah, Joe. You okay?'

'Fine.'

'How's Marty holding up?' he asked. I started to talk, but he went on: 'Judy went over to the house last night and dropped off some food. Casserole and a cake. She sat with Marty while Pop went out for a few. Think he needed to blow off some steam after what Donald pulled. Hope you're okay with the way Marty's been looked after. We'd have been more involved, but Judy had to be at an appointment at the medical centre and I needed to get things sorted out here.'

'It's fine, Ted. Tell Judy I appreciate what she was able to do.'

Didn't feel like getting into the whole deal about Donald, either. I couldn't handle much more of anything. Ted would have hell and all questions for me to answer if I gave him the

344

time. Donald would apologise eventually, and he'd want to speak with Marty so he could smooth things over. From there we could call it even.

'You okay?'

'I'm fine, Ted. But I need some time with Marty. He's been feeling out of it for a while. We're going to stretch our legs and talk. Maybe give him a warning of the kinds of things people will be saying about me. Won't get in to the office today at any rate. You okay with that?'

'You just take care of that boy.'

'Plan to. He's been getting the short end. When they're tough as Marty it's too easy to believe they can survive anything.'

'They'll always learn what they need to survive, Joe. The kid's a good one.'

'Suppose you may be right,' I said.

'I'm getting old, Joe. Of course I'm right. See you tomorrow, and take your time with him.'

'Alright, bud.'

I hung up. Filled the kettle and put it on the boiler. Went for the cabinet where Pop keeps the instant coffee. I didn't have time to filter anything. Reached my hand out and turned my attention to the cabinet. Force of habit. Got used to finding notes. Started expecting them wherever I went. Looked on cabinets and doors for a message of some kind.

'Dad?' Marty called from down the hall. His voice seemed normal again. He had energy and life in him. I didn't want to ruin it.

'What is it, bud?'

'You think I need to double up on my clothes? Storm's still building.'

'Doesn't feel that bad to me. If we get cold we'll walk fast. If we don't go soon, it won't matter anyhow.'

He came down the hall. Came into the kitchen and I got a good look at his eye. It was swollen, and where the skin was stretching it took a yellow shine under the light. Side of his face was red from his jaw to his ear. A smudge of something reached up from his eyebrow to his hairline.

'You took a lickin'',' I said.

'And I keep on tickin'.'

Probably laughed more than I should, but it felt good. I needed it. And the way Marty caught on, it sounded like he needed it too. I leaned against the counter and kept chuckling out the laugh. Marty had his shoulder pressed against the door jamb and watched his shoes. We didn't move until the kettle whistled. Pulled the thermos and coffee from the cabinet. It was all quick and efficient. Marty pitched and pulled out the snacks he wanted to take along. We didn't speak, just packed and headed out the door to the van.

We were down the road before I spoke. Marty was singing along with a song on the radio. I'd never heard it before. He'd changed the station when we got in. A college station that faded in and out. I turned the radio down. He kept on singing – under his breath now.

'When did you get back to the house?' I asked.

'Pop brought me back about lunchtime,' he said.

'When was it Donald left?'

'Last night. Right after he shoved Pop and hit me. He just up and went.'

'Anybody come to the house while you were sitting around?' I asked. 'After Pop went out.'

'What do you mean?'

'You get any visitors?' I kept my eyes on the road. 'Anyone other than Pop?'

'Nope.'

He turned the radio up again. The song finished. Something else started that I didn't recognise. I drove down to the picnic site at Cedar Creek. Pulled into a parking space. It was just me and Marty, the van and the tracks our wheels had cut in the snow. It was a long walk to get to the creek. A good way to ease into a conversation. Gave us both time to consider what we wanted each other to know. No need to jump in just to keep a conversation going.

The clouds were layering again. Dark grey rolling into black. Winds had trailed off and the trees sagged with a heavy fall of white powder. There was a silence. A calm. It was interrupted by the distant sound of cars passing on the highway. Traffic hidden by the hills and trees to the east. Our boots pressed through the snow. Made almost no sound at all. Like a brush sweeping over sand.

'I used to come here all the time with Pop. He brought me down here before that path was paved,' I said. 'Before the road went past the ranger station.'

'So it was just forest,' he said.

'That's pretty much it. No picnic tables. Frisbee golf hadn't made it to Henderson back then.'

'Probably wasn't even invented,' Marty said. He was smiling. Made me feel like the day was worth something. So I reached out and set my hand on the back of his neck. Squeezed it. Nothing hard. Just enough to get a response. He jumped away and laughed some more. Made like he was ready to box me. Confidence back in force.

'Things weren't all that different for me, Marty. You've probably got this idea in your head that I lived in a black-and-white world. But that's not the case, bud. I was a kid like you. Making mistakes. There were some good times. Mostly with Pop and Mona. When they brought me here it was better.'

We walked a while without talking.

'Pop even had hair back then, full dark hair.'

Marty laughed.

'That's like Homer Simpson with a toupee,' Marty said.

'You're not far off, bud. He was just like that.'

We laughed. Kept walking. Hands in pockets and chins to our chests. Marching into the forest. Down the path and kicking through fresh snow. Marty left a skid path behind him.

Zigzagging the trail like an Olympic skier. Made the swooshing sound of skis cutting a frozen crust. Arms up to his sides. Invisible skis out behind him. He stopped and walked back to me.

'What was it like for you when Grandma died?' he asked. 'Not Mona, I mean. Your real mom.'

'That's a tough one, Marty.'

'Sorry,' he said.

'Don't be. It's the kind of thing I need to be asked. You know, it's weird, but I'm always glad when people ask about your grandma. It's hard to think about her. But I don't want to not think about her. Can you understand that?' He nodded his head. 'She was a strong woman. I don't say that just 'cause she was my real mother. She had something most women don't have. Most people don't have. Not that I can put a finger on it. Maybe it's just something that's stuck in my head 'cause of the end. When she was getting even weaker by the day. She was just a shell. Seeing her get away from my father like that was something. I idolised her for doing it. Being able to slip away. There was a kind of power in that.'

'You think Mom was strong?' he asked.

'She's strong, yeah.'

'You don't think she's dead?'

'Marty,' I said. 'You should have hope that she's alright. She's not here right now and that's tough. But she's not dead.'

'You know that for sure?' I nodded my head without looking at him. 'You seen her in town?' he asked.

I stopped. He walked a few more steps and followed my lead. He went a way before he finally stood still and turned round to face me. Lifted his chin from his chest. He was sucking at his bottom lip and frowned like he was waiting for an answer.

'No, Marty, I haven't seen her.' I kept my eyes on him. Waiting for a reaction. Hoping he'd spill what was on his mind.

Knowing this time, if he didn't, I'd have to start prying. 'Tell me what's going on, bud.'

'Nothing really.'

'You'd tell me if you've seen your mom? If she's come back to the house?'

'No,' he said. His hands came from his pockets and opened up in front of his chest. He rubbed them together and looked away from me. Pushed his hands back down in his pockets and stared at the prints we'd left in the snow. 'I mean I'd tell you, yeah. But, no, I haven't seen her.'

'So what's this about?'

'It's nothing,' he said. Turned and started walking away. I followed. Fought an urge to grab the hood of his jacket. Swing him round and bring him face to face with me. Same as my old man would have done. Have him give me the details. All of them. Man-to-man. Have him spill what happened yesterday. *Why did Donald hit you? What did he say? What is everybody else saying?* But I didn't go for him. Instead I walked. Kept pace with him at first. We passed the third marker. Six markers to the creek bed – where the path headed south. We were on an incline. He slowed to keep his footing. I caught up with him and almost went down on the path.

'You alright?' Marty asked.

'I'm fine. Just kind of shocked it out of me. Twisted something.'

I grabbed at the side of my boot. My ankle was shooting a pain back up the length of my leg. A signal that something was wrong. The body's internal telegraph to find a comfortable chair 'cause you'll be resting a while. Figured it was a good sprain that was going to swell up the minute my boot came off.

'Neil Podie was telling the guys at school that he saw Mom.' Marty was breathing heavy. White puffs of smoke came from his mouth. There wasn't much of a break in the rhythm. He was staring down the hill. Kept his attention on something

349

else so he wouldn't have to look at me. 'He swears she's been all over town.'

'So what did you tell him?' I said.

He shook his head.

'That's from Donald,' he said pointing to his eye. He moved his finger across his face and stopped when he got to the red around his jaw. He said: 'That's from Neil Podie.'

'When did you get in a fight with him?' I asked.

'I went out with Pop to the hardware store. When Pop went inside I went to talk with the guys. They were up looking in the window at Howison's. They've got a load of new model tanks in. They were all talking, and when I came up to them they went quiet. Stepped away from me like I was a disease. Then Neil Podie called me Casper.'

Almost laughed, but stopped when I saw how upset Marty was getting. I was just pleased they didn't give him hassle for being the son of a criminal. The offspring of the only jailbird Henderson had to display. I'd disappointed him. My response wasn't what he was expecting. Shook the smile off my face and finished pressing my ankle into shape. Stood and tested it with my weight. Seemed alright. Probably just the support from my boot. Take it off and let the swelling commence.

'Sorry, Marty. It's just I don't understand.'

'Casper's the friendly ghost. Neil Podie says Mom's dead and everyone knows it, but still everybody's seeing her. Nobody's spoke with her all the time she's been gone. They say it's weird that everyone says they've seen her, but nobody is talking to her. So it's going round that it's her ghost that's here. Not really Mom.'

'Marty,' I said. 'I'm real sorry about the Casper thing. You're not a kid who gets wound up easy, so I expected a girl was involved. Something different. Anyway.' I made a waving motion with my hands. Brought one down on Marty's shoulder. Used the other one to emphasise the point I was about to make. 'It's crazy. This ghost thing. Your mom took a break. For whatever reason. I can't give you a good one. But she'll be back. We'll hear from her soon.'

Sure about that, Joe? Don't forget the blood in Jules Lewiston's car. Her blood and her purse.

We walked a way farther. Marty went off ahead of me again before doing a slow zigzag back. Look on his face gave me the same warning as before. He'd loosened me up with the Casper story so that what he had to tell me next didn't come with the same anticipation. Wasn't feeling the same twist in my gut. Wished I had, 'cause the impact might not have taken the wind out of me so easily. Could have used a moment to prepare.

'I've got to tell you something else, Dad,' he said. He looked tired. Looked like he'd been holding on to whatever it was for too long and needed to finally get it away. Drop it and let someone else take the weight for a while. 'I feel real bad about keeping this from you. But I kind of needed it to keep secret. For Mom more than anything.'

We walked back towards the van. I took it easy 'cause my ankle was starting to throb. Even with the pain, I found I was walking faster. In part 'cause of the snow falling and in part 'cause I was trying to move away from what he was about to say. Trying to outrun bad news. We walked – feet slipping on the new snow that was settling onto the path. Marty was usually the one to look back. Always checking to see if there was anyone coming up behind us. But he was thinking hard. He was trying to get his words together before he told me everything that was on his mind. I was waiting for him to speak. Feeling anxious about what I was going to hear. Thinking there was something coming – something on the way – that was going to make it hard for me to go on with things.

'We went to a place called Maritime,' Marty said. 'When we told you we were going to see Grandma and Grandpa last. We went up to Maritime. We went there a few times. Mom told me not to say anything to you. Said you'd get really mad. Said it would bring back too many bad memories that you were trying to forget. So I didn't tell you. Only I can't sleep some nights 'cause I keep thinking about us making those trips.'

'Okay,' I said. There wasn't anything behind us. The hill ahead was looking steep. I put my hand on Marty's shoulder and he stepped up the pace. The snow was coming down hard again. The winds picking up. 'So, tell me about this trip. What did you think of the place?'

'It's big, I guess. Bigger than Henderson anyway.' Marty hung his head. 'We went by a shopping mall. Drove round some of the schools. Some of them were okay. Others were kind of rough-looking. Then we went down to a lake.' I nodded my head. Marty didn't like the silence, so he said: 'I wanted to take a boat out, but Mom told me it wasn't allowed. Said it wasn't the right season.'

'She was just trying to protect you,' I said. 'So what else did you see?'

'Not much.' Marty lifted his head. Punched his hands into his pockets and tilted his face to the sky. Snow fell on his eye lids. He looked pleased. Like he was okay now that he had told me all about the trips he'd taken with Carole. Seemed like it was enough for him to confess he'd been involved. I needed him to keep talking.

'I'm glad you let me know, Marty. Sometimes your mom needs to get away for a while.' I took my hand away from his shoulder. Clenched my fingers to get the blood flowing again. Restore some of the feeling the cold had taken away. 'Henderson's not home for everybody.'

'That's what she said.'

Marty was looking at me again. He wasn't smiling, but he looked like he wasn't far from putting something on his face. Even if it was just to make an impression. We walked faster, slipping over the path. It could have been a good time. I could have let that one go. Forgive Carole and Marty . . . But, Marty spoke again.

'Mister Muniz says small towns make some people feel uneasy.'

My teeth came together and my jaw tightened.

'Mister Muniz told you that?'

'Yeah,' Marty laughed. 'He and Mom were always talking about it. Mom told him how everyone in Henderson wears the same clothes. You know, 'cause we all shop at the same stores. And she said the only culture we get is in high school when our football teams travel to other schools for games. Mister Muniz said it wasn't much culture, being they were other local small towns.'

We made it to the top of the hill. The van was still the only car in the lot. Yellow arcs of light fanned down from the two street lamps. They'd been triggered by the dull skies. We walked a while. Marty was whistling by then, so pleased with the way he felt after clearing his conscience. Sensing things were returning to Henderson-normal. I didn't want to spoil that feeling. Didn't want him to lose what he had at that moment. But I needed to find my own good feelings. Needed to know who the hell Muniz was and what game he was playing. Needed to know how I could get to him to get my wife back.

'Marty,' I said. Tried to make it sound like I wasn't eaten up by the whole thing. I called out his name like I wanted to tell him a joke. Like there was something funny about to follow. He looked at me and we kept walking towards the van. 'I know Mister Muniz, don't I?'

'It's Mom's friend from Columbia,' he said. 'Mom says you were friends a long while back.'

I nodded my head at him while I ran through my memories like I was searching a pile of keys for one that was going to open a locked door. Only all the keys looked the same. There was nothing unique about any of them. Shook my head.

'I can't remember him. Of all the names and faces I've got

353

in my head, I can't picture a Muniz. What's his first name? Can you remember that?'

'Mom called him Carl.'

'Oh, yeah. Carl. That rings a bell.' I was chewing my lip hard. Sparkles of pain kept my mind clear while I figured a way of throwing Marty a curve ball. Let him think that what he was telling me I needed to hear. That it was good for him to keep revealing all his mother's secrets.

'Carlos Muniz,' I said. 'I'll be . . . That was a long time ago. Is he still fat?'

'Nope,' Marty said. He jumped ahead. Back-pedalled and watched my face while he spoke. Looked real pleased with himself for being able to tell me all about my old friend Carlos. A guy I didn't know from Imhotep's third cousin. A man who met with my wife and son on a trip I didn't even know they were taking. Some soneofabitch that called me from a road-side diner playing like he was my old man's lawyer.

While Marty danced backwards and spoke, I felt a strange sympathy for him. He was in the middle of something that could split his family. He had been part of something that *had* split his family and he didn't even know to stop talking. To stop dancing.

'Carlos isn't a real big guy. Was he fat when you knew him, Dad?'

'Well, Marty we were in high school. Some guys are slow starters. But, yeah, he was fat. Kind of on the short side too.'

'He's not as tall as you,' he said and made his feet skip a few steps. Spun round and faced me. 'He's got his own company, though. Drove us around in a new car. It was foreign, so I can't tell you what kind it was. But it smelled new. Mom kept telling him it was a nice one.' Then, like he remembered who he was speaking to, he added: 'She was in the back seat with me.'

'Oh,' I said. 'Where were you guys going?' Marty stopped walking backwards. He turned and watched the path. Bowed his head and kept ahead of me. I asked: 'Did Carlos take you to see the schools?' He nodded his head. 'You remember the names of any? You visit Hampton Academy? You remember that one?'

He nodded. 'That's one of the rough ones. I had a bad feeling when we were walking around it.'

Nothing changed there, Joe.

'Why did Mom have Mister Muniz take you to all the schools?'

'We were going to the house, and I guess we were passing by them in his car. He pulled in and gave us a—'

'What house are you talking about, Marty?'

'It was on . . . I can't remember the name of the street.'

'Westchester?' I asked.

He nodded his head.

'That was one of them.'

'You go to another?' I asked.

He nodded. A dry sort of feeling clouded up in the back of my throat.

'You remember the street that the house was on?' He shook his head. 'How about the name? Anything on the door or the mailbox of the house?' Marty nodded his head. His eyes were looking up the path. He was walking faster. I kept up with him. 'Was the name Gillespie?' I asked him. He shook his head and picked up the pace.

'Lewiston? Was the name Lewiston?' I asked.

I had to walk faster to keep up with him. Wanted to grab him by his collar and pull him back, but I didn't. *It's not his fault, Joe. He was only following Carole.*

Marty nodded his head. Then he took off running. I watched him run across the parking lot. His feet leaving a trail leading to the van. I didn't have the energy to chase him.

Chapter Thirty

Marty was leaning against the passenger side of the van, kicking at the snow. I opened the doors and got in and started the engine. I wanted to tell him he'd been right to spill his guts about everything. Knew while I looked down at him that I should swallow my pride and give him the reassurance he needed. Trouble was I couldn't bring myself to give him that or anything else. It's a bad way to deal with your kid, but I can't find comfort in being any other way. I'd tried and it never felt natural.

'You're angry with me, aren't you?'

I shook my head. He was just like Carole, always wanting to talk things out. Sometimes it's best to keep silent and let time run its course. Let it age and weaken and soften the problem.

'Then why are you looking at me like that?'

Pulled the van out of the space and started driving. Marty was quiet in his seat and that suited me alright. Almost wished he'd done his usual thing and disappeared into the back. Sometimes he liked to lie down on the gurney while I drove. I'd strap him in with his arms folded over his chest and his legs tight together. When he laid like that I'd take the back roads home. Long, swaying bends in the hills. Marty would lie back there and stay silent until we hit the dips and then he would laugh. Some of the dips make your stomach jump – same as a roller-coaster.

'Sure you're not wanting to go in the back?' I asked him. Maybe I asked partly because I knew he liked it. But I needed him away from me. There was a big part of me that needed to be alone. A part that had started resenting Marty. Sure, he'd done what he thought was right and seemed pleased when things fell into place. But I had to consider what these small trips meant to the big picture. And looking at it that way, Marty wasn't the blue-eyed boy any more. He was involved in everything that had happened.

Gripping the wheel and watching the road, I could hear their voices speaking inside Carlos Muniz's car. Laughing and joking. Speaking about Henderson and all the small-minded small-town people. Marty cutting up right along with them. Beyond it hurting to think of my son doing just that – pitching out jokes about the only place he ever knew – it hurt to imagine him with Carole and another man. I'd been hundreds of miles away, picking up bodies in a white van, thinking Carole and Marty were with the in-laws. Sitting in a house in Cumberland listening to Paul tell stories about an old war.

You called them, Joe. That night when they were away, you called over there to speak with them. It almost came out. I almost said it out loud. It was too much of a thought to keep inside. Held tight onto the steering wheel and pushed the accelerator down hard. We moved faster over the snow. Had to keep it from making its way out of my mouth. Not telling what else would come out once I'd started.

You phoned them up, Joe. You called them that night, and Frances told you that they had gone out to see a movie. You left a message with Frances, damn it! And Carole called later to tell you about the movie. Some film you'd never seen. Some movie you could never question her about.

'Why are you driving so fast?' Marty asked.

'I've got a lot on my mind, Marty. You can understand that, can't you?'

'Yeah,' he said. 'I'm sorry. Things were different when Mom

was around. When we went up to Maritime it didn't seem like anything was wrong. It didn't feel like we were doing a bad thing.'

'How's it feel now, Marty?' My voice was shaky. There was emotion in the words. I was trying to keep from letting it all come out. Something I've practised over the years. Something that's not easily controlled. 'You feel any different now?'

'Feels wrong.'

'Sure it does,' I said. My head was nodding. I stopped it and corrected the wheel. I'd been steering off the road. Hit the gravel on the shoulder. Wheel turned into a jackhammer in my hands. Pulled the van back in line and started nodding my head again. 'When you do something like this, it's got to feel wrong. That's a big lesson for you to have to learn.'

'Why are you yelling at me?' he asked.

'I'm not yelling!'

Marty fell back into his seat. Pushed himself towards the door and hid his face. Pressed it close to the window. I made it to Main Street and waited for a logger truck to make it past – rushing up towards the timber mills. Marty was crying heavily by the time I got the van heading up Main.

'Marty,' I said. 'Hush things up, bud. Look, I'm just upset is all. It was good for you to tell me all this stuff. It's something I needed to hear. I'm upset more because it was kept from me for so long. This is the kind of stuff I need to know. Maybe something you just told me will help to find her.'

'You're looking for her?'

'Yeah, Marty. I'm looking for her in my own way. May not look like it, but I'm real damned close to finding her too.'

He nodded his head and sat up straight in his seat. Used the sleeve of his jacket to wipe a line of snot from his lip.

'I'm not angry. I'm disappointed.'

Marty crossed his arms. Set his hands in his lap and looked ahead for a while. His shoulders heaved, but I didn't hear any sounds. He was on his own to deal with the thoughts his mind was churning out. Sometimes that was a good thing. He'd work through as much as he could handle on his own. Then we'd talk again. By that time I'd have a plan. By that time I could deal with what he had to say.

I might be able to offer him something in return.

Made it to Pop's house and pulled the van into the driveway. Shut the engine off and looked over at Marty. He was fast asleep.

Chapter Thirty-One

The black mesh of the screen door folded over like a curtain in a window. The white frame it was once attached to was still in place. The imprint of a shoe, too big to be Pop's, marked the outside of the door frame. I suspected it belonged to Paul Quincy. Same as I figured the small black circles belonged to the bottom of his cane. Must have hammered like mad at the door to get Pop's attention.

I shifted Marty up to get a better hold. His legs dangled over my left arm. His head burrowed into my right shoulder. He was out and sleeping heavily. Carole always said he gained ten pounds when he was asleep. Carrying him from the van to Pop's front door, I knew she wasn't far off. She never was. I pulled the screen door open and tried the handle of the main door, expecting it to be locked. It turned and I pushed it open and went inside. Scoped out Pop's front room for a place to set Marty down. The sofa looked like the scene of a crime. The engine from the snow-blower was sitting on an old rug on the floor where Pop usually kept the coffee table. He'd covered the cushions of the sofa with old towels. Set the hoses and belts from the engine lengthways on the towels. Sausages at a butcher's stall. I hefted Marty on my shoulder while I looked at the mess. Smelled the oil and grease and knew Marty wouldn't be sleeping on the sofa any time soon. Went down the hall and set him on the bed in Pop's guest room. Left him in his coat and covered his legs with the quilt. Backing out of the room, I hoped Marty would be out until the morning. Give me time to get some distance before he had a chance to ask any questions.

I went up the hall to the family room. Called out to Pop and waited for a response. Heard the glass door to his back patio slide open, and I gave it a few seconds and called out again.

'Hey, old man, you around?'

'Out here,' Pop said. 'Outside getting some fresh air.'

I followed his voice. Went through the kitchen and saw he'd stacked a few more plates to his collection. The tower was getting bigger and the fungus was getting thicker. Passed the clutter and went through the glass doors to the patio. The doors were smudged with crusted white snot from a dead mongrel Pop had called Spick. He'd found it while fishing along the river during the spring months, brought it home and kitted it out with everything. Ironic 'cause it was a useless beast. It would bark for hours at the artificial palm in the corner of Pop's living room, then slink away at the sound of a knock at the door. But Pop had a connection with the animal. For some reason he couldn't do enough for it.

I stood outside and got a better view of the marks on the glass. Imprints like rubber stamps, smudged up in long sweeping streaks. It was thick in places, flaking off like dried paint in patches. Before going out the door I spotted the print of the nose. Almost perfect. Two teardrop nostrils painted in cream.

'You enjoy your first day of freedom?' Pop asked. I nodded. 'A full day of fatherhood.' Took my eyes off the glass and looked at him. Showed him I didn't get what he was saying. At least how he knew what I'd been doing. 'Ted called me. Found me over at the Tavern. Told me you called from here and that you were taking some time with Marty.'

Pop looked out at the yard. I followed his lead. Moved my hand to touch away the string of bulbs he had hung up on the roof. He'd continued with the bulbs in the yard, stringing them up along an otherwise empty arbour in the middle of the lawn. 'You both need that, Joe. More than just today too.'

'Maybe,' I said.

'You want to knock back a few?' Pop was already opening the new box of beers while he spoke. He stuck his hand in to fish out a pair of cans. His hair was falling out from under his trucker's cap. He brushed it back with heavy fingers. It fell again and this time he left it. He brought up a can and handed it to me. I got one of the folding chairs Pop had stacked against the house. Shook it open and set it next to Pop. Sat down and looked out at Pop's white lawn. Looked at how the snow was already melting on his green artificial grass.

'Jesus, Pop,' I said. 'It's like a football field.'

'Yeah,' he said. 'Just like it.'

I raised the can and took a heavy pull. Downed half of it before stopping.

'Where'd the real lawn go?'

'They dug it up and took it away.' He popped the top of his beer and drank. He was sweeping his hand in the air. It was a motion that made me look out at the long, wide yard. All green plastic grass. 'It been that long since you came over here?'

'Yeah, Pop.' I took a drink and when I was finished I kept nodding my head. Moved the can away from my mouth. 'I'd sue the assholes for that.'

'I asked for it. Got tired of the real stuff. Tending to it all the damned time.' We both sat watching the yard. A wind blew and something shifted on the roof. A sheet of snow fell down and landed on the lawn, hit the ground a few feet away from us. Pop stood up and looked at the new pile of snow from another angle. Then he sat down again.

'I'll fix that screen door if you've got some duct tape,' I said.

Pop looked at me. His forehead was wrinkled up with deep lines. His eyebrows settled after a few seconds and the crevices planed out. Then his head nodded forward before he took a drink from the beer can.

'I take it Paul kicked it in when he was here the other night,' I said.

'Nope. Donald did that damage.'

'Sorry to hear about that,' I said. Watched Pop shrug his shoulders. 'He's got a lot in his mind. No good reason to shove you, but he's hurting.'

'Sure he is.'

Pop laughed. I took another drink and said: 'That's a riot, Pop.' I drank again, so Pop wouldn't expect a laugh in return.

'There was no controlling him. Tried to get him to stop talking all that nonsense. Went to get the phone off him.' Pop shook his head. He was looking at the lawn with a new wet filling his eyes. 'He was not Donald that night. He was all fired up about everything. Like everything hit him all of a sudden. One big whoosh of realisation.' Pop's head was moving from side to side, ducking punches that came with the wind. 'Wouldn't have got that far if you'd been here. That's what set him off.'

'I'm here now, Pop.'

'Those idiots arresting you like that. The hell was Nat thinking?'

We drank. Pop pulled two more cans free from the case. He handed one across to me and pulled the tab of the second. Tossed the empty cans out to the artificial turf.

'How'd they treat you?'

'It was a show. Deputies getting caught up in the moment. Lasted the night through.'

'They wouldn't let us in to see you. I called up there and talked to Nat. He was leaving to go to Maritime and he told me the place was crawling with folks. Told me it was best to keep Marty away.'

I nodded my head. Glad he'd made the decision.

'Any ideas about what Carole's playing at?' he asked.

363

Yeah, Pop. According to Herman Dorlund, she's trying to make it end with my old man. But, then she's hanging out with some guy named Muniz. How the hell that's going to play out . . . Your guess is as good as mine. I kept shaking my head and watching the can.

'You checked her credit cards?'

'Nat checked them after her purse was found in that car in Maritime. They authorised the release of the records. Can't see it being of use. Don't need to know where she was before she got separated from her purse.'

'How's Marty seem to you?'

'He's shook up about Donald. You see the knocking he gave Marty before he left? Swollen up. Kid took a good one.' Pop was sitting with his arms balanced on the chair rests. 'How'd Donnie get up to his dad's?'

Pop shrugged his shoulders.

'Probably should call and make sure he made it up there. After all the yelling and shoving, I couldn't bring myself to taking him anywhere. After what he did to Marty especially.'

I didn't say anything. All of a sudden I felt like I'd lost someone else. Donald was gone and I was alright to leave him gone. But I started feeling sorry for myself. *You're more alone now, Joe. Carole. Then Donald. Who's next . . . Pop or Marty?*

'She's got no right to do this to those boys,' Pop said. 'They're good kids. Thing like this can turn them bad.'

Pop moved the can of beer so it was sitting between his knees. His arms weighing heavy against the red plastic armrests of his chair. His neck was sagging now. His face had started falling a couple of years back. Gravity taking no prisoners. Veins pushing farther out on the tip of his nose and scattering through his cheeks. And his eyes – under the thick fur of an overgrown brow – were yellowing same as old paper. They spun to the side and caught me looking.

'Yeah, Joe,' Pop said. 'I got old.'

'Happens.'

'Even quicker when you lose what you need.'

'I'm feeling it.'

'Just the facts, man,' Pop said. He laughed. This time I joined in.

'Thanks, Pop.'

'Don't turn out like me, son. Keep part of yourself. Don't hand it all over to something that can go away.'

'That what happened to you?' I was still smiling. Even now that Pop wasn't in it for the laughs. I still smiled, thinking: *Pop's turned a corner now.*

'Look at that mess,' Pop said. He tossed a thumb over his shoulder. I looked where he was pointing and caught sight of the glass doors. All the shapes in crusted white. White swirls shaping the nose of the mongrel dog.

'Spick left a hell of a mark,' he said.

'Yeah, he did, Pop.'

'And I can't bring myself to wipe that shit off. I bought a bottle of glass-cleaner. Heavy-duty stuff. Made with vinegar, it said. Best stuff to keep glass sparkling. It's amazing, it said. Even bought new rags.' Pop sat there shaking his head. 'Who the hell buys rags? They're rags 'cause they're worthless. Christ! And can I get myself to spray the stuff on the door? Can I wipe those marks away?'

'He was a good dog, Pop.' I thought it's what needed to be said.

'He smelled bad in the end. Last six months. Had that thing come up on the centre of his head.' Pop tapped at his scalp with a single bony finger. 'Big black thing. It'd flake off and underneath it was pink. Then it'd go black again. Vet didn't know what to do. Freeze it, he said. Cut and cauterise. Finally gave me cream and I'd lather it up and Spick'd rub it off all over the curtains.'

'Another beer?'

'Yeah,' Pop said. He finished the can he held. Dropped it to the ground and reached for a couple more. He handed one to me. I took it and watched him. Seemed Pop was turning to dust, but still had some substance that was binding him together. Keeping him from blowing away.

'Six months should be enough.'

'They're just nose marks, Pop.'

'Yeah and they're from Spick.' Pop watched the yard and drank his beer.

I joined him. The urge to say something was controllable for a while. Then the sound of a neighbour starting up their car brought me back. Made me want to talk. My thoughts were filling up inside. Layering and compounding and looking for a way out.

'She's not coming back,' I said and listened to the car moving out of the driveway. Onto the street and down the road. 'Not on her own anyway.'

'I know that, son.'

'I'm leaving tomorrow.' Threw my thumb over my shoulder. Got Pop looking at the sliding door. The ghosts of Spick's nose swirling on the glass. 'Kind of worried that something like that's going to happen to me if I don't make a move.' Toyed with the idea of telling him what Marty had shared with me. Thought better of it 'cause Pop would do all he could to keep me from leaving with the new information. A new anger burning. He'd play through a couple of scenes in his mind of how I'd deal with this Muniz guy, none of them ending with a laugh and a handshake.

Watched Pop while he nodded his head. Looked past me the way he always did when the subject was something he didn't find comforting. When I was planning something he didn't agree with. Approval from Pop came in a direct sort of way. He'd look at you and wish you all the best. He'd be sincere about it. *Pop, I'm going to ask Carole to marry me, Well, that's the best damned decision you have ever made. I'm moving into the TP for a while. Me and Carole need to work some things out. Oh, come on, Pop. Don't do that. Look at me . . .* When he had other thoughts, he'd look way out somewhere. In the distance, and he'd wait for you to try and convince yourself that you were on the right track. It was a hard thing to do.

'You're heading out to Maritime, I take it.'

'Yeah, Pop. She's there and I need to bring her back.'

'Well, you keep on the good side of this,' Pop said. He'd given up on keeping me straight. Must have figured the same as me – that the time for peace had passed. Acting the soft touch had got me nowhere. Gave a lot of people in town the false impression. I had no intention of storming round town when the morning came. I'd had enough of the people in Henderson. Had it up to overflow with the looks and the rumours, and what was ready to spill out was going to hurt anyone it touched.

Pop looked me in the eye. Felt sort of uncomfortable to see him that way. His chin down, splaying his beard out like the fur of some great white beast. His eyes looked thoughtful and tired.

'She hasn't been shacking up?'

'Can't see Carole pulling that one. Not in Henderson anyway.'

Mister Muniz's not as tall as you, Dad, but he sure does drive a nice car. Not going to give that one to Pop to chew on are you, Joe?

'Don't do anything stupid. Tell me you're gonna keep your head this time round.'

'I'll keep it tight, Pop.'

Drank heavy from the beer and almost finished it in a oner. Like an afterthought I raised the can and held it towards Pop. We clinked the cans together. They made a hollow sound.

'Hope you find her and bring her back home.'

'I will, Pop.' I took a drink and let the silence settle between us. 'I'll find her alright.'

'Leave Marty with me. No need taking him home tonight just to drop him back in the morning,' he said. 'I'll make sure he's got something to keep him going. If he asks where you are, I'll tell him you had some business to deal with.'

367

Nodded my head and got up to leave. Felt my head going soft with the beer. Leaned towards Pop and tapped his shoulder before pulling the sliding door open. He went back to watching the white snow covering his lawn. Hiding it from sight.

Went inside and headed for the front door. Looked down the hall with a quiet guilt for leaving Marty behind. Saw the light coming from under the door. Walked back to the guest room and opened the door slow, hoping Marty would still be sleeping. I found him lying across the covers, reading through the pages of an old comic book. It was the same comic he'd read the last twenty times I'd dropped him off to spend time with Pop. He looked up when I came into the room.

'You alright, bud?' I asked.

'I'm okay. How about you?'

'You don't have to worry about me.'

He flipped through a couple more pages and finally shut the thing when I sat on the side of the bed. He moved it to the corner of the bed and sat up, made his legs like an Indian. He turned his face into the old wise-man thing he does so well. So natural. It is a face that makes it difficult to lie to him.

'I've got to go out and do a few things in the morning. Then I have a few important things to take care of after that. You're okay to stay here with Pop for a couple of days. I'll come back and we'll catch up on some missed time.'

'You're going to find Mom in Maritime,' he said. 'You don't need to get angry about it. I know Mom wasn't doing anything wrong. Remember, I was there, and Mister Muniz was just trying to find a house for us. Mom didn't want to tell me why she was doing it, but I think it was just so she could get away. All of us, I mean.'

'Away from what?' I asked.

'Henderson. She really wanted to leave. She said you wouldn't go because you have all your history here. She told me you wouldn't leave unless she . . .' He looked at me. His eyes wet and heavy. 'She said you would only leave here if you had to leave. Then she told me there wasn't going to be a choice.'

I wanted to tell Marty that his mother had filled his head with lies. I wanted to tell him that I'd come to Henderson from a bad past in Maritime and there was not a chance in hell that I'd go back to that place. Things had been good in Henderson. Still wasn't sure I wanted to leave, but Carole . . .

She's going to end it.

Just what the hell was she going to end?

'You don't want to leave here because they protect you,' Marty said. 'Mom didn't say, but I kind of know. You have people who look out for you here.'

Not too much now, Marty. They arrested me, remember that? Some of that protection's gone and will never come back.

It didn't feel like I was talking to my eleven-year-old son. Maybe I'd disconnected myself from the subject. As the subject. But Marty hit it on the head. He knew more about me and my place in the world – about my life – than I knew about him. He was bright and he preferred building models to playing football in the park. He liked black-and-white horror movies and couldn't sit through a whole sitcom without calling it brain-numbing. He could fix whatever problems I was having with my computer. That's what I knew about Marty. But he had other things going on upstairs. A lot more that I didn't know about. He had to – or else he couldn't know so much about me. Chewed my lip while I looked at him. Chewed hard to keep myself from talking.

'They can't protect you when you leave,' he said.

'I better get going.' Reached over and put my hand on his head. Pushed his hair away from his face. 'We can talk about all this when I get back.'

He moved under my hand. Slid over and grabbed me in his arms. Pulled hard like he did when we wrestled.

'Don't forget I'm here, Dad.' He must have sensed that I

didn't feel comfortable. I wasn't pushing him away, just loosening his arm. Getting space between us. He let go and sat back. Moved to the corner of the bed where he'd been before, sitting like a small pale Indian.

Chapter Thirty-Two

I pulled the van into the garage. It's not something I usually do, but I figured I'd be leaving early in the morning and didn't want the cold to keep me from getting a fast start. I wouldn't have to deal with the ice. Waited in the van for the garage door to come down. *Keep eyes off you, Joe. Best thing for you to do is keep out of sight for a while. All those fuckers Verring's convincing that you're a killer will be looking for you.* Went into the house.

It was dark. I kept the lights off and went through to the kitchen. Thought about making coffee, but I needed to crash. Sleep would help get my thoughts in order. Hoped it was going to help keep me from doing something crazy when I started meeting with people in Maritime.

Opened the fridge door and looked at the beers. I'd got down to the four bottles. Looked at them and heard Marty's voice echoing again. Telling me to do the sensible thing. Do the reasonable thing. So I closed the fridge and moved away from it until a chair hit the back of my knees. Sat down and looked up at the cabinets. No notes. No pictures and no warnings. No threats of what was going to come next. I sat there in the dark, a slanting light from the street lamps washing across the cabinet doors.

'What are you doing, Carole?' I asked.

Heard a trap go off – snapping shut under the kitchen sink.

I hadn't loaded them for a while – not since Carole had disappeared. Wasn't expecting the sound. Harsh metal against wood. Something was moving round under there. Small claws scraping at the wood floor where the linoleum wasn't covering. Just dust and crumbs and cobwebs. A sad place to die.

'Probably just nerves,' I said. It's what I would have told Carole. Something to ease her mind while the small legs kicked in circles. The last of its life-juices running a circuit through the muscles.

Carole would be yelling.

God, that makes me sick. Did you hear that? Something just died. Stop smiling at me, Joe.

It started up again. Went into a frenzy, scraping at the floor and dragging the trap along for the ride. Metal bar wrapped round its neck, and there it was pulling it along so it wouldn't die in the dirt and dust.

Get it, Joe. You need to clear that. Now! Take it out and put it out of its misery.

'Sure thing, Carole.'

The mouse banged again.

Goddamn it, Joe!

Sat and listened to the mouse bang against the cabinet. Sound of the small claws working away at the wood floor. Trying to set itself free amongst the crumbs and the dust and the cobwebs. Manoeuvring round in the dark with its head jammed in a vice.

It went silent.

Waited for it to get its energy back. Took some time. Finally heard it scraping at the floor. Kept going at it like it was about to break free. Like it'd found a weakness in the trap. I kept my eye on the floor, on the sink cabinet where the mouse was struggling. Half-expecting the bottom of the cabinet to tip over. Mouse tumbling out with a trap on its neck. Listened to the poor bastard scrape. Then it was all quiet. Everywhere.

Like the world had closed up shop for the night and all sounds in the place went dead. All at once.

It had played itself out. The mouse had worked so hard to stay alive that it went faster. Should have sat and waited and breathed the best it could until its energy came back. But animals don't do things like that. It's nature. Harsh. Cruel.

It struggled until the end, Joe. It's not weak when it struggles. When it fights. I leaned down and pulled the bottom of the cabinet away. The mouse was a small thing. Grey and still trying to breathe. One back leg was shaking and the other was making a slow pawing motion. The guillotine had come down across the nose and held down one arm with it. It had snapped the arm at the shoulder. I looked at it for a while, wondering what the hell I was going to use to snuff it. Carole wasn't around to give me hassle. She wasn't going to come in and see what I was doing.

Took the mouse by the tail and lifted it along with the trap. The trap weighed more than the mouse. Watched as the body grew and then faded with breath. Its legs moved. Front paw scraped. It knew the fight was over, but something kept it alive.

Let the mouse dangle with the trap clipping its head and I reached for a knife. Slipped the knife in and loosened the guillotine. The mouse slipped from the trap. I let the trap and the knife fall to the floor and I raised the mouse to the sink. I held it there, swaying by its tail – upside down, the mouse became a pendulum. Didn't last long. The blood flowed to its head and the thing choked. When it stopped writhing, I set it down inside the sink. Pulled the knife from the floor and slipped the trap from the blade.

Turned on the water and watched it flow in a circle round the sink. Remembered a piece of carrot and a spider at my old man's place. Westchester Drive. Just me and my old man and a spider. The swirl of the water had collected the spider and took it down into the disposal. I'd flipped the switch and ground the spider into nothing. It went down into the disposal with a piece of carrot. It was the carrot I'd heard grinding to pieces. The spider never made a sound.

I stood there for a while, watching the water spinning. Listening to the garbage disposal churning away. Catching something hard on occasion. Chewing through it. The sound told me it was still together. The blades hadn't ripped it apart, not all the way. Not yet.

Listened to the water gurgling. With the disposal off, the sounds were smooth. Soothing. Then I heard the sound of a key fitting into the lock of the front door. The handle turning and the door pushing open. Closing. Footsteps on the hard floor moving towards the kitchen. I stepped back away from the sink. The light came on and someone shouted. I don't think it was me, but I can't be sure.

The room was too bright. I'd have closed my eyes against it, but I couldn't blink. I couldn't take my eyes off of her standing in the archway to the kitchen. My muscles went numb as the face moved into the room. Familiar, yet sunken. This and . . . So afraid.

'Carole,' I said.

'Oh, my God.'

She was gone. The sound of her feet moving against the wood floor brought my muscles to life. I pushed off the cabinets and moved after her. She was at the front door when I got to the family room. She had both hands on the door. Her head was moving back with each pull. The door came open and swung in and slammed against the side table. Sent the phone and the empty vase to the floor. She was onto the porch, moving away when I got through the door and went after her.

'Oh, my God!' she was yelling. 'Help me! Somebody help me!'

'Carole! Jesus Christ, Carole. Come here!'

I got to the sidewalk and was closing in on her. My foot slipped on the snow and I hit the path hard. A shot of pain ripped through my wrist, sending a wave of fire all the way to my shoulder. She was standing by a car. Some kind of sedan. *Goddamned Muniz. She's driving that fucker's car, Joe!* Got to my hands and moved to my feet. Tried to get some kind of traction. She was juggling keys in her hands and trying to get the one she was after before I got to her. I ran to the driveway and moved round the front of her car. She started back-pedalling. Looking at the keys instead of me. Her head down. Hair falling over her face. She was moving towards the road. Still looking at her keys. Moving towards the circle of yellow that the street lamp was throwing on the ground.

'Come in the house.' I was calm. Thought I sounded calm. My breathing was off. Heavy from the shock. From the pain in my arm. And she was still moving away from me. I wanted to get her inside. Get her out from under the street lamp where she would be making a show for the neighbours. I wanted them to see that she was home. Wanted them to know that much, so they could spread the word around. But I didn't want them to see her acting that way. Screaming and afraid.

'That's far enough. Come back.'

'Oh, God,' she said. Her hands were shaking. Keys splayed out on the ring as she kept picking through them.

'Stop that, Carole and come inside.'

She looked up and threw the keys at me. They flew over my shoulder and, when she turned, I was already going for her. She slipped and went down hard. Hit the circle of yellow and her feet kept scraping at the snow. Moving in the dirty grooves tyres had cut into the road. She was on her hands, feet still moving when I caught her from behind. Slipped my arm round her waist and pulled her off the ground. She struggled more.

'Oh, God! No! Somebody help me!'

I grunted and pulled her into a tight hold. My arms cut into her thin waist. She wasn't heavy, but she was moving too much. I was losing my balance. Squeezed tighter and shook her. She stopped moving and made a sound like she needed air. I walked faster towards the house, dragging her feet through the snow. Looked once at Edith Krantz's house. Saw the curtain of the front window open. The room was black, but Edith's small face was looking at me. She had a phone to her ear and her mouth was moving.

'You see, Krantz!' I yelled at her. Kept walking and turned so she could get a look at Carole. 'You see her, Krantz!'

Moved through the door and into the house. Carole was breathing heavy. Lungs filling and falling. Chest moving out and in. Kicked the door shut with my foot and tossed Carole loose. She went stumbling towards the sofa. She was screaming something on her way down. Breathing too hard to get a good scream going. Something about God again. Then she was calling for help. Really screaming her lungs out.

I walked round and sat in my chair. Sat on the edge of the cushion in case she moved. If she'd tried to get away, I'd put my weight on her until she tired herself out. That was the plan. I was ready. She didn't look like she had the intention. Didn't have the energy to make that getaway happen. She was wasting too much of her energy clearing her lungs.

'Scream yourself out.' Reached over and took hold of her knee. It felt thin inside her jeans. I wanted to get up and turn on a light. I wanted to get a better view of her. What was coming through from the kitchen wasn't enough. I couldn't make out what was wrong with her. Moved my hand farther up her thigh. So thin. 'The hell—'

'Get your hands off me!' She sat up. Hair moved away from her face. Cheekbones high on her face. Skin sunk back to her teeth. There were dark crescent shapes under her eyes. Her head dropped before I could get to her. Before I could see how bad she'd fallen since I'd seen her last. Stood away from her and she went back to hiding. Slipped behind the thick brown hair. Moving her hands up like shields. 'Stay away! I swear I'll kill you, Joe!'

'What happened? What's going on?'

'Get away, you fuck!' She stood up and I moved over her. My hands reaching out. Ready to take hold of her shoulders. She moved up and hit me in the chest. Felt the thump on my right side, and before I could reach her she was hitting me again. Stomach. Leg. Arm. Anywhere she could reach her hand out, she took another shot. 'Get away!' she kept yelling. She connected. Moved away. Connected again.

'Stop hitting me.' I grabbed at her and got her shoulders. They moved into a thin blade of light and I saw the red. It glistened. Wet and red. Warm and flowing. 'There's blood,' I yelled at her. 'Carole, where's the blood coming from?' It was on her face. She kept moving. Hitting me. Tried to touch her again and move her into the light. My arms reaching. Her mouth opened and she was screaming again. Blood on her neck. On her face. More spraying, arching and covering her coat. A white coat. Red dots falling on the white. Red soaking in. Dots moving together.

'You're bleeding,' I said. She screamed at me. She screamed and kept hitting. Hand connected. 'Why are you bleeding?'

My hands reached her shoulders. I shook her and her mouth opened in a long shape. She looked to the side and I couldn't hear her scream. I heard a siren, far off in the distance. It was a long way off.

'I have to hold you, Carole. They need to see you're here. They need to see you're alive.' She moved and I fell onto her. Moved her back onto the sofa. 'I'm not a killer,' I whispered in her ear. 'Carole, look at me. Look at me. I'm not a killer.'

Her face was red and her mouth open. Hair pushed back. Skin tight on her cheeks. And she screamed. She screamed and the sound of the sirens mixed with her voice until they came together.

'Why are you bleeding!'

She moved against me. Grabbed her and pulled her in and she couldn't get away. She hit me and tried to stop me from leaning on her. She pushed and I was moving her. Trying to keep her on the sofa. She was so strong. So much stronger than me. Pushing against me. I fell and pulled on her and she came up over me. My back found the floor. Her knee came up and caught my balls. Felt a knot swell up in my guts. Hunched over and still I held onto her.

'Stay with me, Carole.'

She was still moving and struggling against me. Fighting against my arms. It took all I had to keep her. My hands were weak and they were burning. Pins and needles set into all of my fingers. Piercing deep into the meat of my palm. Tried to grab her, but there was nothing.

'Don't, Carole,' I said. 'You can . . .'

She was screaming the sound of sirens. Filling the room and making the dull air swept clean with a blade of red. A blade of blue. Her siren-scream was in my head. Heavy in the air around me. Burning and hot. I watched her moving and her mouth growing with the sound, and a hand fell against my neck. A line of knocks punched into my face. Her small hands were moving against her own face. I held her tight and I moved her. I moved on top of her and the sirens were louder. And a hand was on my neck and it was holding me tighter.

'You can't leave me.'

And my head felt heavy. Heavier with each blow landing. My face wet. Turned and saw Jody Verring standing next to me. His mouth is open and he is making the siren noise. He is moving closer and my head is pulsing again. Siren isn't getting any louder. Red and blue sweeps of colour behind him. Moving forward. He grabs at my arm and the pins and needles go in deeper. Look down at my arm to see his fingers sink into my shirt sleeve. Blood seeping between his fingers.

'She's here,' I said. My voice sounded weak. Not as strong as I needed it to be. Not as heavy as I hoped. 'She's here!'

His fist fell down and caught my eye. Head went to the side. Brought it up to feel the second punch connect. Fell to the side and hit the sofa again. Carole wasn't under me any more. Something was at my legs, knocking them apart. Knocking them so hard the rest of me moved. Slid from the sofa and hit the floor. Looked up at Verring. He stepped back. Carole moved to his side. Moved past him and disappeared into the blades of colour.

'Don't let her go.'

Chapter Thirty-Three

When I came to, I couldn't move my arms. Tried my legs and they were strapped up just the same. Moved my head forward to get a look down my body. Saw the sweeps of blue and red moving across the windows at the front of my house. A hand came up and held my forehead. It was a cold hand. Covered in plastic.

'Keep your head back, Mister Pullman. Relax,' a woman's voice said. Looked to my right and saw a face. Someone I didn't recognise. She was wearing the light-blue button-up of Meridian Ambulance Services under the company-issue navy coat. She was smiling at me, but that wasn't enough to set my mind at ease. They'd strapped me down enough to keep King Kong on a gurney. 'We'll be moving you out in just a minute. Hold tight for us.'

'The hell is going on?' Twisted again, trying to get my hands free. The woman started to look less confident. Dropped her hand to the straps. Gave them a couple of hard tugs before calling out for the sheriff. She called a few times before I joined in.

'Nat, get over here,' I yelled. My ribs ached. My head throbbed. I kept at it. Coughed and felt something well up inside me – hot like lava. It ran down my side under all the clothes and covers. Tried to suck in deep breaths, hoping it would make the sick feeling go away. Nat showed up and hung over me. He set a hand on my shoulder and mouthed something to the paramedic.

I shook my head 'cause I couldn't shake his hand off my shoulder. He pulled his hand away. I coughed a few times and got out what I needed to say: 'She was here. I swear to Christ, Nat. She was here tonight. Verring had her at arm's reach. That sonofabitch had her. Tell me he didn't let her go.'

Nat stepped away from the gurney and waved a hand at a deputy standing in the front door. He was the same guy who had come into my house and sat looking dumb and useless while I reported Carole missing. The deputy looked at me and went through the door into my house. Nat stepped towards me again and kept coming until he was right up over me. 'You take it easy, Joe. Got more slices in you than a danged pack of cheese.'

Tried looking down again, but my neck took a cramp. I dropped my head back to the shallow pillow. Looked up at the ambulance and felt my guts binding up.

'You got her, didn't you? Verring didn't let her go?'

'Take it easy, son. We got the woman who did this. She's in a car and we're getting ready to take her down to the courthouse. First thing, though, we need to get you off to the medical centre.' He dropped his face down close and put his hands on the metal rail at the side of the gurney. Looked at me with a strange kind of sympathy that I wasn't used to seeing. Not the sort of look people were putting my way of late. 'You may be taking a ride into the city before the night's over. Won't know until they check you out fully, but those cuts may have gone deep.'

'What cuts?'

'She got you good, Joe. Must have stabbed that blade into you ten times. Maybe more.'

'What's happened to her, Nat?' Turned my face so I could get a look at him. He was staring at my chest. It was like his eyes had some kind of control over me. I took in a heavy breath to test my lungs. Test the depth of the blades by how well my body was still working. Felt a long burn open up inside. Let the breath leave me fast. Shook my head and said: 'She's not the same woman.'

'You're right about that. She's about as different as can be.'

'You got her,' I said.

'We got her, Joe.'

That woman ambulance driver started pushing the gurney. Said something to Nat that I didn't catch. Something about urgent care. Needing to get me to the medical centre just in case. Had a moment when I worried about the knife Carole used on me. Worried it had been long. Wanted to ask, but I didn't want to know. It hurt to breathe, but it got worse after Nat told me I'd been stabbed. Tried to block it out of my mind, but it wasn't easy. Tried to breathe shallow breaths, but I needed more to keep from feeling sick.

Another paramedic came rushing up from the back of the van. He grabbed hold of the bottom of the gurney and said something that sounded like a prayer. I caught sight of Verring standing on the porch. Had his hand pressed up against a column at the front of the house and was looking out at the cruiser sitting in my front yard. He stood there watching the lights spin round. Hypnotised by the colour it threw against the house. They wheeled me towards the back of the ambulance and Verring looked at me. His expression didn't change. He was full of thoughts and none of them were easy for him to sort out. Stood for a second staring at me waiting at the back of the ambulance, when I heard him call out. He'd decided not to hold back after all.

'It's not Carole,' he yelled. 'Before you get too comfortable tonight, Pullman. That woman in my cruiser is not your wife.'

'What's he talking about?' I asked. I tried to lean my head back so I could see the paramedic. She was still pushing the gurney. Saw her hand close to my head, but I couldn't see her face. 'What the hell's he talking about?'

Leaned my head forward and felt the burning pain in my chest. Still, I leaned forward. Needed to find someone who would tell me what was happening. If that wasn't Carole in the cruiser, I needed to know who it was and what the hell she'd been doing in my house.

'Who the fuck just stabbed me?' I kept yelling. The small glove came over my shoulder and pulled my head back. Wasn't a heavy hand and it didn't press on any of the parts that were burning. Vital places. The hand landing made me consider the wounds. Was like they lit up with fire in an instant. Strange sort of push-button pain. A series of small fires that ignited on my chest and stomach.

Must have stabbed that blade into you ten times. Cuts may have gone deep.

'Hold tight, Mister Pullman,' the guy pulling the gurney said, steering his end to the open doors of the ambulance. He looked back to make sure his partner was following his lead. My head came back round. Looked at the guy's face as he nodded. Fast shove sent me backwards. Something clicked underneath and I saw the walls of the ambulance closing in round me. Watched the guy take hold of a door. Reached for the other. Just before he swung them shut, I saw a road-boat pull up slow and steady in front of my house. It was gliding to a stop next to Verring's cruiser.

'Paul,' I said.

The paramedic jumped in and pulled the doors closed behind him. He knocked on the ceiling and we started a slow crawl backwards. Siren wailed. The paramedic leaned over me. He lifted the blanket covering my chest. Put something cold on me and leaned his head down. Moved the thing round my chest to a few places. Brought it out and covered my chest again.

'You're lucky it wasn't a longer blade,' he said. 'Number of times you've been stabbed . . .'

'How long was it?' Had a feeling he was going to raise a

Ziploc bag to show me a red-greasy pocketknife. Instead he made a gap with his finger and thumb. Not a lot of space between the two. Enough so I could see his eye on the other side.

'Too short to get the important stuff.' He dropped his hand into his pocket. Pulled out a silver pen and used it to flash a light in my eyes. Used his thumb to hold my lids open. Gave a swipe of light to each eye and moved away again. Heard the sound of Velcro and something wrap round my right arm. A sucking sound came before I felt pressure on my arm. 'You seem to be holding up okay. Never been stabbed before, have you?'

He looked up from my arm and saw the expression on my face. His face melted and he gave my arm more attention.

'You hear who it was?' I asked. He kept staring at my arm. Frowned for a moment and squeezed more air into the bag. Pressure on my arm increased. 'Quit dicking around with that thing and talk to me.'

'I don't know anything about the attack,' he said. 'There was a small knife at the scene. I looked at the blade and recorded the length. That was it. We don't get into the police side of things, Mister Pullman. We help the injured.'

'You heard them talking,' I said. 'All the time you were there. You must have heard someone talking.'

He moved away and wrote on a clipboard. Set the board down and looked at his watch. Lifted a phone from the wall of the ambulance and put it to his ear. 'ETA,' he said. He paused and nodded his head at what he was hearing. Then he said, 'Stable' and hung up the phone. I was still looking at him and he knew it. 'Some of the deputies were talking while I got the bus ready. I didn't hear enough to tell you exactly what they were saying.'

'What'd you hear?'

'Something about your sister,' he said.

Shook my head. 'I don't have a sister.'

'Like I said, I didn't hear enough to give you anything.'

'There must have been some names.'

'Quincy,' he said. 'That's a name that came up. Mean anything?' Nodded my head. Thought he was going to give up at that. 'Carole. How about that one?' Nodded my head at him again. This time I let it rest on the pillow.

'That's my wife.'

'Okay,' he said. 'Well, that was one of the names they said. Then they talked about your sister.' He moved his hands so I couldn't see them. He was messing with something below the gurney. 'But you don't have a sister so that doesn't make any sense. Other than that, they talked about a guy named Paul. Then it was about Lynda. After that they were off to—'

'What about Lynda?'

'That's another name they threw around.' His hands came up and he showed me the green gloves were still on. Still unmarked. 'Can't give you any more than that.'

I didn't say anything. Just leaned my head back against the thin pillow and hoped like hell the ride was going to end soon. Wanted to get clear of the straps on the gurney and get out of the medical centre. Didn't care if they taped the puckered wounds shut. They could have the time to stitch the things together if it meant I'd be able to get out of there before the morning came. I had a long drive ahead of me. The urgency of the trip was starting to build. The more the ambulance slowed – the more the sirens wailed overhead – the more I wanted to be behind the wheel of my van, hauling ass to a place I'd wished I'd never have to see again.

Chapter Thirty-Four

It took two hours for a doctor with a German accent to push a needle through all the gashes in my skin. While she worked I had a steady stream of visitors. Nurses mainly, but there were also folks from the community. Strange thing about people of faith is that they feel the need to repent for everything. They see you as being a bad person and they feel justified in delivering to you a steady stream of shit. Deliver it with the same faithfulness as a baker delivering bread. The only things they delivered at the hospital were well wishes and soft voices. Bunch of damned hypocrites.

The doc frowned at my gashes. She pushed at the wounds.

'We are almost finished.'

'That'll be fine.'

When she moved away I sat forward. Had a mix of numbness and sharp pains. Made my body a patchwork of sensations. Swung my legs off the bed and moved my feet in circles, stretching out my ankles. They had a strange feeling outside my boots. My ankle was still sore from the tumble I took at Cedar Creek, but it was a small concern with the rest of the pain. Looked at the red stains between my toes where the blood had soaked in. Didn't have any idea where my boots had gone. Suppose it didn't matter. Pop was coming with a change of clothes. I'd told the nurse who had him on the phone that whatever he brought needed to be comfortable and loose-fitting.

More nurses came in and spoke to me. I didn't respond because I didn't want the rage that was filling me to go away. Didn't want to turn it on any of them. I'd already met all of the nurses on the night-shift when Pop finally showed with my clothes. I heard him come into the trauma unit. He talked with the nurses, asking where I was. He went through half a dozen of them, wanted to know if I was getting moved to the city or if I was alright to be here. My nerves were short and I didn't want to wait for him to get the low-down from people who didn't know.

'I'm over here, Pop!' I yelled out. 'And I'm needing some goddamned clothes.'

He came through the curtain. His face told me he'd been expecting me to have a room with real walls. After a hesitation he moved in and handed me a bag and a winter coat. I took them both and set them on the bed. I hopped off the bed and turned as Marty pushed through the curtain. He looked like he wanted to move to me. Like he wanted to put his arms round me again. Instead he stood with his hands away from his side. His eyes were fixed on my chest, staring at the short tracks of a railroad puzzle that hadn't been pieced together all that well.

'It's alright, bud,' I told him. 'Don't get all worried about it.'

'Why'd she do that?' he asked. His hand moved away from his side again. Started towards me. He stopped and dropped his hands back to his sides. He slid them into his pocket. 'Why'd Aunt Lynda stab you like that?'

''Cause she was doing something wrong,' I said, grabbing my shirt from the bag and pushing my arms into the sleeves. Started buttoning it up. 'I caught her doing something in *our* house and she went nuts.'

'Marty, you go outside,' Pop said. 'Go find Ted and tell him I'll meet you two in the café.'

'I don't want to go to the café.'

'Marty, I'm not going to tell you again.'

387

Marty looked at Pop. He wasn't used to the old man giving orders like that. Not used to Pop's voice going mean and getting forceful that way. He didn't like it any better than me, but he took it. His eyes met mine once more and he slunk out through the curtain. His shoes made a noise while he moved down the linoleum corridor. Pop looked up at me and we stayed like that – eyes not blinking. Kept at it while we listened to the sound of Marty's shoes fade.

'What's the plan, now, Joe? What's the next thing you're going to get yourself into?'

Pushed a leg into the jeans Pop had brought me. Hopped off the bed and pushed the other leg in, hiking them to my waist and gritting my teeth while I fastened the button. Lynda had caught me just above the waistline. The doctor had convinced me it was shallow, but it was deep enough to 'cause some serious hurt. Took a few deep breaths and hopped up on the bed again and pulled a pair of socks from the bag. Snapped the knot loose and raised my foot. The burn spread across my gut.

'I'm heading to Maritime,' I said. 'I'll get there by morning. Should be able to meet Sheriff Wilcox and start things moving.'

'The hell do you have to start moving out there?'

'I need to find her, Pop.' He watched me pull the socks on, struggling through the pain. He stood with his arms crossed, thinking the pain was going to make me rethink what I was about to do. He had another thing coming. 'She's in Maritime, Pop. Nothing's changed about that.'

'Marty told me about the Muniz fella. He told me about the house and the school. Everything he told you.' Pop stepped forward and took the boot out of my hand. Set it back down in the bottom of the bag. 'Whatever she was doing there is not important. Not any more it's not. Paul Quincy is in the courthouse taking the same amount of shit you've already taken. He's got cops all round him, Joe. Lynda's in a cell, and it's your turn to press the charges.'

I took the boot out of the bag again and pulled it over my foot. Started lacing.

'What happened tonight doesn't bring Carole back, Pop.' Worked on the bootlaces a while and kept swallowing down the sick feeling that was coming over me. Could have been the pills they gave me for the pain. Could have been thinking about going back to Maritime. 'Carole will still be gone and the questions will come in like another damned storm.' Took the other boot and slipped it on. 'I'm not waiting round for that to happen.'

'And what happens if you can't find her?'

'I know where to look,' I said. Hopped down and tested my feet in the boots. Twisted at the waist to make sure the stitches were going to hold. I lifted the coat from the bed and pushed my arms through the sleeves. 'Got a real bad feeling that I know exactly where to find her.'

'I don't like the sound of that, Joe.'

'Neither do I, Pop.' My hands was shaking so bad it took me a couple of tries to get the coat zipped up. 'I don't like the sound of it, either. Not a damned note of it.'

Chapter Thirty-Five

Got to Maritime before the morning cars found the roads. Wouldn't have been much of a traffic jam even if I'd pulled into town during rush hour. Came in on State Road Nine. It wasn't a scenic route, but I wasn't coming to Maritime as a tourist. Went past the picnic areas where families usually gathered at Wild Lake. Snow covered the benches, turning them into great white beasts. Small patches of black bench jutted out, revealing bones of the monster underneath. The weatherman on the radio had been saying that the coming days were going to be warm for the season. He was expecting the snow to thaw.

'Let's see what that snow's been hiding from us these last few weeks,' he said. 'Maybe find some things you forgot you ever had.'

I wasn't in the mood to listen to the idiot, but his voice was better than silence. Had too much going on in my head and I needed someone else to interrupt my thoughts. Move out some of the images that I didn't want showing up at random. Flashes of memories brought back by Maritime landmarks weren't helping much, so I turned up the radio and let the weatherman talk cheerful about the snow melt.

Drove past the welcome sign stuck up at the intersection of Main Street. Felt a nostalgia I hadn't been missing. A familiarity with the way the town was set out; the location of the shops and buildings was the same as I had left. Watched the faces of the few people who were moving up the main drag. Almost expected them to stop and stare while I drove by. Point, the same as folks did when Nat Upshaw and Jody Verring had dragged me into the courthouse in cuffs.

The freak's come back to town.

Only took passing a few of the locals to start feeling that I wasn't recognised. To feel that maybe my past in the town had been lost over the years. It was easy to make myself believe it from behind the wheel of the van – moving along Main Street in a slow crawl. I thought about finding a café to stop off and take a piss and buy a coffee. My head was feeling hollow and my mouth had dried up from the blasting air of the van's heater. Pulled up to a red light and spotted a cruiser in my rear-view mirror. It pulled out of a side street as I idled at the light. The cruiser rolled up behind my van and the lights spun once without sound, then again with the noise. I rolled down my window and waved an arm to get him to pass. The cruiser pulled up next to me and it didn't keep going.

I looked down at the cruiser and waited while the window slid open. The cop in the passenger seat had a moustache that curled over the corners of his mouth. He motioned with his hand, like he wanted me to lean closer to him.

'You after something, Officer?' I said.

'We've been expecting you, Mister Pullman.' He had a deep voice. His words came out in grey clouds. They scattered fast. He pointed down Main Street. 'Follow us back to the courthouse. Three streets up and then left. We'll keep it slow so you won't get lost.'

I let them get out ahead and followed along. The courthouse was the last place I'd seen before leaving Maritime. It was the last place I'd stood as a member of the town. Had a green-apple feeling churning up my guts, and it churned harder the closer we got to the courthouse. I made the left onto

Liberty Avenue and it was a straight shot to the building. The cruiser took it slow and I held my distance. When the patrol car pulled into the parking lot, I followed the tracks it made in the slush and brown snow. I pulled into a space reserved for official visitors.

The courthouse didn't look any different. It wasn't any more inviting. I sat in the van for a while looking up at the building. It was more like a church than a courthouse. I remembered thinking the same thing when I was escorted through the doors by the social worker and the cop who'd knocked my father out cold. With that last memory in my head, I got out of the van and walked up the path. I looked at the cruiser that had escorted me from Main Street and saw the two cops still sitting inside. I took the steps to the building and went into a small lobby. Pushed through the next set of doors and found Maritime's finest waiting for me. A line of cops standing with their arms crossed. Guns and clubs dangling from heavy black belts. Sheriff Wilcox was sitting on a bench in the middle of his men. He stood when I walked towards him.

'Joseph Pullman,' he said. His voice slow and cheerful. His head shook the way you would expect from a man as he greeted a long-lost friend. He made a try at a laugh. It didn't sound right, but I could deal with that as long as it made his men feel uncomfortable. 'Boy, we've been expecting you.'

I wasn't too easy with the enthusiasm he was showing me. Even less pleased because of the way his deputies stood in that choreographed way. They weren't big guys, but I'd started sizing them up along with my chances. Might have been out of reflex. Old habit. The town didn't do much for me when I was a boy, so I couldn't see it changing for the present.

'Sheriff,' I said. 'You'll know why I'm here.'

'We heard about the trouble you were having out there

in Henderson. That and the find we made down at the lake . . .'
Two of his deputies traded glances and turned to look at me
again. 'I don't know how much additional assistance I can be
to you. I can show you her purse and such, but it's evidence
in a missing person's investigation. I can't let you have it until
we locate her.'

'I understand that.'

'Well, I'm sure you do. Now listen, if there's anything
you need before we sit down to talk . . .' He hesitated for a
second, like he was waiting for a translator to give me what
he said all over again in another language. I shook my head.
'Nat called and told me how you'd been sliced up last night.'

'That's right. I don't need anything. I'd just like to get out
to the Lewiston house and have a look around.'

'Oh, yeah?' Wilcox took a step back and shifted his weight
between his feet. He reached a hand down and tried to slide
a thumb between his belt and his gut, but there was nothing
doing. He settled for clasping his hands behind his back. 'What
do you hope to find at the Lewiston house?'

Wilcox leaned forward and used a slow hand to scratch
the back of his head. He kept scratching and made a weird
kind of animal sound in his throat. When he brought his
head up again he looked relieved. Eyes almost rolling in his
head.

'We went by there to make sure it's locked up, after we
got word of Jules' accident. We've since made enquiries about
his next of kin . . .'

'But you've been inside the house?'

Sheriff Wilcox let his hand hover at the side of his head. I
turned to look at the deputy standing to his right. Wilcox
stepped towards me and dropped his hand to his side.

'We have been in his apartment, and the RSPCA has
removed his cats. Jules Lewiston lived alone. His possessions
are secured and will remain that way until his next of kin
comes to town to claim them.'

'Lewiston didn't live in an apartment. He had a house, a few streets over from my father's.'

'What makes you interested in that place?'

'My wife and son came to Maritime and they met a man named Carlos Muniz. He showed them around and he took them to the Lewiston house.'

'Muniz . . .' Wilcox turned his head so he made contact with each of his deputies. They all watched him make the rounds, but none of them motioned like they knew what I was talking about. 'And he took them into the Lewiston house?'

'That's right,' I said. 'Have you been in the house?'

'Well, Jules has been renting that place out since he went into the apartment. We checked that residence to ensure—'

'You checked the apartment. What about the house, Sheriff? That's all I'm interested in.'

'You can bring yourself in line. Drop those hands for one, and lower your voice. We want to help you, but there's a way of going about asking for that help.'

I dropped my head. Felt my body starting to sweat and the painkillers were wearing off. I thought about all the places Lynda had hit me with that blade and a fire-show of two-inch burns lit up all over me.

'I need to find my wife.'

'Alright. Well, last we spoke with the neighbours, they hadn't seen anyone coming or going. I've asked them myself and my deputies have made their rounds, and no one has seen anything out of the ordinary.'

'Well, I'd like to have a look. Just long enough to see with my own eyes, Sheriff. I have a feeling that the tenant in the Lewiston house is somehow connected with my father. The man in that house has called me and he has made contact with my wife on sever—'

'And you're sure there's nothing going on between your wife and this Mister Muniz?'

'No! I'm certain. She came here to trade him information. I don't know what it was that she had, and why it was so important. But I believe something happened to her . . .'

Wilcox moved his hand like he wanted me to step towards him. There wasn't enough space. He was already there. We were already together.

'Let's go back to my office, Joe. I'll get you a coffee and some pain pills so you don't have to keep holding your chest like that.' He turned and started walking and I followed him. He motioned to a pair of deputies as we passed. 'Go over to the Lewiston house and see if there's anyone home. Let me know what you find.'

He walked through a doorway and pointed out a chair in front of his desk. I sat down and loosened my coat. Pulled it away from my body as best I could. Wilcox went around his desk and sat down. He hit a button on his phone and watched me while the thing made a humming noise. He hit the button again and it went silent.

'I guess there's no one in the break-room just now. I'll go get us something to drink in a minute.' He opened up a drawer and took out a large pad of paper and a pen. He set them down on the desk and stretched out his neck. 'Now, let's do this. I'll fill you in on all we know about your wife's situation here in Maritime, and you can do the same from Henderson.' I didn't have time to protest. He went straight into his side of the bargain.

'Your wife came to see me. Nat will have told you that already. She wanted to know if we had any additional information about the Gillespie case.' I frowned at him and nodded my head. Tried to make a show of it, so he would think I didn't already know so much.

'She came in with a folder of information already,' he said. 'She had a map of the open spaces and another of the town. Then she showed me a map of Delaware Glen. She'd even marked where the crate was found in the bog.' He used his hand to make a circle in the air between us. 'And a path that went from the Gillespie house to Delaware Glen.'

He gave me some wide eyes for a while. Then he dropped his head a notch like he was wanting me to respond.

'I heard she was looking into the murder,' I said.

Wilcox reached his hand out and hit the top of his desk with the back of his fingers. Made a swatting motion that sounded loud against the wood. Must have seen me wince 'cause he held his hand in the air for a moment and, when he started talking, he did it with less enthusiasm.

'I asked her what the little dotted line was for,' he said. 'And she told me it was the path Dean Gillespie had taken on the morning he was killed. That path went to your father's place first. Next to the house she'd written 'picked up crate'. From there she'd drawn two squiggly lines. One line running parallel to the other.' He touched the collar on his shirt and pulled it away from his inflated neck. He dropped his other hand down and rubbed it along the lower rim of his belly. He frowned.

'We always assumed that your father had put Dean Gillespie in the crate at the house. From there we'd believed he'd loaded the crate into his car while it was parked in the garage and then he had driven it out to the glen.' Wilcox made a sucking sound with the side of his mouth. 'Somehow your wife came up with this new idea – a new version of what happened that day, that answered some of the questions we'd been asking for years. One of them is where your father had parked and how he had walked the crate to the bog. Her version went in an entirely different direction. You have any idea how she was able to come up with the new sequence of events?'

'She'd been speaking with my father,' I said, looking at Wilcox and trying not to let emotion take me. Anger because of his Hollywood cop routine, and fear because of Carole showing off the ideas of a dying man who had become a sort of collector. A thinker. A man who had had twenty years in a cement box to piece together the events in a way that would set me in his place. Events he had been manipulating and honing while he searched for a sympathetic ear.

'My father's had a good long time to imagine a way out of prison. Now that his time's running short he's beginning to show off his wares. My wife got sucked in by his story.'

Wilcox raised his hands to his chin and made like he was praying.

'She was looking for some kind of response from me,' he said. 'I let her have my time, but I didn't give her anything more than that. I just nodded my head once in a while and told her what she had was interesting. And then I asked her if she knew how much the crate weighed. She started flipping through her yellow pad of paper. This legal pad she had filled with notes.' Wilcox's hands broke apart. The prayer had ended. 'She didn't have a clue. Eighty-nine pounds. That's what I told her. Then I reminded her that she had to put the Gillespie boy in that crate and, when she did, she'd have added another hundred to it. That's almost two hundred pounds, I told her! Who is going to be able to carry that weight along your squiggly line?'

'How'd she respond to that?' I asked.

He breathed out hard and leaned over the desk and pressed his weight down on his elbows.

'She told me that Dean Gillespie wasn't in the box at that point. Said that he was helping to carry the crate.' I tried to show Wilcox that I thought it was as wild a story as I'd ever heard. Only I couldn't get my face working the way I needed it to work. 'It is a far-fetched story. Isn't it, Joe?'

'Sure it is,' I said. 'Dean wasn't a strong kid. Besides, he was stubborn like any boy that age. How do you think he was convinced to carry something that heavy? Specially if he couldn't use it in the end?'

Wilcox moved his head forward and back again. His straight-line mouth got shorter.

'Good point. Something I've been asking myself over the past few nights.'

'Did Carole leave any of her papers with you?' I asked. 'Something I can look at to see what she was working on.'

'She left nothing with me.' He went back to praying and made his eyes real sad. I sensed there was something coming that was going to be painful to hear. 'She had the map and the guy had a briefcase, but he didn't open it, so I can't tell you what was inside.'

I stared at him and he gave it back to me. Only his eyes weren't interested in a fight. He was interested in seeing how Joe Pullman was going to react.

'What guy was that?'

'Carlos Muniz,' he said. 'He didn't say much while they were in here. He just listened to what she was saying. Once in a while he made a sound that stopped her speaking. I took it that he was a lawyer of some kind. She started off the meeting by telling me she didn't want to incriminate anyone, but that she needed the truth to be seen. She told me that he was helping her piece all the story together.'

'You ever see this guy before?'

Wilcox turned to the window and waved a hand in the air. I turned my head and saw his deputies were lined up again, this time by the wall outside his office. One of the deputies was walking towards us.

'He wasn't a local. I had the two of them in here talking for almost two hours. I just thought she was getting things together for her story and then she'd be off. But every time she went to leave, he would say a little something in her ear and she'd start talking again. Or she'd show me another map and start the whole thing over.'

'And what was Muniz doing all that time?'

'He was sitting with the suitcase on his lap. Tapping his fingers on it. Not doing much of anything but listening.'

'You didn't think that he was controlling her?'

Wilcox put his hands out. Made like he was ready to stop a bus. He didn't like the look of what might be on the way. He was wanting to stop the thoughts before I got too much steam behind me.

'Hold on there, Joe. There wasn't any sign of that kind of thing between them. He was all business. Dressed in a sports jacket and had a long coat on over that. I told you already, I took one look and pegged him as a lawyer. Maybe a private investigator, but either way he looked like he was getting paid. The only thing out of place was the briefcase. It looked old. He'd be the kind to be carrying leather if he wanted it to fit the rest of him. This was just hard plastic.'

My stomach was rolling again and I didn't want to leave a mark on the tile floor. Wilcox moved forward in his chair and reached out like he was going to straighten me up. He pushed me back so I had to look him in the eye.

'You need to see someone? I can take you round to the hospital. You maybe need to get some fluids in you.'

'How about that coffee, Sheriff?' I kept my eyes on him and managed a smile. 'After that, maybe a trip over to the Lewiston place? If nothing else, we can drive out there and see if it's just an empty rental. If so, there's no harm done. No foul. Of course, if it's not empty . . .'

'What do you have to connect this Muniz guy to your father?'

'I don't have anything. I just know that Carole has been drawn into this, and the only person with anything to gain is my father. And the only thing he has to gain is one last go at me before he dies.'

Wilcox touched his lips with the back of his hand. Looked like he was about to turn round to test the idea with someone else. But we were alone and Wilcox had his own concerns. His own ideas.

'You ride with me,' he said. 'We can talk as we go.' He came round his desk and opened the door. He called into the hallway:

'You guys come on back here.' We waited until the officers assembled around his door. 'I need three units to follow us out to the Lewistons' place. No lights. Keep it off the radio.'

We left his office and Wilcox guided me through a series of doors that brought us out to a parking lot full of police cruisers. I followed him to a brown Chevy Malibu with thin blue and red lights in the dash. I sat in the passenger side and Wilcox got behind the wheel. He started up the car and drove out like he didn't have any intention of keeping the other cruisers at a close range behind him. We sped along the roads that looked too familiar. Wilcox watched the road and I kept one hand out – almost touching the dash. It didn't make the ride any more comfortable.

'Why did Lewiston come to see you?' Wilcox finally asked. 'I ask because it's something that's given me problems. Lewiston was a quiet man. Not really someone who takes it on himself to make problems.'

'He was in a diner eating a meal when I showed up, and he tried to start up a conversation. Asked me about my scars. Seems that's how he knew me.'

'What kind of things he say?'

'Nothing important.' Wilcox made a grunt sound in his throat. Figured it was a cue for me to try again. He wasn't buying what I was selling any more. Nat must have filled him in on Sheila's side of the Lewiston story. 'He told me about his memories of Oscar. Said something about trying to get him talking . . .'

'He say anything about how Oz died?'

'No,' I said and looked at Wilcox for a clue. Tried to decide if that was going to be enough of an answer to satisfy him. Look on his face told me he was expecting more, so I gave it to him. 'Just that he didn't have to keep the game going any more.'

'We'd been looking for Jules for a few weeks when your

Sheriff Upshaw called. Pathology report on Oscar came back from the state labs shortly after he died. Toxicology reports took a while to make their way to us. Results suggest he'd died of a drug overdose. It was either that or manual suffocation. Leading up to Oscar's death Jules had been erratic, to say the least. That was understandable, with all the years he's been living with Oscar.'

'When did Oz die?' I asked.

'Couple months back. Since then Jules has shut himself in that apartment. Wasn't one to socialise over the years. He was stuck to the boy and, when he went, a good part of Jules went with him. Kind of to be expected. Devote that much of yourself to a case like Oz and you don't have much left.'

I started doing the maths. Placing events on a calendar in my mind. Carole's questions about Oz. Her growing interest in my past. Progressive. Constant. She started taking more night-time craft classes that didn't produce anything. Nancy Lowell huddling up with Herman Dorlund for a psychic chant about Dean Gillespie. All the small details were adding up. Phone call from Carlos Muniz about my old man's parole hearing that was never going to happen. He was just testing the waters for a reaction. Making sure I was at home in Henderson and keeping well away while my wife was digging up Maritime. The days and people were falling into place. It all started to feel coordinated.

'Will my father get a parole hearing?' I asked.

'Your old man won't be seeing any parole hearing.' I looked at Wilcox and found his eyes on me. He moved them back to the road as we turned onto another street. 'Child killers with life don't get parole. I'd know if they were giving him a hearing. They'd contact me. And I'd be present and I'd make damned sure he didn't see the sun shine without the shadow of fence links shading his eyes.' He looked at me and, when I didn't speak, he continued. 'When's the last time you saw your father, Joe?'

'His sentencing.' Reconsidered. 'There was a photograph in a paper a few years back.' I shrugged my shoulders to show him that I didn't have a need to see my father. Didn't have the need to meet him again before he died. 'No telling how old that picture was.'

'Let me tell you something that may bring you comfort. If your father was on parole this afternoon, he wouldn't be attending. If they opened the door to that prison and told him he was a free man, he wouldn't be able to get to the door on his own two legs.'

'That bad?'

'Look, Joe, I'm sure you'll take this the right way. But we are all waiting for the day your father dies. He's the last of the bad seeds this town sent to the wind.'

His last word was performed more than spoken. There was a lot of emotion behind it. I didn't say anything. Wilcox pulled the car to the kerb. I looked over and recognised the Lewiston house. Almost the same as it had been. The weather had beaten it, but it was almost the same.

'Whose car is that in the driveway?' I asked.

'Don't know. Rental, from the looks of it.'

'Where are the deputies you sent out here earlier?'

'I'm not sure, but I'll find out,' he said.

Wilcox went first and I followed. We walked down the driveway and came to the snow-covered path. He put his hand back and patted at the air between us. I slipped my boots in the prints he left in the snow. He made it to the front door and pulled the screen open. He knocked and listened for a while. He stepped back and let the screen door shut, then leaned over and looked in the window beside the door. He pressed the doorbell and a chime sounded from inside the house.

'Looks like there's no one here. I told you, Joe, Jules was living at the apartment. Now, he's been out of this place for weeks.'

'Can we walk around and have a look? See if there's anything to cause concern?'

'Knock yourself out,' he said. 'I'll check with the neighbours and see if they know of anyone coming and going these past few days.'

Wilcox went one way and I went the other. Struggled against the slush-slick snow as I made my way to the side of the house. Went past the pine tree and up the small mound. First window looked into the garage, and I couldn't see anything out of the ordinary. Tools on the workbench and an old bike hanging from a hook on the ceiling. Through the next window I saw a tumble drier and a washing machine.

After that I came to the sliding doors that led to the kitchen. There was a glass table with four chairs at one end of the room. Two chairs were set away from the table. I stepped onto the raised porch to get a better look. I saw that a brown ring marked the table in front of the farthest chairs. It meant something. And I stood with my head close to the glass and felt my breath leaving my lungs. I felt the burn of each small cut marking my chest. Tried to even out my breaths as I looked at the small brown circle on the glass table. I stared at it and wondered how long it takes a ring of spilled coffee to go dry. To turn to a brown powder.

'Sheriff!' I called out. *He's at the neighbour's, Joe. Be loud and get him over here.* 'Sheriff, you there?' Nothing. He wasn't calling back. *You need to make more sound, Joe!* I grabbed the door handle and pulled hard. It came with my hand. It moved for a second and stopped. Jolted me as it clicked in place. Pushed it back and pulled hard again. It was loose, but was catching on a security bar. It moved just enough to raise hope, but that bar was stopping me.

'I'm going, Sheriff!' I yelled. 'I'm going inside!'

I took a step back and ground my boot in the snow. Found the cement porch underneath. Wilcox came round the corner.

He was hunched and huffing towards me. He saw my leg rise up and launch forward, and he shouted with all he had as my foot made it towards the door. His voice was loud. So was my boot hitting the glass. But it all seemed dead silent when the gunshot rang out from inside the house.

Chapter Thirty-Six

Glass shattered.

I dropped down and rolled away from the door. Wilcox was shouting again. Yelling for me to get out of the way. I turned on my side and tried to move. My feet were slipping over the ice. Spinning in place. Kept kicking and my boot found traction. Got to the side of the house where Wilcox was struggling with his gun. It was still in the holster. His hands were moving over it, but weren't getting it out. I ran past him and pulled at his arm. He grunted and turned and ran behind me. We moved up to the road.

I leaned against the side of the cruiser and looked over the hood and watched the house. I expected more gunfire. More windows to get blown out. We waited there until another cruiser pulled up. The deputies came out of the car and ran to Wilcox.

'Get down!' he yelled. 'We've got gunfire coming from inside the house. Single shot from the back right. Secure the side and rear until backup arrives.'

Two deputies made a slumped-run down the side of the house. One with a shotgun. The other with his pistol. Both aiming at the house. Wilcox pressed himself against the trunk of his cruiser. His breathing was off. His body wasn't reacting well to the excitement.

'Did you see him?' I asked.

Wilcox shook his head. Closed his eyes and kept breathing heavy through his mouth. Another cruiser pulled to the kerb and two more deputies came running out. Wilcox ordered them to the other side of the house and the deputies went without slowing down.

'He's coming out,' a deputy yelled. 'Freeze where you are!'

The front door moved in and the screen door stayed closed. A light behind the figure shined bright. The black outline of a man showed in the mesh of the door frame. His shoulders were drooping. Arms dangling low. The right arm of the silhouette hung longer than the other. It was a thinner shape on the end of the arm. A line that touched all the way to the ground.

'Joe Pullman,' the voice called out. 'Is that you, Joe Pullman?' A white cloud puffed out from the silhouette's head. It formed and floated into the glow of the dim grey light of the day. It died off and disappeared in the cold air. 'You left it too long, Joe.'

'Who are you?' I stood and moved away from the back of the cruiser.

'It's Colin Lowell.' The silhouette bent forward again. Regained himself and raised a hand to the door. The deputies moved against the car. Handles of pistols scraping against the metal trunk. Elbows pressing against the cruiser to keep the guns steady. 'It's too late. You left it too long.'

'I got here as fast as I could. I went to get help.' I turned and looked at Wilcox. He was nodding his head and rolling his hand like he wanted me to keep talking. 'I couldn't do it on my own. I came here to find Carole and . . .'

'She's here.' His voice was low. Almost too low to hear him.

'That's good, Colin. Now, listen to me . . . I'm here to help. You can use my help, can't you?'

'Not so much now.'

'What do you mean?' I called out.

'It's all finished.' He was quiet a while. Wilcox was looking at the front door. His hands wrapped tight against the handle of the pistol. I looked back at the deputies on my side of the car. One of them had swapped his pistol for a rifle and was leaning against the butt of the gun.

I moved away from the car and started towards the house. Wilcox reached an arm out and grabbed my jacket. I pulled hard and broke free and kept on walking. *Colin wouldn't shoot you, Joe. He's harmless and useless. Sure, you kicked the shit out of him . . .* I shook the thought out of my head and kept moving for the front door. Remembering how Colin had taken the stories I'd fed him. Drunken nights when I needed to talk about what I'd been through. Nights when I'd convinced myself that the only way to get rid of the pressure was to confide in someone. I'd chosen Colin Lowell. Same as I'd chosen Dean Gillespie. A friend. An awkward and lame friend who would be controlled by the threat of my temper. Only Colin was too much like Dean. Too eager to hear more. Too ready to be like me.

'Colin,' I called out. 'I'm coming in. I need to see Carole.'

'You don't want to see her, Joe!'

I stopped and looked round. I'd made it to the middle of the lawn. No place to hide. No place to dive if he started shooting. If he decided that the beating I'd given him wasn't justified. I put my hands in the air.

'I'm right here, Colin. Alright? I don't need to come in,' I said. 'But I've come out here to get Carole back. I want to take her home.'

'Carole's not going anywhere,' he said. 'Not until they come in and get her.' He started making sounds that I didn't like. Some kind of suction sound, all wet and pained. A sort of gurgling.

'Is she alright?'

'I've been a bad husband, Joe. You know that, as much as everybody else. But what you see in this house wasn't me.

You remember that, because what is in here was already done.' The silhouette hunched and when it stopped coughing it moved straight again. 'Has Sheriff Upshaw got to town?'

'Not yet, Colin,' I said. The shadow figure tilted to the side and leaned against the doorway. 'He'll be here soon.'

'When Upshaw gets here, ask him what he thought was going to happen next? After the hand showed up in the snow, I mean. Ask him what he was expecting to show up after that. You ask him what part of her needed to be dragged back by a family pet before he started looking for the rest of her!'

I started walking again. The sound of Colin's voice moving me towards the house. I walked and felt a harsh ache moving through me. It was no longer the burn of the wounds Lynda had made. It wasn't my wrist, or my ankle from falling on the ice. This was deeper. I needed to get inside the house or it might never go away.

'Colin,' I yelled. My voice was loud. I couldn't control it. My hands reached out in front of my body. A reflex. A human instinct for survival, a weak shield from danger. 'I'm coming up to the house, Colin. You can tell me what's on your mind and we can talk a while. It's a cold day, man. But I can stand out here with you. We can talk all you want . . .'

'Stop there, Joe.'

'I can't, Colin. I need to—'

'Colin,' Wilcox called out. He'd sneaked out from behind the cruiser. I looked for his voice and found shrubs off to the side of the house. Wilcox was inside there with the dark shadows. 'It's Sheriff Wilcox here. From what I'm hearing, it doesn't sound like you're thinking all too straight. What I say we do is—'

'You've said enough, Sheriff. While I'm talking to my friend here, you can go take a quiet breath. You'll need it. You'll be real busy soon. My wife, for one, is a real—'

'This isn't going to solve anything,' Wilcox called out.

'Maybe not for all of you.'

'What did you do?' I called out.

'Nothing,' he said. 'It was done when I got here.' He moved in the doorway, shifting his weight from foot to foot. 'I got a call from a man who told me that Nancy was here. He said that she was staying with another man. He told me that all the nights she'd been at those classes with Carole, she'd been meeting with this man. Then she went away and I couldn't find her, and everyone in Henderson was talking about Carole. Then there was that article in the paper and the rumours kept spreading. And they grew, and I didn't say anything about Nancy because I didn't want that same thing to happen to me. And when I finally tried to find her . . .'

'I went to see him too, Colin. Herman's why I'm here.'

'So he spoke with you? Well, he shot me. Asshole coward did it, and then he ran away. I was sitting in Sinai Hospital with tubes coming out of me and I was thinking about Nancy. I was wondering what I would be coming back to. And out of the blue the phone rang and it was him, this man. He told me Nancy was here and that she was with Carole.'

Colin hit the door with the palm of his hand. I stopped moving. The ache was gone. I was feeling numb. Sick in my guts.

'I thought about telling you, Joe. But I came out here to deal with it. I wanted to take care of things for you and me.'

'Who called you?' I asked. 'Who made that call?'

'The man with a soft voice.'

'How did he find you at the hospital, Colin?' I resurrected my walk towards the house. Moved with a purpose.

'I don't know. But it doesn't matter.' Colin moved into the light again. 'It's finished, Joe.' His silhouette was taking aim. 'Stop right there or I'll have to put a hole in you. Not something I want to do.'

'Settle down, son.'

'Time's right for you to go quiet, Sheriff.'

I turned to see Wilcox move from behind a tree. He was

closer to the house and moving down the driveway. He was under the oak tree, from where he could aim a black revolver.

'I'm going back into the house now, Joe. Before I do, I need you to tell me that you don't think I did any of this. Remember when you came to Henderson and you had nobody. I listened to you, Joe. I need you to listen to me now. I didn't do this!'

'Okay. But, you need to tell me, Colin. Where is Muniz?'

'I don't know.'

'He's the man who was living here. The man Nancy and Carole were coming here to see. Where is he now?'

'I don't have any answer for you, Joe.'

'Alright,' I said. Wilcox was moving out from behind the tree. I turned towards the house. Colin was still in the doorway. Silhouette slumping. 'I need to know about Carole.'

'She's here, Joe. But you don't want to see her. When this is all over, you stay out there.'

'What does that mean?'

Go to the door, Joe. Run for that sonofabitch and get inside the house. Get Carole.

'You do a good funeral for me, and another for Nancy?'

'Sure,' I said. Took a step towards the house. Put my hands up in the air and kept walking.

A crack came from behind me. Sound of a bug – some big thing – whizzed past my ear. It felt close. Hair moved on the side of my head as it passed. Colin's silhouette jerked back a few steps. Two flashes came from the middle of the silhouette. Two flashes pounding sounds and pain deep inside my head. My hands moved to my ears. My body fell back. Two jagged mouths had opened up in the screen door. The ground came up and met me hard. My eyes stayed on the screen. Amazed by the sound of the gun. Ears ringing.

'Shots fired!' Wilcox was yelling from somewhere in the trees. He kept shouting it over and over. His voice making it into my head, rattling around in there. I rolled to my side. My ears ringing, mixing with the deep pulsing sound inside my head. Then the gurgling in my guts moving up and sticking in my throat.

'Joe!' I heard someone calling. It sounded far away. An underwater sort of sound. Someone was calling my name from the surface. I looked at the oak tree and saw Wilcox moving away from the trunk.

My hands were shaking over my ears. Took them away and the ringing was growing louder. The muffled voice was still calling me. Snow had covered my lips. I licked and it was in my mouth. Cold and melting fast.

'Joe!'

'Colin?' I looked at the door. Backlight from somewhere down the hall was coming through the screen. Small, round lights finding a home in the screen's two mouths. Smoke rising all round the door.

'Yeah, Joe!' His voice made it through the ringing. Found a way to get through the pulsing deep inside my head. 'You do a good funeral for me and Nancy.'

Another shot rang out. This one louder than before. It stopped the ringing in my ears. For a moment everything went silent. Then the small siren deep in my head started working its way to the surface. It built up to a high squeal. A shriek that fell back deep inside my head. Fell back to the same place the small siren had started. I got to my knees and straightened my back. Crunching sounds of feet coming to my side. Moving through snow before settling somewhere behind me.

'You hit?' Wilcox asked.

'No,' I said. 'He wasn't shooting at me.'

Chapter Thirty-Seven

Wilcox came out of the house and found me sitting on the front step with my feet spread and my hands dangling between my knees. That's the way I'd been since they'd left me to go into the house. Since the deputy with the moustache and the big arms wrestled me back to the ground. I'd gone for the door and he dropped me. Kept calling to the side of my head to *calm down. Calm down, Mister Pullman. It's over.* Wilcox went inside and I sat on the step and watched the neighbours gather along the street. They stood in a line behind the yellow police tape and they stared and they talked. I watched them and I listened to their chatter while the cops went in and the cops came out.

'Jesus Christ,' one of the cops said. He stumbled out the door and bent at the waist. Made a few loud heaves over the shrubs. He finally stood straight and breathed like he was about to take a dive in a pool of cold water.

'You alright?' I asked.

He looked down at me and shook his head. Stopped after a couple of seconds.

'I'm real sorry, sir.' He had his hands together. Palm to palm. Wondered if he'd learned that from Wilcox, or if what he'd seen in the house had brought him closer to needing God. He kept talking to me and I watched his hands. They were unflinching. That unknowing prayer must have been bred into him deep.

Wilcox came out while I was watching his man bend over the shrubs again. Wilcox moved in front of me and cut off the view I had of his deputy. He stood there with his right hand sitting atop the ledge of his belly and made a sound like he was going to speak. I looked up at him and raised an eyebrow. It was enough to stop his hands from working that circle motion over his gut.

'You going to let me go inside?' I asked. He shook his head and started his hand circling again. 'You can at least let me see her.'

Wilcox shook his head again.

'I understand how difficult this is for you, Joe.' He turned his head and looked at the deputy. Watched the guy breathe in through his nose, trying not to heave again. Wilcox turned to me. 'Nat Upshaw is on his way. He's been on the road a few hours. He's on the highway with his lights on, so it'll be soon when he gets here.' We watched his man throw up what he'd been hacking on. It covered the top of the shrubs in a cream-coloured frosting.

'If you want, I can call and get you a room in town,' Wilcox said. 'We've got a few motels. Guest houses.'

'No, it's not necessary,' I said, standing. I made like I was going to move up the path. Turned round so I was facing the house. So I was looking into the screen door with the puckered marks from Colin Lowell's shotgun blasts. Wilcox looked past me. His deputies were working hard to keep the neighbours in one place. They were calling out and making a lot of commotion. Wilcox made like he was deaf to all their calls.

'Did you see her?' I asked.

His chin moved up and down, slow-motion-style.

'You're sure it's her?'

He nodded again. 'I recognised her from the licence we recovered from her purse. It is definitely Carole.'

'How bad is she?'

'If you are considering going in that house . . .' He looked at his deputies who were standing in the doorway. He finally brought a hand to his face and pulled it from forehead to chin. His thumb and index finger held his chin for a moment. Then he moved his eyes so they locked up with mine. 'I mean this with all sincerity, Joe. You need to keep what you have of her, and leave this where it is. Leave what is in there to us.'

'I don't think I can do that.'

'You wanted to know where she was, and you found her. What happened to her?' His shoulders moved up and fell down again. 'You can know without having to see it. You have to leave that here.'

'I appreciate the sentiment, Sheriff. But I need to see my wife.'

He didn't try to stop me. As I moved past him he stayed where he was, holding his chin with his fingers. He didn't move aside to allow me past, but he didn't step in front of me as I went by him, either. He made that animal sound in his throat and let out a breath. I'd made it to the porch step, had my foot off the ground when he spoke.

'I'll ask you not to touch anything.' He turned so I could hear the last of what he had to say. 'We need to process the scene before you take anything away. Before she goes back to Henderson with you.'

I nodded my head and felt my legs giving way. The cold had slowed my blood and the tone of Wilcox's voice didn't help. He was weak and I could feel myself going that way. Pulled the screen door and stepped up into the house. My feet landing on the laminate floor, making wet sounds as I walked through the foyer and into the living room. It was sunk down a step. There were two brown sofas and a large television in the corner. On the largest wall there was a shelf with a line of photographs on it. I couldn't bring myself to look at any of them. Didn't want to see Oz and how the years had changed him. How they had made him older even when his mind never moved on from the summer of 1987.

There were voices coming from the other room farther down the hall, towards the back of the house. Voices of the deputies, nervous and excited as they described the moment when a shot rang out. They spoke with loud voices. One deputy came into view from where I was standing in the hall. At his boot was the corner of the white sheet covering Colin Lowell. 'Wilcox let fire and I was squeezing,' he said, with his hands out, clasped together. Two fingers making the barrel of the gun. 'Could have ended it. Sent one off. Sent it into him.' His hands broke apart and he put a finger to his chest.

I turned and made my way down the hall. Walked to where two doors stood open. Something told me to try the door on the left. I'd remembered the few times I'd been in the house with Oz. Once when he was picking up a box of pellets so we could shoot at the birds in the forest. He'd gone into the last room on the right. That had been his room, and I couldn't go in there yet.

Turned left and reached my hand inside the room and flicked the switch. The light came on. It was a bedroom with cream-coloured walls and a white chair rail. A border of flowers was up near the ceiling, otherwise it was plain. It was clean and sparse. I walked to the bed. It was the only piece of furniture in the room. I stood with my knees pressed against the mattress and I looked down at the remains of Nancy Lowell.

She'd been centred on the mattress with pillows set around her. She was a doll on display. A single bed sheet was sitting just below her shoulder line. Beneath the sheet she was naked. Her curves moulded into the white sheet. She looked peaceful and staged. I wondered how much time Colin had spent with her. How long he'd looked down on her, once he had moved her into place.

What was she like when he arrived, Joe? That's the question you should be asking. You're already shaking and you haven't even got to Carole yet.

415

I set my hand on Nancy's leg. Touched her calf and lifted it. I wanted to know if she was only just dead. I wanted to get a feel for rigor. I lifted the leg with a hope that the skin was still holding warmth, a slight run of blood keeping her alive. I raised it a few inches above the mattress. When the leg came apart in my hands I didn't fumble to keep it together. I looked down and was amazed at how it landed. How the parts of Nancy Lowell were mismatched. She was a puzzle fit together by a child who had lost the pieces. I lowered the rest of her leg to the mattress.

There was a pulsing starting up in my head again. Pounding and painful as they signalled danger was present. A warning . . .

My chest heaved with each breath I tried to take in. Reached for Nancy's left arm. The drums were gaining speed. Picking up that tempo and growing louder and closer. Lungs started to burn as I lifted her arm. Below the thin sheet I watched where the clean stump formed at the end of her wrist. I dropped her arm and it made a dull sound as it hit the mattress. I stepped back and moved away from the bed and tried to get myself through the door. Tried to move out of the room without taking my eyes off Nancy Lowell. Her body forming under the white sheet – how it gave shape to the single sheet – shapes missing under the—

'Are you finished, Joe?' Wilcox asked.

'She's missing her hand. We've got her hand in Henderson.' I raised my own like he wasn't going to understand. Like we were men from two different places, speaking different languages. Wilcox looked at my hand and nodded his head. 'Doctor Maitland has it in storage. A dog brought it back. The owners called in . . .'

'Slow down, Joe,' he said. 'You've seen enough. One of my men will take you back to the courthouse. Or maybe you want to go to the hospital and have them look at your stitches. All that moving you did in the snow could have pulled you apart. You looked at yourself?'

I glanced down and saw small black circles shining through my shirt. Pulled my jacket open and felt the sting. They were everywhere.

'I need to see my wife.' Wilcox was standing in front of the open doorway. He reached a hand out and grabbed at my coat. He took my shirt with it. Got hold of something on my chest. I pushed through him and he let go. I was inside the room and I felt every scar on me, old and new, ignite. I walked into the darkness and looked around at the shapes. So many shapes.

I could see the large bed. A frame reaching up around it, starting from the floor and moving up until it almost touched the ceiling. Something was hanging down in the centre of that frame. A harness. Some kind of swing. There was no fan in the room, nothing to move the air around, and so everything was still. It was calm. The smell of chemicals was strong. Cleaners. Bleach and ammonia. I stepped farther into the room, moving towards the bed. To the right was a desk. It was clear except for a notepad and a pen. My eyes were adjusting and it took me a long time to look up from that pen. I wasn't sure I wanted to see what was behind the swing. The small shape that was a mere shadow amongst the shadows.

'Carole,' I whispered and waited for a response. I called again and waited. Nothing called back. Nothing moved on the bed or reached out to try and find me. I felt along the surface of the desk and found a lamp. A twist of the dial and it came to life. The room took on colours of childhood. Of clowns and balloons. Of tropical fish and . . .

Closed my eyes and gave them a moment to adjust. I waited with my eyes closed. Waited for the sound of her voice. A low hum of sound that could become more. A scratching at the covers. Hair pulling across the bed sheets. *I know you, Carole, and you make no noise when you sleep. You can be sleeping now. You can . . .* I waited with my eyes closed until I found some remaining strength to see what had been hiding in the shadows. I looked down at the desk and the pad sitting on it. My name was written at the top of the page:

Joe
    Listen to the ocean and watch the storm come in.
    I love you, Marty.
    C

As I turned from the table I watched the ceiling. It was made to look like the bluest sky. There were a few clouds hanging. Nothing threatening. Just a blue sky with a sun some-where out there. I watched the sky and the clouds and I went to the bed. I took hold of the cold metal railing and guided myself around it. I took a breath of the blue sky above and I watched the clouds as I moved past them. My nose burned with the ammonia and the bleach and the . . .

And I looked down at her and I wanted to see nothing.

Light from the small lamp cast a yellow glow on the side of her face. The other half of her was in the shadows. She was light and dark in one. She was alive and she was dead. I moved to the mattress and I leaned close to her. I reached out and ran the back of my fingers along the soft of her hair. My hand fell on her shoulder and held there. Her skin was elastic. It slid over the bone.

Her eyes were closed and set back in her swollen face. White skin as smooth as marble, a pale, glassy sheen. The harness over the bed looped down and touched the swell of her breast. I moved it away, wanting to rip it from the ceiling and throw it across the room. But I held it instead. I held it and looked down on Carole and the sunken pocket of her stomach and her arms tightened down to the bone. Lines of rubber strap-ping pulling her forearms down against the mattress. Her back tight against the headboard. More of those bands holding her in place – cutting hard lines across her body. Lines that fell in deep crevices like there was nothing left inside her.

Carole was sitting upright in a long white shirt. It was a thin cloth that exposed her. I followed the line of her body to her bare legs. The shirt was pulled up to her hips. She was wearing nothing underneath. I reached and drew the shirt down until it would go no farther. I set it against her thighs and I looked up at her face. At the dried lips. At her sunken eyes. I touched her leg and I wanted to leave. But my hand was on her and what I was touching brought back the beating in my head. The deep rhythm that I didn't want to hear or feel. I peeled the white cloth away from her thighs and the rhythm set in louder. I breathed in through my nose and looked down at her. At the single wound on her inner thigh. Large enough to push a finger inside.

'Joe,' Wilcox said. 'Come out of there. Your people will be here soon and you can help them come to get her.'

'Where is it?' I asked. He didn't answer, so I asked again.

'Where's what, Joe?'

'All of her blood.'

He didn't answer me.

'There's a hole in her leg,' I said. Wilcox came into the room and grabbed my arms. He pulled and I got to my feet. He moved me towards the door. 'He took her blood.' Wilcox moved me and I tried to struggle, but Wilcox kept pulling.

I looked at Carole as Wilcox wrestled me through the door. She was sitting up in the bed. Her face made from porcelain. She had been a beautiful woman. And like my mother, I had ruined her. My mind held on to that final moment. That last scene. I would have her in my memory as the shell of the woman she had once been. She would be the pale and empty thing for ever. Eyes sealed shut. Lips glued together. A crude practice of embalming. Someone had taken the time to read about it in a book and they had tried their hand on my wife. My only hope was that she was dead before they'd started.

But I knew otherwise.

'Why did they strap her down?'

'Let's get you out of here, Joe.'

Wilcox walked me out of the house.

Chapter Thirty-Eight

The call came through four days after Carole's funeral. Marty was sitting on the sofa with a pillow pulled to his chest. An old werewolf film was playing on the television. The monster had a dog-face. I don't remember anything else about the movie. My eyes were on Marty more than they were on the film. He kept lowering his chin to the pillow. He had it wrapped up in both arms. He was squeezing it with all he had. He'd raise his head once in a while when the action picked up on the screen. He finally looked over at me and saw how I was watching him. He went back to the movie without so much as the blink of an eye. I got up to go through to the kitchen when the phone rang. I stopped on my way to lift the handset.

'Hello,' I said.

'May I speak with Mister Joseph Pullman?'

'You got him.'

'Mister Pullman, my name is Eric Henry. I am the assistant warden at Baltimore Correction Facility. I am calling you with some bad news, I'm afraid. Mister Pullman . . .' He paused. The poor man had been trained in this sort of thing. He was taking his time and allowing for a sombre feeling to move in between us. I'd been waiting all those years for that moment, and Eric Henry was holding the line in silence. He hadn't made too many calls like this one. I gave him the time. It was time I used to steady myself – not from the shock of it, but from the anticipation.

'Mister Pullman, it's about your father. I regret to inform you that he passed away this morning.'

'How much can you tell me about it?'

'Pardon me?'

'How much can you go into detail about his last moments?'

'Well, Mister Pullman, it's a difficult thing to discuss over the telephone. You see, I'm the assistant to the warden. He is on vacation and until he is fully briefed about the incident we cannot make anything public.'

'Incident?' I said. My voice climbed up and I wasn't able to bring it down.

Marty lifted his head from the pillow and looked at me. I shook my head at him, but he was still watching me. He sat forward and I moved my hand towards him and realised it was my expression that had him so curious. Damned if I couldn't help it, I'd been waiting for that man to die for a long, long time.

'I'm sorry, Mister Henry, but I was expecting this call under different circumstances. He's been sick a long time. I'm sure you know all about that. And now you're telling me it wasn't the cancer got him in the end?'

'No, sir. Your father was in an altercation this morning.' He went away for a moment and came back on the line. 'A fellow inmate went to see him in the infirmary. Your father has been complaining of nausea and he was bedridden at the time of the . . .' I heard papers moving close to the phone. 'Yes, I see he went into the infirmary close to three weeks ago.'

'Is that common practice?' I asked.

'For the severely ill. Your father was working on a plea to be released for health reasons.'

There was a long silence on the other end of the phone.

'Mister Henry?' I said.

When Eric Henry came back on, he was more shaky in the voice.

'I am here, sir.' He didn't seem like the kind of man who had the balls to run a prison. He took a sip of something and came back on the line. 'I have been in contact with the authorities and can assure you that an investigation is under way.'

'Well, I thank you for that. But, I only need to know one thing . . .'

'Yes, Mister Pullman?'

'What's the name of the man who did it?'

'Well, I can't give away that information at this time.'

Marty stood from the sofa and walked to where I was standing. He moved up against me, and I dropped a hand and set it on his shoulder. Out of reflex I started to push him again. He looked up at me and I pulled him close and moved my hand between his shoulder blades.

'Can you tell me if it was an old cellmate?'

'Your father has had many cellmates over the years.'

'Sure. They serve their time. They don't deserve to get put through the ringer. But you had a convict in your prison and you paroled him. Maybe not you personally, but your prison let him out.' I gave him a few seconds to retaliate. To start a defensive. He sipped on something and stayed quiet. 'The short of it is, Mister Henry, that your convict murdered my wife.'

'Yes, I read about that in the . . . the paper.'

'Good,' I said. 'You have all of those details and you know the prisoner. You know how he was released and you know how he was caught.'

'I know about the story, Mister Pullman.'

'Don't go all sheepish on me, Henry. I just want a simple answer. Was the man who killed my father related to the man my father sent to kill my wife?'

'The details . . .'

'Let's fuck the details, Henry. Carlos Muniz was pulled over on I95 and in the course of the arrest he got himself killed. Those are details straight from the paper. Interesting? Not really.'

'Mister Pullman . . . Can I get back to you with more information?'

'How about you leave the phone for a minute or two and you go and collect yourself. Come back when you're ready, and come back with an answer to this . . . Did the man who killed my father have a connection with Carlos Muniz?'

Another long pause. This time Eric Henry was making a lot of noise. He was moving things around and the racket wasn't doing anything to settle my nerves. A couple more thumps got me moving. My hand gripped the handset harder. I looked down and saw Marty struggling to get away from me. I'd taken a handful of his shirt. I let it go and he dropped back a few steps.

'Mister Pullman, I'll need you to hold the line for another moment.'

'Sure thing, bud.'

There was more sound. A clink when he set the phone on the desk. A few seconds later a door shut. Scraping when he pulled the phone off the desk again. Lifted it to his ear.

'I apologise for the way I'm behaving, only this is awkward. It is a difficult situation to have to deal with over the telephone.'

'Don't sweat it. I'm glad my old man is dead, if it makes your day any better.' I gave him a few seconds to respond. I got tired of the sound of him breathing. 'Do you think Carlos Muniz had anything to do with my father's murder?'

'Yes, it would appear to be the case. Witnesses are hard to come by in these instances. We have video of the attack, but there is no audio. I can assure you that your father's killer will be prosecuted.'

'I'm not concerned about his killer,' I said.

We ended the conversation after Eric Henry gave me the

details of how to collect my old man's body. I wasn't going to drive up there and back. I'd have paid for it to be delivered, but I didn't want to spend money on him. While I wrote the directions to the morgue, I thought about Ted and I figured he'd be game for a drive up there and back. He'd feel like he was doing something for me. I'd tell him there would probably be the press to speak with. That would give me a good excuse for not tagging along. It'd give him something to consider on the drive to Baltimore.

I stood next to the phone for a long while after I set it back on the receiver. Marty was making noise and moving around me, so I looked at him. He was still adjusting his shirt where I'd pulled it tight round his neck. His fingers played round the collar and pulled it away. I saw a thick red line where the cloth had dug into him.

'I'm sorry about that, Marty. Got caught up in the call. Didn't know what I was doing.'

'It's alright, I guess.' He was quiet a while. When he stopped touching his neck he looked down at the phone and asked me: 'Is your dad dead then?'

'Yeah. He died this morning.' My voice sounded weird. Sounded like there was some kind of emotion in there. Some kind of weakness in the back of my throat. A sound that I wasn't too comfortable hearing. 'Kind of weird to think that he's gone. After all this time. All the waiting.'

'Are you sad about it?'

'No. There were things I'd like to know. Questions I still have for him. But I wasn't going to go up there to ask him. Didn't want to be in a room with him. I had all the time I needed when I was a kid. Took all the beatings I could handle.'

'Is it alright if I think it's sad?'

'You can think whatever you want, Marty. But you should save your sadness for your mother. Don't waste it on that sonofabitch.'

'It's not for him.'

'Alright then. Whatever you need.'

He walked back to the sofa and picked up the pillow and set it on his knees. His chin fell into the edge of it. I watched him while he watched the television. He raised his chin now and again and took breaths so deep his back moved almost straight. He let the breath out slow. Before long the tears were falling and I stood there waiting for him. Expecting him to need me again. After a while I figured he had it covered. Whatever was happening in his head, he was living with it his own way. I turned round and went into the kitchen, opened the fridge and took out a bottle of beer. Topped it and sat down at the table.

'To my old man,' I whispered. 'And the bastard who got him.'

Chapter Thirty-Nine

Ted came back with the van. My father's body was strapped to the gurney in the rear. I'd been keeping busy. Dropped Marty off at school and spent a while in Ted's truck with him. Ted had loaned me his F-150 when he took the van and Marty had touched all the dials and played with the heater. He was stalling, not wanting to go into school. I wasn't pushing him out of the door, either. He stopped messing with the levers and sat back on the bench seat.

'When's Ted getting back?' Marty asked.

'Late morning.'

'And you still think I shouldn't see Grandpa? I'll never get to meet him any other way.' Marty picked at his nails until he found a piece he could pull off. Scraped off a crescent shape from his middle finger and threw it on the floor. Sat for a second and looked at the finger. The nail started to bleed.

'You don't need to know him.'

'You don't think I need to know him.'

'He did this to me, Marty.' He looked up and saw where my finger was pointing. He looked at my eyes. Looked at the scars surrounding them. The deep signatures of a bad few years. 'Do you really want to know the man who did this to me?'

'Yes.'

'I don't understand you,' I said.

'Doesn't matter.'

We sat there a while longer.

'We can talk about it tonight. I won't be doing anything with him before we talk. Deal? If you can . . .' Shook my head. He seemed more interested. More alert. 'If you can convince me that there's a good reason for you to see him, I'll take you in. I'll keep you off school for the day and we'll go in and see him.'

'You'll take me off school too?'

'Yeah,' I said. 'I don't think you'd be able to concentrate in Social Studies after viewing the remains of Richard Pullman.'

He left the truck with a smile on his face. Turned at the sidewalk and waved. Took the steps to the main entrance of the school two at a time. When he was inside I sat there and waited. Wondering what I was going to say to him that got me out of showing him the body. *Too damaged. What they did to him in prison . . . He wasn't the man I remember.* All the things that would make Marty want to see him even more.

Went to Darnell's after that and had a coffee. Sheila came to the table and turned over the mug. Filled it to the top without speaking. When she was finished she stood a while and looked down at me. Made like she was writing on her order slip. She was writing way too much.

'Thanks for the coffee,' I said.

'You take your time. I'm real sorry to hear about your father. So close to Carole, it has been a tough spell for you.' She started saying something else, but stopped. Kept scratching on her pad and stooping over me.

'His passing gives me solace. Strange kind of solace anyway. What he didn't do for me in life he did for me by dying.'

Sheila stood with a sick sort of look on her face. Pencil hovering over paper.

'I don't . . .'

'Relief,' I said. 'An overwhelming sense of relief.'

She left the table with a new look on her face. Walked up

and down the counter taking orders from outsiders. Looked over at me now and then. I drank the mug of coffee and left before she could make it over to fill it up again. Set two bills under the mug. Waved as I went through the door. She waved back, but not with her usual energy and smile.

Rest of the morning I spent in my office. Sitting at the desk with the papers piled in front of me. Good intentions of getting stuck into the pile. Whittling it down to what was priority and what was junk. Which went in the square file and which went into the round file. Instead I sat in my comfortable chair and looked at the square urn Charlie Himple had left me. The two hearts on top and the too-black colour of the thing. Sat back in the chair and looked at it until I couldn't look at it any longer. Closed my eyes and fell into a deep sleep. Sound of the garage door woke me up.

'You haven't been napping on me, have you?' Ted asked.

'It's been a wild few days.'

'I understand. You head off, Joe. I'll get someone to help me here.' He walked up to where I was sitting. 'Get it while you can.' He set a large manila envelope on the desk in front of me and moved round to the other side. He took a seat in the chair. I looked at the envelope and waited for him to tell me what it was all about. 'Your friend at the prison gave me that. Big enough to fit a damned body.'

'Yeah,' I said. 'Beat to hell too.'

'It's not in the best of shape. Your old boy's been carrying it round all his days. Everything he owns is in that envelope. All of his drawings, writings, photographs, everything. Guy who came down to see me handed it over. Asked that you get it.'

'What guy was that?'

'Man named Henry. Second name anyhow.'

'Assistant warden,' I said. Ted nodded his head. 'Spoke with him on the phone after the old man died. He was shaken. Seemed real concerned about having to spill the news.'

'Nice enough guy. All suited up and business-like. He asked me to give that to you, and I've got a bag of the clothes your father wore when he went inside. Few of his other possessions. Not much, but it's all in a bag if you want to see it.'

'Later.' Went to open the envelope. Ted sat there watching me. Pulled the flap open and looked inside. Hundreds of sheets of white paper all wrapped up and bundled. Held in place with a heavy rubber band. Some photographs had slipped down in the bottom. There were two pencils, with another rubber band keeping them together. What took my eye was a small black book. Looked like an address book. Reached in and took it out. Looked at both sides of the cover. No words or title. A small red ribbon stuck out from the bottom. 'You looked through this stuff?'

'Nope. Set it in the seat beside me and left it there while I drove back. You recognise something?'

Shook my head. Opened the book and read the first page:

It has been suggested that I should write my confession in a book like this one. Putting words on pages of an expensive journal are supposed to mean more than writing on random pages. I have been writing my ideas on leafs of scrap that I find on my rounds. What I have concluded as I write this is the want for other expensive things. The desire to own better than I own now. I want back the things that have been stolen from me. Things I would still have if I was not in here. But, this is not a rant and I am not making excuses. This is supposed to be a confession. And so it goes:

I am guilty of a catastrophic oversight. I am guilty of idiocy. I am guilty of letting down my guard. I am guilty of taking away from a boy who was more capable than I suspected. I am guilty of beating his body to misshape his mind. I am guilty of a monster.

430

'Joe? You alright?'

'Yeah, Ted. It's just something my father writes here.' I held up the small black book. Felt like a preacher with a member of his congregation sitting before him. Waving a book of damnation. Shaking it to make the shower of fire and brimstone scatter far and wide. 'Guess this whole thing is filled with his confession.'

Ted was nodding his head. He sat forward and made like he was going to reach out a hand and take the book from me. He stopped when I pulled the book back and closed it. Opened the pencil drawer in my desk and dropped it inside. Ted leaned back and crossed his legs. He looked at the floor and acted all pathetic.

'It's not that I don't trust you with it, Ted. It's a personal thing he's writing about. I was close to the boy he killed. Me and Dean were one and the same really. So, it's still a tough thing to deal with.'

Ted nodded his head.

'You want to give me a hand with the gurney?'

'I'll come out and help you. Give me a few minutes.'

Waited until Ted was out of my office. Turned the envelope up and let everything spill out on my desk. Pages wrapped up. Could date the pages by the absence or presence of yellow. Stack of pages had the same striations as a rock. Could tell when he found them. Somehow he shuffled them into the stack out of order. Looking at it, I figured that one day I'd take the time to look through it. Sit with the time ahead of me to pull them apart and see where the rationale was in the order. Until then I set the pages aside.

Lifted the photographs and found an old picture of my mother. Looked like it was in the Seventies. She had on bell-bottoms. Her hair long and straight, pulled away from her face with a middle parting. She was holding a small globe. The picture was too small and I couldn't see what was inside the globe. The picture was too blurry. The colours faded with the years. Still, I looked at her. At the smile on her face and wondered when it had changed. When she had changed. When the moments began and the bad days took her away. When the screaming started. Screaming that led my old man to take her to the place where she swung herself from the tree. That peaceful estate for the mentally deranged.

With the photograph of my mother were snapshots of Maritime. One of Delaware Glen. Looked like the wetlands anyway. The place where the ground floated with the movement of leaves on water. Along with this was a snapshot of the tunnels leading under Grant's Road. Tunnels me and Dean had walked a hundred times that year. An easy way to pass over to the Glen without being seen. Flipped the picture and on the back I saw a handwritten note:

Two boys carrying a crate. Can they fit through this tunnel?

'Sure they can,' I said. 'With space to spare.'

Flipped to the last photograph and had trouble keeping it steady. Had a hard time holding it to get a good look at it. Carole was a young woman. She had long hair and it was flared out on the sides. There was a kind of bleary light. May have been a studio shot. It was from a time before I knew her. A shot they hadn't got from me. A picture my old man wouldn't have received from Carole, either. I turned the photograph over and read the words out loud.

'Carole Quincy. Married Joe in '00. Have son, Martin.'

Lifted the phone and dialled the number without setting the photograph down. Listened to the ring while looking at my wife from a time long gone. How she looked so young. Almost innocent, but I knew Carole hadn't been innocent for a long time. Long before she met me. The ringing stopped.

'Hello?'

'I need to speak with Paul,' I said.

'Joe? Is that you?'

'Yeah, it's me, Fran. Now put Paul on the line.'

'Jesus, God, Joe. I still can't believe what's happened.'

'Put Paul on the fucking line!'

Commotion followed. Plastic on wood. Shuffling. Fran shouting and moving. Then someone else started in on the noise. Then the phone scraped against wood. Paul cleared his throat. Sounded tired when he breathed into the receiver. Settled himself and spoke.

'I can't take this call right now.'

'Well, if you're talking to me you're already taking the call.'

'It all got out of hand.'

'You're right about that, Paul. Goddamn, you're right about that! I'm holding a photograph of Carole. Of your daughter. She's young, Paul. From before when I knew her. And the thing that's troubling me is how this photograph got to be in the possessions of my father. You have any ideas about that, Paul? You know how a man in prison got a photograph of my wife? Your daughter? She was your daughter in the photograph, Paul. A young Carole.'

'I can't do this.'

'You can do it, Paul! You did do it! You did this to Carole! Everything happened because of you, Paul. What were you hoping? How did you think this was going to end?'

'He was going to tell me what you did. He told me that you killed the Gillespie boy. He claimed to have information that would put you away. And so I went to meet him. I went up to Baltimore and I sat with him. He told me stories. He gave me versions of what may have happened that day the boy died. I went up two times and he kept telling me different stories. And that last time I went he'd asked me to take pictures of Carole and Marty. He said he would give me all he had on you, if I showed him the family he had on the outside. He wanted to be connected with something again.'

'So you gave him Carole?'

Paul was making wet noises on the other end. I wanted to keep talking, but I wanted to hear him suffer. Let him take the moment and I felt no pity for him. Listened to his pathetic moment.

'I took several photographs. I let him hold them. He talked and I listened. He must have kept that picture. I didn't give it to him. I didn't plan to leave him anything.'

'But you did, Paul. You left him her face. You left him a motive. I had something he didn't. I had something he wanted. And he went after her, Paul. You led a killer to your daughter.' I let out a laugh and he made more wet sounds. 'All this time you were coming after me. You were putting all of your energy and time in following me. Making me feel responsible. Did it make you feel better, Paul? Did it make you feel less remorse for killing your own daughter?'

'I didn't kill her!'

'You started the machine.' He choked on something. Words he wanted to say. Some kind of protest. Some kind of affirmation to himself that he had done the right thing. 'And did she confide in you, Paul? Did she tell you what my old man had sent her? Did she tell you what her man Muniz had given her when she went to Maritime? When she took our son to Maritime?'

'No.'

'What was that, Paul? Did you say something? Did you say no?'

'Carole gave me nothing.'

'Do you know why? Do you know why Carole gave you nothing, Paul? Because she went to Maritime to protect me. She went up there to see what they had as evidence. She went up to disprove the lies my old man was creating. The lies you were so desperate to believe in.'

434

'I didn't know it would go so far.'

'No. You wouldn't know a thing like that, Paul. You would think only of the moment when Carole returned to you. When she came back to you with Marty. When your little Carole was returned to the homestead. Away from the monster and close to the father that sheltered her from a world gone mad. You were waiting, Paul. Waiting for that moment to happen. But your machine swallowed her. I saw what your machine did.'

'I did not do this!'

'You killed her, Paul! How long can you live knowing you killed your daughter?'

The line went dead. I set the phone on the receiver and waited in silence. Looked at the stack of paper and the photographs on my desk. The pencils my father had used to write out his thoughts. His versions of what had happened to Dean Gillespie. Two decades of pencil etchings of scenes and scenarios. Scratchings of a man driven by revenge.

'One last talk, old man.'

Stood up from my desk and leaned over the papers and the photographs. Shifted the pile around until it looked like it was ready to fit back into the envelope. I set Carole's photograph on top of the pile. Then I was ready.

I went through to help Ted with the gurney.

Acknowledgements

Some people are fortunate to have the support of family. Others have a network of experienced and talented friends and colleagues. I am the guy who's got both. I want to thank those people who have helped me along the way. Willy Maley, my mentor and most constant source of critical support. John Coyle, introduced new lenses that help me see literature with more clarity. Rob Maslen and David Punter asked the simple questions that pulled out the complex answers. Robin Robertson and Ellah Allfrey edited my work from the beginning, but always left the final word to me. Alex Bowler helped clear out the last of Henderson's clutter. Special thanks goes to my agent Gill Coleridge and all of the RCW crew who got me on the road and continue to trust that I know where I'm going (no matter how long it takes me to get there). The always hearty, Richard 'Beardy' Henderson, who lent his name to a town and continues to inspire. I would also like to thank my colleagues and friends, in particular Addae Moon and Jackie Jones, for continuing to ask how the writing is coming no matter how deep I am buried in papers.

Of course, my family needs more than a nod. My parents tolerated my past mistakes, knowing that I needed to figure out the meaning of stupidity on my own. I thank my children for not turning off the computer in the middle of too many writing sessions and for letting me have the days (locked away in the study) to get this book finished. Finally, I thank my wife Elaine for putting up with my quirks and always encouraging my imaginings. This book wouldn't have happened without you . . .

The writer acknowledges support from the Scottish Arts Council towards the writing of this title.